Clutch START

Keith Michaels

Published in Australia by Sid Harta Books & Print Pty Ltd,
ABN: 34632585293
23 Stirling Crescent, Glen Waverley, Victoria 3150 Australia
Telephone: +61 3 9560 9920
E-mail: author@sidharta.com.au

First published in Australia 2021
This edition published 2021
Copyright © Keith Michaels 2021
Cover design, typesetting: WorkingType (www.workingtype.com.au)

This book is a work of fiction. Any similarities to that of people
living or dead are purely coincidental.

Michaels, Keith
Clutch Start
ISBN: 978-1-925707-61-8
pp546

iii

To the thousands of boys and girls propelled into adulthood through the RAAF's Engineering Apprenticeship Scheme, and to those who nurtured us.

*Thanks to Rel Smith for helping turn words into a story
and to our fellow Thirty Three Intake Apprentices
for the inspiration and encouragement.*

Disclaimer

While some of the events described in this book are real, the majority are works of fiction. All names and characters are fictional. Any resemblance to actual persons, living or dead, is purely coincidental. Where real events are used, the author has made all reasonable efforts to ensure accuracy. The author welcomes any alternate views.

Contents

I come to, wondering where I am. The rain is heavy on my face and my left leg is aching. I'm on my back and the leg is jammed under the bike. I can tell my ankle is at a weird angle in comparison to my knee and it's not a good sign. The bike is wedged under the side of the Mazda and now I remember.

The water has overflowed from the gutters on either side of the street, like a huge lake. It's two inches deep around me and, for a short moment, I am worried I might actually drown. But the monsoon drains in Penang are pretty efficient; the water isn't rising.

Saunders is lying a few yards to my left. He's out cold, but his chest is rising and falling; he's not dead. The baseball bat is beside him and there is a twang of pain in my side as I remember the bat going into my ribs — bastard.

I try to think whether I could have done something differently. I didn't have to follow him. Was that bravery, bravado, or something else? I replay the accident in my head.

The Mazda is in front of me, it's pissing down, and I am on a bike that handles like a cake of Palmolive Gold in the shower. I decide to lay it over rather than impacting directly and going over the bars. Maybe I should have taken the other option?

As the bike hits its side, my arse hits the bitumen and I can feel my jeans ripping. There is no pain, just jeans tearing and skin scraping along on the gravel.

This is going to hurt.

I can hear sirens now and I am lying there, waiting, hoping help is on its way, the rain in my face and the pain rising.

How the hell did I get here?

A myriad of thoughts go through my head: the farm; grandma and grandad; mum and dad; the girls; Louise, Nev and the boys; Allison; and Liz. Oh, lovely Liz.

I start shivering and I know it's the shock setting in. My mind starts to wander. I remember my first day in the Air Force.

How young and naïve was I?

My most vivid memory of that first day is the ride to Wagga Wagga on the C-130 Hercules. A frightened fifteen-year-old from the bush, among a bunch of other wide-eyed teenagers.

The engine noise changes slightly and the nose of the C-130 dips. It seems we are descending now. I look around and everyone else is wide-eyed, alert, observing the scene within the aircraft with no idea of what's happening or what to expect. It's unlike any vision of any aircraft I had ever imagined or seen on television. There is a row of seats along each side of the plane and two rows, back-to-back, facing out, along the centre. The seats are made from an aluminium frame with a red nylon webbing covering, a bit like those aluminium beach lounges. The walls are covered in a silver-greenish padding material and there are a couple of small windows along each side.

One thing is for sure, the padding is doing nothing to dull the amount of noise in here, you can't hear yourself think.

I am in a seat along the left-hand side and I can see blue sky out of the windows opposite. The cockpit is in an elevated position on my left and I can see various electronic boxes and wiring like woven ropes below it. The floor is a pretty rigid structure with various locating lugs and hooks. There are rails with rollers on them stacked up on either side of the plane. The ceiling has a couple of air-conditioning ducts and cables running fore and aft. In the centre is a structure with lights and it supports the posts holding the centre two rows of seats. At the back is the ramp with our bags strapped to a pallet. This side of the ramp, there are two doors, one on either side behind the wings.

A guy in green overalls is seated at the back sipping from a cup. When we boarded, he told us he was the Loadmaster and we should follow his every instruction to the letter. He is wearing a headset with microphone connected to a black cable. It's a long cable, coiled up, and hanging from some bracket above his head. He speaks into the microphone every now and again, obviously to someone up front in the cockpit. Most of the time it looks like he's taking a nap, a tiny bit more comfortable in there than we are.

It's my first time in an aeroplane. Looking around, I feel sure most of us are in the same boat. I feel the pressure in my ears building as we descend. Instinctively, I hold my nose and blow, clearing my ears. One of the guys sitting opposite has thrown up into a white paper bag — he's looking about the same colour. The smell fills the cabin and invites the rest of us to consider whether we need a bag too, it's powerfully contagious.

The overhead light goes red and the ride gets bumpy; lots of eyes looking around nervously. There are sounds like a hydraulic pump, something mechanical turning, and the vapour from the air-conditioning looks like smoke emanating from the vents. The noise of the engines increases and the aircraft banks steeply. All I can see out the window is dry, brown paddocks, and it looks hot, uninviting. The aircraft levels out again, still jumping around in the heat.

The noise in the cabin seems to be building, crescendo like, and then there is a sudden jolt as we hit the runway hard. Mr Loadmaster looks relaxed, I guess this is normal then. Soon everything stops shaking around and the engine noise changes. It's like take-off again, only this time the engine power and propeller blades are being used as brakes to slow us down. We are all falling on top of each other the opposite way, completely unprepared for this. It's unsettling but probably looks funny to Mr Loadmaster.

The aircraft slows and the engine noise returns to the same rhythmic frequency of the taxi out to the runway in Sydney an hour ago. It turns a hundred and eighty degrees and backtracks up the runway, turning right onto a taxiway. The Loadmaster is busy opening the two doors and the upper portion of the ramp. The heat floods in and hits us immediately while vapour pours from the air-conditioning. Out the back of the plane I can make out low hills beyond the runway and those brown paddocks. The tarmac is a mirage of shimmering heat; it looks like we may have descended into hell itself.

The aircraft swings around and comes to a halt. The Loadmaster drops the ramp and a figure wearing blue overalls and ear protectors appears. They exchange hand signals and Mr Overalls disappears again. There is another sound like a jet starting and the engines start slowing. The Loadmaster makes his way through our legs to the front left where we entered. When the engines stop, he hangs up his headset, opens the main door, and makes his way back down between our legs to the ramp. It's obvious he has done this a thousand times before. We might as well be sheep or pallets of cargo as far as he's concerned.

A forklift appears at the back of the ramp and there is a flurry of signals as the baggage pallet is pushed back and onto the fork. It disappears out of view.

A figure in a brown uniform and ear protectors appears at the main door. The protectors are on his head at an odd angle, cups on the side of his head behind the ears, and the bar holding the two cups across his forehead. His moustache is twisted and curled up at the ends.

He announces himself as Squadron Leader Banks and welcomes us to RAAF Base, Wagga Wagga. He instructs us to gather all our personal items and exit the aircraft over the back ramp, a softer touch than I was expecting. We file out and hop down onto the tarmac. The heat hits me instantly and I feel like I am in a furnace. Then the yelling starts.

There are about three, maybe four, people dressed in green military uniforms all yelling various instructions.

'Move, move, move,' screams one.

Where am I moving to?

It seems I'm not the only one; lots of bewildered looks. The noise of the aircraft and the oppressive heat adds to my cloudy mind. I see some guys walking to the pallet gathering their bags, I follow; more yelling, now intermixed with swearing. The soft touch didn't last long.

We board a bus and I take the first seat I can find. We sit there bathed in our own sweat while the men in green talk with the Squadron Leader.

There are about forty of us on the bus, about half were at the hotel last night. I am guessing the rest are from Sydney as the first time I saw them was at the recruiting office this morning.

I had caught the train down from Dungog yesterday and got into Central at about 7.00 pm. I had walked up Pitt Street to the Westend Hotel, the same hotel they put us in when I went for the selection process in August. I had never stayed in a hotel before then.

There were a bunch of nervous faces at breakfast in the hotel this morning. One guy had his dad with him. I was jealous. When I checked out, there was another guy just finishing his check-out. He said 'Hello,' and asked if I was joining the Air Force. I said 'Yes' and he looked relieved. He said we can walk around to the recruiting office together.

His name is Merv, he's a stocky barrel-chested kid, looks a bit like one of those wrestlers on TV, and he's from Cootamundra. I asked him where it is and got a geography lesson along with a turn by turn description on how to get there. I wonder why the hell they had to bring him all the way to Sydney and send him back again. The wonders of military logic have started to make me curious, and I am not yet a part of it.

I am carrying my personal effects in my old school port. Merv also has his. He asked me where I am from and I told him our dairy farm is about eight miles out of town on the Fosterton road. He said he knows Doug Walters is from Dungog and asked if I get bored with people asking me if I know him.

'My mum went to school with him, but he was a couple of years behind her.'

They completed a medical check and we pledged our unconditional allegiance to the Queen and country, on the Bible, 'so help me God'. I am not religious, but it's a solemn pledge. Then, we were put onto a bus to Mascot airport where the C-130 was waiting. Holy hell, I have never been on an aeroplane before, much less a military transport.

Grandad had dropped me off at the train station in Dungog nearly twenty-four hours ago. He got out of the car and opened the boot without a single word. I grabbed my bag and put it on the ground, extending a hand. He gripped it strongly and told me to be a good boy; stay out of trouble. He mumbled something about getting back to the milking, got back into the car, and drove away without a look back. A man of few words, my grandad.

Grandad is a veteran of World War Two and fought in New Guinea on the Kokoda Track; later in Borneo. He's President of the local Sub-Branch of Returned and Services League, the RSL. They operate a licensed club in Dungog and he's also the Secretary of the local branch of the Country Party. Grandad is a big deal in our little town.

The goodbye from grandma was a little more emotional. She fussed around all morning making sure I had this, that and the other. Grandma always made sure you had clean underwear in the bag. She cried when I kissed her goodbye at the back door. 'I am only going to Wagga Wagga, grandma,' I reassured her.

Grandma is one of four girls on the Dennis side of the family. She had a brother. He was a Mid-Upper Gunner in a Lancaster during World War Two. Their aircraft was shot down over Stuttgart on their third mission. The letter from Buckingham Palace sits pride of place on the mantelpiece at home. When I said I wanted to join the Air Force, there was hell to pay. She gave me a stern talking to and it took some time to convince her I would be ground crew and had no plans to be a gunner.

The engine of the bus erupts into life disturbing my reflection of the past twenty-four hours. The Green Men have stopped talking to the Squadron Leader and are now in the front of the bus. It moves off through the Base.

The place looks kind of sleepy, but everything is neat and tidy. I see a large number of aircraft hangars with corrugated iron walls; the major feature is the large water tower with its large, flat bulb at the top. The bus weaves its way between various buildings before coming to a stop outside the middle of three, three-storey buildings; more yelling.

'Move, move, move.'

Where are we moving to?

Off the bus with bags in hand, we are herded under a tree and told to wait. Another C-130 roars overhead. Noise, heat, yelling and swearing seem to characterise my first few hours in the military. Move, move, move, then wait, wait, wait. There seems to be an unnecessary waste of energy in this place.

Sitting around, Merv and I strike up a conversation with one of the other lads. He's from Woolloomooloo in Sydney, I ask him where it is.

'Near the Cross, Kings Cross.' Never been there, but I've heard the stories.

The green men come back and start reading names. It's alphabetical, so I sit back and wait till the end. A couple more rounds are called and there are four of us still sitting there. One of the green men returns.

'Okay boys, I should have a Stevens, Sutton, Walsh, and a Walker.' We each acknowledge our names and he asks us to follow him. We enter the middle one of three buildings and as we walk into the foyer, the green man points out a set of double doors on the right.

'The ablutions are in there,' he says.

I guess he means toilet?

We turn left and there is a set of stairs on the right before we enter a long corridor. The man in green stops at the first door on the right and turns.

'My name is Corporal Kennedy, but you can call me Corporal,' he says, grinning.

'Yes, Corporal,' Stevens says, a little too quickly.

He's done that before.

Corporal Kennedy looks at the rest of us inquiringly, prompting us. We join in together with a loud collective.

'Yes, Corporal.' He looks pleased with himself.

'Right, Stevens, you are in here, first bed on the right.' He walks to the next door and Sutton is allocated a bed. Down the hall he stops at the second last door on the right. 'Walker and Walsh, you guys are in here. Walker on the right, Walsh in the next bed. Get comfy. I'll be back in a while.' We step inside.

Right in line with the door is a wooden partition dividing the room into two halves. There is a window on each side of the room separating identical steel-framed beds, four to a room. A desk and chair are at the foot of each bed. The wall back against the corridor has four identical built-in wardrobes, each with four drawers, hanging space, and an overhead section. I drop my bag on the desk and turn toward the short little aboriginal guy.

'Nev Walker from Kempsey,' he says. The accent reminds of something off TV, a classic blackfella. He's a thin kid, built like a halfback. 'Where are you from?'

'Dungog.'

'The only time I ever been to Dungog was when the train stopped there on the way down yesterday.' We talk a bit about how far it is from Kempsey to Dungog, where the train stops, and then talk turns to football. Nev is a Balmain supporter, I'm a St George supporter, just like grandad.

We hear more aircraft landing and I open the window to hear better as the door opens. It's Corporal Kennedy again.

'That bed there, Watson,' he says, and disappears again.

We introduce ourselves to the new guy and find out he's Michael Watson from Melbourne. The talk goes back to footy; he has no idea what we are talking about, he's a St Kilda supporter. I have heard of St Kilda, but have no concept of where it is, other than Melbourne. As for the footy, they have a weird game down there. I have seen it a couple of times on TV, but can't understand what is going on.

I wander down the hall to the toilet and back. I can hear noises emanating from most rooms — nervous chatter, new friendships being made. Shortly after, one more addition is made to our room.

'James Wenke from Roma,' he says, in a slow drawl. 'Most people call me Jim, or Jimmie.'

'Where's Roma?' Nev asks.

'About three hundred miles west of Brisbane.' We mustn't look convinced. 'Halfway to Longreach,' he clarifies. I am no wiser.

A little while later, shouting from the hall grabs our attention. Nev opens the door and we hear someone yelling.

'Everyone outside, move, move, move, outside.' We are herded outside and there are green men yelling from various directions. I can see Corporal Kennedy, and I wave to the others to head in his direction. We go and stand before him.

He counts heads and leads us to a shady tree. We take a seat. He does a roll call with Stevens' name coming first. He responds with 'Corporal' and we all follow suit. Corporal Kennedy looks pleased again. Not too hard so far.

He explains we are Number Seven Flight, of the Thirty-Third Engineering Apprentice Intake of the RAAF, known as Thirty-Three Intake. He will be our host, instructor, guardian, mother and father for the next ten weeks.

Looking around I can see five of the other six flights. They look like us; groups of boys surrounding a man in a green uniform.

'How come you guys are dressed like army soldiers,' asks one of our new seven flight inmates.

'I'm an Airfield Defence Guard,' he says. 'We're known as ADGs, or ADGies. Our job is to protect airfields from ground attack. It's why we wear jungle greens, camouflage.' I look around at the brown hills surrounding the Wagga Wagga airfield.

Somehow, I think we are going to be free from an attack by the yellow hordes tonight.

Corporal Kennedy briefs us on working routine, meal times at the Mess, stand to, stand down, lights out, and other matters.

'The Apprentice Club's over there,' he points toward a large, old, fibro building. 'You can get supper in there each night at 1900 hours. The base canteen is ASCO. It's past the Apprentice Club, that way,' pointing north. There is a list of don'ts.

'Don't walk on the grass, don't put your hands in your pockets, don't fold your arms, don't walk across the parade ground, don't meander and no wanking.' We all laugh, some nervously. He proceeds to tell us about his mate who got caught wanking in the shower. 'He said, it's my dick and my soap and I will wash it as hard as I like.' We all laugh again. Corporal Kennedy is now looking us all up and down, stopping at a tall guy with long, dark hair and a heavy brow.

'Hey, Lurch, didn't they tell you it's short back and sides here?' The guy looks at him slightly stunned. Corporal Kennedy scans again stopping at another guy who has short sides but has left it long at the back. It's a silly look.

'Curtains, you and Lurch take a walk to the barber, it's next to the canteen. The rest of you follow me.' He leads us inside while the two long-haired guys wander off dejectedly.

We are told to wait inside the foyer while he sets up a bed. 'You will be issued with two sheets, a pillowcase, a mattress cover, a pillow, four blankets, a quilt, and a mat,' he commences. 'You are expected to have your bed made whenever you are not in it. There will be consequences for those with unmade beds, at any time.' He looks around at us, 'Got it?'

'Yes, Corporal,' came from most of the boys.

We are getting good at this 'Yes, Corporal' stuff.

He then proceeds to give us detailed instruction on making a bed, military style. Everything is tight, precise and includes hospital tucks. Halfway through the demonstration, Curtains and Lurch reappear. Lurch still has some of his long locks in his hand, almost in tears.

What the hell were they expecting?

It's now mid-afternoon. Looking outside, I can see that there has been no decline in the furnace-like heat. Corporal Kennedy issues us with our bedding and we have to sign for it. He directs us to make our beds and says he'll come and get us for dinner at 1630. Nev looks at me.

'It's got to be forty degrees out there; why the hell do I need four blankets?'

Just before four-thirty, the yelling starts again. We file out and join a long line of our fellow Apprentices heading toward the Mess, and being Seven Flight, we are last. Inside, there is a blackboard with the menu and we shuffle along to a serving counter. Each person picks up a plate and indicates which selection they would like. The cooks smile at us and place a scoop of our desired substance onto the plate. I am having sausages with onions.

Some of the cooks have a talent for flicking food onto the plate. The girl on the mash potato is really good; I reckon she was a good foot away. I follow the others into a huge dining hall and sit with Lurch. We eat in silence.

When they said I was going to Wagga Wagga, I didn't really give much thought about where it was or what we would be doing. I am not sure I like this. All they have done is yell at us. Uncle Bert told me to expect a tough time. 'Part of the process,' he said, but it's still unsettling.

I don't feel hungry, but I have been schooled in eating what is on my plate. I can hear grandad now.

'There are people in this world who don't get any food, so you eat what is on your plate.' I reckon grandad may have first-hand experience there.

In the early evening, a steady stream of guys in blue overalls flow into the buildings either side of ours. The noise level increases commensurate with the inflow of people. Not long after, our door flies open.

'Where are you from, Sprog,' asks some guy, obviously not much older than me.

'Dungog,' I say. He screws up his face.

'What about you, Sprog?' pointing at Jim and the same

questions to Nev and Mick. He seems disappointed with the answers and disappears.

The theme continues for some time, the general question being, 'Where you from, Sprog?' Some ask additional questions to clarify. No one seems to know where Dungog is, so I start to say Newcastle. If they question further, I know they are semi-local and then clarify it's actually Dungog.

A few of us decide we are going to find the canteen and walk down past the Apprentice Club and through a car park. The car park is filled with a mix of sedans, station wagons, panel vans and bikes. Holdens and Fords predominate, with a couple of Valiants and a smattering of Jap cars and Kraut Wagons.

'Where I come from, this is called Cow Shit Green,' says Jim, pointing at a green Centura. A guy pokes his head up from under the bonnet of a Cortina.

'Hey, can you Sprogs give me a push,' he yells, closing the bonnet. He climbs into the driver's seat and we push it back out of the car space. As we walk to the boot, I notice it's a '68 or a '69 Cortina 440. I only know it's a '68 or '69 because dad had one once.

We lean into the Cortina and it starts rolling, getting quicker as we break into a jog. I can feel the load as he drops the clutch and the engine starts to turn over, then it fires and stops, then fires again.

The car accelerates away from us, coughing and backfiring, a right hand out the window waving appreciation.

He's not going far with it missing like that.

Inside the canteen, we find a milk bar-style hot food servery on one end, drinks and a counter in the middle and a small supermarket type operation on the other end. I grab a can of Coke and, walking to the counter, I see a local newspaper on display, the Daily Advertiser. The thing that catches my attention is the photo of Doug Walters on the front page.

Apparently, World Series Cricket was playing a match in Wagga Wagga that day and Doug is a member of the Cavaliers team playing the World XI. I grab a copy.

Two Dungog boys in town on the same day, a good sign?

Back in the block, the interrogations continue. One guy is from Adamstown in Newcastle. He seems a genuinely nice fella and he sits with us for some time to explain the finer points of life at RAAF Base, Wagga Wagga. He's a Second-Year Apprentice.

Most of the guys visiting our room are Second-Year Apprentices. From Number Thirty-Two Intake, they've been here a full year. There are some Third-Year Apprentices here from Number Thirty-One Intake, but most have already graduated. Apparently, we are Sprogs, second years are Super Sprogs and third years are King Sprogs.

'It's all a bit pointless. The adult trainees and instructing staff refer to all Apprentices as Sprogs. There's about three hundred Apprentices here, and twice as many adult trainees. We call them Thicks, because most of them are as thick as two short planks.'

Some of the Second Years calling past are welcoming, some are arrogant, and some are flat-out threatening. Some sense they have an advantage they are about to exploit. You can tell by their mannerisms. The interviews continue till the lights out at 10.00 pm.

We lie there, sweating, listening to the hum of the building subside. Nev interrupts.

'Hey, did you hear the one about the Englishman, the Irishman and the Australian ...' It's been a huge day, probably one of the biggest in my life, and despite the heat, I sleep soundly.

Day Two, I wake at the usual time and lie there for an hour enjoying the early morning cool. At 6.00 am the yelling and swearing starts all over again. Our door swings open.

'Hands off cocks and on socks. Shorts, t-shirt and sandshoes, gentlemen. Fucking move.' As I dress, I am thinking about home.

Grandad and Uncle Bert will be well through milking by now. I wish I was there.

We follow Corporal Kennedy in a slow jog going east around some sporting fields. After a while, a golf course appears and we follow the perimeter fence arriving back at the Apprentice Club. After cooling down, we are told to bathe, shave, and be ready by 0700.

There are nearly fifty of us on the ground floor. It's quite comical trying to get through one of the six showers, dressed, and outside in less than thirty minutes, fighting for space; some dick comparisons being done.

Seven o'clock, we're escorted to the Mess for breakfast. It's a spectacle — hundreds of people all trying to get some toast, a cuppa, and cereal. Afterwards, we're told to clean our teeth, and be ready by 0800. They are imposing tight deadlines on us. The yelling starts again at ten-to-eight.

'Outside, outside, everyone, move, move, move.'

Shortly after, seven little clumps of Apprentices are assembled on the dirt road outside our accommodation. Corporal Kennedy picks out the tallest guy in our flight, Lurch, who is probably six foot eight and tells him to stand in one spot. He picks another two tall guys and tells them to stand behind Lurch. The rest are then organised according to height; tall people on each end, short guys in the middle. He then walks through the ranks inspecting us.

'You haven't shaved,' he roars at one guy. 'Try again, GO.' It gets repeated every third person.

'Did you shave this morning, Sutton?' he bellows.

'Yes, Corporal.'

'I suggest you stand about three fucking inches closer to the razor Sutton. Do it again, GO!' I'm also told to have another go.

Shit, another go? I have never shaved in my life and don't even have a razor.

We run inside and I go to the ablutions and beg someone to let me use theirs. I don't know where to start and so I just scrape my chin, hand the razor back, and run back outside. Corporal Kennedy says if we ever turn up for parade again without shaving, he will charge us. I don't know what it means, but it sounds bad.

He then goes through the routine of instructing us in the art of standing *at ease*. Feet about six to eight inches apart, hands behind the back, right hand in left hand, with right thumb over the top of left thumb. He walks around and checks each person's stance, physically correcting errors. Doesn't feel much like *At Ease* to me.

'Your elbows are out too far, Young. It's not a fashion parade, push your fucking hands down.' He is satisfied.

After a while, we are going from *Attention* to *At Ease*, turning to the left, the right, front and rear, and right dressing. The Right Dress is a way of getting everyone into straight lines at equal distances apart.

It occurs to me how rampant the swearing is. In less than twenty-four hours, I think I have heard the 'fuck' word more than I have ever heard it so far in my life, and in more ways than I ever would've thought possible.

Corporal Kennedy tells us we are going to go marching. When he yells '*By the left, Quick March,*' we are going to step off with our left foot and proceed down the dirt road toward the Mess — not too difficult really. Corporal Kennedy clears his throat and we pay attention.

'Seven Flight,' he commands. 'You should be standing *At Ease.*' We adjust ourselves. 'Seven Flight, *Attention.*' Not too bad, we all got there, together, more or less.

'Seven Flight, *Into Line, Right Turn*'. Most of us go the right way, one guy turns left.

Corporal Kennedy marches smartly over to Wilson. He hasn't yet remembered all our names and so nicknames are in use. He gets two inches from Wilson's nose.

'Sticks,' he screams. Wilson is one of those guys with long legs and slim body. 'Somewhere, there is a village in search of their idiot and I think I have just found him.' There are a few sniggers in the group.

'As you were.' We face the front again. This time he raises his right hand and points to our left. 'Seven Flight, *Into Line, Right Turn.*' Three more guys turn left as well as the previous disobedient mortal. 'The other right, you idiots,' he screams, but there is a grin lurking, he's enjoying this. Third time we get it right.

'Seven Flight, *By the Left, Quick March.*' We all step off. 'Left, left, left, right, left.' The tall boys out the front are watching each other's feet. Everyone is in step for about ten yards before it descends into chaos. The corporal yells 'Halt', which brings us to a stop, well most of us, eventually.

We work on the marching for the next two hours, to little avail. It appears everyone over six foot is totally uncoordinated.

Perhaps the blood can't pump all the way to that altitude?

We shuffle the batting order and a couple of us, who have some semblance of natural rhythm, get to the front.

'Seven Flight, *By the Left, Quick March*.' We are off.

'Left, left, left, right left'. I am on the right, Watson in the middle, and Thompson on the left. We march on for several hundred yards, wheeling left and right, all the time Corporal Kennedy calling the step like he is singing. The cadence is a bit like twelve bar blues and I hum a Beatles tune in time with our step.

Wow, we're now walking, together, military style.

It's getting hot again and Corporal Kennedy suggests we should take a break before lunch. Nobody argues. With lunch done we spend most of the afternoon lounging under a gum tree, a few of the guys lighting up a smoke the moment we sit down. Corporal Kennedy calls it 'Plan B'. We are lucky. The other six flights are getting drill lessons most of the day. From what we can see they are all struggling just like us.

In the evening I go back to ASCO to get the newspaper. I am keen to see how many runs Doug Walters got yesterday. It's a disappointment; Trevor Chappell and Rick McCosker chased down the 167 runs without losing their wicket. Doug didn't even get a bowl, but Dennis Lillee took seven for twenty-three against the West Indies at the SCG yesterday.

How good is Dennis Lillee?

Grandad doesn't think much of World Series Cricket. He would say it's not about players being paid what they are worth, its more about Kerry Packer trying to buy the TV rights. He has a radio in the dairy; it's tuned to the ABC, and only the ABC. Whenever there is a Test or Shield game, we have it on — no World Series Cricket on the ABC.

Friday, 26th January 1979 is Day Three and we get issued with our Air Force kit. The civvies get packed away and won't see the light of day for a while. There are two pairs of overalls with a name tag over the right breast pocket and Apprentice flashes on each sleeve. There is a towel; some strange underwear; sports clothing including sandshoes; safety boots; safety shoes; black dress shoes; socks; turtle neck jumper; V-neck jumper; two long-sleeve blue shirts; two pairs of trousers; a dress jacket; great coat; tie; belt and various adornments.

Corporal Kennedy instructs us on how to wear the various forms of the uniform and what has to be polished. We are then instructed on how to arrange our uniforms into our locker. Corporal Kennedy says if this is not done correctly, we could be charged.

At lunch time, we are served a selection of fish, chips, mash, peas, or salad. The Mess is unusually quiet and, throughout the afternoon, there is a steady stream of cars going down the main drag. By the evening meal, the one hundred and sixty-odd Sprogs of Number Thirty-Three Apprentice Intake are the majority of the people in the Mess.

Our mentors, the band of corporals, stay with us over the weekend and our induction continues. It's mostly marching around and around, dispersed with the odd lesson in first aid, who to salute, who not to salute, how to salute, how to present our room and locker for inspection and how to make a bed roll.

We must have our bed made at all times, but for Tuesday

morning stand-by-beds inspection, there has to be a bed roll added. The bed roll consists of three light-blue, striped blankets, folded so the stripes on each blanket are exactly in the centre of the fold, and, of course, with the stripes perfectly aligned. Two sheets are neatly folded and sandwiched between the three blankets. The last blanket is the wrapping around the sandwich, stripes positioned centrally around the package, all perfectly proportioned.

The bed roll is placed at the head of the bed, pillow on top and our service dress cap on top of the pillow. It's a spectacle to behold. This little ritual will be played out every Tuesday morning. Every other morning, the bed is made with hospital tucks and everything pulled tight and flat. If it's not right, your bed gets flipped over.

The bed is a military standard issue, steel bed in three pieces, the mattress a four-inch bit of foam covered in plastic. The main part of the bed has spigots on the four corners, they seat into receptacles on the two steel end pieces, the weight of the person on the bed further pushing the spigots into the mainframe. When the bed is inverted, gravity has the opposite effect and the bed collapses onto the floor in three pieces.

Monday morning, the drill practice gives way to instruction on cleaning. We are taught to clean toilets, hand basins, shower rails, urinal, floors and cupboards. Every metal surface must shine, hallway vacuumed. Even the taps behind the dunnies and in the showers have to be polished.

Tuesday morning is stand-by-beds inspection and every square inch of the building must be spotless, thus Monday night is known as Panic Night. Each room is assigned a task in the common areas, as well as cleaning their own room. Our room is assigned the showers and we knock it over pretty quickly.

The foyer floor, and the floor in each room, are lino and they must be highly polished. There is an industrial-grade polisher on each floor and it takes some work to master operation; it's a beast with a mind of its own. Pull the handles up, it goes left, push them down, it goes right. Sometimes, it just goes wherever it likes. It must be shared around to each room.

By Monday night, the Base has filled back up and the evening meal at the Mess is more crowded. We have spent the day cleaning, organising our locker space, and waiting our turn to get the polisher onto our floor. After dinner, our turn arrives, and we hurriedly try to turn the dull floor into something resembling shiny.

Guy Randall from across the hall comes in and tells us our time is up.

'We've still got ten minutes left,' argues Nev, but Randall shoves him aside and unplugs the polisher. I walk over and go nose-to-nose with him, just waiting for him to swing. Nev steps in the middle.

'We are fine, just take the damn thing.'

Randall and I stay in place for a few more seconds; I am not budging.

He smiles, turns, and drags the polisher out the door.

We get our singlets out and rub the floor bringing up a reasonable sheen. Nev's diplomatic skills have avoided what was certainly going to end in a punch-up. I give him a wink. He smiles and nods knowingly. Seems to me he's seen more than his share of this sort of thing.

'So,' announces Nev, 'why did the chicken cross the road?' I shrug. 'To get to the other side. Why did the chicken cross the road?' He persists.

'To get to the other side?'

'Nope, to see Gregory Peck. Why did the rooster cross the road?' I shrug again.

'To cock-a-doodle-doo something. Why did the dinosaur cross the road?' A shake of the head from me.

'Because chickens hadn't been invented yet.'

Tuesday morning is stand-by-beds inspection. We are milling around when Corporal Kennedy and Flight Sergeant Gardner arrive. We all stand beside our beds, at ease, and await the inspecting officer entering the room.

Our room is toward the end and throughout the inspection we can hear yelling and beds being overturned. After what seems like an eternity, Flight Sergeant Gardner enters the room closely followed by Corporal Kennedy.

'*Stand Fast,*' yells Nev, and we snap to attention. They go left to Jim and Mike's side of the room.

I can see Flight Sergeant Gardner looking intently at Watto's locker. The second drawer is pulled out and overturned on the floor.

'Re-panic,' he says. I can hear two more drawers overturned from Jim's locker. Shortly after, I hear a bed being overturned.

'Re-panic,' he says again.

He comes to our side of the room and looks into Nev's locker. His finger wipes across the top of the mirror, looking for dust — nothing. He looks around the rest of the locker, apparently happy with what he sees. He comes to my locker and looks around.

I have put a lot of effort into this. All my uniform shirts have been ironed, socks neatly rolled and placed in rows, singlets precisely folded, every inch has been dusted. He tests the top of the doors for dust, finding nothing. Inside one door I have taped the front page of the Daily Advertiser with Doug Walters picture on it. He stops and reads.

'Didn't get a bat,' he says. I nervously respond.

'No, Flight Sergeant. I reckon Chappell and McCosker are looking for a spot back in the Super Test Team.'

'You are probably right, but it's just pyjama cricket,' he says. 'Where are you from, son?'

'Dungog, Flight Sergeant,' I say with some pride that Doug Walters and I share the same hometown. He turns and looks straight at me.

'No room for sentiment here, young Dougie,' he says. 'If I find that newspaper clipping here tomorrow, I will scrunch it into a ball and shove it up your arse. You understand?'

'Yes, sir,' my arse clenching nervously at the thought. He does a double take and walks toward me extending his hand, finger pointing at my nose.

'And, don't call me sir. I work for a fucking living.' There is real anger on his face.

I'm going to stay clear of this guy. He's scary.

He walks over to my bed roll, tells me it's shit, and throws it around the room. Nev's bed is next and, despite an intense examination, he gets through completely unscathed.

How the hell did he do that?

On his way out the door he turns to Corporal Kennedy.

'Re-panic for the whole room,' which means we will all do it again tomorrow, in spite of Nev's unblemished performance. Nev is not happy with the rest of us.

The next day, the inspection is repeated without blemish. Nev has had a hand in constructing the four bed rolls in our room. Corporal Kennedy takes the opportunity to point out the common mistakes people have made with inspection preparation and cleaning. My mind isn't there.

Grandad and Uncle Bert will be finishing their morning tea about now.

'You bloody listening, Dougie?' he yells, staring at me as if reading my mind.

The constant heat and drill leave us exhausted at the end of each day. It's like every bit of energy gets sucked from our bodies. There are not too many evening pursuits except for some TV at the Apprentice Club, or a game of cards. The exhaustive days help us to sleep in the heat. But, it's not always a deep sleep.

It seems one of the favoured pastimes on the Base is setting off the fire alarm at three in the morning. We evacuate the building, form up outside and see if anyone is missing. The Base fire truck screams into view sometime later and the fire fighters run in to check for any evidence of fire. Obviously, there are none, only the broken glass from an alarm.

The Service Police turn up a few minutes later in their white Valiant station wagon. We are then collectively subjected to interrogation as to who let the fire alarm off. They are not exactly a smart bunch.

Why would we let our own alarm off and parade outside our accommodation block at three in the morning?

Our marching improves to the point we are deemed competent enough to be on the parade ground. The surface is much more conducive to drill and we are introduced to the art of changing direction left, right, and reverse, while marching in slow, quick and double time, moving as a group without losing alignment of the ranks, or losing the step. We are starting to rely on each other. Some guys have a tendency to look down at their feet.

'Don't look at the fucking ground,' screams Corporal Kennedy. 'There is no money there. I already looked.'

There is also a tendency to look at aircraft. Most of us have never seen so many aeroplanes and helicopters — may as well be something from another galaxy. When one is flying around, it is extremely difficult to not look up. One of the instructors has a unique method for dealing with the issue.

If one of his charges looks the way of an aircraft, they are positioned at the centre of the parade ground, at attention, and must yell out the identity and relative position of any aircraft in the vicinity.

'Iroquois Helicopter at three o'clock high, Corporal,' one Apprentice screams. If they get the aircraft identification wrong, they have to double around the parade ground.

The other flights always seem to be a step ahead of us in terms of knowledge, skill, and precision. One, in particular, is very advanced — Five Flight. Five Flight's instructor, Corporal Perry, is newly promoted and I overheard Corporal Kennedy say he is out to make a name for himself. Five Flight is on the parade ground for long periods of time, in the oppressive summer heat. One day this week, he had them turning on the same spot for so long, their boots left black marks scoured into the parade ground.

He seems to be in a permanently bad mood; an angry man. I wouldn't like to get on the wrong side of him, I reckon he would get real nasty. He is the exception though, the other instructors are tough, but helpful, and generally jovial.

We have started to adapt to the routine. For me, it has a settling effect and brings some comfort amongst all the yelling. I am used to being up early to milk before school and to help out after school. Some of the others find the incessant tasks and hurrying a little confronting. Paul Van Dijk appears in our room late one evening, obviously in some distress.

'I can't do this, Dougie,' he sits on the edge of my bed, lower lip trembling, 'I've never been away from home before.' He starts to sob. Nev sits next to him and puts an arm around his shoulders.

'It's okay, mate. We'll look after you.' Nev looks at me, his face is not convincing.

By the next week, we gain a level of competency at marching and are permitted to participate in morning parade. Each morning, except Tuesdays, there is a parade for the entire RAAF School of Technical Training, RAAFSTT as it is known. There are six squadrons on the parade with various numbers of Flights, I reckon about eight hundred people, give or take. Being allowed onto the parade is a big deal for us. We have practised and practised this. It's now time to put the practice into effect.

We are all lined up on the eastern side of the parade ground, Standing Easy. The Warrant Officer Disciplinary, known as the WOD, marches onto the parade ground and screams, '*Markers*'. This is the signal for us to stop messing around and stand *At Ease*. With markers in place, the WOD commands, 'RAAFSTT, *On Parade*.' There are two double thumps from the bass drum, the side drums erupt into life, and everyone steps off. As we approach Lurch's position, Corporal Kennedy orders us to halt and left turn.

It all goes pretty well from there. Our drill isn't perfect, but we are at least doing roughly the same things as each other. The Open Order March is almost textbook.

During the inspection, the WOD stalks the parade ground randomly yelling at people, finding details he's not happy with, uniforms, posture, somebody smiling, pretty much anything. He has the pace stick under the left arm with the elbow bent at right angles, the lower part of the arm horizontal to the ground, fingers extended straight from the body. It's like something from a Pommie war movie.

Today he is screaming at some cook who has a dirty shirt. The whole parade ground can hear it.

'This was a white shirt before it was issued to you, AC Ward. It's supposed to remain a white shirt. How did you manage to do this?' I can tell there is a response, but it is in hushed tones.

'Working on your car?' His voice has a tone like someone has challenged the fidelity of his wife. The WOD is screaming back at the unfortunate cook.

'Working on your car?' he repeats. 'The Royal Australian Air Force doesn't allow you to wear its shirt to work on your car. It's your uniform son, not a pair of overalls. You will be in my office at 12.30 pm today with the cleanest, whitest shirt you own, and we can discuss what I am going to charge you with. DO YOU UNDERSTAND?'

'No wonder they call them Thicks,' comes a voice from behind me.

After inspection, the flag is raised, and then the march past commences. Being Seven Flight in Six Squadron, we will be the last flight to step off on the march past and we have to stand still for a long time waiting. You have to wiggle your toes, rock back and forth on your feet and clench and unclench hands to keep the blood circulating all the way up to the brain. Otherwise, you could wake up face down on the tarmac, which won't be pretty. Finally, we step off.

Lurch and the boys at the front are watching Corporal Kennedy like hawks. He has positioned Nev about three ranks back and centre to call the step. It's working a treat till we get to the Eyes Right command on the march past. It all goes to shit from there. We have the heads to the right, but there are feet and arms going every which way. By the time we get the Eyes Front order, there is barely a person in step.

Lurch has gone to full Square Gait. The right arm is swinging forward as the right foot goes forward, and left arm goes forward with the left foot. It's actually quite hard to do intentionally and goes completely against the natural rhythm, but then nobody could ever accuse Lurch of having anything resembling natural rhythm.

Later, we are adopting 'Plan B' under a gum tree in the shade. Some of the boys light a fag and I pick a piece of grass and chew the stump, daydreaming. Out front of the library, I catch sight of Flight Sergeant Gardner and he's giving Corporal Kennedy a dressing down. I can't hear what is said, but there is finger-pointing and our corporal has his head down. I recount the incident to the other boys.

We are going to have to lift our game.

For the next hour, we get off our arses and practise. Stevens gives the commands as we march around. Nev is the umpire, walking around correcting errors and making suggestions. By the time Corporal Kennedy returns, we reckon we have it down pat. He runs us through a variety of drill movements and the session is longer than usual. After an hour, he seems happy with our progress and dismisses us for the day, but we take the early mark to work on a few things with the taller guys who inhabit the front of the flight in the march past. If they get it wrong, we are all in trouble.

The following morning, our parade performance is almost textbook stuff and Corporal Kennedy is pleased. The close presence of Flight Sergeant Gardner throughout the parade tells me there may have been a little more at stake than met the eye.

One of the few respites from parade ground drill this week has been filling out forms. Corporal Kennedy takes us into a classroom where we get issued a stack of forms a good inch thick. Each one requires Surname, Given Names, Service Number, Rank, Date of Birth and then whatever special information the specific form requires. Some require father and mother's names, or next of in. Others require height, eye and hair colour. It's amazing how many people don't know how tall they are. Corporal Kennedy spends some time standing beside guys, looking them up and down, and announcing their height. He calls it his calibrated eyeball.

Others have difficulty remembering their Service Number and he has a list in his pocket. We had to write it on the labels of all our clothes.

How do these guys not remember their Service Number?

Paul Van Dijk doesn't show for parade on Wednesday morning. He got a tough time during *Stand By Beds* inspection yesterday and was in tears half the day. Corporal Kennedy goes to look for him and doesn't come back for a while. When he does, he says that Van Dijk has opted out and we will not be seeing him again. We all have a ninety day 'get out' option, no questions asked, and Paul has decided to take it.

It has a stunning effect. I can see everyone thinking about whether they should also opt out. Silence for an extended period. When we move off, there is some sort of increased resolve in our step. It's like we have just taken a collective hit, but we are going to overcome it.

Our next challenge is adding a rifle to the drill equation. Corporal Kennedy marches us down to the Base Armoury behind the Sergeants' Mess where Sergeant Lane and LAC Dwyer issue us with an SLR and a ground sheet. He takes us to a shady tree where we each roll out a ground sheet and he introduces us to the intricacies of the weapon.

'Listen carefully, lads, you will need to know this stuff in your sleep,' he starts. 'This is the 7.62-millimetre L1A1, Self-Loading Rifle, the SLR. The major components of the rifle are, from the front: flash suppressor, barrel, gas plug, forward sight, gas regulator, forward woodwork, dust cover, carry handle, magazine, cocking handle, change lever, trigger and pistol grip, rear sight, and rifle butt. You got all that?'

'Yes, Corporal,' we all say.

'Okay, now I want you to point at each component as I say them.' He goes through the list and we point while he corrects any errors. He repeats the lesson twice more.

'Okay, now I want one of you to show me the components.' He looks around seeking a candidate. 'Dougie?' he asks me. I get through the first few, but my memory fails after the *Forward Sight*. 'Anyone want to help him?'

'Gas regulator, Corporal,' says Nev.

'Good,' he says. 'Keep going, Walsh.' I manage to get the rest right. Two other guys get the same treatment. By lunch time, we can readily identify all parts. We lock the weapons into a room and head to the Mess. We are last through and the selection sucks; either rice and some sort of Chinese chicken, or sausages with mash and cabbage. The salads have been decimated. In the heat, I don't really feel like either, but the need to fuel my body outstrips the lack of enthusiasm.

After lunch, we start with rifle drill. Corporal Kennedy demonstrates standing *At Ease*, and at *Attention*, with the rifle — right hand and left foot moving in unison. He then runs us through several commands correcting errors as he goes. All good so far.

It gets a whole bunch harder moving from standing *At Attention*, known as *The Order*, to *The Shoulder*. The command is *Shoulder Arms*. You need plenty of leverage on the forward sight to throw the weapon vertically with your right hand and then catch the pistol grip with the same hand, the left hand grabbing the forward woodwork. The left hand then snaps quickly back to the side of the body. If all goes to plan, the *Forward Sight* ends nestled neatly in the armpit area, weapon neatly tucked in between the chest and right arm. The reverse movement back to the order is less difficult.

I am almost six-foot tall and so the long SLR Rifle is not too hard for me to throw around. Poor Nev is only five-four and seven stone wringing wet, it's a whole other problem for him.

Corporal Kennedy allows us some time to practise the movements on our own and I have it fairly well under control within several minutes. Some of the other lads need more time and a little coaching. Once we have individually got a reasonable level of skill, we do it as a group, Corporal Kennedy giving the commands. He has Nev calling the cadence as we go from the order to the shoulder and back, standing at ease every now and again. The perspiration flows freely and most of us have a wet strip down the back of our overalls in no time.

After a quick drink break, he demonstrates the *Present Arms*. The practice proceeds through the afternoon. We are getting tired and I am not sure I can go on much longer, but nobody is giving in, so I dig in for a long innings.

'Seven Flight, *Shoulderrrrr Arms*,' commands Corporal Kennedy. Instinctively, my right hand grabs the forward sight and thrusts the rifle upward. As I am taking control of the weapon and returning my left hand to my side, there is the unmistakable sound of a weapon hitting the ground. We all look toward the poor culprit — it's Jim.

'There is no need for that, Wenke,' screams Corporal Kennedy marching right up into his face. 'What did the poor, defenceless, rifle ever do to you?' Blank look, no response. I have no idea what I would say either. 'Now, rifle above your head, double around the parade ground, GO.' He sets off at a trot, arms extended.

'Anyone else want to drop their rifle?'

While it's obviously a rhetorical question, it has had its effect. We are exhausted; no one wants to run around with a rifle above their head. It strikes me that Corporal Kennedy treats his rifle like his life depends on it and expects us to do the same.

Maybe he has some experience there?

When we finally sign the rifles back into the armoury in the late afternoon, I am totally drained, and I know I'm not alone. We take a shower and grab a feed. Tonight, its schnitzel, mash and gravy, a selection of grey veg, which probably started life being green, and pumpkin to go with it.

Thursday is our first pay day and Wednesday we are put through a practice session. There are two tables set up with Flight Sergeant Gardner sitting at the far right and two LACs on his left. He stands and begins the instruction.

'You will line up to the right here in alphabetical order. When your turn comes, march up to the NCO with the pay books here,' he says, pointing at one of the LACs. '*Halt and right turn.* Tell him your name and service number and he will hand over your pay book. As the line progresses, you sidestep left to the paying NCO here,' pointing at the second LAC, 'where you hand over your pay book. He will put the appropriate amount of money onto the pay book and hand it to the Paying Officer here,' he says, pointing at the place where he will sit.

'You then sidestep left and stand at attention in front of me. I will count the appropriate amount of money out to you. You can then step forward, gather the money in your left hand and step back. At attention, you say 'Pay correct, sir,' salute, left turn and march away. Clear?'

'Yes, Flight,' we say in a chorus. He looks at me.

'Dougie, why is it so important to pick up the money with the left hand?'

'So, we can salute with the right, Flight.'

'Well done that, man,' he says. 'Normally, you should never salute a Non-Commissioned Officer, but for the purposes of this exercise, you can salute me just this once,' he smiles.

The next day, pay parade goes well and I am now ninety-four dollars and sixty cents richer. It's more money than I have ever had in my life.

On the way back to get changed for dinner, there is something not quite right. I can't put my finger on it, but something is wrong. We are approaching the accommodation block when a whole bunch of Second- Year Apprentices come running out screaming, they start to herd us like cattle and pick off the slow ones. It's like a scene from a documentary and the lions have us surrounded.

Once captured, the young Sprog has one leg applied to the water outlet on the fire hydrant, sleeves are rolled down and secured, and the water is turned on. The overalls fill quickly, ballooning with water, then it starts to escape through the easiest means, out through the neck and onto the face. Sprog after Sprog is subjected to the 'Sprog wash'.

It's not an unpleasant experience in the hot Wagga afternoon sun and by the end, there are few left dry.

Thursday is steak night at the Mess. They even serve chips as a bit of a treat. The place is unusually empty. We get to go through without lining up and there's plenty to go around. We surmise people are cashed up on pay night and head to town for take-away. Even some of our fellow First- Year Apprentices are favouring an ASCO hamburger over Mess food. I opt for steak, chips and salad. The boys are chatty this evening.

'Well, I reckon they have just about finished breaking us,' announces Thommo.

'What do you mean?' asks Nev.

'Basic training is all about breaking you down and rebuilding you to do whatever they tell you. They don't stop until we are all doing the same thing, at the same time, without thinking about it. No room in the forces for people who think for themselves.'

'How do you know?'

'My dad was in the army. He did this for a living.'

Pretty much what Uncle Bert told me would happen, although I didn't believe him at the time.

'Have you ever shagged a girl?' asks Lurch, changing the subject. Darryl Turner looks up with interest.

'There was this one *sheila* in the form above me who was the school bike,' he tells a now captivated audience. 'Everyone rode her. She shagged me in the toilet at my mate's sixteenth, then shagged two other guys after me. Slut.'

'How do you shag a girl in a toilet?' asks Thommo. 'There ain't a lot of room.'

He gives us a blow-by-blow account and I slip away before the scant details of my sex life are sought.

Later in the night, there is commotion in the hall and we stick our heads out to see what's going on. There are five Second-Year Apprentices going room to room, and by the sound of it, they are flipping beds. They get to our room and barge in, obviously pissed.

'Get out of the way, Sprog,' one says, before inverting my bed. The mattress lands on the floor with base on top, the two ends collapse easily on top of the base. The other three beds in the room follow quickly and then they are gone. No sooner have we reassembled the beds than another three pissed second years come through the door. The beds are inverted again and I decide it might be a good idea to wait and see if there is a third party.

Ten minutes later, I am not disappointed, but the second years are.

'Who rumbled your bed, Sprog?' one asks.

'Ask your mates,' I tell him. He doesn't seem impressed and kicks my bedding around the room a little before departing.

'Cock,' I yell after him.

Friday rolls around; the day is filled with training on how to fire the SLR. We spend most of the time lying on ground sheets working through endless repetitions of firing commands and what to do if the rifle stops. I reckon I can do this in my sleep. Even lying down, the heat is cruel, and we have a water break every forty minutes. Some of the boys have taken to drenching their green giggle hat under the tap. They are generally dry again before the next break, except for the band of sweat around the inside rim.

Lunch, as usual on Fridays, is fish. Fried fish, fish fingers, there is even a fish soup. I cannot bring myself to try the soup. Fish fingers on bread with salad are accompanied by four large glasses of cordial from the silver drink urns. These drink urns are amazing things. Bare metal exterior, about eighteen inches square and two feet high, they must be constructed like a thermos because the hot drinks come out fucking hot, and the cold ones fucking cold.

After signing our rifles back into the armoury, we all hit the showers. This afternoon, we are going to be allowed off Base for the first time. The dress is Blue Service Dress, known as 'blues', with long sleeves and tie. Two buses fill quickly and we snake our way to the main drag and toward the main gate. We have not been permitted this far down the main drag before. There is a service station on the left and a large oval on the right, roller on the turf pitch out in the centre.

Then there are houses on both sides of the road. Each has a neatly manicured lawn, fence, and a name plate attached to the letter box, Squadron Leader this, Flight Lieutenant that, all very organised.

The guard house at the main gate is a two-storey, brick structure. There is a guy in blues watching each vehicle go out the gate. Our bus creeps through and turns left onto the highway. A Meteor and Sabre Jet are parked between the wooden fence and the road; fighters that used to be the first line of defence.

As we go down the hill toward Wagga Wagga, I can see a hill with a tower in the distance. The road is straight for a while, then meanders past a drive-in picture theatre and some industrial buildings, before becoming dead straight again.

We reach a set of lights before the road dips under a railway overpass. As we turn right, I see some wag has spray-painted the tin fence. The inscription is, 'Give Fraser the Razor'. I reckon grandad would agree with that. He is always going off because the Liberals have a majority in their own right and Fraser doesn't listen to the Country Party. I can hear him now, 'Doug Anthony doesn't have the bargaining power he had against McMahon, and Fraser is squandering his time. At least Gough had a bloody red hot go at it. Fraser needs to get on with something, or get out of the way.'

We get dropped at a park on Morgan Street and told to be back by 1645 hours; bus leaves no later than 1700.

Bayliss Street, Wagga Wagga is long and straight. We wander up and down looking for music and electrical shops. Almost everyone wants to price a television, record player, or cassette player. Most of us can't afford any of it just yet.

It feels funny being in a uniform walking around a country town. The locals seem to be used to it, but some of the people our age give us a snigger, others are almost hostile. Most of them still have their long curls, so even without the uniform we would definitely stand out.

Nev and I find a music place and I buy a cassette. It is Wings at the Speed of Sound. It's a sentimental purchase. Mum loved Paul McCartney. Nev tells me I'm a dick because I don't have a cassette player. He's got something there.

Back in the park waiting for the bus, we all compare purchases and I have time to look my fellow Thirty-Three Intake Apprentices up and down. It's a real mix. There are the tall and thin, the tall and thickset, and every combination down to the short and thin, like Nev. There are various shades with a good smattering of boys with a dark Mediterranean complexion, Greek and Italian, some with big noses. There is even one Chinese looking guy from Townsville, though his accent is more Aussie than mine.

I have started to notice that there are variations of the Aussie accent. The guys from South Australia having a particular weird thing happening like a little English accent amongst the Aussie. West Australians have a variation I can't quite put my finger on. The funniest ones are from Queensland. They have a long, slow, drawl and many sentences end in a 'hey'. Nev reckons they all talk with their lips close together so the flies don't get in.

The spread of attitudes is likewise varied. There are the quiet ones who keep to themselves and read. There are those who like a chat, sometimes endlessly talking about the most childish nonsense. There are the cool kids, or at least they think they are, and there are the spoiled brats who squeal when they don't get their way. There are boys who have money and let you know how much money they have, and there are those who have obviously had it tough at some point. Some are scroungers, always trying to get something for free in every deal or make a quick dollar off you.

While I am looking around considering the varied characters, Randall walks into view with a couple of his henchmen in tow. He is clearly looking for a target. He picks up a shopping bag belonging to one of the smaller guys.

'Get yourself a little dolly, did we, Cooper?' His mates laugh. Cooper gets up and tries to retrieve the bag.

They throw it around for a little while, Cooper running after each throw, but they get bored quickly and move along, the bag discarded on the ground. Guys like him make my blood boil and there are more than a few of them smattered throughout the various flights. I feel the need to provide them with a response, via my fist in their face.

Randall will keep, at least for now.

The next week, they let us onto the rifle range. One and two flights go first, and we watch on from a distance, continuing our rifle firing tuition under a gum tree, interspersed with General Service, Maths and English lessons. I wonder why we need maths and English when the selection standards to become a RAAF Apprentice are pretty high. Our teacher, an education officer, explains the curriculum around Australia differs between states and the RAAF just wants everyone at the same standard — sounds fair enough to me.

General Service training includes instruction on the history of the RAAF, the various aircraft, squadrons and bases. It also includes instruction on basic hygiene, bush medicine, and more general medical issues. We are giving a stern talking to about visiting prostitutes and the prospect of venereal disease.

The guy doing the hygiene training hands out condoms. Being red-blooded teenage boys, the condoms get a workout. Over the ensuing days, movement around our accommodation is undertaken with some care. At every turn, someone is throwing a condom full of water, from second floor windows, from behind trees, from doorways, everywhere.

The other party trick is to entice someone on the ground or second floor to stick their head of the window. This is normally accomplished by yelling till someone puts their head out to see what the commotion is. Once the head is outside, the boys on the third floor pour a bucket of water on the unsuspecting victim.

Late on Tuesday afternoon, we are waiting to return our rifles to the armoury watching members of Six Flight on the range. Sergeant Lane is the officer-in-charge of the practice with Corporal Butler acting as his assistant. The 'fire' command is given and there is sporadic fire from the six Apprentices on the mound. Being relatively young and scrawny, it's actually quite hard to hold such a large, heavy weapon up on the shoulder long enough to get a good and somewhat steady sight of the target. The bigger guys appear to be getting their rounds away more easily and with a level of confidence beyond me.

Through the smoke, I can see Steve Rose fiddling with the action. He has a stoppage. He gives the weapon a shake and can't clear it. He starts turning around asking Corporal Butler a question through the gunfire. No one can hear him and the muzzle of the gun is turning with him.

In an instant I hear, 'Cease fire, get down.' Sergeant Lane throws himself at Rose, separating rifle from shooter in a swift movement and knocking both to the ground solidly. Everyone within fifty yards is on the ground covering their heads.

I look up toward the mound as the rifle smoke clears, Sergeant Lane is getting up dusting himself off. He hands the rifle to Corporal Butler and picks up Rose. He's holding his ribs and crying. Lane picks him up with ease and carries him into the shelter, sitting him down. The water bottle comes off his belt and to Rose's mouth. A handkerchief appears and is soaked, Sergeant Lane wipes Rose's forehead, cradling the boy in his arms.

LAC Dwyer comes running from the armoury. There is a quick exchange of words before he runs back to the armoury. Corporal Butler has cleared the mounds and he and Corporal Kennedy are busily clearing each of the weapons. A few minutes later, the RAAF ambulance roars into view, sliding sideways in the dirt as it turns toward the range. It skids to a stop and a medical orderly and nursing sister exit. Rose is taken away at a pace.

Corporal Kennedy comes back over to us and instructs us to form up. We are commanded to place our weapons on the ground and Stand Easy.

'Did you guys see that?'

'Yes, Corporal,' a couple of us respond.

'So, what golden rule did you see broken?'

'The loaded weapon is always pointed down range, Corporal,' says Watson.

'Exactly, Watson. You guys will be using the range tomorrow. I don't want to see anyone turn around with a loaded weapon in your hands. If you get into trouble, keep the weapon pointed down range and put your hand in the air. If you are lying down, put your foot in the air. Is that clear?'

'Yes, Corporal,' we say as one.

Wednesday morning, and it's our turn on the range. The range is a twenty-five-yard affair. A firing point at one end and a large mound of dirt behind the targets at the other. The targets are on white, cardboard cards, representing targets at ranges of 100, 200 and 300 metres, the cards held onto a wooden board by rubber bands. The symbols on the cards have some resemblance to an Asian person wearing a san pan hat; maybe they are leftovers from the war in Vietnam.

I have fired the shotgun on the farm before so the kick of the SLR isn't too frightening, albeit a big kick. With the earmuffs on, the sound is somewhat subdued, and I reckon I could almost hear the breach block and slide move back and forward, ejecting the spent case and picking up a new round on the way through. Although my eyes are focused on the sights and target, I pick up the cases flying out the right side of the weapon in my peripheral vision.

After the first three sighting rounds, I feel fairly comfortable. Holding it firmly into the shoulder means the kick is absorbed a little and it doesn't feel like being hit with the butt. It also makes it easier to keep it still when taking aim. After the fourth and fifth rounds, I am able to concentrate on hitting the target without worrying about the kick and noise.

Firing from the prone and kneeling positions allows me to get good control over the rifle and I can just make out movement in the dark symbol as the round goes through. It's much harder from the standing position as there is nowhere to rest our arms and we have to support the full weight of the rifle. As I aim, the muzzle is waving around and I can't seem to keep it still; I just don't have the strength. I think to myself, the longer this goes on, the harder it will be. I manage to squeeze off the five rounds, but can see dark marks outside the symbol on the white target card.

I rest the rifle and wait for the others to finish. Two up from me on the mound, I can see Nev struggling. He's only a little fella and the muzzle is wavering all over the place, the rifle probably weighs more than he does. I can tell he is letting off rounds as his sights are hopefully moving across the target, not the best strategy.

With everyone finished, we make the weapons safe and move forward to the targets. I have managed to get four hits on the 300-metre target, and five on the 200-metre target, but there are only two on the 100-metre target. It's the standing position I have to work on. After the scores are recorded, we move back to the mound, pick up our rifles, move to the shade under the gum tree, and nearly everyone lights up.

We are all comparing notes. Watto has managed to score thirteen from the fifteen scored shots, I have eleven. I seek out Nev. He's sitting on his own contemplating his cards.

'How'd you go, mate?'

'Fuck it, Dougie. I hit four on both the prone and kneeling, but couldn't hold it up standing up.'

'I could see, mate. Watto is pretty strong and he scored four standing and only missed one prone. It's all in the strength of your arms.' Nev and I decide we are going to work on our strength to see if we can get our scores up. We do curls with buckets of water each night.

Friday morning, we find ourselves lined up like sheep outside Medical Section filing through for a cocktail of inoculations. Military medical care is nothing like what I remember of going to the doctor in Dungog. There is a distinct lack of bedside manner, sympathy, or empathy. We leave feeling like our arms have been used for darts practice.

After lunch, we get another go on the range. This time Nev and I both score three from the standing position. He scores eleven in total and I have twelve. Watto has a perfect fifteen. It's progress, and we'll get another chance to improve next week.

Saturday morning, I am feeling like crap and get up early.

Maybe a shower will help?

I am burning up with a temperature and my left arm hurts like shit. It's in the spot where that Flight Lieutenant poked a needle into me. She had the touch of a Front Row Forward. I reckon she's probably on the Officers Mess darts team.

I try and wake Nev for breakfast, but he's in a worse way than me. He can't get out of bed and so I make him a bacon and egg sanga. Over the course of the day, we bring him food and drinks from the Mess, but most of it ends up in the bin.

By 1600, I am getting really worried about him. He hasn't

held down anything during the day and he isn't lucid. Jim and I decide to take him to medical section.

Flight Lieutenant Brooker greets us with a snarl. She's the same one that jabbed me in the arm the other day; I recognise the heavy makeup.

'Sick Parade was this morning,' she says, abruptly. 'Come back tomorrow.' She turns to walk away.

'Ma'am, he hasn't held anything down all day and he's burning up,' Jim pleads.

'He's delirious,' I add. She stops and looks around.

'Bring him in here.' She rolls her eyes, then sits him down, examining him. She puts a thermometer in his mouth, waiting for it to register. She pulls it out and looks.

'Shit.' She is running now, calling for help. In no time, a medical orderly with a stretcher appears. We help them lay him down. She is giving orders quickly, the Orderly setting up a drip, and she pushes the needle into his arm. Nev is wheeled away.

She comes back a half hour later looking a little dishevelled.

'The doctor is with him now. His temperature has come down and he will be okay. Thank you so much for looking after your friend; he was in real trouble.' A smile comes to her face and I realise she not as scary as she seemed an hour ago. She is actually quite pretty.

Maybe she should ditch the makeup.

Most of the guys have been affected by the inoculations. Some of the less affected Apprentices take some delight in slapping or punching others in the affected arm, Sanders being one of the main culprits — dickhead. It is quite excruciating, and I get really mad, but don't have the strength to do anything about it.

By Monday, most of us are not much better. Rifle drill on the Wagga Wagga parade ground, in the February heat, is no fun at the best of times. Running a temperature and having a throbbing arm makes it even more enjoyable. At least Corporal Kennedy takes pity on us. He says the smallpox vaccine affects everyone differently and he elects to commence our bivouac preparation under the shade of a gum. It's map reading and navigation using a silver compass, in the midst of a haze of cigarette smoke. I am wondering if I should just take it up with the rest of them.

The lessons are about patrolling in the bush, hand signals, silence, and no talking. Corporal Kennedy starts to teach us contact drills.

'*Contact Right,*' he yells. We all turn and run yelling to our right. Run, drop, fire, look, run again. We are going on bivouac soon and the drills must be executed right. He also instructs us on survival techniques. Where do we find water? What can we eat in the bush? How to make a shelter. He keeps telling yarns about how they did this in Vietnam. Trouble is, we aren't going on bivouac in Vietnam.

The mail comes in each day and we pick it up from the Orderly Room. Most of the guys get a letter about once a week. Mine are a little more infrequent, but high in quality. I can tell it's grandma doing the writing and I can just imagine grandad dictating from the kitchen table over morning tea. 'Tell him about the corn crop.' Grandma's letters aren't the only ones, Louise gives me the school gossip.

Between lessons, the talk turns to any subject, football being one of the main topics. There is heated debate about which form of football is superior. The southern states guys are unable to contemplate any supremacy of rugby and Rugby League over Aussie Rules.

As the week progresses, the pain in my arm eases and the festering sore turns to a scab. Nev re-joins us on Wednesday morning, back to his usual chipper self.

'Dougie, did you hear about the scarecrow who got an award? He was outstanding in his field,' laughing at his own joke.

Wednesday afternoon, we are parked under another tree awaiting another tactics lesson. A few of the boys light up a smoke and the talk turns to parents.

'So, what's your old man do for a living, Nev?' asks Stevens.

'Don't know, I haven't seen him for five years,' he tells Mark, with a frankness bordering on dislike. 'Prick just up and fucked off and didn't tell anyone where he was going.'

I can see from the look on Mark's face this is an alien concept to him.

'How does your mum cope?'

'Oh, she's okay, they're divorced now. Mum's been working for a local solicitor for years. The old man used to piss all his money up the wall, so mum decided to get a job to feed us kids.'

'Your mum works?' There is a hint of superiority in Stevens' tone. Not only is Stevens stuck up, he's a suckhole too. Anytime Corporal Kennedy is nearby, he's just behind him. Prick even irons his overalls.

'Yes, mate, we'd have gone hungry if she hadn't. What's your old man do?' Nev returns the question.

'Works in a bank in Sydney.'

'My parents are divorced too,' Thommo jumps in.

'Mine too,' adds Youngy.

Turns out, three quarters of the boys are from divorced, or at least separated, parents. It must be tough being the meat in the sandwich when parents split.

I don't recall this many guys from my school having separated parents. Maybe I am not the only one running away from something.

During the day, we tell Corporal Kennedy about the Service Police trying to finger us for setting off our own fire alarm.

'Fucking elephant trackers,' he says, and we giggle. 'Don't take too much notice. They aren't the brightest crayon in the box. Some of those guys couldn't track an elephant in snow.'

Thursday, the first day of autumn, no change in the weather though, still fuckin' hot. I have developed a deep tan on my neck and arms where my overalls aren't shielding the skin from the sun. Nev reckons if we could shade around our eyes, mouth and hands we could do a Black and White Minstrels show.

Thursday also marks five weeks since we've been in this man's Air Force. Only eight years and forty-seven weeks to go.

We are doing final preparations for our last time on the range. Things are becoming quite competitive and it's probably going to take a perfect score to win. There is a fair amount of tension as we prep our rifles. Watto looks smug as he checks his weapon.

We get to the mound; ammunition is issued. Sergeant Lane briefs us on the nature of the practice then instructs us to put our hearing protection on.

'Three rounds in your own time, at the top left, target, fire.' Almost immediately, I let a round off and follow quickly with two more. I can make out three rounds hitting the target.

After 'safing' the weapons, we go forward to check the fall

of shot. I don't need to adjust the sights on my weapon, others make minor adjustments. We put two more rounds into the top left target, just to make sure. There will be no excuses today.

From the prone position the five rounds go into the bottom left target and I am feeling good. We go to the kneeling position.

'Five rounds in five seconds, at the bottom right target, fire.'

On the second shot, all I get is click as the hammer strikes the breach block. 'Fuck.' I instinctively start the procedure they have hammered into us.

Cock, lock, look, fuck nothing. Let the working parts go forward and continue firing.'

I get the other three away, no problem, but I am conscious that I have a live round on the ground beside me. I put my left hand up. Corporal Kennedy comes over, one earmuff cup off his ear.

'Stoppage, Corporal,' I say, pointing at the unfired round on the ground.

'We'll come back to it,' he says calmly.

As we are standing for the last part of the practice, I can feel the perfect score slipping away from me.

'Five rounds in five seconds, at the top right target, fire.

I let go and see a black spot appear on the white part of the card, shit. I get all five rounds away and see one blacker spot appear.

Shit, shit, shit.

'Unload,' Sergeant Lane yells. We all go through the motions. Corporal Kennedy has a quick word with the sergeant, comes over and hands me another round. Sergeant Lane gets me to put the round into the magazine, adopt the kneeling position, and commands me through a single round at the bottom right target.

It hits okay, but I am devastated. I know there are at least two missed shots here, and possibly more.

When we check the cards, my worst fears are confirmed. I have actually missed three — a score of twelve. Nev proudly boasts a perfect fifteen. Even Watto has managed to cock up one round. Nev is triumphant and don't we get to hear about it.

For the next three days, we get a constant stream of one-liners.

'Can you give me a hand with this, Nev?'

'I'll take a shot at it.'

'You coming to the Apprentice Club, Nev?'

'One hundred per cent, mate,' or, his absolute favourite, 'I'll aim to be there.'

If only I had kept my cool when I had the stoppage, I wouldn't have to put up with his crappy jokes.

The next day, backpacks, ground sheets, sleeping bags and houtchies are issued. We are ready for bivouac.

A week later, I am sitting in a hole in the ground somewhere east of Tumbarumba. I relieved Thommo in the gun pit around midnight and I have my eyes peeled, looking back and forth up the road, not that I can see much. There's no moon. My SLR is resting on the sandbags and I have my hands loosely around it.

Fuck, it's colder than a witch's tit.

It's been so hot in Wagga that I had almost forgotten to bring a jumper. It was only at the insistence of Corporal Kennedy that I put a jumper and greatcoat into my pack. Lucky, I did. We can't be far from the Snowy Mountains. I have a couple of lollies from the ration pack to keep me company.

Around 0230, I think I see something on the road to the south. There is definite movement, but I can't see what it is. I wish I could communicate with Youngy in the other pit and ask if he can see anything, I tighten my grip on the pistol grip of the rifle, and watch. They did say anything moving outside the perimeter should be shot. I look more closely, straining my eyes to make out a silhouette, anything. A little while later, the kangaroo hops back into the scrub and I have a little smile to myself.

Suddenly, there is gunfire to my left. It's about four or five shots, but a fair way off. A short time later, all the boys start filling the pits.

'We've been ordered to *Stand To,*' says Lurch. He takes over prime position in the gun pit. We sit, scanning the dark bush for movement, nothing. Around 0500, it gets colder. I would do anything for a hot cup of tea.

How the fuck did I get here?

Four months ago, I had just finished fourth form at Dungog High School. Now, I am hundreds of miles away in the Snowy Mountains, freezing my arse off, with a rifle in my hand. I could do with a few hours sleep.

Fuck, I am so tired.

Lurch is beside me. He has not rested since we *Stood To* at 0300 hours, pivoting the SLR from left to right, eyes peeled. He might be a little 'un-co', and sometimes doesn't appear to be the sharpest tool in the shed, but by hell, he is persistent. And, he certainly isn't dumb.

We are ordered to *Stand Down* as the stars give way to the growing light. The fire is quickly lit and a billy on the heat. Cups of tea get passed around to reinvigorate everyone and we warm some food. So damn tired, my eyes feel like they have sand in them.

I look around. The elevated position allows a view of the bush, mist rising into a clear sky, stunning. I wrap my hands around my tin mug, close my eyes and think of home.

After morning brief, we patrol the area to the south of our position. The mission is to flush out any insurgents. Thommo is the Patrol Commander and I am his 2IC and Navigator. Sticks is carrying the radio and Lurch is Tail End Charlie, watching our back door. We are to zigzag our way down a grid square.

Nev is out in front as our Scout, he seems to be a natural at this, stepping silently through the scrub. He and Thommo exchange signals every now and again, while I keep an eye on the map and compass to make sure we are on the right heading. We stop every hour, double check our location, do a SITREP by radio, and eat if we need to.

Around 1400, we are coming to a creek and there is a rise beyond, not a lot of cover. I can tell Nev doesn't like it, he's moving quite slowly, then stops, shaking his head. He signals we should wait while he circles around in heavier cover for a look, then disappears.

He's been gone a while. I am scanning the bush at the top of the rise for a sign he may be there, but nothing. Thommo doesn't seem worried and is sitting back eating a survival biscuit.

'Can you see him, Dougie?' he whispers.

I am shaking my head in the negative when a twinkle of light flashes from the top of the hill. I look a bit harder and can make out Nev, just. I signal back to him.

'Thommo, he's about ten feet to the left of the Iron Bark over there. He's sitting behind the clump of blackberries. Can you see him?'

'Tell him to smile, Dougie,' he whispers, with a grin.

Nev is well concealed and Thommo has to look closely. Looking, looking, enlightenment coming to his face, he signals Nev and they exchange information silently.

'Seems there are three enemy troops at the top. He wants us to come around to the left there, the same way he went. We'll follow you, Dougie.' He clicks his fingers a few times to get the attention of the others and indicates they should follow me. I move off and cross the creek, keeping in the trees to conceal our approach. When we get to Nev, he is chuckling uncontrollably.

'Dougie, you guys couldn't sneak up on a deaf, dumb and blind bloke in a dead sleep. It was like a herd of elephants heading towards me.' We all look at each other. We thought we did pretty well. Obviously, Nev has a different standard to the rest of us.

'Okay, there's a couple of guys dug in at the top of this rise,' he says, pointing. I need someone to come with me and sneak around behind them, and I do mean sneak.' I put my hand in the air, volunteering. 'Not you, Dougie, you've got feet like Dumbo. Lurch, you come with me. The rest of you guys stay here. We'll start shooting at precisely 1500. When you hear the first shot, you come running up and catch them from the other way, got it?'

We're all nodding and giving him the thumbs up as he turns and picks his way through the scrub, and to be fair, he's a lot quieter than we were. We fan out and await the shot.

It's only a fifteen-minute wait, but it seems like an age. In the last few minutes, as the time closes in on what we agreed, we check our weapons and ammo. Right on the stroke of 1500, gunfire breaks out and we start running. There are now a number of weapons being fired and it's starting to intensify.

As we get to the top of the hill, I can see two figures in green behind a log, with backs to us, shooting into the bush. Another figure, behind a tree, shooting in the same direction.

I am sizing up the situation when Thommo stops, holding his fist in the air. We all stop in our tracks. He drops to one knee and indicates to the boys on the left to cover the two green guys behind the log, and we should cover the guy behind the tree. The shooting subsides.

One of the guys stands and turns around. It's Corporal Perry and, by the look on his face, he didn't have a clue we were there. He swears loudly and the others turn around. It's LAC Dwyer and some guy I have never seen before.

'Weapons on the ground and hands in the air,' demands Thommo.

Nev and Lurch appear out of the bush, Lurch goes to take Perry's rifle from him. He is shoved away.

'Fuck off.' Perry turns and walks off into the bush, his companions a few steps behind. We all break into laughter as they retreat.

'Fucking hilarious,' announces Nev, with the biggest grin. 'It was the most fun I've had in years, the look on his face!' I find myself patting him on the back along with the rest of the boys.

'And that, my friends, is what you call black magic.'

For the last two days of the bivouac, we are treated as mini heroes, particularly Nev. We are the guys who ambushed Corporal Perry. No one likes him, and it's cause for some celebration. Even Corporal Kennedy gets us to relate the story to him several times, just so he can laugh some more.

2 – Nothing Glamorous About This

Sunday morning, I am sitting on the dunny with a sharp pain in the belly. I have been here for a while, but nothing is budging.

Bloody ration packs.

There are a few whispers and giggling outside my stall and shadows moving around on the floor. I am about to yell out when something rolls under the door, a flash, and the loudest bang I've ever heard, complete with a shock wave. The stall fills quickly with smoke and I have to evacuate, coughing my way out.

Back in the room, Nev is sitting on his bed reading a magazine, looking a picture of innocence. The Bee Gees coming from the radio, Nev joins in the chorus.

'Ah, ha, ha, ha, barely alive, barely alive.'

As I comb my hair, I can see him in the mirror. A cheeky little grin slowly coming to his face.

'You little prick, Nev, you scared the crap out of me, literally. What the fuck was that?'

'A matchbox bomb,' he grins sitting up and pulling out another match box from the desk draw. 'One of the Gunnies off 32 Intake showed me how to make it.' He proceeds to give me the ins and outs of match box bomb construction. 'Brilliant, hey?'

'Good for the bowels, mate,' I frown.

I reckon the boys now have too much time on their hands. The practical jokes are starting to escalate. Dipping the hand of a sleeping Apprentice in warm water to make them piss themselves, shortsheeting a bed, and Glad wrap over the toilet bowl are the favourites. You have to stay alert.

At work, we finish off our final military lessons and exams. Corporal Kennedy announces that we won't be seeing as much of him anymore. It's a shame, we have come to rely heavily on his advice, navigating our way around both the RAAF customs, and certain personalities on the Base, without getting into trouble. I think he is also a bit sad at seeing us move along.

April, we start our engineering training proper and the first subject is Technical Drawing. It's precise work and the Corporal instructor is demanding of cleanliness on the paper. It's not my forte, on the farm the way we do things is agricultural in more ways than one. I struggle through the two weeks but thankfully manage to pass with a little help from Nev who did it at school.

Saturday afternoon, Nev and I head to the Apprentice Club, grab a couple of cartons of Iced Coffee from the fridge and a piece of fruit cake. The cake's a day old and has the consistency of a house brick. A couple of sips of milk makes it edible.

In the Snooker Room we start a game on the table closest to the car park. Neither of us are particularly adept at playing on a full-size table and the game is drawn out, not too many coloured balls going down.

A couple of Second Year guys come in and start playing on the other table, they're chatting about nothing in particular. One of them walks around near Nev as he lines up a red ball. Before he can shoot, there is a quick jab on the end of Nev's cue and the white ball rolls down the table aimlessly. My blood instantly starts boiling.

'That was fucking stupid,' I blurt. He is short and has attitude, ignoring me, taking a shot before looking back at me.

'Take it easy, Sprog, or I'll give you a lesson in manners.' Now the red mist is really descending, it's like being back at school and the other kids are teasing me. I walk toward him, fists clenching.

'Let's go,' Nev says with some urgency, stepping in my way. He grabs me by the shirt and drags me from the room. I eyeball the idiot all the way out while he makes wanking motions at me with his right hand.

'If you let cocks like him get to you, it will end badly, Tim. You need to let them go, mate. If I had a dollar for every puffed-up cock who tried to punch me?' He leaves the line unfinished.

'And, when you're a black fella, the cops always take the other dickhead's side, no matter what. It will be the same here, mate, just leave it.' Through the red haze, my mind starts to clear and I realise he's right. But, I still think this Second Year needs to be taught a lesson. I will bide my time, for now.

I spend the rest of the day stewing about it and sleep finally comes, but not before a lot of tossing and turning.

I wake with a sudden shudder, my jaw hitting the lino floor followed milliseconds later by the bed landing squarely on top of me. I manage to extract myself from under as the door slams shut.

'Bastard' I mumble, no prizes for guessing who had just rumbled my bed. As I reassemble it, I decide I am definitely going to teach him a lesson. Nev has been woken up by the clattering of the bed frame. He switches his bedside light on.

'Whose taken an interest in you this evening?' I shake my head at him and finish making my bed.

In the next week, I see him strutting arrogantly around the Mess more than once. He has corporal chevrons on his overalls and the name tag reads Faulkner, 32 Inst. Corporal Apprentice Faulkner from No. 32 Apprentice Intake training as an Instrument Fitter. I am not normally vindictive, but this guy has now become a pet project.

Easter arrives. A lot of the guys take the train to Sydney or Melbourne, some fly to further places. Anyone living locally manages to go home for the break.

The few of us staying in Wagga Wagga are billeted out for the weekend. Lurch and I stay on a farm west of town. We were briefed to stay clear of the girls when the farmer picked us up and, whilst he doesn't seem like the sort of guy who would shoot us and throw our bodies in the river, I'm not going to take any chances.

Unfortunately for us, his daughters had a different idea. The older daughter, Debbie, manages to get Lurch into a clinch more than once behind the tractor shed. The middle daughter, Tracey, keeps chasing me around. She's only fourteen but pashes like a veteran.

Our weekend is spent stacking feed for the sheep, riding dirt bikes and spotlighting for rabbits, that and kissing the farmer's daughters.

'Dougie, she went off like a cracker when I slipped my hand into her pants,' Lurch tells me. I give him a slap on the back like he's just scored a try, but I have no idea what he's talking about.

Tuesday we are back into the day-to-day. The next subject is Turning, and we are in the machine shop for a few weeks. The mysteries of various threads UNC, UNF, UNEF are revealed. The art of setting up a lathe, knurling, cutting a thread, lubricants, feeds and speeds come to light. It's amazing how quickly I have become expert at manufacturing some pretty complex bits and pieces.

Who would have thought?

Our instructor is an older Englishman, Sergeant Moriarty. He talks with a funny accent and most of us have trouble understanding the language, it's certainly not English. He leaves out words and says others strangely. Nev has developed an impersonation which is almost perfect.

'Ah, thee's best be goin' oop on t'roadh to Mess, lad, and on tha dinner.' Nev has a knack for that stuff.

Although he is hard to understand, there is nothing he doesn't know about making stuff. He tells us a story about making engine parts for Destroyers in the UK.

'Ay, lad, made steering block fer Type 21 Frigate and Type 42 Destroyer.' Nev jokes that it was engine parts off the Titanic, he is so old.

The call is made for volunteers to join the drum band. Whilst there is an audition of sorts, I think all applicants are accepted. Nev and myself are going to be side drummers and Lurch a bass drummer. Lurch might have two left feet when it comes to marching, but somehow, he has rhythm and much to our surprise he takes to it like a duck to water, keeping a steady and sustained beat.

Each Monday, Wednesday, Thursday and Friday morning at 0730, we collect our drums at the Band Room near the Chapel and march to the Parade Ground.

'RSTT. Onnnn ... Parade,' screams the WOD.

The Lead Bass Drummer give it two double hits, and we start two rolls of three beats each on the snare drums. The waiting Airmen and WRAAFs step off onto the Parade Ground. It's only a short little refrain and the Drum Major hold his arms indicating we will stop playing at the end of this particular repetition. As it comes to an end, the Lead Bass Drummer gives it two double hits again, just to make sure everyone is awake, and we all stop on cue.

During inspection, there are a couple of slower little pieces played, with tenor drummers twirling sticks around like a pipe band. Then, there is a General Salute as the National Flag is raised, then the March Past.

Our previous experience on the Parade Ground has been from the back. The band's vantage point offers a very different, and close up, view of the world. The various uniforms and the sheer number of people parading is something to behold.

It takes some time for all of them to March Past. The Flights come west in trail toward the Medical Centre, two left turns, before heading east past the Reviewing Officer and flag, then off the Parade Ground to start work for the day. At any given moment, there are around ten Flights marching, all carrying little blue bags in their left hand, and all in step, which makes it a quite mesmerizing sight.

The band plays over twenty different little refrains, each

one played three times over. At the end of each one, we watch our more senior Apprentices to ascertain which refrain is to be played next, then join in. The Bass Drummers set the speed at 120 beats/minute and the Trainees marching past keep step with the beat. Well, most of the time.

My Apprentice Flight, Number Seven Flight, is the last to go past and the Drum Major sticks the mace into the air, pumps it twice and we step off. We do a right turn, and 'eyes right' as we are the last to go past the Reviewing Officer, ADGies hovering close to see whether we have shined our boots and stood close enough to our razors.

Being a member of the Drum Band has certain advantages. Practice times are Tuesday morning, during the routine block inspection, and Friday afternoon during clean-up. Playing drums is a much better option than mopping hangar floors. This is looking better by the minute, and the guys who thought we were crazy for wanting to be little drummer boys are now more than a little jealous.

Late May, and it's starting to get really cold. The roll- neck jumper and the four blankets they issued us are starting to get a workout. After morning parade, we head to the basic training hangar and hang off a file all day, every day. Apparently, we are going to make a small vice and each component has to be hand-crafted, but it just seems like we file chunks of metal into meaningless shapes, to extremely close tolerances. The routine is well and truly established, we are becoming machines, we wake, eat, march, learn, file metal, and sleep.

Our living habits are also becoming ritualistic. Some guys like a shower straight after work, others wait till morning. Some turn in early and others are up half the night. Some guys are private about showering and changing, some quite brazen. Gary Sheen takes great pride in walking down the hall from the ablutions to his room with just a towel over his shoulder, and his wet pack in his hand. Plenty to be proud of has Gary.

It's a long Mess line on Monday night and I am keen to get back to the lock and finish my cleaning duties. Nev and I finally make it to the servery when two second- year guys walk up and tell us to stand aside. It's Faulkner and another guy from the Instrument Fitter course.

'The back of the line is that way,' I tell them pointing.

'You and your little Abo mate can fuck off,' Faulkner says shoving me back against the wall. The back of my head hits it hard and my teeth involuntarily clamp down on my tongue. 'Matter of fact, I am amazed they let the little black cunt in here at all.' He laughs.

I get three punches in quickly. The first one smears his nose across his face, one on the cheek and the last on his jaw. He goes down without a swing in my direction. There is blood pissing everywhere and the whole place stops abruptly, everyone looking at me. My tongue is throbbing and there is a dull throb at the back of my skull.

'Now fuck off back to the end of the line like I said,' I tell them. Faulkner's mate helps him to his feet and half carries him away. Faulkner is wobbly on his feet as they retreat. A Cook's Assistant arrives quicker than seems feasible with a mop and bucket to clean up the blood. Nev is giving me a look. I know what he's thinking and he's probably right. But, smart arses like Faulkner deserve all they get.

You can't follow the rules only when it suits you.

The Elephant Trackers turn up at my door an hour later. I am escorted to their white Valiant station wagon and taken to their office on the other side of the train line. This is looking like the wrong side of the tracks for me. I make a statement clearly outlining the racist slur and the shove into the wall, the fact I was only retaliating, defending myself and my mate. I show them the fresh marks on my tongue and let them feel the lump on the back of my head, but it seems it's to no avail. They tell me Faulkner had to be treated at Medical and will be there overnight for observation. I will get the charge sheet tomorrow. They let me go and I trudge slowly back to the room knowing this was not the smartest thing I've ever done.

Sure enough, I am summoned to the Orderly Room the next morning and handed a green Charge Sheet. It will be heard by Squadron Leader Banks at 1000 the next day. Everyone crowds around to have a look. It reads *"Conduct unbecoming an Airman. On or about 1720 hours on Monday 21 May 1979, Apprentice Walsh assaulted another Apprentice at the Airmen's Mess."* Nice and simple.

Later, we are sitting around our room polishing our shoes when the door flies open and there is a large guy standing there. It's Dave McGlashen from 32 Intake. He is more commonly known as just 'Lash'. There was a rumour circulating that, in his first week at Wagga, he punched the shit out of a third-year Apprentice who was trying to rumble his bed.

'Which one of you Sprogs thumped Faulkner?' he demands. I meekly put my hand up thinking I am probably about to receive some degree of revenge.

'He's got a broken nose and a black eye. What did he do to deserve that?' he asks ominously. I tell him the story. He looks at Nev and then back at me. 'Fair enough,' he says with a sly little smile. 'Faulkner is a cock sometimes.' He goes to leave and stops, looking back at me.

'Take a word of advice, Sprog. I can tell you from personal experience, they don't like that shit around here. Keep your hands to yourself, and only do what you know you can get away with.' He looks over at Nev. 'And, if anyone gives you any more shit about being black, you come and talk to me.' And, silently he was gone.

Sure enough, they didn't take too kindly to me punching another apprentice, a Corporal Apprentice at that. Faulkner's offsider gives evidence it was a totally unprovoked attack. Nothing said about racism and shoving me against the wall. The Squadron Leader asks me if I have anything to say in my defence and I tell them what really happened.

'Even if your version of events is true, the response is unquestionably excessive,' Squadron Leader Banks says. When I ask what an appropriate response to racism and being shoved into the wall would be, he appears to get annoyed.

'Fourteen days loss of pay, and fourteen days Confined to Barracks.' He says before signing the charge sheet and leaving the room. I am not sure whether he is annoyed at my accusation of racism in the ranks, or irritated that I might question him. It doesn't matter, this has not gone well from any angle.

Being Confined to Barracks, also known as CB, is a right royal pain in the arse. You have to be dressed and up to the Guard House at the front gate by 0600 each day. It's over a kilometre away. There are another four trips to the Guard House each day, once before we eat at midday, another after work at 1700, another at 2000, and the last at 2200. The 2200 trip must be done in Blues, long sleeve shirt, jumper and tie. On every visit I report to the Guard Commander, get inspected, and have my name ticked off.

Each night after the evening meal, I get to ride shotgun on the Chunder Wagon in the Mess. It's not really a wagon as such, just a large trolley with a stainless-steel top, trays for used plates and cutlery, and a big bin for all the scraps. The task is to clean each table of plates, scrape the leftovers into the bin, and wipe the table. The title comes from the urge to vomit when you put your nose near the bin.

It's a great opportunity for your mates to hang shit on you, or leave a special surprise on the table, like a dog turd. Someone even superglued all the plates onto a table one evening, pretty funny actually. Every day, I await what delights my fellow apprentices and supposed mates can leave for me.

CB is one thing, but fourteen days loss of pay hits hard. A first-year Apprentice only gets one hundred and thirty odd dollars a fortnight. Forty of it goes on Rations and Quarters, or R&Q as it is known, which is food and lodging, and it only leaves ninety a fortnight in the hand. When they take away fourteen days' pay, it's the whole amount and it leaves you in arrears on R&Q for the fortnight. So, your next pay is only fifty dollars in the hand, bastards.

It can be hard to make it through CB without further indiscretion. Guard Commander is a rostered duty for the Senior NCOs of the Base. Some of them are Technos and so they don't take the whole military discipline thing too seriously. But you often get someone who wants to make a name for himself.

I manage to get to the Guard House for all my calls and avoid further trouble. One of the Thicks doing CB with me is not so lucky and gets charged again for not shaving before the 2200 visit. He gets another week on the Chunder Wagon for the crime of a stubble.

The following week, we are walking back to our block after watching a movie in the Apprentice Club. There's a Service Police white Valiant station wagon parked out front, the occupants are obviously inside making some Apprentice's night.

'The idiots have left it unlocked,' announces Jim with a look of excitement. 'We'll have some fun here,' he says as he runs to the driver's door, quickly opening it and popping the bonnet. At the front of the car, he adeptly opens the bonnet, leans over pulling the distributor cap off, extracting the rotor button. The distributor cap and bonnet are returned to their original positions just as quickly. We are into the foyer when the two Service Policemen come down the stairs, an earnest looking Sergeant, and a Corporal who looks like he's our age. It's a race for the back door to witness the impending events.

Outside, we stick to the shadows and edge towards the front of the building. I can see the two of them in the car with the light on, one of them is writing something. The notepad goes onto the seat, seat belt on, and the starter motor comes to life. He turns it for a good five seconds before trying again. I can tell he is pumping the throttle.

'The idiot will think he's flooded it, fuckin wet behind the ears little twat,' whispers Jim with a grin. The starter motor turns over several more times before we hear the bonnet catch. The Sergeant gets out and opens the bonnet, shining a torch around the engine bay.

I sense movement beside me and my jaw drops as Jim breaks from the darkness and walks casually to the car.

'Something wrong Sarge?' The Service Policeman turns his head toward him.

'It won't start.'

'Probably flooded it.' He walks to the passenger side window. 'Hold the pedal flat to the floor, Corporal, and try it again.' The car turns over several times more.

'Must be something more serious than just flooding.' Jim leans over the engine bay, wriggles a few leads and fiddles with the carbie.

'One more time, Corporal.' It's turning over and of course, it isn't going to start, the rotor button is in Jim's pocket.

He scratches his head.

'Got me fucked. Sorry I can't help Sarge,' he says wandering off. We sit and watch the two super sleuths discuss options, then lock the car and wander off into the night.

Back inside, we run around laughing and carrying on. Jim grabs a piece of paper and a texta and scribbles a sign. The sign and a plastic bag containing the rotor button are pinned onto the noticeboard inside the main door to the building.

WANTED

A good home for the rotor button in the bag.

Best suited to a VJ Valiant wagon.

Contact Corporal Sims at the SPs Office.

When we get back from work the next day, the Valiant is gone. Apparently, the MT Fitters turned up, fitted a new rotor button and drove it away. It took thirty seconds to diagnose it.

The following week, things go bad for me. We're close to finishing the running plate of the meticulously crafted vice, and my mind is wandering, filing, filing, filing. Mid-year leave starts next week and I get to go home for two weeks. I am thinking about grandma's cooking, my bed, and Louise.

The thoughts of Louise catch me out a bit. I had engrossed myself in my new life and tried to block out everything else. But it's inevitable I will see her when I'm home. I can't ignore it.

I pick up my little block of metal and apply the micrometre to the section I had filed.

'Fuck it.' The guys around me look up.

'What's up, Dougie?'

'I am ten thou over.'

'Not good, Dougie,' says Lurch walking over. He takes my job, picks up a micrometre, and makes an assessment. 'It's fucked,' he announces.

'Can't I just make the other side of ten thou over?' I ask pointing to the opposite side.

'No, mate, this block runs up and down the Base plate and butts onto the two end plates. It'll look like shit, and I doubt you will get a pass. You have to start again.'

'Fuck it.' The job is due tomorrow afternoon and there is about four days' work in it. I am going to have a shake a leg.

The boys help me cut a new piece of metal and those more adept with a file take the new piece down to within twenty thou. I will take it from here and stay back an extra half hour to get the bottom square and the width right.

Walking home alone, I am so engrossed in my predicament I don't immediately spot the carnage. The fire hydrant has had a workout and a few of the boys are peeling off their waterlogged overalls. I look around for an escape and realise it's too late. My only chance is to run for the safety of our accommodation block.

I take off quickly and sidestep a few of the slower Second Year Apprentices, but there are too many blocking the way, I circle and let the hyenas chase. Out of the corner of my eye, I can make out a large figure. A quick glance tells me it's Lash.

I can outrun Lash.

I make a tight turn toward Lash assuming his momentum will take him past me, wrong. For a large man, he has agile feet and I can sense him right behind me. I now feel a hand on my back and my overalls being lifted. I can feel my overalls tighten in the crotch and my body rises. Whilst I am still running, kind of, I am being turned and guided toward the fire hydrant. About ten yards away, he lifts and throws me into the mud in front of the hydrant. From there, a group of the hyenas tapes the ankle and cuffs of my overalls and the other ankle is attached to the outlet.

As the tap is opened, I can feel the cold water filling my clothing. It happens quick, just like jumping into a cold bath. The overalls swell and suddenly the jet of water starts to exit the front of my overalls and collar and hits me in the face. They hold me there long enough to make breathing a difficult manoeuvre, and for my testicles retreat to somewhere completely unknown to me. This is what I call "Spanner Water" and it is to be avoided at all costs in the future.

Friday, late June, it's a bus trip home for mid-year leave.

Everyone is up early, dressed in Blues and packed. The buses start arriving at 0800, they are bound for Melbourne, Adelaide, Brisbane, and some beyond. The guys from Tassie, WA, and North Queensland get to fly.

Our bus goes up the Olympic Way through Cootamundra, Bathurst, to Sydney and then up the Pacific highway via Gosford and Newcastle. A couple of us from the Hunter get dropped off at Hexham. I shake hands with Nev on the way off the bus, he stays on for the ride up the Pacific Highway to Kempsey.

Uncle Bert is there in his HJ One Tonner. It's 2200 and we are over an hour late. I apologise and he tells me not to worry, he expected it from the RAAF.

I do all the talking on the way home, he drives and listens, there's no back and forth. We've never been close. I am grandad's shadow and he keeps a distance, only offering comment or guidance in exceptional cases. Grandma reckons he was never the same after going to Vietnam.

When we get home, grandma gets up and makes a pot of tea and a toasted sandwich. Boy, have I missed grandma's toasted sandwiches, the best food ever. I say goodnight, grab my RAAF duffle bag and head for my room, through the lounge room past grandad and grandma's wedding photo on the wall, and mum and dad's.

I wake late and realise milking is nearly done. Stepping into my civvie overalls, they pull in the crotch. I must have grown a bit in the last five months and put my RAAF overalls on. By the time I get my gum boots on and over to the dairy, it's clean-up time. I help out and grandad mumbles something about the Blue Orchards making me soft. He's usually cautious about chipping people and so the dig is heavily felt.

Over breakfast I catch up on all the local gossip. Mrs Maybury had a stroke and died, Johnny Raymond got caught cheating on his wife and she threw him out, Douglas Grocers have a new delivery truck, it's an International, and young Tom Charlton over on the Stroud Hill Road joined the Navy.

'Did you see the bloke from Sydney bought Maybury's farm,' grandad says looking at Bert. 'He's going to build a house amongst the trees up on the ridge above the dairy.'

'He wants to watch out he doesn't get his backside burnt,' observes Bert.

'Yer, I've seen fires go through there twice in my time. If a westerly gets a hold, they'll never stop it. Bloody Pitt Street farmers, you can't tell them anything.'

We spend the day mending a few fences before doing the afternoon milking. The herd is mostly Friesians, big- boned black-and-white cows. They are quite productive, but we keep a few Jerseys and Guernseys as well. The Jerseys keep up the cream level in the milk and are good breeders. They can be cranky though. One of the older Jerseys, I call her Shit Head, has a habit of standing on my foot. She doesn't let me down this afternoon.

Many of the girls have nick names. Mavis, the old girl of the herd produces more milk than most. There is another always sticking her head up looking around and inspecting what you are doing. We call her Dorrie Evans.

After clean-up, it's into town to the RSL for few beers before dinner. Well grandad and Uncle Bert have a few beers, grandma has a glass of Ben Ean, and I have a lemon squash. Grandad fills out the form for me to join the Sub-Branch. I sign it and he hands it to the Secretary, Mr Moore, who says I am not yet eighteen and cannot be a member. Grandad argues my corner and Mr Moore disappears to the office to check the rules. It's not the first time Mr Moore and Grandad have disagreed on membership, or a number of other subjects.

I remember a couple of years ago they disagreed about membership for guys like Uncle Bert, who had served in Vietnam. Mr Moore told grandad it wasn't a real war. I think it's a bit rich coming from a bloke who was in the Ordnance Corps and never even heard a shot fired in anger.

Grandad doesn't care if you were in the Ordnance Corps. In his book, "if you have ever had to pull on a military uniform, and or got shot at by the bad guys, then you are in on principle." Mr Moore comes back and says I have to be in the Forces a minimum of six months. We'll resubmit the paperwork when I come home at Christmas. We have a couple more drinks and grandad drives us home. Grandma serves up rissoles in onion gravy with mash potato and pumpkin, and beans. Bread and Butter Pudding for dessert, the tastes, the experience, familiar, comforting, I'm home.

I make it to the start of milking the next morning and we knock it over pretty quickly. It's not that milking cows is quicker with an extra hand, but the supplementary work is done more efficiently. After a cuppa, we get into grandad's Valiant and go to see Mr Rienhart further up Fosterton Road. We talk about the weather for a while and the price of heifers at the Gloucester sale. Grandad would like to borrow his bull to service some of the beef cattle and they agree on an exchange of hay for the service.

On the way home, we go past the Carmody's place. Old Man Carmody and his son Michael are out fixing a fence and he stands up and waves. Grandad pretends not to notice the wave and just keeps driving. Grandad reckons Old Man Carmody is a flog. It's the worst name I have ever heard him use. None of the women in the district will go near him and I remember mum saying he was a creep. He has three kids, Michael, who is my age, and two daughters. The two daughters are a little weird.

Mr Bennett is in his front paddock ploughing. The tractor stops and he climbs down. Grandad slows the Valiant.

'Morning, Jack'

'Morning, Les.'

'What are you putting in?' grandad asks.

'Just a bit of lucerne,' Mr Bennett replies. 'Hello there, Tim.' He looks at me.

'Lou is up in the house if you want to say hi'. I take the tip, get out of the car, push down on the second fence wire, slip through, and make my way to the house. Grandad and Mr Bennett continue to discuss the weather and the price of heifers at the Gloucester sale.

I kick my gum boots off at the back door before knocking. She comes to the door and there is an awkward moment when she realises it's me.

'I heard you were home,' she says.

'Nice to see you too,' I say, with just a touch of attitude, regretting it instantly.

Louise Bennett and I go back a long way, as long as I can remember. Her mum and my mum were best friends. We went to Kindergarten, Primary School and High School together. I have partnered her to every social event in the Dungog district for the past ten years. She is my confidant and best friend, well except for Dave McLachlan.

Lou is an only child and I am the chosen one. I am sure there is some sort of covenant where we get married, I start farming with Mr Bennett, we have children, and live happily ever after. The Air Force has put a spanner in the works.

We go inside and Mrs Bennett is in the kitchen. She gives me a hug and big kiss on the cheek, which makes me blush. She looks me up and down and asks if they are feeding me, puts the kettle on, and get some slice from the fridge. After a little more chat, she disappears to the laundry.

Lou and I sit there for a bit and she asks me about Wagga Wagga. I tell her about the local wheat farms, the town, the Base, the Air Force, our living routine, the food. She sits and soaks it up. After a while the talk turns to the school crowd. She recounts various stories about our friends and teachers. Apparently, Lisa McKay is up the duff and not sure who the father is. There are a couple of boys ducking and weaving.

'It's not surprising. She was always one for playing doctors and nurses. She put the hard word on me at last year's end-of-year dance. What's Dave up to?'

'Oh, he's okay. He is chasing Michelle Blande and she is playing hard to get. I reckon she'll fold though, he's rather handsome.' She pauses.

'Why haven't you written to me?' There is a long silence. '*Good question,*' I think to myself. I stutter something about being busy, but it's not true and Lou knows it. As she is about to speak again, the horn on the Valiant blasts. You can tell its grandad, it's a long blast. Not one for doing anything in small measures my grandad.

'How about you come for dinner tomorrow night,' I invite.

'We are already coming for lunch today. Didn't your grandmother tell you?' She looks at me with forced bewilderment. Grandma is one of the main conspirators in the Covenant.

'Okay, see you soon then.' I run out the back door and grab my boots, don't want to keep grandad waiting. Grandad thinks patience is something to do with a hospital.

When we get home, Uncle Ron's LTD is parked at the back of the house. I run inside and find Amy and Susan in the lounge room reading. They jump on me and give me a big hug, it's been too long since I last saw them. We size each other up and I ask them how school is going, what they are up to. While they are my sisters, we haven't spent much time together since mum and dad passed. It doesn't seem or feel right, but there's nothing I can do about it.

The house smells of baked dinner. Grandma demands grandad, Uncle Bert and I wash up and change our clothes, and make it snappy. The dining room table is set. We only ever use the dining room table when something important is on.

Mr Bennett's HQ pulls up out the back. It's a crappy brown colour and I can imagine Jim referring to it as 'dog- turd brown'. It has louvres in the back window, I bet they rattle when he gets out on the highway, Mrs Bennett in the front and Lou in the back. I rush out and open the door for Mrs Bennett. She fusses over me and says they mustn't be giving me enough to eat. Lou and she go into the kitchen to help with the finishing touches. Mr Bennett and I join grandad and Uncle Bert on the front verandah. There's more talk of the weather. If you're a farmer, there's always talk about the weather.

Talk turns to crops. What they intend to plant for the spring, which paddock will get which crop.

'It's been pretty dry, I might put the vegies down by the river this year,' says grandad. The danger of putting anything down near the river is we lose the whole lot if we get a flood, and it's a regular occurrence. But, in a dry time, you can use the irrigation to get some water onto the vines. Mr Bennett nods and asks about the corn crop.

Lou pops her head out the front door and announces lunch is ready, we file in behind her. Grandad always sits at the head of the table nearest the window, I reckon it's so he never has to get up for anything. Grandma's seat is at the hallway end. I am told to sit next to grandad with my back to the fireplace, Uncle Bert in his usual spot opposite me. The plates start to come out of the kitchen, roast chicken, potato, pumpkin, sweet potato, peas and gravy. I tell everyone they don't make it like this in the Mess. Grandad mumbles something, but I only catch Blue Orchids.

The ladies take their seats, Lou next to me, Aunty Elsie and then Susan. Mr and Mrs Bennett, Uncle Ron, and Amy sit opposite. There is no grace in our house, we aren't particularly religious. Everyone adds salt and pepper to the meal and dig in. Lou pushes her thigh against mine, it feels so naughty being intimate in such a public place, but I'm not complaining. Mr Bennett enquires about life in the Air Force.

'The first couple of months was the hardest,' I tell him. 'Wagga Wagga is really hot in the summer and we spent a lot of time on the Parade Ground, which just radiates the heat back at you. Lots of drill, marching up and down.' I tell them Corporal Kennedy's joke about a village missing an idiot. 'Now Basic Training is finished we are spending most of our time in a hangar filing bits of metal. Apparently, we are making a vice.'

'Bloody RAAFies have enough vices,' Uncle Bert says without a laugh. 'Do you know why RAAFies stay in five-star hotels?' He doesn't wait for a response. 'Cause they haven't invented six star hotels yet.' Everyone has a laugh, Uncle Bert remains dead pan. Uncle Bert did National Service in the Army. He isn't complimentary about the RAAF.

Something happened in Vietnam. I am not sure what, he doesn't talk about it, but he is a little strange.

Maybe he was always a little strange?

The main course finishes and dessert comes out, Grammar Pie and ice cream. Lou's thigh is warm against mine, it feels great. The teapot goes onto the table and everyone pours a cup. Grandad starts pontificating about football and whether the young St George side can win the premiership again.

Lou and I finish our tea and start to clear the table, disappearing to the kitchen to wash up. She loves telling silly jokes and starts a roll.

'How many elephants can you fit into a Mini Minor? Four, two in the front and two in the back. How do you know there have been elephants in your fridge? There are footprints in the butter and a Mini Minor parked outside.' We giggle, me mostly from a sense of politeness, the jokes are bloody lame. Another car pulls up out the front. It's a bit flash, one of the new Commodores, a Calais, top of the range. A familiar figure gets out, it's Milton Morris from Maitland. He used to be the NSW Transport Minister. I open the back door and greet him.

'Good afternoon, Mr Morris.'

'Hello, Tim, how's the Air Force treating you?' Never misses a trick Mr Morris, keeps his finger firmly on the pulse of what everyone is up to.

'Very well, thanks Mr Morris.' He makes his way to the dining room and takes a seat at the table. I get him a cup and saucer and the women excuse themselves from the table. The discussions turn serious, pre-selection, Liberals running in a safe National Party seat, preferences, and more.

Lou and I escape down to the river. We lay in the grass with the winter sun and full belly making us sleepy. She curls up in my arms and we nod off for a little while. On the way back to the house, we talk about how much longer I have in Wagga Wagga and where I might go after that.

'If you come back to Williamtown, you can live at home,' she proposes.

'Yep, that'd be really good,' I say unconvincingly. I don't mention Malaysia. The Air Force has three Squadrons at a place in Malaysia called Butterworth. There are two fighter Squadrons and a Maintenance Squadron. My chances of getting to Williamtown are good, and my chances of going to Malaysia are almost certain if the first posting comes off.

Back at the house, Mr Morris has left and grandad and Uncle Bert have changed for the afternoon session. I rush to catch up. Lou kisses me goodbye on the lips and I go weak at the knees. They drive off in the 'dog-turd brown' HQ Holden. Mr Bennett has his own milking to do. Uncle Ron packs the LTD up and he, Auntie Elsie, and the girls all head off back to Newcastle.

The next two weeks follow a similar pattern. Two milking sessions a day, farm maintenance, Saturday night drinks at the RSL, and Sunday lunch at the Bennett farm or the Davidson farm. On the second Saturday night, Louise, my best mate Dave McLachlan, and Michelle Blande join us for drinks at the RSL. Grandad is chaperoning. Dave and Michelle are close and hold hands continuously. I can see Lou edging closer to me and she slips her hand into mine. I like it and go weak at the knees again.

The third Saturday night is my last night here, we stay home for a baked meal and the dining table is once again set with the good dining set and cutlery. After dinner, Lou and I sit on the front verandah in the cold. She cuddles up and we kiss. It's pretty intense and the breathing gets heavy.

Why did we wait until I have one foot on the bus back to Wagga?

All too soon there is a cough from the front door. It's Uncle Bert, subtle as ever, the embrace is over.

"Time to head off, Tim, you've got a bus to catch." It's the same as last time. Grandma crying like she'll never see me again.

'I am only going to Wagga Wagga, Grandma.' Grandad firmly shakes my hand, only this time I have Mrs Bennett fussing too, and Lou looking stunning in the cold night air, the feel of her lips on mine still all too fresh in my mind.

The bus picks us up at Hexham, Uncle Bert shakes my hand earnestly like grandad, and we are off into the night. Nev is already on the bus and we exchange leave stories. I tell him about

Louise and how pretty she is. My only dilemma is the expectation we would get married and I would go back to the farm.

'I don't want to be on the farm, Nev, it's why I joined up, to see a bit of the world and be something different.'

'I know what you mean, Dougie, same here. I had to find a way to get out of Kempsey, make something of myself, stand on my own two feet. Otherwise, I am just another black fella waitin' to go to gaol.'

I think about her all the way back to Wagga Wagga, she even manages to invade my dreams when I nod off for a while. It's six degrees when we arrive at 1100. Nev and I head to the Mess for Sunday lunch, Beef Stroganoff. I'd rather be eating grandma's roast with Lou's thigh against mine.

3 — That's What the Fuss Is About

The wind is sometimes out of the south. It cuts through us like a razor-sharp knife. When it's not windy, there's often a heavy fog, it doesn't lift till two in the afternoon. The Fokker Friendship from Sydney circles the Wagga Wagga airfield tirelessly waiting for a visual on the runway.

Do they ever had to turn around and go back?

The working routine starts to get zombie-like. Up at six and shower, 2WG playing Air Supply or Kenny Rogers — you never hear The Angels — Mess for breakfast, then morning parade. Playing drums on parade in these circumstances is painful. Don't bump your fingers on the rim, they might just shatter into a million shards. Most of the day is spent in Hangar 68 where we continue to hacksaw and file meaningless bits of metal, over and over again.

Are they trying to bore us into some sort of submission?

Work is usually followed by dinner, a shower, and then a little TV, the *Muppets* and *Dallas*. We hate JR even more with each episode.

One bright interlude in the work routine is the week of Blacksmithing. I never knew how satisfying it could be to get a hunk of metal red hot and bash the crap out of it with a big hammer. I get a Distinction for Blacksmithing.

The tension with John Faulkner continues. He's been promoted to Sergeant Apprentice and thinks he has a renewed power to push First-Year Apprentices around. The prick's favourite trick is to bait people with smart-arse comments, time and time again, until they snap. Then, he puts them on Mess duty for being insubordinate. During inspection one morning, he tells me I have fluff on my overalls. I just glare at him with the 'go fuck yourself' face. I am itching for another chance; the CB would be worth it.

The weekend ritual includes either playing or watching football, rugby or Aussie Rules, depending on who is short of players. I have come to adopt a begrudging respect for the southern game and take some tips from the boys on drop punting and torpedo kicks. I am a hopeless marker of the ball and have to get clear to take a mark on the chest. Tackling also takes some work to master. I give away free kicks for either going too high, around the legs, or for in the back.

I have spent some time trying to figure out what 'in the back' is. It appears it is illegal to get anywhere near another player's back, unless of course you want to jump high and put your knee between someone's shoulder blades to take a specky mark. Regardless, there is some perverse pleasure in driving some smart-arse into the dirt, even if it does cost a penalty. Those Aussie Rules guys can't tackle anywhere near as hard as a rugby player.

Every second room in our block now has a stereo. You can walk down any hallway, on any floor, and hear a variety of songs all competing, louder and louder. The predominant albums are the ones supplied by record clubs. Australia Post has these advertisements for three albums for ten bucks. Trouble is, the options are limited — *Stranger in Town*, *Van Halen*, *Bat Out of Hell*, and *War of the Worlds*. I know 'Paradise' by the Dashboard

Light off the top of my head. Some of the guys manage to get into town to buy new stuff, but it's mostly repetitive.

On Tuesday, Padre is instructing us on filing our first tax return. I never knew fifteen-year-olds had to do a tax return. At the close, he casually informs us that he has organised a dance this Saturday night. Sounds like fun. Nev jokes that we will look really good dancing with each other, and he adopts the lead stance, I take the lady's position. We waltz a few steps and he ask me what I am doing on Saturday night.

'Do you fuck on the first date?'

'Depends whether you can get it up,' I respond, laughing. The boys call us bloody poofters. Some have serious concerns and give us a wide berth for a few days.

We are all a little sceptical about whether we'll be dancing with someone of the opposite sex, or with each other. But as Saturday night rolls around, we drop the doubt, get cleaned up and dressed up in our best. Jim has some Old Spice aftershave, and we share it around before wandering over to the Apprentice Club.

'Holy shit,' there are at least twenty girls in the place. The padre is in the corner with a record player, a couple of speakers and a grin on his face. He has contacts in high places, our padre.

We nervously approach a group of three. I say 'Hello' and introduce Nev, Lurch, Jim and myself. The girl on the left introduces Janine, Robyn, and herself, Julie. I strike up some small talk with Janine and before we know it, everyone is paired off. Nev loses out.

Padre puts on a Chuck Berry tune to groans from the crowd. Someone runs out and comes back a couple of minutes later with a couple of albums. 'Lido Shuffle' comes to life and the crowd cheers.

Janine is in Year 11 and plans to go to Uni to do an accounting degree. She's not a tall girl, slim, and made-up to cover the acne marks on her face. While not pretty in a classic sense, she is sure of herself and that self-confidence is quite attractive. She has gaps between her front teeth which reminds me of Melissa Jones from Dungog.

After a couple of dances, Janine waves her hand in front of her face and asks me if it's hot in here. She suggests we get some air. We go out the back door into the barbecue area. It's about two degrees outside. She finds a dark corner and shoves me back against the wall. She kisses me strongly slipping her tongue in my mouth — zero to one hundred miles an hour in two seconds. I am weak in the knees. She has a hand groping around on my crotch.

Holy hell, what do I do here.

I am figuring she likes the kissing and move my mouth from her lips to her neck. She moans. I have never heard a girl moan before; it's exciting. She grabs my head and drags me back to her mouth before turning her neck to put her ear in my mouth. I nibble the lobe, she moans again, and then the Nazi floodlight comes on.

We separate and stand up straight. There are two other couples in the BBQ area. You can almost smell the guilt. Padre opens the back door and orders everyone back inside. I have a bulge in my crotch and have to avoid the main room while it subsides.

When I get back, Padre is playing Bob Seger. Janine is waiting and we dance some more. Lurch and Julie are in a clinch in the corner, and Robyn and Jim are not to be seen.

Around 10.00 pm, Padre announces the girls' lifts are here and we are to escort them to their ride. As we walk out, Janine and I busily exchange phone numbers. She says that she will call.

Outside, Padre is thanking everyone for coming and we all stand and wave as the cars disappear into the night.

On the way back to the block, we compare notes. It's not so much bragging to each other as discovery. I tell the boys about Janine moaning.

'If she does that when kissing, what's she going to do during a root, Dougie?'

I've never thought about that.

'Where did you and Robyn disappear to, Jim?'

'She wanted to play World Championship Wrestling in the TV room. She's got a better sleeper hold than Killer Carl Cox.'

It's a new experience, well, for some of us.

Sunday is a drag, cold, wet and dreary. We run to the Mess and back for each meal. Late afternoon, we are sitting around watching a silly American beach movie in Lurch's room with Frankie Avalon and Annette Funicello. The door flies open.

'Dougie, there's some chick on the phone for you.'

I wander up to the foyer and pick up the handset. It's Janine. We chat for a while about nothing in particular.

'What are you doing Saturday?' she asks. 'I am playing netball. Do you want to come and watch?'

'Sure, why not.'

Janine has asked her mum to pick me up from the front gate. I walk out the main gate and stand out on the Stuart Highway at midday. I don't want to piss off anyone's mum by being late. About 12.20 pm, a Toyota Crown turns toward the main gate and completes a U turn back toward Wagga Wagga. It stops in front of me. The bright face in the driver's seats waves at me and I open the door.

'Tim?' I nod. 'Hello, Tim, my name is Margaret. Jump in, luv.'

She's very trusting.

After getting myself buckled in, I look over at her. She's got a black-and-white work uniform on, stockings, black skirt, white blouse, and a black cardigan. She tells me she has just knocked off work at David Jones. I get the third degree on the way into town.

Where am I from? How old am I? How long have I been in the Air Force? What do my parents do?

'They are dead,' I tell her. Shock registers on her face and apologises. I really need to come up with a more subtle answer to the question.

I break the nervous silence with some information on my grandparents and their dairy farm. It lightens her back up and she is off again talking about Janine and her dream of going to Uni.

We arrive at netball as the girls are warming up, sandshoes, short skirts, and long sleeve tops. Janine sees me and comes running over to give me a hug. The other girls are looking on with interest; seems they have been briefed on my arrival.

I hope I rate.

Janine wears a WD on her shirt for Wing Defence and she plays a wow of a game. She takes several passes from her opponent and gets the ball away quickly and cleanly. She seems to be a class above most of her teammates. After the game, its congratulations all round and we head back to her house.

The rest of the afternoon is spent sitting at her kitchen table doing schoolwork. I help out with physics and history stuff, but I am hopeless at chemistry. Margaret is watching a John Wayne movie on TV — *Rio Bravo* with Dean Martin and Angie Dickinson.

How hot was Angie Dickinson in her day?

Grandad never watched commercial TV, only the ABC, except for when *Policewoman* was on. He reckoned Angie reminded him of grandma in her day, but he doesn't say it in front of her. I ask Janine where her dad is and she gets tense.

'He's down at the club drinking. He will come home at eight, demand his dinner, slap mum because its overcooked, and go to bed. Same thing tomorrow.' I swallow, more than just a bit uncomfortable.

Later in the afternoon, she shows me around the house. It's not as big as the farmhouse. Mum and dad's bedroom and lounge room at the front, kitchen off the lounge room, laundry and toilet at the back of the kitchen, two bedrooms down the hall, with the bathroom between the main bedroom and the smaller ones. She takes me into her room and pushes me against the wall and kisses me hard — it's intense again, hands and tongues going everywhere. It's going to get loud and we break it off, panting, looking at each other. She's got a funny look on her face, almost crazed.

Margaret makes a dinner of braised steak and onions with mash. Straight after dinner, she asks Janine and me to get in the car and she'll drive me home.

Obviously, before the old man gets home and flogs her.

I ride in the back of the Crown with Janine holding hands, Margaret in the front. The images of what might happen later are running around in my skull. The thought of a man beating his wife is alien to me. Of course, I had heard that it happens and I had seen my parents argue, but there was never any thought of physical violence. It is troubling.

She pulls up at the spot I was standing at this morning. I peck Janine on the lips and jump out, thanking Margaret for the ride.

The scene gets repeated the next weekend. Only, this time, Margaret has to go round to Auntie Lizzie's to pick up something or other. She's not out of the driveway ten seconds when Janine grabs my hand and we head for the bedroom. She is as aggressive as before, pushing me against the back of the now-closed bedroom door. The kissing and moaning start again but this time she is pulling off my clothes, that crazy look on her face.

Why the hell not.

I help her out of her jumper and top. She looks sweet in just jeans, socks and a bra. We giggle as we take off each other's jeans, but it gets serious from there on. She instructs me on how to remove a bra with one hand and soon we're free of our clothes, save the socks. She lies back on the bed and pulls me toward her. Her small breasts are wonderful to touch and kiss. Next thing I know I am sliding into her and, holy shit, now I understand, that feels way better than my hand!

'Don't get me pregnant,' she gasps between moans.

Fuck, how did I forget that?

It diverts my attention momentarily but it's my first time and now I need to think about pulling out before it's too late, and that won't be long! She moans loudly which is adding to the sensory overload. My brain is saying one thing, and my dick is saying something else completely. It's over quickly and we lie there for a while in each other's arms before she pushes my hand between her thighs and says she's not finished. She shows me where to touch her and with some further instruction on a tender approach, she sighs and shudders, almost sucking my lips off.

That was awesome!

We get back to the homework before Margaret returns.

'How's it all going?'

'Very well, mum, we are making great progress,' she says, coolly. I can feel my face get hot, blushing.

The third visit is like the previous ones. Margaret picks me up, we go to netball, and then on to the house. Margaret excuses herself again. This time, she has to go into work for a couple of hours to do some stocktaking. Janine looks at me knowingly and I wonder whether there is some collusion.

Inside her bedroom, I confess last time was my first. She giggles and admits the same. I pull a couple of condoms out of my pocket and the giggling stops; she is on a mission. With clothing hastily discarded, things slow down, and we take some time to discover each other's bodies. I try some stuff I have read about in *Penthouse*; it goes well indeed. The intercourse is more satisfying for her and less intense for me given the rubber. All round, we are both happy indeed, and starting to get an inkling of what all the fuss is about.

I come out of her bedroom, whistling. Still combing my hair, I look up and freeze. There is a tall, thin man in his mid- to late-thirties standing at the end of the hallway. He looks just a bit older than Uncle Bert.

'What the fuck is going on here?' he asks.

I hear, 'Oh, shit,' from the bedroom and Janine pops her head out the door. Luckily, she is dressed and composes herself quickly.

'Oh, hi, dad, didn't think you'd be home yet. This is Tim. I was just showing him my records.' He huffs and walks to the kitchen.

'Records, my arse.' He's obviously pissed and I can hear the fridge door open.

Looking for another drink?

'Where's your mother?'

Janine explains the trip back to work for stocktaking as she cleans up the schoolbooks for the kitchen table. I stand back, shit scared, and try to melt into the wall. Janine says we were just heading up to Kooringal Mall to pick up some fish and chips.

'Do you want anything?'

He shakes his head and lifts the top off a large bottle of Flag Ale.

Hasn't he had enough? Grandad reckons if you need to drink at home after being at the pub, then you are a pisspot.

We disappear out the front door. Janine is relieved, not just that we nearly got busted, but she says he has a quick temper and liable to go off when he is pissed. We take our time at Kooringal Mall. On the way back, Margaret pulls up in the car. Janine and I get in and she tells her mum the Old Man is home. Margaret curses under her breath.

'You go home, darling, and keep him busy. I'll drop Tim home, just so he has no one else to go mad at.' Janine agrees and we drop her on the corner near their house. I hop in the front.

She is pretty silent on the drive back to the Base. Obviously has some serious thinking going on. The last rays of sunshine come through the back window of the Crown and light her hair. It's the same colour as Janine's. The facial features are similar too. I note, for a woman in her mid- to late-thirties, she is in pretty good shape. Small frame, nice legs, and breasts a little larger than Janine's.

I wonder if she moans like Janine? Don't be an idiot, Tim.

She pulls up at our spot on the road outside the Base, leans over, and kisses me on the cheek. She smells great.

'Tim, I am so sorry you met Roy like that. He's normally a really nice bloke.'

'That's okay. I hope everything works out well.'

As she drives off, I reflect on the kiss and have a few butterflies in my stomach.

This is a bit weird.

I show my ID at the gate and head for the Mess. The sex has made me hungry. As I walk through the doors, they are locked behind me — in by the skin of my teeth. There's not much left but I salvage some chicken casserole and veg, and head to the dining room. Nev and Mike are sitting at a table gasbagging.

'How's it going, Dougie?' Nev asks.

I am still troubled and thinking about Margaret and Janine and whether Roy is bashing them up right about now. I mumble I am okay. They shrug and go on with their conversation as if I'm not there. It's fine with me.

Sunday night, best get my washing done or I am going to be in shit tomorrow. I have brought a stick book with me and there's a story about a bloke screwing a chick on the kitchen table. It all sounds so believable, at least in the story. My washing is coming to an end and the washing machine starts to vibrate as the spin speed increases, really rocking. The whole machine walks across the floor in the process. There is a momentary glimpse of Margaret on top of the washing machine and we are doing it. I shake myself. Maybe I've been reading too much porn?

This is more than just a bit weird.

Tuesday night, I get the routine call from Janine. I sit on the floor in the foyer making small talk and she is making light of the meeting with her dad on Saturday. I don't believe her, but don't say so.

'It's my sixteenth birthday on Friday,' I tell her. Born on 14th September 1963, few in this Apprentice intake are younger. In contrast, others are already seventeen.

'No way,' she says. 'I am six months older than you. We'll have to do something special.'

I have some thoughts about what might be special, I read about it in a Penthouse magazine.

'Netball is finished for the year, so I am free all day Saturday and mum and dad are going to a wedding in Uranquinty. John is staying with Aunty Lizzie, so we'll be alone.'

I spend the next few days reading *Penthouse* magazines and playing out various scenarios for Janine and I in my mind. I have a semi hard-on the whole time, lucky there is plenty of room in our overalls. The soap's getting a workout in the shower.

Saturday morning rolls round and I get a hot breakfast in. The spring air is a welcome treat after the long winter months. I make sure I borrow some Old Spice from Jim and have a couple of condoms on me.

As I stroll up the main drag toward the front gate, I notice the Elephant Trackers hiding behind a tree with a radar gun. They're pulling up anyone doing one kilometre over the 30k limit.

Thank God they are on the job, I'll sleep better tonight.

I get to the front gate and wait to hitch a ride, a Thick picks me up almost immediately. There might be some argy-bargy between Thicks and Apprentices, but it's mostly show and we generally get along pretty well; everyone has the same challenges. As we go down the hill, I can see the fog clearing over the city. It's going to be a warm day. On the way in, we laugh about the Elephant Trackers and talk about the weather. He drops me at the Farmer's Home Hotel and I walk up Lake Albert Road enjoying the sun. There isn't a car in the driveway and I go to the door and knock.

'It's open,' she calls from inside. I walk in and she is standing in the kitchen doorway. Left arm up the door frame, right hand on hip. She has her hair pulled back, heavy makeup, lips red, and wearing her school skirt and white blouse. The blouse is open at the front exposing her bra, and she is in high-heels and white school socks.

Fuck me dead.

She comes over, pushes the door shut, staring intently at me, the half-crazed look in her eyes. The kissing starts immediately, it's like she is on a mission; passion and intensity, clothes coming off. She suddenly breaks the embrace and announces, 'Happy Birthday.' She pushes me back into the lounge and takes me in her mouth, I nearly lose it right there.

Fuck, this is amazing.

From the lust-filled haze, my mind registers I am going to need some contraception pretty soon and I reach for my jeans. She sticks her head up, licking her lips, and quite matter-of-factly asks what I am looking for. I tell her.

'Don't worry about it, Tim,' she says, climbing on board, 'I'm on the pill now.' She starts thrusting her hips, moaning loudly, and I am grinning from ear to ear.

The afternoon is a blur, lounge room, bedroom, kitchen. At one point, we are on the kitchen table and she is so loud I am worried the neighbours will come over and enquire if anyone is hurt.

'I have an idea,' I say. She's not used to me dictating terms and it takes her by surprise. I take her to the laundry. She is looking puzzled. I sit her on the washing machine and turn the dial to spin, pushing start. I kiss her as the machine comes up to speed. She gets the idea.

The rocking of the machine and her moaning are at the same frequency. She grabs my hand and thrusts strongly. Before she loses it, she pulls me to her. Her legs, with white socks still on, are wrapped around me and we both go off quickly. In the panting aftermath, I push the stop button and we laugh.

'Well, Tim, you have excelled yourself there,' she says.

The afternoon teaches me a few little lessons about patience, women, a gentle touch, and knowing when to up the ante. She is precise about what she wants and when. About 9.00 pm, I think it's time to make an exit. I certainly don't want to be here when Roy gets home. She tries to persuade me to stay and she'll hide me in her room, but the chance of another meeting with Roy is unthinkable.

It takes me about half an hour to walk down to Sprogs Corner. The heat of the day is gone and it's fresh. I wait for about twenty minutes before a couple of WRAAFs pick me up. They are on a Clerk Supply course and will be graduating in a few weeks. I am jealous that they get to come and go to the real Air Force so quickly.

On the Tuesday night phone call, I am invited to dinner. Apparently, Roy is out of town for a couple of nights and Margaret wants to cook me dinner. She'll pick me up at 6.00 tomorrow night.

The Toyota Crown crested the hill promptly at 1800 hours. I hop into the passenger seat and she leans over and pecks me on the cheek, then moves the T-Bar to drive. As we head down the hill towards town, I look her up and down, dressed in jeans, blouse and jumper. The conversation in the car is casual and easy; she's good company. Upon arrival in Kooringal, she leaves the car in the driveway and I follow her into the house. My eyes are wandering.

She fills those jeans out pretty well, for an older woman.

Janine is there to greet me. Margaret orders Janine and John to get out of their school clothes while she goes straight to the kitchen and starts dinner. I wander around the lounge room looking at photos and checking the paper to see what's on TV.

Harry Butler, fuck, I hope Margaret isn't a Harry Butler fan. The only thing worse would be Alby Mangels.

She starts talking again and I take up station at the table, chatting away. Janine joins me, grabs my hand under the table and leans over whispering.

'How did you like the school uniform?'

I have read about guys getting girls to dress in school uniform, but it's usually the older guys. I wonder why Janine thinks it turns me on and, for some reason, I nod and smile.

I don't need a school uniform to get me going.

The schoolbooks come out and we get into the homework, more mathematics, John is watching Dr Who.

'Did you see that new clip on Countdown, *Video Killed the Radio Star?*'

'No.'

'Oh.'

Maybe she doesn't watch Countdown?

'How do you rate Paul McCartney's songs after The Beatles?'

'Paul who?' Alarm bells are ringing in my head.

Fuck, how can someone not know who Paul McCartney is?

Margaret sets the table around us and shortly after declares five minutes to dinner. Janine clears the homework and we all obediently attend the bathroom to wash our hands. When we get back, four plates are on the table with crumbed cutlets, mash, peas and gravy. I tell Margaret it tastes much better than the Mess, which is true, and she smiles modestly and says 'thank you'. This is a homely meal, just like grandma would probably be serving in Dungog tonight.

Janine and I do the washing up while Margaret and John settle into watching *The Sullivans*. When we are finished, Janine declares we are going to her room to finish the homework and listen to some records. Margaret waves her hand.

'Okay, sweetie.'

She puts Peter Frampton on the turntable. The crowd noise starts coming through the speakers as she comes to me. A big pash to get things underway, her tongue darting around in my mouth. I slide my hands down her back, resting on her backside. She has no knickers on under the skirt. She lifts a leg to allow my hands greater access. She is wet and when I touch her button she starts moaning.

Fuck, the door is wide open.

No doubt about it, Janine has a fast motor and if I don't divert my attention, it will be over all too soon. I start thinking about cars — she's quicker than a XU1 Torana, nought to sixty in 8.4 seconds. I try to make sure she is happy. It doesn't take long. She has to bite her lip to keep quiet. With a degree of cold efficiency, she disconnects from the embrace, silently closes the door, undoes my jeans and leans back on the bed, pulling me on top. As we rock back and forth, I put my hands up her top and use her boobs to pull her back and forth. She loves it. I have this weird thought about whether Margaret would love it and I am brought back to my senses by the noise of the bedhead hitting the wall.

It becomes a balancing act knowing I can't thrust too quickly, or too hard, for fear of the bedhead bashing the wall, and Janine's clear instructions to go harder. I manage to grind my pelvic bone onto her button more adeptly and she gets off again.

We both rearrange ourselves and she opens the door again as silently as she had closed it. Frampton has finished and I can hear the closing theme to *The Sullivans* on the TV.

'Tim, can I run you back to Base now? I'd like to get back to watch *Dallas*,' Margaret yells from the lounge room.

'That's fine, thanks, mum,' says Janine loudly.

I shower when I get back to the block. The soap gets a workout and I have a picture in my head of the skirt pulled up, my hands on her breasts, and the bedhead knocking the wall. Only it's not Janine's face in the fantasy.

Fuck, Margaret, she's twice my age. No more Penthouse, *Dougie.*

September brings the football finals and the spring weather seems to lift everyone's spirits, invigorating the arguments over best football code. I keep telling everyone that St George must be the best team ever seeing as they won eleven premierships in a row, and this year is their fifteenth. No one seems to care though. At least grandad will be happy.

Most people disappear over the October long weekend and there are only a few of us left to watch the VFL Grand Final and Bathurst. Nev and I aren't that captivated with the VFL, but check in on the score every now and again; that and kick a footy around.

'Not going to town, Dougie?'

'Na, Janine's mum and dad are visiting her nan in Griffith this weekend. I have been given the weekend off duty.' He gives me that Nev 'do tell' look. 'Is it weird that I am relieved about that?' He looks at me with concern.

'You're getting laid, aren't you, Dougie?'

'Yer.'

'Well, what's to complain about?' I contemplate the question for a while.

'She doesn't even know who Paul McCartney is, Nev. You know me, I love the Beatles. Aren't you supposed to have something in common with your girlfriend, or is this girlfriend thing just for sex?' The concerned look turns up a notch.

'Are you sick, Dougie? Of course, it's all about the sex.' He is forceful and it causes me to think again.

'I don't know, mate. Have you ever rooted anyone?' His expression changes.

'Er, um, no, mate.'

Sunday, we are watching the Torana procession at Bathurst.

'Did you know there's seven A9Xs in the top ten grid positions?' Nev asks as they line up.

'Really?' My lack of interest shows. The flag drops and there is the usual jockeying for position into the first corner, Brock in front. They head for the foot of the mountain.

'I was thinking about what you said yesterday, Dougie.' I look over at him. 'You know it's okay to just have sex. It's not like you are going to marry her or anything, is it?'

Marriage, fuck, I am only sixteen. No, I don't want to get married.

'No, mate.'

'Good.' He appears satisfied with my response.

By four in the afternoon, there's a small crowd huddled around the TV in the Apprentice Club watching the red-and-white Marlboro Torana cross the line.

Fucking Peter Brock! How do you pass seven cars on the last lap, and still break the lap record?

Tuesday after work, cricket training starts. The coach, Warrant Officer Mal Thomas, is a short, thick-chested, man. Mal puts us through fielding drills before a long net session. The net pitches are concrete and covered with matting. I have never seen this before — in Dungog it's just plain concrete in the nets.

Flight Sergeant Gardner turns up at the end of training and addresses everyone — apparently, he's the Club President. He gives a nice welcome to the club speech, talks about the competition, practice and game day arrangements. He has that firm military air about him, no nonsense, but not pompous.

At work, we are chained to a bench with a file in hand most days. The interesting part is we can start to see the vice we are making come together, but shit, it's a slow and painful process.

What the hell is wrong with power tools?

Weeknights is either cricket training or the cinema. Weekend routine has changed to cricket on Saturday and a visit with Janine on Sunday. She has developed a taste for outdoor sex and we have a few secluded spots to indulge her new interest. She always dictates the time, place, and method of engagement. It strikes me that this is becoming a little too organised. There's still the crazed passion, but she has a plan for each disciplined clinical move. I'm not complaining, well not much.

Mid-October, Janine suggests I stay in town after cricket and hang out with her and some of her friends. I am to meet her at a takeaway just down the main street from the railway station. When I get there, she is with four other girls, one with a boyfriend. He's about my age, long hair over the ears and down over his collar. He nods an acknowledgment of my existence, but it's just not cool to hang out with RAAFies.

Everyone is dressed in a uniform: blouse, tracksuit top, jeans, and sand shoes. Chatter is based around cute boys, cute teachers, and cute musicians; John Paul Young and Lief Garrett are high on the list. Everything is cute.

Megan manages to get a side conversation going with me about pretty rockers.

'Christie Allen is quite attractive,' she says.

'Yep, I kind-of like Linda Ronstadt, she can really sing. Her and Stevie Nicks.'

'Most of the guys I know are still drooling over the blonde from ABBA,' she harrumphs.

I can see Janine looking daggers at Megan and decide it's probably a good idea to not get too deep in a separate chat. Megan seems to have an interest in me and I am not sure whether it's a real interest in what I have to say, or just trying to make Janine jealous.

On this occasion, I decide it's probably better to bail out. She gives my tonsils a workout before I depart. I think it's more for the audience than me. The stroll to Sprog's Corner takes me about fifteen minutes and I manage to thumb a ride a short time later.

Early in November, she tells me she has a better idea and things step up a notch. Saturday night, we go back to her place and I wait outside hiding in the dark, cricket bag stashed in the garden. I wait outside and can hear her greet her mum and chatter for a little while. I am guessing Roy is already pissed and in bed.

Shortly after the lights in the house extinguish, she comes to the back door and lets me in. I can make out her slight frame as we go down the hall. She is in a dressing gown. The bedside light is on in her room and she sits on the bed patting the space beside her. As soon as I take the assigned place, the kissing starts, the usual zero to one hundred. And, as usual, I am trying to slow her down. I want to make sure everyone in the house is asleep.

The gown is silky and the feel of her body under it has me excited quickly. I manage to pop a small breast out and kiss the pink nipple softly. It's swollen. She starts moaning, pushing my head down, and parting her legs. I slow her down, trying to draw it out and shut her up a bit. But she doesn't have time for that, changing position, hands on my head pulling me in, thrusting. No patience, this girl; instant gratification required and expected.

Afterwards, she's panting, recovering, but still has the crazed look in her eyes. I know she isn't done. I get pushed back onto the bed as she gets up, recovering some long socks from her cupboard. She comes to me kissing my chest and tummy, soft breasts brushing against me. There is the odd flick of the tongue across the tip, but she mostly leaves the direct touching to a minimum.

She straddles me, rubbing herself without any penetration, back and forth, slowly tying the socks to my wrists. The other end wrapped to the bedhead. While she rocks back and forth, she pulls the sock up tight, and fastens the other end. I can't move my arms.

What the fuck is she doing?

She reaches up and starts to play with her nipples, caressing her breasts. Still rocking back and forth, its driving me crazy, and I thrust upward. She cocks an eye, pulling away. She is going to make me wait.

Dismounting, she moves to the stereo speaker and sits. The bedside lamp is dull, but enough light to see her. Out of reach, but close, I can smell how turned on she is.

She starts rubbing her breasts and tummy. One hand goes between her thighs and she is quickly engrossed in self-manipulation. Her legs part and I get a good view of fingers rubbing her clitoris and moving in and out of her. It's a spectacle. After a little while, the speed of the hands increases, she throws her head back. I can see the muscles in her legs spasming.

That is one of the most amazing things I have ever seen.

After the spasms subside, she gets up very matter-of-factly, straddles me, and starts riding. The bed creaks loudly, but after the display, I am in a heightened state and orgasm is almost instantaneous. She unties me and we cuddle just as the toilet flushes.

Fuck, I hope whoever is in the toilet didn't hear us.

Next morning, she smuggles me a cup of tea and some toast, then finds an opportune moment to let me out the back door. I recover my cricket bag, jump the back fence, dodge a nasty Alsatian dog, thankfully on a short chain, before finding my way to Sprogs Corner a while later. On Sunday morning things are slow in Wagga Wagga and it takes over an hour to score a lift back to Base. It gives me time to consider whether Janine is worth the various risks I am taking.

It's a serious consideration. After all, we have very little in common except bonking each other's brains out.

That afternoon, I have become so worried about the whole situation I seek Nev's advice again. He is usually sensible about this shit; doesn't muddy the water with his own dramas.

'She did what?' He looks at me in disbelief. 'Fuck, mate, most of us would give our left one to get something other than our own hand, but ...' He searches for words and then changes tack.

'My Uncle Dennis once told me; you should never fuck anyone crazier than yourself. I recommend you dump her,' he pauses momentarily. 'What did you say her phone number is?' now laughing.

'It's not like she is crazy,' I conclude. 'She just likes sex and knows what she wants, I don't have to guess.'

'If she was a guy, you'd be slapping her back as some sort of hero. Just go with it, Dougie.'

'Yer, but it's just that I need to feel some connection and it's just not there. I am literally just a rooting machine to her.' He gives me that look like I am from outer space. 'I am going to tell her it's over next weekend.' He shakes his head in disbelief.

Monday is the beginning of the end of our basic fitter training.

We finish the base plate on the vice. The holes are drilled and countersunk at just the right depth. We need cutting fluid to keep the heat down on the larger holes. As the bits are bolted together there is some filing to remove any misfits, but not too much. I continually use the micrometer to make sure I am within tolerance. I just make the cut and submit on time.

It is also the week we get assigned our trade. I am going to be an Armament Fitter for the next eight years. Armament Fitters are known as 'Gunnies' and Nev is also going to be a Gunnie. On our midweek phone call, Janine tells me we are going to the pictures on Sunday afternoon. I am determined that it's going to be our last date and start thinking through the breakup speech.

Sunday morning is a slow start, I lounge around before getting an early lunch and hitching a ride into town. We meet out the front of the picture theatre. It's the latest James Bond movie this afternoon starring Roger Moore.

'I reckon Sean Connery is a much better James Bond than Moore.' She just shrugs her shoulders.

'I don't think I have ever seen a Sean Connery movie.'

What! Have you been locked in a cupboard for the last sixteen years?

My mind wanders as the movie muddles along, not really keeping my attention.

Should I tell her now and walk out, or wait till after?

I am contemplating the options when she leans over to me.

'Julie Relf told me her boyfriend played with her boobs at the pictures,' she whispers, nibbling on my ear.

I am apprehensive about starting anything, but the nibbling

has turn to a full-on pash. Involuntarily, my mouth opens accepting her tongue, with a little sigh from her.

She reaches over and grabs my hand, pulling it inside her jumper. Her hand over mine cupping a breast over her bra. She squeezes her hand and I respond with a soft massage. Her breathing intensifies, my mind no longer on breakup options.

Her hand comes off mine and moves to my jeans. She starts rhythmically kneading, bringing things to life.

Fuck, you can't do that here!

I guess I should be thanking my lucky stars, but I find myself wanting to shrink into the seat and disappear. Janine is on a mission, undoing the zip, freeing my now swollen member. Her hand now rubbing me, faster and faster, my hand now inside her bra, playing with her nipple. If anyone were to turn their head one degree away from the movie, they would get a much more pornographic show, but they seem unbelievably entranced with Roger Moore's campy efforts to stay alive.

I know I'm about to lose it, and Janine senses it too. She makes a cursory effort to restore my modesty, grabs my hand and drags me out of the seat. Before I know it, we are in the girls' toilets with her bent over the cistern moaning loudly. I have both hands on her breasts. It's a short event and she still has the crazed look when we get back to our seats, just in time to see Roger Moore save the world from yet another disaster.

As we wander out onto the street, the afternoon heat is fading, the low sun creating long, sleek shadows. Janine whispers in my ear that she still needs something rather urgently and, just for a moment, I start looking around wondering where she is going to seduce me next.

Surely not on the main street?

Moments later, Margaret pulls up to the kerb in the Crown to take Janine home. Surprisingly, she gets out of the car and comes over. She gives me a little hug and a peck on the cheek. I can feel her breast firm against my chest. I am aware of it being larger, fuller than Janine's.

'You look tired,' she tells me. Janine stands back, a wicked smirk on her face. 'Can we give you a ride home?'

Margaret is chatty on the way out to Forest Hill, asks how the course is going, where do I hope to get posted to. It suddenly strikes me Janine and I don't discuss this stuff.

Perhaps we don't have anything in common at all? Maybe, this is just how relationships are normally like? Fucked if I know.

The subject changes to music. What do I think about the Rolling Stones, the Who, The Easybeats, who are the best solo artists. I am enjoying the conversation. Margaret is obviously a music lover. Janine is looking annoyed at being left out, but isn't taking part or offering any opinions. There isn't a kiss at the drop-off.

Back at the Apprentice Club, I manage to find an iced coffee and some fruit cake, Nev walks in.

'How'd you go, mate?' he asks, sitting down.

'Not good.' I tell him about the afternoon at the pictures. 'I couldn't really break up with her after that,' I plead.

'Maaaaattttteee,' he says. 'It's okay to just have sex, you know.'

'No, mate, this is not going to end well. I am going to let this cool off for a while.'

Funnily enough, I don't get the mid-week phone call and I am relieved. The only other departure for the routine comes

Thursday after lunch. We are marching back to work. Well, it could be described as marching but there is a lot of fuck-arsing around. Suddenly we hear loud yelling.

'That Flight there, HALT,' the voice says. We stop and look around, but there's no one in sight. We are just about to take off again when a figure in jungle greens drops down out of a gum tree. It's Corporal Perry. Some of us are chuckling at the turn of events.

'Right, you lot, you are on CT,' he says, taking out his notebook and writing down our Flight and Intake number. He spots me with a smile on my face and comes up in my personal space, noting my name as he approaches.

'Find something funny, do we, Walsh?' he asks. I am stifling the laughter, but it's not easy. If he asks me if I have something better to do, I am going to lose it.

'No, Corporal,' I respond loudly with my best straight face.

'Right, get the fuck out of here,' he barks and we march off, a little more militarily than we had before. I look back and catch sight of Perry climbing back into the tree.

The guy must have a screw loose.

A couple of the boys have a trip to Melbourne planned for the weekend and have a whinge about the CT causing them to be late for a party. With no visit to Janine on the dance card, I have a leisurely weekend ahead. It's only going to delay my Friday afternoon net session with Nigel and Lurch, so I frankly don't give a flying fuck.

At cricket on Saturday afternoon on the oval near our block, I get three for fifteen off five. Sunday is an all-day TV session at the Apprentice Club, day two of the First Test against the West Indies in Brisbane.

It's the first test with a full Australian side after World Series Cricket. I keep my transistor radio with me to check the Sheffield Shield scores. Dougie didn't make the Australian team, David Hookes got the number six spot and Doug played in the shield match against South Australia in Adelaide. He took two for and made forty odd runs in the first innings, probably not enough to get him back in the Test team.

The next week, we get the results of our final assessment on the assembled vice. Mine is a pass, enough to get by. I was never going to get a great result with such fine hand work required, just not my thing. The end of the year cannot come fast enough and the expectation of seeing grandma, grandad, and Louise is growing day by day.

The last Saturday for the year we played our match on the turf pitch on the main oval at Base. There is a distinct green tinge to the pitch and I get some nice movement off the seam. We knock them over for one hundred and seven and I get four for twenty off six. We chase the runs down with two wickets in hand. The barbie gets cranked up, beers in hand.

We're sitting on the grass recounting key points in the match when Flight Sergeant Gardner walks over.

'Who needs a beer?' Yogi puts his hand in his pocket and gives him a dollar note.

'Nige? Dougie?' he asks. We look at each other in slight disbelief. He knows how old we are.

'Thanks, Flight,' I say, handing over a two dollar note. 'For both of us, Flight.'

'Dougie, its cricket. My name is Bob,' he says. He returns a short time later, hands out cans of Tooheys New and we discuss the Australian number six spot. I tell him Doug Walters should be there. He says Rick McCosker and Peter Toohey got hundreds for NSW at the WACA yesterday. Dougie isn't playing.

'I reckon they'll pick Toohey at six for the first Test against the Poms,' he says. We then went on to select a bowling attack.

'Spinner,' he asks.

'I think Kerry O'Keeffe is just about finished. Not sure there are any decent leggies getting around, though; not that O'Keeffe was much of a leggie.'

'I think they'll stick with Ray Bright, even though he didn't do much against the West Indies in Brisbane,' he says, as a woman about his age comes to his side. She is quite pretty.

'Dougie, this is my wife, Nancy,' he says. I shake her hand politely.

'My real name is Tim, but everyone calls me Dougie because I am from Dungog,' I clarify.

'Oh! Pity about Walters missing selection,' she says.

A very informed lady indeed this one.

Nige asks Bob if we can have another beer and he okays it.

'No more than three for you two, though,' he commands, in his best military voice.

'Yes, Flight,' we say in unison. Nige disappears into the shed to get the beers. The selection discussion turns to opening batsmen as we grab a piece of bread and a snag from the barbie; onion and tomato sauce on top.

We finish the beer and I go into the shed for my shout. There is a girl sitting on a green army chair behind a camp table, with tubs of beer and soft drinks behind her. She is reading a book.

'Hi,' she looks up and smiles. I am instantly taken by her.

She is about my age, dark hair, almost black, fair skin and a beautiful face.

'Double! Double toil and trouble,' I say, glancing down at the book.

'Are you trying to be Macbeth or trouble?' she asks, smiling.

'Depends on the situation. It's a bit of an odd mix, Macbeth and serving beer?' I enquire.

'Oh, I have to read this over the summer holidays for school next year. And this,' she said, pointing to the drinks 'is to help dad out.'

'Flight Sergeant Gardner?' I ask.

'Yep.' She's still smiling, looking me up and down. 'You don't look very old, are you a First-Year Apprentice?'

'Yep,' I echo. 'Are you in Year Twelve next year?'

'Yep,' she hasn't lost the smile.

'How did you go today?' she asks.

'Won by two wickets,' I tell her, and she nods knowingly.

'You bat or bowl?' she continues.

'Bowl, first change. Got four for,' I brag a little.

'Very good.' We stand there looking at each other for a bit, eyes locked, searching for the next discussion piece. It's not awkward, just oddly silent. Nige sticks his head in the doorway.

'You bloody brewing that beer, Dougie?'

'Oh, yer, two beers please ...' I ask, seeking her name.

'Allison,' she answers with a smile. 'There ya go, Dougie,' emphasising the accent and the name, not mocking me, but taking the piss out of the macho-ness of it.

I give her my best smile and head for the door. I am trying to get another look at her as I go down the stairs and stumble. I can see she's amused, and I am definitely intrigued.

The conversation at the barbie has turned to the Australian team captaincy after Chappell — Hughes, maybe Yallop? A little later, she appears beside her father.

'Nige, Dougie, this is my eldest daughter, Allison,' Bob says.

'Allison, this is Nige and Dougie.'

'My real name is Tim, but they call me Dougie 'cause I am from Dungog,' I repeat. She also appears to understand the link; very much the cricket family.

Nige jumps in with some small talk about what year at school she is in, what she is studying, and ambitions. She talks with confidence and tells us she is heading to Uni to be a lawyer.

'It'll take a good HSC score,' I say. 'Over four hundred, maybe four twenty?' I ask.

'Yep,' she says again. 'I think I need four thirty.' Both Nige and I whistle and raise our eyebrows. I manage to carve him out of the conversation after a while and get her one-on-one. It's getting late and I ask if I can call her.

'That's fine,' she says. 'We live on Base so you can use the on-Base phones.' We are about to depart when she asks my last name.

'Tim Walsh,' I say, and her smile disappears in an instant.

'The great Tim Walsh, hey,' she says with scorn.

'Yes,' I reply with some bewilderment.

'Every girl at Kooringal High School knows who you are. Had any adventures on the washing machine lately, Dougie boy?' she asks cynically.

Bloody Janine, the blabber mouth.

'Don't bother calling,' she says, walking away.

Shit, that didn't exactly go to plan.

There is a heat wave the next week, and the Wagga Wagga sun is brutal. Our basic fitter instruction is finished and we have been assigned shitty little jobs, or SLJs for short, sweeping hangars and painting rocks. In the heat, we try to keep the effort to a bare minimum. Every afternoon is spent cooling off at the pool, trying to outdo each other in the bombing competition. I have a lot of time to think, especially about one Allison Gardner.

She has me transfixed. Every time there is a spare moment, the smile and sense of humour come to mind, followed quickly by the burn of her scorn. I wish I had a way to rewind and start over with a clean slate. The images of her are not sexual, like Janine, but ones where we are laughing and smiling at each other, having a conversation, just enjoying each other's company.

Thursday night rolls around, Christmas leave starts tomorrow and there is an air of excitement. After our swim, we get a bit of dinner from the Mess and head to the cinema. As we approach, I notice a group of girls out the front and one of them is Allison. I am not going to miss an opportunity like this and I lead our group to theirs. As I get within earshot, she looks up and sees me.

'Hey, look girls, it's Doug the Stud.' They all turn and laugh, and my face goes red.

'You should take it easy on him,' says one of the other girls, 'he'll be heartbroken.'

'Why would that be?' I ask.

'Oh, haven't you heard?' she says. 'Janine has a new flame to keep her satisfied. You've been dumped.' More giggles from the group.

That's actually a relief.

There's an awkward moment as the two groups size each other up, uneasy glances being exchanged. Finally, Lurch breaks the ice, and soon after we start to pair off. Allison and Nigel are deep in conversation and I try to get in between. She keeps manoeuvring her back to me. Michelle Wright tries her best to corner me.

We all end up sitting through the movie in pairs, Nige and Allison, Nev and Heather, Lurch and Isabelle, and Michelle and me. I find myself continually looking over to see if he puts his arm around her.

Will she look over and smile at me like she did last weekend?

As we part ways, there is a collective, 'Merry Christmas, see you next year.' I watch Allison disappear into the night.

Fuck it.

The buses arrive to take us home around eight the next morning and in typical military fashion, there is a lot of yelling and hurrying, before a long wait. It takes an hour to sort people into the right bus, load up, and move out. We are on the road by 0900 hours.

I have the transistor radio and manage to find the cricket on ABC. Bloody Botham has taken three early wickets, and there was a stupid run out with Wiener. Eventually, Hughes digs in and takes charge.

It has me stumped why Botham gets so many wickets, I just don't rate him.

It's around 2200 hours by the time we get to Hexham. Uncle Bert is parked there waiting and, for the second time this year, I need to apologise for being late. He just puts it down to good old RAAF planning and we discuss the cricket on the trip to Dungog.

Even though it was a late night, I am up at 0430 hours the next morning, not going to be late for milking. I am into my work shorts and shirt. It's definitely a squeeze into the shirt now. A cup of tea and then I'm into it. Shit Head doesn't disappoint and Dorrie Evans looks me up and down several times as I get the cups onto her. We are in the kitchen just after seven and grandma has fried tomato and onion bubbling away. I sneak a peek into the pot, salivating at the smell.

'Your tomatoes, grandma?' I ask.

'Yes, Tim. It was a warm winter and your grandfather got them in nice and early. There are plenty,' she leans over and whispers, 'but, he doesn't know how to tie them up properly, the silly old bugger, I do all of it.' Over breakfast we go through the local gossip and the plans for Christmas.

'We'll be going into Maitland for the Christmas shopping on Thursday if you want to come.'

Despite the recent turmoil with Janine and Allison, I ask grandad if I can take the Valiant and go and see Louise. I don't have a licence, but I have been driving the tractor since I was seven, and the car ever since I could reach the clutch. He just waves acceptance and off I go.

It's a short trip up the road and when I get there, she comes running out and jumps into my arms. This feels a little uncomfortable, given recent events, but it is good to see her. I give her the download on my training to date, and my cricket achievements, leaving out the nocturnal events. She shares all the school gossip; Lisa McKay had a little boy and has moved into Michael Latimer's house with his parents. Mrs Bennett comes in and hugs me. It's all nice, but I am not feeling at all like the boy who left here a year ago.

It's day one of the holidays and I have slipped easily back into the local routine. After the afternoon milking, there is a trip to the RSL for a drink, then we sit around the radio listening to the last session of the Test from Perth — Brearley and Dilley are defying our bowlers. We need to knock them over quickly tomorrow if we are going to get a first innings lead.

By bedtime, my first year of marching, filing, polishing floors, and RAAF Base, Wagga Wagga, seems like nothing more than a dream, and maybe even a bad one.

On Christmas Eve, we finish the milking a little early, get cleaned up, put on our good clothes, and head to the Bennett's house for dinner and drinks. Grandma makes it plainly obvious I need to be spending time with Louise. I go along with her to keep the peace, but it doesn't feel the same.

I am now sexually active, and I look at her differently than I did six months ago. Yes, she's definitely attractive; she is blooming and growing in all the right places. I so want to share the excitement of sex with her, but I am feeling guilty.

What would she think about me if she knew what Janine and I have been doing? I can't tell her. And, then there is Allison Gardner. I am feeling torn.

Why is it I get so bloody emotional every time we head back to Wagga Wagga?

Christmas leave was so much fun and now I am both loathing and excited by the prospect of another year in the RAAF. There is the immediate memory of four weeks leave, longer term memories of my sometimes troubled first year in the RAAF, and the exciting prospect ahead of learning a career as an Armourer.

My heart tells me I should be back on the farm with grandad. He's turning sixty this year and gran is turning fifty-nine. Both are fine physically, but I wonder how long they can keep it up. The whole operation is not a one-man thing and all three, grandad, grandma and Uncle Bert, are needed to do all the work; it's a real team operation.

Grandma gets out there, harvesting corn, feeding poddy calves, the chooks and the pigs. She is from a respected and hardworking family and, as the oldest, was the quasi mother for many of her siblings, all eight of them. No slouch, my grandma.

Grandad would happily have me home, but knows that a trade is the best thing for me in the longer term. Farming isn't the profession it once was and there is constant pressure now just to make ends meet. Dairy farming is becoming an endangered occupation. On the other hand, I'm pretty sure Uncle Bert does not want me home.

There are, or were, three children: Uncle Jim, mum, and

Uncle Bert. Uncle Jim joined the PMG after fourth form and left home. It's how dad and mum met. Dad was with the PMG and Uncle Jim and him were mates. He went to live in Melbourne.

I have heard talk that when grandad passes away, the farm gets divided three ways, the girls and I will get mum's share. I also have heard talk Uncle Bert wants to keep the farm in the family name. Not sure how it might work, and at this point I guess I don't really need to know yet.

Another issue pulling at my heart is Louise. We had a great time over Christmas. She was at our house most days, or I was at hers. We joked, milked cows, picked cucumbers, swam in the river, and changed the irrigation pipes. There were intimate moments and I got a sense she would have been happy to consummate the relationship, but I played dumb.

I've got no idea why. Maybe I just don't want to upset her? Why didn't I push it? It's not that I'm not attracted to her.

I could have easily been drawn back into this lifestyle, but there are two other things on my mind. I want to see the world and experience things I would not experience living in Dungog. There is some burning need in me to go beyond the dairy and the farm. Sure, life would be easier. I could live up to the family name, and I have no doubt Lou would be a great wife, but there is this nagging desire in me for more, a whole lot more.

The second thing on my mind was one Allison Gardner. She has been invading my thoughts almost daily. I feel like a cheat when I kiss Lou because I have a picture of Allison in my head and I am kissing her. It's really not fair on Lou. On the bus, I tell Nev about my torment.

'I know what you mean, mate. Most of my family were born in Kempsey, live in Kempsey, and will die in Kempsey. Most of the boys have been in gaol at one time or another, and Uncle Dave is about to go back for the third time. I don't want to be just another alcoholic black fella. I want to be someone, to do something more. I know there's a lot of people happy to see a black fella fail, but that only makes me more determined.' I realise that I don't see Nev as a black fella. To me, he is just one of the boys, a mate, but the odds are definitely stacked against him. Nev is on a roll. I can almost see his brain ticking over.

'And as for the chick thing, you are in a lot of trouble there, mate. No right or simple answer there,' he continues.

Everything he says is confusing, but, he's a good sounding board and it's good to get it off my chest.

We start to talk about what we are going to do after Wagga Wagga. There are a few options. If we go to Amberley, it will be to work on F-111s. They are glamorous aeroplanes and living in Queensland sounds pretty exciting to both of us.

Edinburgh in South Australia has two Squadrons of P3 Orions which also sounds like fun in some ways, but South Australia seems a long way away, and they are a little weird down there.

Being Gunnies, there is little chance of getting a posting to Richmond. They mostly fly C-130 transports and there isn't a big call for bombs on a C-130. The only possibility is No. 2 Aircraft Depot, known as 2AD. That wouldn't be a good first posting. Come to think of it, no depot would be good. 2AD, 3AD, or No. 1 Central Ammunition Depot would all be a disappointment; not exactly the pointy end.

As it turns out, both of us are attracted to the French lady, the Mirage Fighter. There is something about the Mirage which is in oddly desirable — you just want you to get your hands on it. It looks like it's going a thousand miles an hour standing still. The bonus is, the only Australian fighter base is at Williamtown, near Newcastle. Newcastle looks to have a good lifestyle and is close enough to home to make it easy to visit, but just far away to not make it obligatory. And, the girls live there too, so I can see them regularly and have some role in their lives as they grow up.

Back in Wagga Wagga, we slip back into the routine quickly, Mess food, the dry heat, shining shoes, belt buckles, and making bed rolls. It's all still ordinary and in some way comforting, secure in a way it didn't feel last year.

The work, however, has ramped up a notch. After parade on the first Monday, we pack the drums away and march up to the Electrical Trades Squadron building. From there, we divide into Electrical, Instruments, and Armament sections. Nev, Gus, Mick Gilmore and I enter Armament Section and join the other lads.

There are eighteen of us, all up. I know most of them, but not all. The two Kiwis, Phil Beach and Warren Fraser, are there; Justin Arnott and Jim Brown from One Flight; Stan Cooper and Gus Edwards from Two Flight; Mick Gilmore, Jerry Holmes and Merv Humphries from Three Flight; Peter Johnson from Four Flight; Nixon from Five Flight; O'Reilly, Ross, Sharpe and Smith from Six Flight; and Nev, Watson and me from Seven Flight. We are seated at our desks chatting and sizing each other up, when two Sergeants walk in.

'Sit fast,' orders Phil Beach. We all straighten our backs, arms outstretched, fists clenched on the table, knuckles down. The two Sergeants stand along the wall. Then, a Warrant Officer and Flight Lieutenant walk in.

'Thank you, Gentlemen, *Sit Easy* please. My name is Flight Lieutenant Sanders, and this is Warrant Officer Foley,' with a gesture. The next fourteen months are going to test our brains and your powers of concentration. If you can maintain your academic performance, you will join the highly respected trade of Armament Fitter.' He lets it sink in, looking around.

'As Gunnies, we'll have a privileged position in the RAAF. Not only will we be assembling weapons, loading ammunition, and servicing weapons systems, but we also become egress system specialists. Pilots' lives will depend on our skill and attention to detail. The standards are high, and we should always be striving for excellence.

This scares me a little. Last year, I had struggled with the precise nature of the filing and turning tasks. I am much more at ease with a hammer, the bigger the better.

He hands over to Warrant Officer Foley who gives us instruction on our new day-to-day working routine and disciplinary matters. He reminds me a bit of grandad, a man of few words, but those words will carry a lot of weight.

He also announces several people are to be promoted to Corporal Apprentice. Promotion is based on our academic and disciplinary record, as well as our general behaviour.

'Congratulations to Apprentices Beach, Nixon and Smith,' says Warrant Officer Foley. Nev looks upset. He did well in every subject last year and should have been in the mix. It's a tough call whether the other guys deserved it more.

Maybe their results were better?

The Sergeant orders us to Sit Fast again, and the Flight Lieutenant and Warrant Officer leave the room. He introduces himself as Sergeant Harrison and looks to the other Sergeant,

'This is Sergeant Delamont,' he says. 'For the next three weeks, we are going to explore the delights of Explosive Regulations. On your desk is a copy of those regulations.'

I look at it with some reservation. The book has a butter-coloured, hard binder and is about four inches thick.

It's a lot of regulation.

At smoko, we get to mix with the Gunnies from their other courses including the Senior Apprentice course from 32 Intake. Sitting around in the shade of the building, many of the boys are lighting up as Faulkner walks out the door.

'Hey,' he shouts. 'You should Stand Fast when a Flight Sergeant Apprentice comes past,' he says, puffing his chest out. We are uneasily shuffling into something resembling standing fast when Lash appears from nowhere. He walks over to Faulkner staring him straight in the eyes.

'You Sprogs don't have to Stand Fast for dickheads,' says Lash, leaning down to stand nose-to-nose with Faulkner. He can't get away quick enough. 'Twat,' says Lash as a send-off.

This Gunnie thing has benefits.

On Thursday night, we are busy swapping rooms. They want the Apprentices from each trade living with each other. Apparently, it helps improve our study. Nev, Watto, and I have become very good mates with Jim and we are a little sad to be shifting. I can tell that he isn't too captivated by the move either. Nev and I have been assigned a room on the second floor with Gus Edwards and Merv Humphries. They seem like nice enough guys. Around 1930 hours, Nigel finds Nev and I wrestling our foot lockers up the stairs.

'Hey, guys, I just got off the phone with Allison. She and a few of the girls are going to the pictures tomorrow night. Are you guys in?' I feel a strong twinge of jealousy at the mention of her name.

Did he ring her, or did she ring him?

'Is the Pope Polish?'

On Friday, Nige and I have a hit in the nets before some food and a run through the dip. The pack departs around 1830, finding the girls waiting outside the chapel.

I doubt it was one of us who chose the meeting place.

As we approach, I am desperately seeking out Allison's face. That pretty face framed in the dark hair.

'Hi, Tim.' I am distracted. Michelle walks forward, lifts her face, and plants one right on the lips. I can smell her perfume, sweet and musky. She steps back, pulling the fringe over her ear, smiling. Unconsciously, I look her up and down — a nice, white skirt and flowery blouse, her breasts noticeably pressuring the buttons.

'How was your Christmas?'

'Good! Yours? Did you go anywhere?' She starts recalling a trip to Melbourne to see her grandparents. I look around to see what the others are doing. Three couples are in idle conversation. It seems I was the only one to get a kiss. I can overhear Allison talking to Nige about the HSC.

Nev is regaling Heather with some tale of his Christmas adventures, complete with actions. He has her captivated. She's a taller girl with shoulder-length brown hair and freckles. She's not fat, but quite a large frame, big-boned I guess is the expression. She is wearing a simple sleeveless dress, and has smaller breasts than Michelle.

I find myself comparing the breasts of the four girls. Michelle has an ample pair, Heather's are small, Jenny is a petite girl so they are small, and it's hard to tell with Allison, who's not petite but she doesn't have big boobs either.

She's talking to me and I have to shake myself out of the trance. It's okay to have a quick look but no gawking.

It's the Twelfth Commandment. Thou shall not get caught gawking at other girls' breasts.

The movie is a soppy Dustin Hoffman film. The girls go all teary at the end and Michelle grabs my arm and puts her head on my shoulder.

Mental note, soppy movies can be good for your love life. Learn to live with them.

It prompts me to check what Allison and Nige are doing. Thankfully, not too much action there.

After the movie, the four couples take the slow walk up the main drag, some holding hands, others not. I am behind Allison hoping she and Nige don't get too close. Michelle has snuggled into my shoulder, arm around my waste.

At Ward Street, we disperse, Michelle and I walking several houses up to her front gate. She doesn't wait, wrapping her arms around me and lifting her face to me; soft lips and the musky perfume, the hot evening air adding to the intensity. She opens her mouth and her tongue pushes into my mouth.

My mind is racing. If I am going to have any chance with Allison, I can't let this relationship blossom. But her breathing has hastened, and my mind wonders. I find myself wrapping my tongue in hers. She moves from my lips and presses my face into her neck — a sweet taste of sweat and perfume.

The front light snaps us out of the little frenzy, and she steps back from the clinch, straightening her skirt, everything apparently under control. The screen door opens, and the tall figure of Squadron Leader Wright appears.

He was probably standing behind the door watching.

'It's late, Michelle.'

'I was just coming, dad.'

'See you at the same time tomorrow?' she enquires. I am not sure what to say and just nod. She turns and heads for the front door and I get a sick feeling in my stomach like I am getting into something I shouldn't be.

The following week goes slowly. At work, the Explosive Regulations studies are going fairly well. The trick is knowing where to look in the book. I am doing well in the progress tests and funnily enough, it's interesting. You can't store certain types of explosives with others. Detonators and high explosives in the same building are a definite no-no. There are also loads of rules around what can be done in certain buildings and with certain stores like electrically initiated explosives.

We are introduced to the rules of managing stray current. Stray current is where radio transmissions, radar, or other sources, might induce an electrical current in a device or a cable. The result is the device is set off at a most unexpected time and this is really important as a lot of explosives are electrically initiated.

Sergeant Harrison gets out the 16mm projector and shows us a US Navy film titled HERO, Hazards of Electromagnetic

Radiation to Ordnance. It shows a fire on the USS Forrestal in the Gulf of Tonkin where one hundred and thirty-four sailors were killed. A Zuni Rocket loaded to a F4 Phantom went off and hit the side of an A4 Skyhawk starting the fire. A hundred and thirty dead sailors is sobering and it brings home to us that this is not a game.

As Armourers we are going to be at the pointy end of things, preparing and loading weapons designed to knock down an enemy aircraft, or destroy them on the ground.

We're not in Kansas anymore, Toto.

The other significant event of the week is the arrival of the new intake, Number 34 Intake Apprentices. We spend much of Wednesday night going from room to room asking the new Sprogs where they are from. I don't find anyone from Dungog, but there is a guy from Newcastle, one from Maitland, and another from Forster. It's close enough to home to be neighbours. They are wide-eyed, and seem so young compared to us even though it's only a year ago we were in the same position.

Over the ensuing days, it's funny to see the way the ADGies break them of civilian habits and build basic marching skills — discipline. I recall our first days twelve months ago and the mixture of feelings. Excitement of getting my first uniform and firing a military rifle. But also, the absolute dread of the drill in the summer heat on the parade ground, and the constant yelling and swearing — intimidating. The new Sprogs are wearing the jungle-green giggle hats. We have now moved onto blue berets. I would have preferred to stick with the giggle hat; it definitely offers more protection from the sun.

What is the point of the beret? We're not French.

With the new Sprogs here, I also have a feeling of being a seasoned campaigner. We have been on the Base at Wagga Wagga longer than most of the other trainees. The clerical trainees come and go quite quickly, and the engineering trainees are only on Base for around twelve months. When 32 Intake graduates, we will be the longest serving students on the Base.

It's the Australia Day long weekend and the Base does its usual clean-out on Friday afternoon. There is a repeat performance at the pictures, and afterwards. Michelle and I make a detour to the golf course for some serious pashing, even a little fondling, before I walk her to the front gate, Squadron Leader Wright interrupting the goodbye again. Back in the block, I find Gus playing one of his new albums, *Breakfast at Sweethearts*.

'You wait, Dougie. These guys are going to be huge. Maybe, as big as the Rolling Stones.'

'You sure, mate? The Stones?' I ask, frowning.

'Well, maybe not that huge,' he reluctantly agrees. 'Their last album was pretty good, though. It's not commercial shit, just good, old Aussie rock 'n' roll, great storytelling.' Nev arrives a short time later. He looks a little pale.

'She stuck her tongue so far down my throat I thought she tickled my tonsils,' he goes. 'Does it always get this intense?' he says, looking at me as if am somehow an authority on the subject. I shrug and tell them I am hitting the sack. In the shower, I recall the moment earlier with Michelle. She had her hands on my jeans. I start to think about Allison and it's her and me in the passionate embrace. The soap gets a workout.

Being the Sunday of a long weekend, the Mess is so quiet that

I get asked how I would like my steak cooked. The cook even throws a fried egg and chips on the plate.

'Don't get used to it,' he tells me, with a grin. I catch the last few overs of the Test at the Apprentice Club. Australia nine for two hundred and one at stumps. Lairdy, Hughes, and Border make runs. I reckon they need to get rid of Wiener and Ian Chappell.

Bloody Ian Chappell! How does he get a run and not Dougie?

One of the Third-Year Apprentices changed the channel to the ABC. Countdown is on, Christie Allen singing.

'Those are definitely bigger than goose bumps!' says someone from the back. I find myself transfixed to the screen for a while trying to watch two breasts which seem to want to go in completely different directions.

I am not sure when the fixation with breasts started, probably around the time they started sprouting on our female classmates' chests. It was certainly noticeable in high school when we had swimming, not sure which year. They looked so soft and I reckon swimming costumes are designed specifically to taunt young men. They reveal just enough to give an insight into what they might look like naked, without the exposure.

Monday afternoon and the Apprentice Car Park has started to fill. On our way to the pool, we check out the new arrivals, a brown XW Falcon and a red HQ Holden SS.

'They should never paint a car that dog turd brown,' observes Merv.

The girls are there before us. Michelle and Heather rise and Nev and I get a welcome kiss. Both are wearing one-piece togs; Michelle's are stretched across two large lumps.

No gawking, Tim.

After spreading our towels on the grass, the bombing campaign commences, a variety of techniques on display. There's one where you lean back with one knee bent and held in both hands, entering the water feet first. Another with the chest flat and arms extended before crunching prior to entry. Most of the action is off the low springboard, but Merv likes to pose from the three-metre board. He can pretty well bomb anywhere in that half of the pool from the high board. A bunch of boys try desperately to impress a bunch of girls.

Once safe in the knowledge that half the pool has been emptied, we retire to our towels, baking in the afternoon sun.

'School starts tomorrow,' she says, somewhat gloomily.

'Uh, ha.' I am watching Allison. She's in a bikini lying face down next to Nigel. They aren't touching or anything. As a matter of fact, I haven't actually seen them hold hands.

Maybe there is hope for me yet?

'Tim!' She shoves a foot into my leg. 'You haven't heard a word I said.' She looks over at Allison accusingly.

'Sorry.'

'Come on,' she says, getting up wrapping the towel around her waist. 'You can walk me home. See you guys later,' she waves. I scurry after her and we walk in silence for some time before she stops.

'Tim, I think it's time we called an end to this.' I don't respond. She is obviously not happy. 'Fair dinkum, it's bloody hard going out with someone who spends the entire time goggling someone else.'

'Sorry.' Her eyes roll and she sighs loudly.

'Sorry,' she says in resignation. She starts walking again. 'Dead set, Tim, you are annoying. Most of the girls think you're hot stuff, but ...' She can't find the words.

'Even Allison?'

'Even Allison,' she repeats, with some resignation in her voice.

Well, that is nice to know.

I am contemplating how to get Allison into a private conversation when she walks over and leans up to me offering a cheek. A little peck and she turns for home.

'See you later, Tim,' she waves.

I think I just got dumped.

It's a funny feeling to be dumped and be happy about it. On the way back to the room, I get to check out more new arrivals in the carpark; a cream-coloured Corolla and a burnt-orange Datsun 120Y. I just don't understand why anyone would buy a Corolla or a Datsun 120Y. They are ugly, and sound like bloody sewing machines.

At the Apprentice Club, I grab an iced coffee and check the cricket score. The West Indies are having another day out in Adelaide, Viv Richards and Alvin Kallicharran the main destroyers. It's the speed they score that gets me — three hundred in a day again — and making it look easy.

By dinner time, the Mess is humming again and I get the rundown on various adventures over the weekend. Lurch and Rosco have been to Tumut fishing and rabbit shooting. There is a discussion on the merits of a 22 versus a shotgun for shooting bunnies. Apparently, the shotgun has a greater kill ratio, but the 22 is cleaner and the price for a head-shot bunny is a lot more than one with a bellyful of pellets. Not exactly something I have spent time pondering. My mind is on Allison Gardner.

The studies into Explosive Regulations continue and the final exam is first up on Tuesday morning. Because there are so many regulations, the exam is open book. The hardest thing to get a grip on is all the forms they use. There is a form for everything, even an empty container form, which is, in fact, a sticker. The bloody military loves its forms; millions of them. Much to my surprise, I get a distinction.

Who would have thought paperwork could be interesting?

Well, interesting might be a stretch, but I am happy with the result.

Tuesday proves to be a bad day for the Aussie cricketers. The West Indies make four hundred and forty-eight and we are seven for one hundred and thirty at stumps. The way it's going, we will lose by four hundred. I bet Clive Lloyd is remembering the '75–'76 series, where Thommo and Lillee tore them apart. Revenge is sweet. Nev is all over it.

'I reckon you and I will get the call up pretty soon, Dougie. Looks like our boys have forgotten how to compete.'

'Maybe! Maybe they're just up against a champion team?'

We have started basic electrical training. I didn't pay attention in science at school. I thought I had no need for it, and so most of this is going to be new. It's a dry subject, but our instructor is doing his level best to add some humour. By Friday, I am struggling. It's a combination of grasping new concepts, the overall technical difficulty and my attention being diverted much of the time to thinking about one Allison Gardner. There is only so much my little brain can cope with.

'What's on the dance card this weekend, Dougie,' asks Gus.

'Pictures tonight, cricket tomorrow, and probably a dip in the pool on Sunday. You?' Gus rubs his chin in thought.

'I think I will head into town tomorrow. See if there is anything new at the record shop. Might join you for a swim on Sunday.'

After work, I catch a bit of the first day's play against England from Melbourne. The boys have had a quick turnaround from playing the West Indies. Botham grabs a couple of wickets and so I decide to give it a miss, scrubbing up and eating before heading to the pictures.

On Saturday, I write a letter home and catch the first half hour from Melbourne before heading to the ground. Another February stinker today, it must be thirty-eight degrees.

What's the line about cricketers, mad dogs and Englishmen?

During practice last week, I had the ball swinging all over the place. Nige and I have been working on a combination of Zinc and Vaseline to see what would happen. We settled on the Vaseline. The ball moves so much that I actually aimed it off the pitch to get it anywhere near the stumps.

So, I am thrown the ball as first change. The first few balls are relatively benign as I try to find my rhythm, but as I take saliva from my mouth, I also get a bit of Vas from my bottom lip. By the fourth ball, it's bending a fair way and on the final ball, I york the batsman, off stump and out of the ground.

It's bending both ways and I have trouble keeping it straight. I end up with four for sixteen off seven and they are all out for seventy-nine. We chase it down in twenty-five overs. Before we head off, Ken puts the cricket on the car radio. Lairdie and Ian Chappell are getting a few, undoubtedly happy the Windies have gone home. They'll have less bruises against this attack. Although the Ashes aren't at stake this time, it's always good to get on top of the Poms.

Sunday, we all head for the pool at about 1400 hours. Walking through the Apprentice Car Park, there is a range of maintenance activities underway: bonnets open, speakers being fitted, wheels and tyres being changed, timing lights and screwdrivers attempting to extract tiny performance improvements from crappy, wheezing, little, rice-burning four-cylinder engines, and big V8s. The chat is about carbies, split systems and extractors, that and cassette players and speakers.

The motor on grandma's sewing machine is bigger than some of these.

We plough onwards to the pool and throw our towels on the grass under a tree. Heather, Michelle and Isabelle arrive a short time later. No Allison; apparently, she is home studying. The girls all get kisses from respective boyfriends. Michelle is going out with Johnno now, which is nice. I get the impression that she just wants to have the trophy to show off. I no longer rate anything more than a little wave.

Round Two of the Bombing Campaign commences shortly after, the girls squealing as we jump in close to them. The water only just cool in the February heat.

I wish Allison was here.

Tuesday night, Nev comes storming into the room.

'I just got off the phone with Heather. Her old man found out she had been out with an Abo and has forbidden her to see me anymore, fucking prick.' I ponder the issue.

'What's her old man do?' I ask.

'He's a Sergeant MTD.'

'It wouldn't be so bad if he was relatively junior, but a sergeant? They all drink together down at the Mess and if you have noticed, the Sergeants' Mess runs this Base. They all know each other and all the wheeling and dealing is done at the Mess. It could end badly for you; a word in the right ear, so to speak.'

Nev is pondering the implications with a glum look. Gus looks up from his book.

'There is more than one way to skin a cat, my friend.' Putting the book aside, he leans forward in a conspiratorial grin and outlines a plan.

'Whenever you go out, you just get Merv to pick her up and drop her off. We mostly all go out together anyway.'

'A stunt double, Nev,' he laughs.

'As long as that is all you do as my double.'

'Yes, mate, understood. Stunt double, not stunt dick!' We all crack up, maybe, just maybe, this will work. Merv is a country boy, loyal to a fault, happy to put himself in harm's way for the sake of the greater good — well, to ensure Nev has a shot here with Heather.

The plan works well in some instances. The pictures is no problem at all; a quick shuffle of seats after the lights have gone down. The swimming pool is more of an issue; they can get close, but no touching. Over the phone is fine. She rings him and just calls him Merv when the need for a name arises. Merv has even got into a good relationship with the old man. He offers beers when he drops by to pick her up.

The major issue is working out how to get them some time

alone together. You can only get up to so much at the pictures, unless your name is Janine, of course.

'She could always take up babysitting,' suggests Sandy.

'Babysitting,' Nev looks at him sceptically.

'Yer, babysitting. I am going out with Carol O'Dea and she does a heap of babysitting in the married patch on a Friday or Saturday night. The kids are normally in bed and asleep by eight-thirty and the parents never come home before ten, mostly eleven. We get a bit of hanky-panky in between.'

'You're a legend,' yells Nev, running out the door.

The weeks start to flick by quickly, and the routine, oh, the routine. It only gets altered by the change in season, which is also the change from cricket to footy. I decide I will try to play Rugby Union with Merv this year. I have never played this supposedly more sophisticated form of rugby before and only played a bit of Rugby League at school. The farm took priority and I never got to play junior Rugby League like a lot of my school mates did. Grandad was happy to adjust the routine to accommodate junior cricket, but not footy.

The first few training sessions go okay. Being tall, and a little slow, I am assigned to the forwards. Chase the ball, get it, give it to the halfback, chase the ball. It's a pretty simple thing. I am hopeless in the line out and I'm always getting outjumped, so I decide to focus on securing the ball after the throw, and just pushing in the scrums. My major issue is learning the rules, there are so many.

Late April, a wet and dreary Wednesday night, Nev comes back into the room with a worried look, brooding.

'She wants to have sex,' he announces, breaking into a grin.

'Apparently, her folks are going out Friday night and we'll have the house to ourselves for a few hours.'

'Is she on the pill?' I ask.

'Fuck, contraception. I never thought of it. I didn't ask.'

I rat around in my cupboard and grab a couple of condoms.

'Here,' throwing them at Nev. He looks at the packet.

'These are all small, Dougie. Do you have any extra-large?' He laughs and I throw my pillow at him. By Friday, Nev is a nervous wreck.

'What if I blow my bolt in the first two seconds?' he ponders. 'What if it hurts her? What if, what if?'

'Calm down, mate,' I tell him. 'She's probably just as nervous as you.' I let the words sink in for a tick. 'Mate, I am no expert, but from experience, you have to fiddle around a little to work out what she likes.'

'How will I know?'

'Oh, you'll know, mate. When you are doing the right thing, there will be a reaction.'

'Yep, okay, thanks, Dougie,' he says, without conviction.

'And Nev, if you go off in the first two seconds, reload and go again, practise makes perfect, right?' Nev looks confused for half a second then gives me a grin and big thumbs up.

I don't have any plans, so I opt for a night at the Apprentice Club watching TV, a Tony Curtis movie, followed by the snooker, the commentator talking in a hushed voice. I decide to call it a night about eleven.

As I walk up to the block, I can see the white Valiant station wagon, three people standing outside the foyer, two in uniform. As I get closer, I realise it's Nev being interviewed. I approach and stand beside Nev to listen to what is being said. There are two Corporals, one in particular doing the talking. He looks at me.

'What do you want?'

'Nothing, Corporal, just want to see if my friend here needs anything.'

'He doesn't, now fuck off.'

Nev interjects. 'But Dougie can vouch for me. I was at the Apprentice Club all night, wasn't I, Dougie.'

'Yep, we watched the movie together,' I add.

'Then I decided to go for a walk to get some fresh air.'

'That's right. Straight after the movie,' I tell them.

'Which movie,' the corporal asks. I jump straight in.

'Houdini.'

'Righto, smart-arse,' he says, looking at Nev. 'Who's in it?'

'Tony Curtis and Janet Leigh,' replies Nev. The Corporal looks at him with scepticism.

'What were you doing down at the Married Quarters?'

'I guess I just got a little lost,' Nev tells him.

The other Corporal has Nev's ID, writing down the details.

'Lost, my arse, I thought you people were supposed to be able to find your way around in the dark,' he says. 'The Married Quarters are out of bounds to all Trainees and Apprentices, unless you're invited. You'll be hearing more about this.' He turns and walks off toward the Valiant station wagon, his offsider handing Nev his ID and scurrying after him. We watch the station wagon disappear.

'Pricks spotted me coming up the road near the WRAAFery. I ducked into the trees, but they were here waiting for me.'

'The corporal doing all the talking looks like a piece of work. I reckon he'll go after you.'

'Yer, maybe,' Nev is still looking after them.

'So, how'd the night go?'

'What?' He looks at me with a blank look which quickly turns to his trademark cheeky grin.

'Fucking amazing, Dougie. Fucking amazing. Do they always go off like that when you stick it in?'

'Like I said, mate, I am no expert, but I think some do, and others like other stuff. I think it depends on the girl and the situation.'

'Well, Heather definitely likes it in, all the way, and seconds are way better than the first time,' he says, dreamily. It's like he's not even talking to me anymore, just replaying the moment in his head.

Do I throw some cold water on him?

'How'd you know who was in Houdini?' I ask, as he comes back out of the dream.

'Oh, my mum is a mad Tony Curtis fan. Every time he come on TV, we would have to watch it. I can pretty well rattle off every movie he's ever been in.'

I am right, Nev gets called to the Orderly Room on Tuesday and given a charge sheet. It reads: 'Contravening Base Standing Orders by being in an out-of-bounds area, being the Married Quarters.' He gets three days CB for it. Nev reckons it was well worth it.

We are studying Aircraft Electrical Systems and Wiring when Warrant Officer Foley comes into the room unexpectedly. Gilmore, Walker, and Walsh, to my office, please. We follow him out asking each other what we are in the shit for. We are clueless, but it doesn't automatically mean innocence either. He closes the door with a glib look.

Warrant Officer Foley explains that one of the Adult Trainees has been killed in a car accident. The funeral is in Canberra tomorrow and he'll get the full military send-off, so we'll be playing our drums at the funeral.

'Go back to your room, shower and change. The car will pick you and your drums up at 1400 hours. Dress for the funeral is full-Service Dress. Go!'

The car ride to Canberra is long and dull. Nev tries out a few new jokes but the delivery needs some work. They give us a room in the transit accommodation at RAAF Fairbairn. Fairbairn is home to number 5 Squadron, RAAF — 5 SQN fly Iroquois helicopters and undertake most of the helicopter training for the Australian Defence Force.

We get a meal at the Mess and hit the Airmen's Club for a beer. At least they have a fire going and we play a few hands of 500. I'm learning you have to watch Gilmore; he likes to table talk. There is a photo on the wall with a narrative. The photo is of Mr James Valentine Fairbairn, Minister of the Air in the Menzies Government, 1939 to 1941. The Base is named after him. It says he died in an aircraft crash to the east of the Base on 13th August 1940 along with another Minister and some distinguished Generals. I could list a few NCOs who should have been on the flight.

We retire for the night, Nev telling his increasingly terrible jokes for what seems like an hour before we finally nod off. Four blankets do not manage to keep the Canberra cold out and we don't get much sleep. When I finally succumb, Allison fills my dreams.

After defrosting in the shower, we find the Mess and enjoy a cooked breakfast made to order. This is a relatively small base and the nice things like orange juice are in plentiful supply, including milky coffee.

The funeral is a sad affair. People in suits, wiping eyes, a woman who looks like it might be this guy's mum collapses in a sobbing heap part-way through the service. That strong feeling of loss comes flooding back to me and I have to stifle my tears.

We play the General Salute and the Catafalque Party fire three volleys into the air. The coffin is put into the hearse and we slow march down the street from the church, our breath vaporising in the cold air with each step. The drums are covered with black cloth and the snares are off, the hollow sound of the drums adding to the solemn event. At the bottom of the street, we peel off and the hearse drives off. I am relieved it's over. It's brought back memories for me and I can tell the others are a little disturbed.

The car takes us back to Fairbairn and we are dropped off at Air Movements. We are greeted by a corporal in a flying suit and he explains he is the Loadmaster for the trip back to Wagga Wagga.

Shit, we are going to get a chopper ride home.

He gives us the full safety brief and directs us to the first Iroquois in the line. Bags and drums are strapped to the floor, and our arses to a seat. Pilots select a variety of switches, pre-start checks complete, start signal and the engine starts to wind-up and rotors start to turn. As the momentum of the blades increase, there's the familiar sound of Iroquois rotors beating, everything is shaking. I can see the pilot pull on the collective and we lift off the ground. He taxies, hovering to his take-off position. I can see him talking to Air Traffic. The nose dips and all we can see out the front of the chopper is the ground rushing past, the noise of the engine changes. As the aircraft speed increases, we start to get lift and gain a little height.

The scene over Canberra is spectacular. The lake dissected by the wide mall with the War Memorial at one end and the white, stately Parliament House on the other. The flight over the mountains reveals a wonderful display of jagged peaks and snow. I feel guilty for enjoying myself knowing I am only here because some young fella, not much older than me, is dead.

Mid-year leave rolls around. It's the same routine as last time, bus to Hexham where Uncle Bert picks me up, two weeks of home comforts, and bus back to Wagga Wagga. There are some intimate moments with Lou, but my mind is elsewhere.

'Are you okay?' she asks me.

'What? Sorry. Yep. I am just a bit worried about some of my exam results,' I lie to her. 'I am struggling with some of the technical stuff, understanding electronics is fairly hard.' Well, it is partially right. I did struggle with the Electrical Theory, but I think it's more because I am torn by my thoughts for Allison, and my loyalty to Louise.

Back in Wagga Wagga, it's back into the routine again, marching, lessons, Mess food and rugby. To be honest, sport is probably the only thing keeping us sane. Most of the boys are playing footy, hockey, tennis, golf or something. Only the odd few nerds doing nothing.

I am not sure what keeps them going?

Sergeant Killer Kilfoyle is our rugby coach. He's a short, stocky, Irishman. Someone said he is from Belfast, and he's pretty tough. You don't pack down in a scrum against him at training unless you want a Liverpool kiss, or in this case, I guess it's a Belfast kiss. He maintains strict discipline and if you shift from the game plan, you get replaced pretty quick.

He's also protective of his team. If any of us get in a bit of shit, he's fast to sort it out, unless you've made a complete dick of yourself. In the latter case, he usually delivers a lecture accompanied with a smack in the ear, which is usually what is deserved.

Killer loves a beer and he makes sure we always have a good supply on hand after the game. Four is about my limit, and it gets me pretty bloody silly. If I have more, the bed does flip flops, and I generally end with my head in the toilet bowl. Some of the other boys don't make it that far and I've had the privilege of cleaning up after one guy spray-painted our foyer with carrots and then fucked off.

Why are there always carrots in spew?

I swear I could go without eating them for a month and they somehow magically appear.

By late August, we have the tough subjects out of the way, Electrical Technology 2 and Basic Electronics. It takes considerable concentration, but with a bit of help from Merv who seems to be a bit of a whiz on this shit, I master all the theory, alternating current, transformers, transistors. We are moving on to soldering, and I am looking forward to the break from the textbooks and getting something into my hands again.

Early September, another funeral. This guy was coming back from Melbourne and wrapped the car around a telegraph pole near Uranquinty. We are bussed into the Wagga Wagga Lawn Cemetery and play the drums during the march from the hearse to the graveside, more crying, ashes to ashes. I ponder the life lost and the things he will never experience. Buried a long way from home, in a town where no one knows him, nor will remember him. It's a lot for a sixteen-year-old to take in.

Saturday night, we are all in the boozer singing rugby songs. Around nine, Killer asks who wants to go to the Shanty and we pile into the back of his panel van. There is a large crowd in the Hotel, fire is going and the music is loud.

Given we are lowly paid Apprentices, we can't spend too much time and money in the pub, but if we've already had a few it works out well. We are also becoming somewhat accomplished drinkers as well, four beers have become five or six, along with the odd cigarette for me. The buzz associated with the booze is enhanced with the rush of nicotine hitting the blood.

Around eleven, the majority of the group decide they've had enough and want to go into town. We Apprentices are just keen to just get a lift back to Base and one of the older guys offers to drop us off on the way past. We file outside and proceed to jump into the backseat of a Ford Fairlane. By the time he shoulders the back door closed, there are about eight of us in the back seat. I can't see how many are in the front.

The car takes off at a great rate, driver crunched up against the door, struggling to change gears. We speed up the hill, past the caravan park, toward the main gate and as soon as he gets to the Base perimeter fence, he slams on the brakes and puts the Fairlane into a four-wheel slide in the gravel on the side of the road. We come to a stop just short of a few gum trees.

'You Sprogs can get out here,' he says.

We unpack ourselves and exit. Gus is the last one out and he smiles broadly and giving the driver a big, 'Thanks, mate'.

'Yeah no worries.' The front seat passengers reorganise themselves into the back seat and they head off into town for a few more.

We jump the fence onto the golf course and make our way toward the sporting field laughing and shoving each there around in drunken playfulness. It's about two degrees but no one is feeling the cold, we've got anti-freeze on board tonight. A couple of lads disappear into the block next to ours, Rob and Gaz into the bottom floor of our block, and Gus and I take the fire stairs to the second floor. We fall in the back door and freeze. Two Service Police standing three doors down turn to us.

'You two, come here,' commands the corporal.

I've seen him before, he's the one who charged Nev, Corporal Schneider. He's a nasty one, and he has a female sergeant with him.

'What are you two doing out this late?' he asks loudly, leaning in on us aggressively.

Gus tells him we've been to the pictures and stopped in at a mate's room in the next block to listen to some music. I am trying to stay quiet and shrink into the carpet. The corporal asks Gus for his ID and the sergeant walks over and asks for mine.

I fumble around for my wallet and pull out my ID. She smells lovely and for the first time I notice her legs. Beautiful legs in dark stockings and low heels to show them off.

Girls in stockings always gets my blood going.

Even in the low heels, she's quite tall for a woman, I am

guessing about five foot, nine inches and maybe short of her thirtieth birthday. The uniform and jumper disguise her shape, but I can see a clearly pronounced chest.

Corporal Schneider is accusing Gus of being drunk and Gus is using his natural charm to quell any thought of it, the gift of the gab lives here. Lucky we were drinking vodka and the smell isn't pronounced.

'Where are you from, Apprentice?' she asks in a slightly hoarse voice and I tell her I am from Dungog, near Newcastle.

'Oh, I know Dungog quite well, my Uncle lives at Vacy just north of Maitland. We used to go there in school holidays. He'd take us to Chichester Dam for a swim.' The raspy voice fascinating me.

'Not too far from our farm,' I tell her.

She hands back my ID and as I grasp it, it drops to the floor. We both drop down to pick it up and we grab it at the same time. I look at her and she is looking back into my eyes. We sit there transfixed for a moment. She has blue eyes, steelier than mine, and they seem to be seeing right into me, into my thoughts. She breaks the stare and stands clearing her throat.

'Okay, Apprentices, into your room and get to bed.' Schneider looks disappointed. 'Come on, Corporal, let's get going.'

They depart down the hall and Gus and I dive for our room. As I go through the door, I take a quick look at the departing service police officers. The sergeant glances back over her shoulder and our eyes meet again for an instant. Shit, she is some woman, not a girl, a woman and an impressive one.

The next weeks drag on. The Wagga Wagga winter chill and the short hours of daylight adding to the glum feel of life. We finish studies into Aircraft Technical Administration. The lack of any colour in the subject adds to the cold feel. The Instructor keeps telling us strict administration is fundamental to safe aircraft operations. I am sure it is, but right now, it's just a bloody drag. His lack of anything resembling a sense of humour is making this particularly boring.

Johnno struggles to pass progress exams and we take turns to tutor him each night. It might help if he would stay off the phone to Michelle. I wonder what they talk about half the night, or am I simply jealous? He passes Tech Admin, but only after sitting a supplementary exam. The tutoring helps the rest of us get the subject matter clear in our minds and we all get credits.

All the time, I am thinking of Allison and what she might be doing. I think of ways to call past her house. Maybe I could tell Bob I need some advice on some military procedural issue, or something. Anything to get a few words with her.

I can tell that the boys are getting bored, there's a lot smoking now, that and a fascination with growing moustaches. Some guys have a really good one. Jim has even taken up waxing the ends of his, trying to look like someone off an English war movie, but most are ratty. Based on what I see in the mirror, I know I'm not ready. It would look like a couple of cricket teams, eleven on each side.

We start studies into aircraft guns and my interest is compulsive. Slowly, over three weeks, the magic of Cannons and Gatling guns unfold, principles of operation, rates of fire and fault finding. The minigun is dissected and we come to know the unique application on a Bushranger Iroquois Helicopter, as opposed to the SUU/11 Pod on a Macchi Trainer. My favourite is the 30mm DEFA Cannon, two of which are fitted in the Mirage fighter. Sergeant Adams adds to the experience with a never-ending set of war stories about gunnery programs. Right now, he seems to be the worldliest armourer ever.

They take us over to the Gunnies' hangar and we start to pull apart a DEFA gun each. I am among the first to have the gun stripped. Sergeant Adams comes past my bench.

'So, Walsh, what have we got here?' He picks up the anti-double feed plate. I rattle off an answer and he nods. A couple of more questions about where we might find cracks in the Gun Housing and he is off to the next bench. We spend a couple of days stripping, scrubbing, and reassembling guns. My overalls are really grubby from all the oil and I wear them like a badge of honour. Most people don't get to do this stuff. I blitz the final exam with 95 per cent, a distinction.

The Wagga Wagga winter finally gives way to spring. I am feeling pretty positive because this means it's nearly cricket season and there will be barbecues after the game. Bob and Nancy will be there and it means Allison might tag along.

I sometimes get a glimpse of her, going past in a car or walking home from school. But, it's at a distance, no chance to talk.

The final of round of footy is played and we get knocked over, just missing the finals. The Aussie Rules boys have fared no better and Gus kicks six goals in a losing team. Last time for beers with Killer after the game, and a few more at the Airman's. We hit the Shanty Hotel about nine and it's a big night on tequila. We get more than our fill and walk back to Base along the train line laughing and shoving each other around. Just as we get to the back of our block, a service police vehicle appears out of nowhere, lights ablaze. We are like stunned bunnies completely mesmerised by the light.

It's Corporal Schneider and another guy, they look pretty pleased with themselves.

This is not going to go well.

'Well, well, what have we got here? Been out drinking, have we, lads?' Not even Gus tries to hide the obvious truth. We just stand there waiting for whatever is going to happen next, resigned to our fate. He asks us for our ID, takes all the details, and tells the others to fuck off. It's has just become personal. He looks straight at Gus and me.

'Right, you two are on a charge for being drunk. I would add AWOL, but I doubt we can get enough evidence together to make it stick'. He gives us a long and tedious lecture on staying out of trouble, leading others astray, and tells us to fuck off to bed. We get the charge sheets Monday morning and the hearing is set for Tuesday afternoon.

Luckily, Squadron Leader Wright is away and Flight Lieutenant Jacobs hears the charges. I played cricket with Flight Lieutenant Jacobs last season and he's a real nice fella. We both plead guilty so there is no need for any evidence to be given, just statements of mitigation. I look at Corporal Schneider and he appears disappointed with our plea. He has missed an opportunity to grandstand here. I reckon he would have loved to give evidence and embellish how drunk we were and try to work a big sentence.

Flight Lieutenant Jacobs is not the same fella I played cricket with as right now he gives us a stern lecture about the health effects of drinking on young minds and bodies, not to mention the illegal nature of our actions. He reminds us the RAAF is our legal guardian and this behaviour is unacceptable. We get five days CB each.

Corporal Schneider is obviously livid we got off so light. If he had his way, we would've got the death sentence and strung up by our balls from the flag pole on the parade ground, just to make sure everyone else knew not to fuck with him.

Under the circumstances, it's not a horrible result. The only downside I can see is the long weekend coming up. I was intending to go bunny shooting at Merv's place near Cootamundra. It will have to wait.

The week is no fun. The usual CB routine up to the Guard House several times a day. It's a real pain in the arse, but then again it is punishment.

On Friday afternoon, the Base empties out quickly, a constant stream of cars heading slowly up the main drag to the gate, while the Screws with a radar are set up behind a tree. It seems ridiculous when the sheer weight of traffic forbids anyone from getting anywhere near the speed limit, bloody elephant trackers.

Gus and I are working in the Mess all day Saturday. It's almost deserted at mealtimes and we get plenty to time to joke around with the cooks. They share a few war stories with us and we are impressed by how seriously they take their role. The military relies on being fed well at all times and in all conditions and they are genuinely proud of their trade. Our elevated view of our own position in the pecking order comes down a few pegs as we get more and more friendly.

Saturday night, and we get into service dress, tie and jumper for the final trip to the Guard House. It all goes smoothly and we are marching back up the main drag for the final time. As we approach the cinema, a few people come out. The pictures must have just finished.

As we get closer, I can see Michelle is one and she stops to say hello. There is a little small talk before Gus says good night. I offer to walk Michelle home.

Her parents gave gone to Falls Creek skiing for the weekend and she stayed at home to finish study for the HSC. Johnno has taken off to Melbourne for the weekend and we talk about how the relationship is going. She knows we have been helping him with his study and she thanks me. We get to the gate, the name plate on the letter box reads Squadron Leader Wright.

'You've been on CB all week, would you like some of dad's whisky?' The opportunity to drink some of Mad Dog Wright's whisky is irresistible and we go inside. The room is warm, the gas heater well alight. Leather lounge chairs and antique furniture around the room.

'Your dad hasn't scrimped on furniture.'

'Not dad, mum's the decorator. The old man wouldn't know a divan from a settee. Mum comes from a well-to-do family in Prahran in Melbourne. Old money,' she says, grabbing a couple of short crystal glasses from the china cabinet and pouring from a decanter. 'They met when he was at Frognall.'

We sit on the lounge and talk about the HSC. She is pretty casual about it, not concerned at all. She is studying because her father wants her to do well, but she really has no career ambitions.

'Going to Uni?'

'I don't think so. Dad is posted to Amberley at the end of the year and I'll probably go back there. Who knows, I might meet an F-111 pilot, and get married? I ask her about a future with Johnno and she chuckles.

'He's lovely, but he's never going to amount to anything.' She pauses, thinking about it. 'I want to live a comfortable life, no scrimping and struggling for this girl.'

She asks me about Allison and I confide, despite not seeing her in a long time, I am still smitten with her.

'It's frustrating, we hit it off so well. I just need five minutes to explain things,' I moan.

'Just cool your heels for a while, Tim. Our Allison Gardner is on a mission. She's going to be someone and not barefoot and pregnant at twenty, like her mum.'

I let the information sink in. It all fits, the studying, the obsession with a good HSC Score.

'The HSC will be over in a couple of weeks, Tim. Just see what happens after that.'

The whisky is going down well and it feeds more talk and laughter. We crack silly jokes and the combination of whisky and the warm room start to cloud my thoughts.

'So, is it true? You and Janine did it on the washing machine?' The question takes me by surprise. Janine, I hadn't given her much thought in the last year. My mind goes back to the afternoon at her house.

'We did it in just about every room in the place.' It brings a smile to my face.

'She bragged about it you know, the washing machine, at the pictures, Wagga Beach. Every time one of the girls got a bit, Janine just had to go one better. It's like a game for her.'

'What's she up to now?'

'Still at it, she just dumped her second boyfriend this year. Apparently, none of them are as good as Old Doug the Stud.'

Fuck me dead, the nickname annoys me. She was a mad rooter and I was just along for the ride, so to speak.

I am having a little flashback of Janine's silky little breasts when Michelle leans over and softly kisses my lips. It feels like a soft, warm, decadent, pleasure, utterly irresistible. She slips her tongue into my mouth and I can't help but have a fleeting thought about the first time Janine did the same thing.

For a few seconds, I think to myself that I shouldn't be doing this. I am in love with another girl and Michelle is going out with one of my mates.

This isn't right.

Next thing I know we are in a mad embrace, the room a blur. She has her hands everywhere and I am gasping. She takes off her top and bra, her ample breasts explode at me.

Nice boobs.

She undresses me quickly and hops on top, sliding down on me slowly at first, then riding me like she is on a bucking horse. In a strange moment of clarity, I think to myself, this is not her first rodeo. We both explode together, but she is not done, not by half. She climbs off and gets on all fours and tells me to hurry. No written invitation required here. She pushes back onto me and moans loudly grinding and wriggling her backside from one side to the other and back, the view from here is spectacular. Her second climax is louder and more intense than the first and we collapse to the floor.

The heavy breathing subsides and my body is recovering. I'm about to say something to break the increasingly awkward silence when she puts a finger to my lips. She stands up, and goes to the door, turn and curls her index finger for me to follow. I get up and follow the shapely bum wobbling from side to side down the hall. Into the shower, we start over again. About 0300 she is sleeping and I slip quietly out of the bed, my thigh muscles straining and it brings a grin to my face. I gather my uniform from the lounge room floor, dress, and let myself out.

Holy shit, that was hot. Now I know what her and Johnno talk about each night.

I wake late the next morning. I can still smell whisky, perfume, sweat, her, and I start to recall the previous night. Man, that was hot. Then, there is an overwhelming sense I have just cheated on my mate Johnno. The thought doesn't last long, she made her career plans pretty clear and they aren't with Johnno. I think I know who is doing the cheating, I probably shouldn't lose any sleep over this one. Then, there is Allison. I don't know how to handle that dilemma and push it from my mind.

After lunch, Gus and I head to the Apprentice Club and down some iced coffee. The place is empty except for the Duty Apprentice and a couple of first-years. We chat a bit before settling in to watch an old British war movie on TV — John Mills and Richard Attenborough saving the empire.

My mind is ticking over and over. I still feel guilty about last night and decide it might be right to apologise to Michelle.

I call the extension for her house and she picks up. After a little awkward chat, I say sorry. She doesn't sound too worried, telling me she's studying this arvo, but offers dinner.

'I've made a heap of spaghetti bolognaise. I won't be able to eat it all, why don't you and Gus come for dinner?

She must have a whole lot of spag bol.

We knock on the door just before 1800 and she opens the door in a lovely dress with a cardigan buttoned at the top, a fifties look. We walk in and Jenny Adams is sitting on the lounge in the very place Michelle and I had kissed last night. I can feel my face going red at the thought, she seems to get the gist and gives me a little smile.

Jenny's dad is the Base Warrant Officer Disciplinary, a WOD. She is also studying for the HSC and the two girls have spent the afternoon testing each other. Jenny is shorter than Michelle and more petite. She is dressed more conservatively in a smart skirt, blouse, jumper and stockings. I haven't spoken with Jenny since our trip to the pool earlier in the year, she always seemed nice, but I can't say I really know the girl.

There are two bottles of red on the table and it's set with the good china, silver cutlery, and a bowl of bread, quite the spread. Michelle invites us to sit and pours us each a wine. She tells us her father has a large cellar and he won't miss a bottle or two. Gus and I giggle like schoolboys.

Michelle brings a large bowl of spaghetti to the table and serves. We eat and drink and talk about everything from being a RAAF brat to politics. Michelle says her father thinks Malcolm Fraser is the best Prime Minister since Menzies and he will be there a long time. She doesn't agree with her father, and thinks Gough Whitlam was the best and wants Bob Hawke to have a go at Fraser. Jenny likes Andrew Peacock and says he would be better than Fraser. I don't share my thoughts about Doug Anthony maybe leading the Coalition. I reckon they just wouldn't get it.

The wine flows and the talk turns to ambitions. While Gus

and I wash up, we admit we have not given much thought to what happens after Wagga Wagga. Being RAAF brats, the girls have lived it their whole lives and have a good understanding of life on an operational RAAF Base. They think we'll go alright. I tell them I want to go to Butterworth in Malaysia and the girls frown.

Not sure what that's about.

We pack away the dishes and cutlery back into the canteen. Michelle grabs a full bottle from the bench and asks how long it's been since we spun one of these. Gus and I look at each other stunned and follow her into the lounge room.

She sits on the rug and pats the floor either side indicating Gus and I should sit either side of her, Jenny sits opposite Michelle. I have this funny feeling that, somehow, we are mere pawns in some master plan.

She leans over, places the bottle in the middle of the circle, and spins it. When it stops, the cork is pointing more or less toward me. She leans toward me and we share a lovely little kiss, nowhere near as intense as last night, but it's still got the blood flowing. She passes the bottle to Gus and he spins it. It points in the general direction of Jenny and the two have a short embrace. Jenny's turn next and it points back at her. She kisses herself on the hand. I spin it and it points toward Jenny. She leans over and we kiss. Her tongue moves into my mouth quickly and there is a little sigh escapes her mouth. I break off the engagement, now the blood is really flowing.

Michelle grabs the bottle again and spins. Before it stops, she grabs Gus and pushes him to the floor with the force of her kiss. It endures a while before she straightens herself. She gets up and announces she is going to up the ante. A deck of cards appears from a conveniently close drawer, definitely part of the master plan. She shuffles them like a pro and sits back down.

'Right, I will deal two cards each. The highest card in the first deal will allow the winner to decide who they will do something with. The person with the highest card on the second deal gets to decide what is done.' A pretty well-rehearsed little bit of instruction there.

She deals four cards. I have a Jack, Michelle a seven, Gus a three, and Jenny a queen. Four more cards are quickly placed beside the first, mine is a two, Michelle's a king, Gus is a six and Jenny a nine.

The girls already have this all worked out while Gus and I have pretty much no clue at all. 'Okay, Jenny, who is your victim?' asks Michelle. She squeals a little before nominating me.

'Right, Jenny, as I have the highest card on the second deal, I think you should kiss Tim for thirty seconds, and he's allowed to touch your boobs.' I swallow. Within thirty seconds things are going to get pretty obvious around here.

She leans over and starts kissing me like before. The same little sigh emanating from her mouth. I reach over and touch her jumper. It's a thick woollen jumper. I slide my hand up looking for her right breast. I find soft warm skin and realise she isn't wearing a bra. I massage her breast which only serves to increase the intensity of the kisses. I can feel my underwear increasingly under stress. And then, the Nazi phone rings. Michelle doesn't miss a beat, stands and picks up the phone.

'Squadron Leader Wright's residence,' she answers in her poshest ascent. 'Oh, Mr Adams. Yes, I'll put her on.' Jenny gets on the phone.

'Yes dad, we are nearly done. There's just two more things we need to go over,' she says looking straight at me.

There is a bit more talk and she says she'll be home by 10.00 pm. As Jenny puts the phone down, Michelle grabs Gus firmly by the hand and disappears down the hall without uttering a word. Jenny comes back to me and starts kissing me and climbing all over me. She's on a mission and there's a time limit.

We get into a fairly torrid embrace and she is clearly excited. I help her out of her knickers and touch her. She's wet and breathing raspy as I slowly move my fingers. Her face nuzzles into my neck, sucking it, then starting to thrust and grind, squealing in delight. She throws her head back as she orgasms, panting loudly.

I relieve her of her jumper and push her back onto the lounge. Strangely, I am aware that I am now having sex in the same spot, with a different girl, in less than twenty hours. Weird.

She is enthusiastic, digging her nails into my back, which I find nice, but weird. Her small breasts have lovely, pink nipples which she squeezes and then pulls my mouth to them. The second time is as quick and intense, her face buried in my neck urging me to do it harder. Judging from the racket emanating from the hallway, I would say Michelle and Gus are also well into round two of the latest rodeo.

Jenny and I get dressed, no conversation. Suddenly, everything is a bit clinical and cold. It's 2130 and I ask her if she needs me to walk her home. She looks grateful, grabs me by the hand, and leads me from the house, shouting a goodbye to Michelle who hasn't appeared yet. There's a little small talk on the way and we stop two doors down from her house. She kisses me strongly again, her hand subtly touching my crotch. She says she'll see me through the week. I meekly agree; what choice do I have?

As I walk back to the room, I worry I have somehow just unwittingly committed to a relationship with Jenny. It would not be good or particularly smart. Her dad, Warrant Officer Adams, is an angry man. Everyone stays well clear of him at all possible times. One of the boys heard a story he is an ex-Apprentice. If it's true, you'd think he'd cut us a bit of slack, but he actually seems to target us over and above others. He has some sort of chip on his shoulder and he's seemingly in a constant foul mood.

Gus manages to find his way home at about 1100 and goes straight to bed for the rest of the day, seems he had a long night of it. The Base starts to fill again from about 1500 on Monday. I wake Gus for the 1700 evening meal. The boy will be hungry, I reckon. We don't talk too much; he is smirking to himself and shaking his head.

Merv walks into the dining hall with a full plate. He spots us and comes over to sit down.

'You two look like you've had a crap weekend. Did somebody die?' We just smirk at each other and nod in agreement. Maybe a couple of rabbits.

Monday night, everyone is back on base and we get about our respective chores, panic night. After Charlie's Angels and MASH, I am lying down with a book.

'I reckon the Angels would be a good root,' announces Merv.

'What, all three,' asks Gus.

'Na, Farrah Fawcett. I reckon she'd give head.'

'No, mate, Cheryl Ladd is the one.'

I like Kate Jackson and fantasise she has nice little breasts with pink nipples. I get a quick flash of Jenny's boobs.

I have to stop thinking about that.

The week starts bright and sunny. It's like the spring buds have just decided to explode into flower. Along with the bright trees, our spirits are high, we know we don't have to endure another Wagga Wagga winter. Our efforts with the drums on morning parade lifts in sympathy, there is a spring in everyone's step.

At work, we're undergoing Small Arms training which means we will learn the whole shebang about the RAAF inventory of pistols, rifles, machine guns, shot guns and other assorted guns. We also get to shoot them all, L1A1, L2A1, M-60s, F1s, and the Browning 9mm. This is not difficult in comparison to some of our other subjects and everyone is focused, no fuck-arsing around.

The mail arrives Thursday and there is a letter in Lou's floral handwriting. The Year 12 Ball is on 18 October. Can I get home for it? I don't have a licence or a car, maybe one of the boys will drive me home? Not sure. The first thing is to get a leave application in. During the afternoon smoko break, I duck into the Orderly Room and fill one out.

I canvass the guys to see if anyone wants to drive to Dungog for the weekend, no takers. We are in the midst of a progress test when I overhear Sergeant Falconer discussing a weekend at home with Corporal Hughes. The word catching my attention is Thornton. I seek him out straight after the test.

'Excuse me, Sarge. I have applied for leave the weekend after next. I have been invited to my old high school graduation and I am looking for a ride somewhere up Newcastle way.'

'Where are you heading?'

'Dungog, Sarge.'

'If you can get someone to pick you up from Thornton and drop you back on Sunday, you got a ride.'

'That's great, thanks Sarge.' I am relieved.

After work, I call home to make the arrangements, they are obviously happy with the surprise visit.

Friday 17th October, he tells me to come back after lunch in civvies with my bag and we hit the road about 1300. Travelling with a Senior NCO has its perks, all the other boys have to wait till 1500 to knock off. We get to Thornton about 2130 and Bert is waiting for me outside the Post Office. By the time we get home and have a cup of tea, it's 2230. Sitting in the kitchen, I feel different about being home this time, my confidence is high.

Saturday morning, talk during milking is dominated by the election. The radio announcers are predicting a tight contest. Bill Hayden has been getting more popular over the past few weeks of the campaign and there is a general feeling Malcolm Fraser is squandering his time as Prime Minister, just not doing enough to get re-elected.

Grandad and Uncle Bert talk endlessly about the local contest. They have to get into town later to hand out How to Vote cards at the school. They are Country Party members and doing their bit to support the local candidate, Bruce Cowan. But Milton Morris is running for the Liberals and a lot of people in the southern part of the electorate near us think highly of him, including grandad.

After milking, I grab a cup of tea and some toast, then press my uniform shirt, run a cloth over my shoes, and check my jacket and cap for lint. All good, I borrow the Valiant and head over to Lou's.

Mrs Bennett greets me at the back door and ushers me into the kitchen, something smells good. Lou is at Mrs Baker's getting her hair done. I am given the timetable for the day's events. There is a formal ceremony at the school, speeches, followed by a sit-down meal and dance at the CWA Hall. Grandad always calls it the Cranky Women's Association and every time he says it, he gets a slap from grandma. It's an amusing if somewhat repetitive ritual. The party afterward is at Bryan Davis' place.

She gives me the third degree about my training progress, when I might graduate, and where I might get posted. Most of it is still up in the air. All I know is graduation is the fourth of March.

'Do we get an invite?'

The question catches me out. I hadn't contemplated this option and just assumed everyone would be busy milking. The thought of my family stepping into my world at Wagga Wagga seems a little intrusive. Till now, they had been quite separate. At times, I greedily used it to almost live a double life. Louise meeting

Michelle, Jenny or Allison would scare the shit out of me. I tell Mrs Bennett I will get back to her about the graduation invite.

Grandad and Uncle Bert get back just before afternoon milking starts. I have ushered the girls up from the river and they take over. Grandad has a bit of spring in his step.

'Lots of people saying good things about Milton. You never know, he might even get enough to take preferences off Cowan.'

I duck off, wash and shave, and put my uniform on, tie, jacket, and cap. We meet at the school and Lou gives me a hug. I haven't seen her since June and she appears to have filled out a little. No fat, just a little curvier, less girl, more woman. She has an amazing silky, crimson, sleeveless dress on, gloves, and high heels. Her hair is up and she is wearing makeup. I've never seen her dress so posh. She is easily the pick of the girls.

With the official part complete, we retire to the CWA hall. The kitchen is awash with matronly women, somehow all managing to speak at once, one clearly in command, Mrs O'Sullivan handing out instructions.

She'd give Bob a run for his money.

Meals are served and the School Captain, James O'Brien, makes a speech. He does it well, complimenting the various teachers on their worldly guidance over the past six years, helping them all grow and develop from school kids into adults.

I'd never really contemplated this before. When I joined up nearly two years ago, I was indeed just a school kid, zits, no whiskers, barely a broken voice, and a virgin. Now I am sitting with my former school mates, beautiful girl at my side, and in a military uniform. I don't consider myself to be overly experienced, but I have already seen and experienced more things than just a dairy farm and Dungog High School, and certainly more than most of my former peers in this hall.

Jim's speech turns to the classic student stuff-ups of the year. Billy Moran splitting his dacks playing handball, the Kennedy brothers being busted smoking behind the weather shed for the umpteenth time, and a fire in the science lab, everyone has a good laugh.

The School Principal, Mr Newton, responds and singles out a couple of students for their dedication to their studies, including Lou. Lou reckons she is going to try and get into New England Uni at Armidale to study teaching, if her marks are good enough. She's going to make a great teacher, smart, patient, loving to a fault.

After the speeches, the noise level in the room goes up as everyone simultaneously starts telling a story or two about school. Lou is in fits of laughter talking with Dave McLachlan and Michelle Blande.

It's weird, but I feel a bit left out, even uncomfortable.

I take a look around, grandma is in the kitchen with the other ladies and grandad is in the corner with his transistor radio and earpiece, tracking the election results. I go over and ask how things are going.

'Sounds like Fraser will get enough seats to hang on. It's touch-and-go with Milton though, he's getting a fair slice of the votes, but I think he'll need a few more to knock off Cowan.'

We sit there, him listening intently to the election coverage, me watching the crowd from a physical and emotional distance. It's the moment I realise I don't belong here anymore.

As much as we all talk about Wagga as being akin to a prison sentence, it's where I have grown up, spent the most important years in my life, and found a place amongst a tribe. Bob, Killer, Ben, and the other NCOs, they've been my parents, my teachers, and at times my friends. My mates are there, Nev, Gus, Nige, Merv, Lurch. We are all like brothers. We've trained together in the oppressive heat, suffered through the winter, played footy and cricket together, been to funerals together, cleaned the shithouse together, and done time on the chunder wagon together, it's a strong bond.

Holy hell, now I think I know why Uncle Bert is a little weird and you can add a war to his list of experiences.

I recount this moment of awakening to Gus the following week.

'Shit, Dougie, this is a bit deep, isn't it?' I can see him thinking it over, 'though, you do have a point. I had a few games of footie when I was home on mid-year leave. It was great playing with my old mates again, but it wasn't the same as when we do stuff here. It's different, I can't explain it properly, but it's like I know what you guys are thinking. It's like there's an invisible link between us all and we all know what each other are going to do next, just with a look. I don't know what it is.'

Friday night before cricket, there's not much happening, so I decide to catch a movie. Just before we go in, Jenny Adams walks in making a line for me with purpose. There is no way I can dodge her, she knows I've seen her.

'I was hoping you might be here,' she says seriously.

'Oh, hi Jenny, how ya been?'

'We have a problem,' she continues ignoring the enquiry.

'Problem?'

'Yes,' she hesitates. 'I'm late.'

'Na. It hasn't started yet,' I tell her and she rolls her eyes.

'Not the movie, you idiot, my period. I'm late.'

The implications start to dawn on me.

'Fuck,' I say looking around hoping no one heard her. 'Can we go somewhere and talk?' I ask her. She turns and heads for the door, me three steps behind.

We walk across the road and stand near the Dental Section.

'I thought you were on the pill?' She shakes her head.

'It was just after my last period. Michelle and I thought I would be fine, but I am a week late.'

'Fuck, what are we going to do?'

'What, after my dad cuts your balls off and shoves them down your throat?' The thought of Jenny's dad finding out just does not bear consideration. Blowing myself into a million bits could be a more comfortable option. 'There is a healthcare nurse at the school. Even though I have finished, I can make an excuse to go back and see her while I am there. I can't be the first girl to get pregnant and need help.'

'What about Michelle? Is she using the same technique?' I ask, trying to hide my apprehension.

'Na, her mum makes sure she has the pill. Her and Johnno are at it like rabbits.'

'Okay. Let me know how you go. We'll work this out,' I tell her. I haven't got a clue how the hell we are going to work it out. I think I may have finally got myself into an irrecoverable situation.

'Don't you mention this to a soul,' she warns with a finger pointed at me. 'Not even Nev or Gus,' she finishes and storms off. I wander down toward the Apprentice Club, lost, shell-shocked.

Pregnant, fuck, I am only just seventeen.

I can't be a dad at seventeen. I can barely look after myself, let alone a wife and kid.

Fuck, marry Jenny? No, I can't do that.

But if her father finds out, it might just be the shotgun marriage of the year. Fuck, she's nice enough, but I don't think I'd be able to live with her, till death do us part. I can just imagine grandad's response.

You'll just have to do the right thing and marry the girl, Tim.

Of course, grandma will be pissed off it's not Louise, but she'll be singing the same tune.

I go past the Apprentice Club and keep walking, thinking it through. She'll be eighteen in February. She can get an abortion without her parents knowing once she's eighteen. Fuck, she'll be five months gone by then, fuck, everybody will know. I don't sleep a wink, tossing and turning all night.

What have I done?

At cricket the next day, I bowl eight wides and go wicketless after ten, a golden duck with the bat, worst day ever.

'You coming for a beer, Dougie, or do you need something stronger?' Ken asks me.

'No, mate, I'm not feeling well. I'll see you at training on Tuesday.' No sleep again on Saturday night.

Sunday morning, I call home to say hello. I don't often call and grandma seems to have a sixth sense that something is afoot, she asks me if everything is okay.

'Yep, fine. I just thought I would call and say hello.' I think I got away with it, who knows.

Sunday night I manage a couple of hours fitful sleep and Monday I am just not with it at all, staring off into space my mind completely consumed.

'You okay, Walsh,' asks Flight Sergeant Bourke, who is somehow now standing right in front of me, I didn't even notice him heading in my direction.

'Yes, Flight, just a bit of an upset tummy, didn't get much sleep.'

Our training is getting serious too, I really can't afford to be distracted. We are well into Explosive Ordnance Demolition, which is blowing stuff up with plastic explosive, and shaped charges, learning how to use safety fuse, crimping detonators, laying detonating cord and getting the timing of the explosion right. Exciting stuff, and potentially deadly if your brain is out to lunch, which mine has been for days. The exam is on Wednesday and we are onto the range actually blowing stuff up on Thursday and Friday. If you don't pass the exam, no trip to the range till you have.

Monday night, we are sitting around reading with the radio on. Bloody 2WG, I wish they would play something other than Kenny fucking Rogers. Gus has his head in the umpteenth book, me flicking through the *Post*, avoiding the textbook like it's diseased. I am thinking through the merits of the whole rhythm method of contraception.

'What do you know about the menstrual cycle, Gus?' He looks at me curiously putting the book aside.

'It has no pedals, Dougie.' I throw the *Post* at him. He knows I am on edge and still can't resist. 'Well, apparently, most women ovulate about two weeks before their period, that is, when the ovaries release an egg and the egg awaits being fertilised until it is flushed out by the period. So, technically, women are fertile for half the cycle. But, it's not an exact science, just ask any Catholic.' I contemplate the answer for a while.

'How do you know this shit?'

'Books, my dear Dougie, fucking books,' he says, waving his latest volume at me. 'Not the drivel you just threw at me.'

Tuesday night, we are watching *Sale of the Century*, studying can wait. Tony Barber is prancing around the place with not a hair out of place as always. Stan sticks his head in the door.

'Some chick on the phone for you, Dougie.' I know its Jenny. My heart is pounding in my chest.

'Hi,' I say tentatively, doing my best to sound calm and casual, when in my stomach the butterflies have turned into a pack of panicked emus, this could potentially be my fiancée in a couple of weeks.

'Hi,' she says with what sounds like some relief. 'Good news. I got my period this afternoon.' I almost collapse on the floor.

Thank fuck.

A wave of emotion washes over me. I think I'm crying.

'Are you there, Tim?'

'Yer. Yer.' I stammer. 'Are you okay?'

'Oh, you know, the usual. Sometimes it sucks being a girl.' I'm not quite sure how to respond and try to make some small talk.

'It's funny you know,' she says. 'I'd almost got myself comfortable with having the baby, and now it's not there.' I am diving for words to console her while trying to conceal my elation, so thankful this conversation isn't face to face. Somehow, I find a way to get off the phone without making an agreement to see her. I am so happy, over the moon, what a bloody relief.

Definitely dodged one there, Dougie.

Wednesday, well slept, clarity of mind returned, I blitz the exam and Thursday we hit the range, laying basic charges at first, then graduating to shaped charges. The detonation of red cord and PE4 is surprising the first time you see it. Flight Sergeant Bourke is in charge.

'Fire,' he yells and hits the button. There is a fast flash and explosion, followed quickly by the crack. Ten times louder than any whip I have ever heard. The delay in between the visual flash and the noise is significant.

Sunday afternoon, we are cordially invited to the Apprentice Club for a barbecue with the CO. He and Missus CO are in attendance, Squadron Leaders Fleming, Wright and Gregory, and Padre Gibson, each with respective wives. Michelle and Jenny are there and the padre also has his daughter in tow, she looks to be about fourteen or fifteen.

The drink of choice is Tooheys Draught, being brandished by the male guests and most of the boys. There is a cup of tea or a can of lemonade for the ladies.

The CO has approved sale of beer to Apprentices considering many of my colleagues are over eighteen. Thankfully, no one is policing the sale to those of us under eighteen. I am on my second can, talking with Nev, Merv and Heather when Bob, Nancy and Allison come through the back door.

I follow her every move, looking at what she is wearing, her hair is in a ponytail. Nev is dribbling something inane in my ear. She captivates me. She takes a seat next to the padre's daughter. They obviously know each other. Bob and Nancy are chatting with the CO and a couple of the suckhole Apprentices.

'Earth calling Dougie, Earth calling Dougie, come in Dougie.'
'Sorry?'
'You still infatuated with her, Dougie?'

'I wouldn't call it infatuation, Nev.'

'All evidence to the contrary, Dougie,' he says, raising an eyebrow 'You should just go and talk to her,' Heather pushes. 'I think she has given up calling you Doug the Stud.'

I gather myself to make the move just as Randall pulls up a chair beside her.

Fuck it, what's that wanker doing?

For the next half hour, I am totally engrossed watching them, making sure they don't get too comfortable. There's a bit of chat between them, but I haven't seen her smile yet. It's a good sign.

The meat starts coming off the barbie and the official party gets first go. Randall tucks into the line right between Allison and the other girl, chatting the whole time. He's all smiles like butter wouldn't melt in his mouth.

Can't she see what a dick he is?

With the meals complete, a few of the ladies make their way inside, they always seem to go to the loo in groups. I figure it's my best chance to bump into her and leave it a few minutes before following.

I am hovering inside the back door waiting for her return, playing it cool. There's a sudden commotion from the next room and I run to the door. Inside, Randall has his arm against the wall, obviously blocking the padre's daughter's exit from the room, he's right in her face. There's a level of fear on her face, trying to push past.

'No,' she starting to cry now. Allison comes out of the ladies' loo and stops, assessing the situation, crossing her arms.

'What's going on, Guy.'

He looks at her and turns his attention back to the padre's

daughter, talking in a hushed voice, ignoring the request. Allison steps forward.

'Leave her alone, Guy,' speaking with force. He's not listening.

'She said to leave her alone,' I tell him loudly. He turns to me a look of scorn coming to his face.

'Fuck off, you dumb shit Gunnie.' It's enough to lift my blood pressure a notch.

Fucking queer traders think they're better than everyone else.

I walk in and pull his left shoulder. He turns and takes a swing. I try and sway out of the way, returning fire, but his fist collects me on the cheek. Mine collects him above the jaw, blood appearing from his mouth. Padre's daughter now starts screaming, Allison pulling her from harm's way. We are now standing opposite each other, fists raised.

A momentary standoff before he throws a right, I duck it and put two short jabs on his nose. Blood now running down to his top lip.

'What's going on here?' Bob Gardner in his best military voice.

'Dad,' Allison cries, running to him pulling the younger girl with her.

'You okay, sweetie?' She nods. 'You and Megan go outside. I will be there in a minute.' He looks at us.

'What the fuck is this all about, gentlemen?'

Cricket the following Saturday, I am at the barbecue talking to Bob about the events of the previous Sunday.

'You were probably lucky it was me that walked in, Dougie. If it had of been one of the Snorkers, you might both have ended up on a charge.'

'But he was interfering with her, Bob.'

He looks at me with knowing eyes. 'Dougie, sometimes being right isn't enough. The world is not always seen through our eyes. The next time you pull out your fists, just be careful about where you are and who is there.'

Maybe Bob has been in my shoes?

It's the moment I see her. She's walking across the oval toward us, he follows my look.

'Beer, Dougie?' he asks.

'Sure, thanks Bob.' I'm not looking at him.

'Hi,' I say.

'Hi,' she replies with a smile. She knows how to make me melt. 'Cold drink?'

'Sure, a lemonade please.' I scurry off, happy to have this unexpected opportunity to be around her again. She is holding my beer when I get back, we trade cans and wander over to a bench seat just off the edge of the field.

'How'd the exams go?'

'Well, I think, but I'm not counting my chickens just yet. I think I will get into law somewhere.'

'Groovy.'

Groovy? What sort of a word is that, you bloody idiot?

'How's your friend Guy what's-his-name?'

'Randall?' I say with disdain. 'He's okay, just a little shiner and a spilt lip. He's lucky that's all he got.' A frown comes across her face.

'You can't go around dispensing justice with your fists, Tim.'

'He deserved all he got.' She changes her frown and shrugs. *His welfare obviously wasn't that concerning.*

'How's the world of Armaments?' she asks, changing the subject.

'Good, we have been blowing stuff up.' It brings a smile to my face and I enter into my description of the shaped charge blowing holes in the half inch plate. She's got a bemused look on her face. I like that look, no, I love that look. I am sure she is thinking boys will be boys.

Somehow, she agrees to a date on Sunday night. I arrive at Bob's house promptly at six, more nervous than an opening batsman in a maiden Test. Allison answers the door. She has a simple, sleeveless, dress on. Her hair is pulled back in a ponytail, no makeup, except lipstick. There's a slight hint of perfume. She looks stunning and smells heavenly.

I am shown into a simply decorated lounge room, wedding photo in pride of place on the wall. I note Allison bears a strong resemblance to Nancy in her youth. By the look of the bridesmaids' dresses, I'd say a similar vintage to mum and dad's wedding. Bob is in the single lounge chair, can of beer in one hand, durry in the other, watching the 6 o'clock news. He hasn't looked up, but obviously knows I'm there.

'You reckon they will stick with Weiner to open against New Zealand?'

'He got a few against Pakistan, they might. I reckon they need to get McCosker back in there.'

'Yep, him and Laird are the two best.' Bob nods in agreement. Nancy pops her head through the kitchen door and says hello with a welcoming smile. She is such a nice lady, but there is always a firm undertone.

'Make sure you are home by ten thirty,' she says.

As we walk down the main drag, I am nervous as hell.

Do I hold her hand? Should I put my arm around her? What are the rules on a first date?

The movie is a spaghetti western. It's full of fart jokes and nonsense. The giggling from beside me tells me she is having a good time. As we get up to leave, she grabs my hand, mine is sweaty. I couldn't be more nervous.

We chat idly strolling back up the main drag. Talk turns to Uni. She would like to attend Sydney.

'I am sweating on my HSC score. Lots of Unis have a Law Degree, but Sydney Uni is the most highly respected and I need at least 430 to get in there,' she tells me. 'I could get a job with pretty much any one of the firms in Sydney afterwards. Location isn't important, I mean, mum and dad could be posted anywhere. Dad wants to go to Townsville.' From the look on her face, Townsville would be seen as a disaster for her.

'I want to go to Williamtown,' I tell her. 'It's close to the farm, and the girls in Newcastle, and I could come to Sydney and visit you.' She seems pleased with the prospect, nodding and smiling.

At her front gate, she faces me and stands there like she is waiting for something. I am not sure what to do.

'There are no washing machines out here, Tim, a simple kiss will be fine,' she says with a grin.

I lean forward and our lips meet for a couple of seconds. My heart is going a million miles an hour. She breaks it off, turns, and says she'll see me next weekend. I watch her go inside and close the door. All the way back to my block, all I can think about is her smell and the feel of those lips on mine. One of grandad's favourite sayings is 'It's a funny old world,' and it is.

Time for a shower.

Early December, world order has finally returned, Doug

Walters is back into the Australian side. He might be getting on, but Dougie's still the best number six in the country. We have commenced our last subject for the year, Aircraft Armament Systems. It's all logic diagrams, wiring schematics, safety interlocks, none particularly complex, but an interesting way to cruise towards the holidays.

Friday morning, we clean up early and are instructed to go back to our rooms, change into civvies, and report to the Apprentice Club. All seems a little weird to us, but the military has never been known to make any sense. Corporal Pike and Sergeant McGleash pull up in RAAF Kombis and we pile in.

We are deposited at a house in Lake Albert and ushered through the carport to the backyard where the barbie is smoking, and there is plenty of meat on the top. A camp table full of bread and salads in RAAF Mess trays, no mistaking who has done the catering. Plenty of beer in eskies, more beer than I have seen at any one place. There is a group of Thicks already there and shortly after our band of Armament instructors arrive, some with wives in tow.

'Yes, dear, would you like a chair dear, can I get you a drink, dear?' It's really funny seeing the big, tough, Armourers fussing over their loved ones. The rigid, often colourful, men reduced to doting husbands.

I wonder if Allison and I will end up like that?

The thought brings a smile to my face.

After lunch there is an official welcome from Warrant Officer Foley, his wife Vanessa at his side. Glasses are handed out and a bottle of port is passed around, Gun Port no less. We all stand as Sergeant Gould delivers the toast.

'According to legend, Barbara lived in the third century and was the incomparably beautiful daughter of a rich heathen named Dioscorus. She was carefully guarded by her father who kept her locked in the tower to preserve her from the outside world.' He looks over at me. 'And the likes of you, Walsh.' He goes back to his notes.

'When Barbara's father discovered she was a Christian, he mistreated her and dragged her before the prefect in the province Martinianus. The prefect had her cruelly tortured and her father then beheaded her.'

That's a little harsh.

'On his way home, the father was struck by lightning and his body was consumed. At Barbara's grave, it is said that the sick are healed and that pilgrims received aid and consolation. In the fifteenth century, the feast of Saint Barbara was commemorated by the French Cannoneers of Lille on the 4th of December with venison, ale and revelry. Saint Barbara is the Patron Saint of Armourers, Coalminers and Fusiliers.' He raises his glass. 'Saint Barbara.'

'Saint Barbara,' we repeat and throw back the port.

That stuff is rocket fuel.

The sun beats down mercilessly, the beer flows and pretty soon some of our instructors are reminiscing about previous St Barbara's days in places far flung, Phan Rang and Butterworth prominent. There are a couple of common threads to most stories, alcohol and more alcohol, bombs and bullets, a degree of nudity, some interaction with the local cops, some of it sounds beyond belief.

As the afternoon progresses, the stories get a little more serious. An accident here, an aircraft crash there, bodies in bags, lost friends, the odd tear in an eye.

It is increasingly obvious this is indeed more like a tribe than any other collection of humanity. These guys are used to a common purpose, close cooperation, a sense of duty, and a sense of belonging. They are loyal to each other, stand up for each other when it's important, drag each other up when it's necessary. There are bonds here that are stronger than anything I have seen in family, school, or sporting teams. I am very happy to be introduced to the club.

By the time the sun is going down, we are loaded into the Kombis. Goodbye kisses and handshakes from new friends. 'Don't any of you Sprogs spew in there.'

It may as well have been a prophecy. Halfway back to Base, Stan covers his mouth, and starts convulsing. Sandy's hand goes over the top in an attempt to stem the flow. The pressure forces a squirt through the gaps in their fingers, high pressure vomit spaying the cabin before we can get his head out the window. Upon arrival, we get some disinfectant from the Apprentice Club and clean up the Kombi.

Saturday, I struggle though cricket, drinking more water than I have ever consumed before. For the rest of the boys, the day is pretty much a write-off, hangovers and sunburn all round. But I am changed forever, and I think from the few words spoken with Merv, Gus, Nev and some of the others, we are all changed. The friendship shown to us yesterday was moving.

Tuesday afternoon is slow, with the summer heat intensifying and less than two weeks to go before Christmas leave, we are in wind-down mode. It's been a long year and even the instructors seem uninterested.

After cricket training, I shower, change, and head for the

Mess. Dave Granger, our new wicketkeeper, is a cook and he has offered to do some steak and eggs for us outside normal meal hours. As I wander in, everyone is in the back of the kitchen, huddled around a TV.

'What's going on?'

'Some cunt has shot John Lennon. He's dead,' Nige tells me. It's like I am hit with a hammer.

John Lennon dead? It can't be true.

I am looking at the TV and there he is in full voice, then a still, then in bed with Yoko, protesting for peace. 'All we are saying ...'

The man of peace, shot dead. What the fuck is wrong with the world?

I thank Dave for the meal, but I'm not hungry any more.

As I walk back to the block, my head is full of Lennon vocals, 'Shake it up baby, I am the egg man', 'Come Together', 'Instant Karma'.

It can't be true.

Some of my first memories are with mum, and she is playing Beatles records. It's like mum, the Beatles and I have a link and no one is allowed to break it, except for mum, of course, and now John Winston Lennon. 'There are places I remember ...' Back in the block, I dig out my *Shaved Fish* cassette and throw it into Gus' ghetto blaster, 'All we are saying ...' It's like a little bit of me has died with him, some part of my upbringing, my childhood enjoyment dead.

Saturday after cricket, we have a few beers on the way back to Base and check the score from the WACA at the Apprentice Club. Dougie and Rod Marsh have dragged the Aussies back from disaster, five for sixty-eight at one point.

That guy Hadlee can bowl.

Showered, into clean jeans and a light, checked, shirt. Splash a bit of Old Spice on and off to the married patch. It's getting dark and I can move around pretty easily without being recognised as an Apprentice. We aren't supposed to be in the married patch, after dark.

Squadron Leader Gregory's house is about six doors up Trent Street, backing onto the oval. It's about eight thirty when I open the gate and knock on the door. She opens the screen door with a finger over her lips signalling the kids have just gone to sleep, ushering me in. The TV is on with the sound down, barely audible.

We sit on the lounge holding hands and without anything being said yet, she leans over and starts kissing me. The smell and the softness of her lips are intoxicating. The kissing progresses slowly and after several minutes her breathing quickens and she pushes her tongue into my mouth, rolling it around. My breathing gets heavier too and there is a bulge in my pants. Several moments later she pulls her mouth away and pushes mine to her neck.

I move to nibble her ears and she lets a little sigh from her lips. The tongue, neck, ear kissing sequence gets repeated several times and I think the time is right. I move my hand from her hip to start to unbutton her blouse, she doesn't oppose the move.

I fumble with the buttons for a while, still kissing her. She must have got frustrated because she quickly does it herself then removes her bra.

'No intercourse, Tim,' she whispers before recommencing the kissing. Her breasts are lovely, larger than Janine's, and soft. She enjoys the gentle massage and light roll of the nipple between my finger and thumb.

When she puts her hand on my crotch, I take it as a cue to up the ante. My hand goes to the button on her shorts and the zipper. As soon as my finger hits the right spot, she starts gasping for air. It all gets hectic from there.

Within minutes, she is thrusting, urging me to finish it off. She nearly takes the wind out of my lungs with the embrace as she comes and I hug her for long time afterwards.

This relationship stuff is making me dizzy. 'You'd better get going,' she says, putting her bra back on and reassuming control. 'They'll be home soon.'

The last week of work drags, we are doing the Gunnie equivalent of painting rocks, which is painting bombs. The instructors knock us off early Monday and we go straight to the pool. We're a pretty close bunch and most of us are there, jumping around, bombing each other, telling the Thick on Pool Duty to 'fuck off' when he tries to kick us out. On the way back to the block, we check out the mob undertaking car maintenance activities and offer some advice, most of it inaccurate, or at the least uninformed.

Gilley has his head under the bonnet of his HG panel van, adjusting the carbie for the eleventeenth time. It's a heap of shit, but the engine is good, and it's his heap of shit. He's proud of it.

Later, at the Mess, Gilley and I are both staring at something resembling Chicken Chow Mein, the odd poke to see if it might be alive. He's lamenting the complete waste of time painting bombs appears to be.

'I reckon no one would know if we were gone,' he says.

'What, all of us?'

'No, Dougie,' he says with a shake of the head, dumb question. 'No, mate, just one or two of us. No one is giving a fuck about us at the moment. I could slip out and go on leave a day or two early, and no one would notice.'

'What about when they tick your name off at the bus on Friday morning?'

'Nope, me and Thommo are approved to go in my van on Friday. We've actually been thinking about whether we could head off after work Thursday. We'd be in Toowoomba by breakfast Friday.'

'Shit, mate, you are playing with fire there.'

Next morning, we are collecting the drums for parade.

'Where's Gilley?' asks Gus.

'Fuck knows, haven't seen him.' As I adjust the position of the drum against my leg, the penny drops and I recall last night's conversation.

They haven't just fucked off on leave, have they? Would they?

After parade, we are sent over to Aircraft Flight. Apparently, they want the ejection seats removed from a couple of old Vampire training aircraft. We are now fairly confident and require little supervision, especially considering the seats have no explosives fitted.

Sergeant Davies drops by after smoko to check progress.

'This is all looking pretty good,' he says, and I ask him for some advice about removing an ejection gun which is corroded.

'You might have to cut the whole bracket with it,' he tells me.

Just before he heads back to the section, he has one last look around.

'Where's Gilmore?'

Fuck, no time to conjure anything.

'A bit crook, Sarge. I think he went to Medical.'

By lunch time, a few of the boys are asking questions. Where's Gilley?

'He didn't look good this morning, I guess they must have admitted him. I'll duck down there and check.' Just in case, I really do go to Medical and check. No Gilley, fuck. I go back past the Apprentice Car Park, no HG van.

Fuck, he must have done a Harold Holt.

I tell the other boys he has been admitted with measles. They won't let me see him cause he's contagious. But fuck me, this story isn't going to wash.

We get the seats out of the Vampires through the afternoon, and start pulling the components off them, they are going to be used as training aids. Sergeant Davies pokes his head in to check progress, then tells us to fuck off for the rest of the day. The pool and car park routine gets repeated. Merv doesn't miss a trick.

'Where's Gilley's shaggin' wagon?' I get him to one side.

'You know how I said I saw him this morning.'

A prolonged 'Yer.'

'Well, I didn't.' Merv's eyes light up. 'I was talking with him in the Mess last night.' I look around to make sure we are not overheard.

Another prolonged 'Yer.'

'He was talking about fucking off on leave early.'

'Fuck.'

'That's what I said.' I can see Merv's mind ticking over.

'What about the measles story?'

'I made it up.'

'Fuck. Sergeant Davies may be getting a bit dottery in his old age, but not even he will miss this. Gilley's really fucked this time.'

Sure enough, straight after smoko Wednesday morning, Sergeant Davies appears out the back of the Gunnie hangar. We are playing cricket with a tennis ball wrapped in Gunnie tape. He approaches Sandy and I get close enough to listen in.

'Where's Gilmore?'

'Got the measles, Sarge. They have him quarantined.' Sandy doesn't know any different. Sergeant Davies nods, casually tells Biscuits to get more front on if he wants to bowl better leg spin, then disappears. A half hour later, he's back and not looking happy, summoning Sandy over for a brief conversation.

'Hey, Dougie,' he yells, tapping his hand on his head. I go over. 'Didn't you say Gilley was admitted to Medical?'

'I said I saw him yesterday morning and he looked like shit. He was heading for Medical.'

'Didn't you say he had measles and he was quarantined?'

'Na, I said he thought he had the measles and I had better keep my distance.' I can see Sergeant Davies smells a rat. I am in Warrant Officer Foley's office within minutes.

'We've checked. Gilmore isn't at Medical and hasn't been near the place this week.' Sergeant Davies in full detective mode, Warrant Officer Foley looking at me over his glasses.

'You want to tell us what's really going on?'

'All I know, Sarge, is I saw Gilley yesterday morning and he was heading for Medical.' Warrant Officer Foley jumps in.

'Look, son, I can understand you not wanting to rat on your mate, but we can tell you aren't telling us the whole story, now come clean. We won't think any the worse of you, but if you keep up the charade, we'll be forced to charge you too.'

Fuck, it's all I need, another charge. I'll end up spending the first week of leave on CB. There's Christmas stuffed.

I think it over for a few seconds, relenting quickly, telling them about the conversation in the Mess. I leave out the bit about the car being missing, they can work this one out for themselves.

Thursday night, Allison and I go to the pictures. It's a pay night, and so it's quiet. We don't see a lot of the movie and it's a pretty emotional goodbye. Friday morning, onto the bus again and off up the Olympic Way.

'Hey Dougie, did you hear they got hold of Gilley and Thommo. They are being brought back to Base to be charged.'

Gilley, he's becoming a master of the screw-up.

The bus ride gives me time to contemplate a few things. In less than three months, I will be at a Base somewhere a fully trained Armament Fitter. If I go to Kingswood, I could go and see Allison each weekend. Maybe, we could even move in together. But it would mean I would have to put off going to Malaysia. There are a number of options and several have merits, but I still think the best option is a posting to Williamtown.

There is one option I am starting to discount, and that is any strong and permanent connection to my hometown. And, although I am looking forward to time at home, there are also misgivings, primarily around one Louise Bennett. I think I am in love with Allison and it's not fair to Louise if I continue to be her boyfriend when I am around, she deserves better. She has been my best friend for a long time and I am not sure how I am going to break off the romance part of the relationship and still stay friends.

Nev is beside me. He's been rabbiting on about getting a car.

'Hey, Dougie, I am thinking about a four cylinder, or maybe a six, what do you reckon?'

'Sure.'

'You haven't heard a word I said, have you?' I shake my head.

'A car, Dougie, I think I am going to buy a car.'

It is one thing I hadn't considered, a car. Fuck, I don't even have a licence.

The next week, I organise a driving lesson in town and a test with the local Police Sergeant. The lesson is just to make sure I haven't missed anything, I can drive. The test with the Sergeant goes well. He's ex-Army and we spend most of the time talking about his various postings. With the licence squared away, I even get to drive grandma to Maitland for a bit of Christmas shopping. The drive back gets a little uncomfortable.

'So, when are you and Louise getting married?' Never one to mince her words, my grandma.

'We are a bit young, Grandma. Lou has to get through Uni and I still don't know where I'm getting posted.'

'Your grandfather and I were married at eighteen, no reason for you two not to get married and start a family.'

Kids, shit. The little scare I had with Jenny Adams was enough, I am not sure I ever even want kids. She doesn't let up.

'Your grandfather and I were married in Christ Church, and so were your mother and father. You can get married there and we'll have the reception at the RSL or the CWA Hall.' She's got it all worked out.

'You got the date set, Gran?'

'Don't you get smart with me, Timothy.'

I better shut my mouth before I get her really wound up.

I've been making sure I am not alone with Lou for a few days now, it can't last. It's our turn for dinner Christmas Eve and she will want to sit out on the veranda. It's a funny situation. We are the best of friends, and she loves me dearly, but we have grown apart.

What happens if I tell her about Allison? It's not going to end well and I'll be lucky if grandma doesn't disown me.

Grandma does baked chicken, ham, and baked vegies for tea. It's the usual feast capped off with pudding and custard. I manage to dodge too much intimate contact on the veranda by telling her about grandma's wedding conversation with me, she laughs.

'I'll ask mum to have a word and cool down the talk. We can't get married till I finish Uni, at the earliest.'

'No,' I agree. I don't say 'no, not ever'.

Coward, there was an opportunity right there.

'When do you know where you'll get posted?'

'They reckon by the end of January. I'll call you as soon as I know.'

'That'll be nice. I reckon I will be heading to Uni in Armidale, so I guess it's going to be a trip for you no matter where you get posted.' I agree while thinking I could get busy trying to maintain relationships with two girls in two separate cities. That won't work, I'm not that guy, I am really going to have to do something about this.

Aunty Elsie, Uncle Ron and the girls arrive spot on ten on Christmas Day. Uncle Ron was in the Army during the war, on the Kokoda Track. An absolute stickler for timing is our Uncle Ron. The girls give me the rundown of their year, producing school report cards full of As and comments like 'exceptionally well behaved and dedicated'. I guess I missed that gene, maybe not, it's more likely to be Aunty Elsie's influence. I am quietly proud. They seem to have adjusted well to life without mum and dad. Maybe it's because they were a bit younger than me.

Amy is in Year Nine next year at Newcastle Grammar School. There had been some talk about sending her to a Sydney School, like Abbotsford, but Aunty Elsie didn't want to separate the girls. Susan will be going into High School.

After lunch, the teapot is put onto the table and questions start, it is relentless. When do you finish your training? March. When will you know where you are being posted? Soon. Where will you likely be posted to? Williamtown. What will you do there? Fix aeroplanes, I leave out the guns and bombs stuff. What sort of aeroplanes? Probably Mirages. They go fast, don't they? Yes, very.

'We are heading to Bulahdelah this afternoon to see mum,' Aunty Elsie says. 'Do you want to come?'

I haven't seen Grandma Walsh in a few years. She a funny old duck, comes across as very grumpy, but has a wicked sense of humour. You just have to pay close attention or you'll miss it.

'How do I get home?'

'Get Alan to drop you to the pub at Stroud, lunch time, on Sunday. I'll pick you up from there,' grandad says.

We pile into the car about 1400, I am in the back with the girls. It's about an hour over the mountains and there are a few cars out the front when we arrive. Uncle Alan and Uncle Cyril are sitting in the back yard eating a water melon, grandma on the back verandah. She gives me the third degree about the Air Force and girlfriends, it's great to be here.

After lunch on Boxing Day, I am sitting around the lounge room, cricket on the television, thumbing through old photograph albums. There are photos of them all, marriages, debuts balls, visits. Grandma leans over narrating names and events. Many of them, I have never met. There is a photo of dad in school uniform.

'Your father was the only one of the kids to go to high school,' she says. 'We lived in the bush up the back of Wootton then. In them days, you went to work as soon as you finished sixth class. Your father was more ambitious than the others and talked Elsie into living with her so he could go to school.' I never knew that.

For a lady with no kids of her own, Auntie Elsie sure has been parenting a lot of people.

I am engrossed in Dougie and Jim Higgs hanging on at the MCG when I hear the horn out the front.

'We're off, see you in the morning, Grandma.'

I hop in the passenger side of the ute and Uncle Alan takes it out of town on the Lake Road, past the farms along the river, and into the bush. As we get close, I can smell the lake, it's like an old friend I haven't seen for a while. He takes an exit off to the left and up a sandy track, emerging in a clearing with a small wharf. The boat is tied up alongside another.

He throws a stack of fish boxes into the boat. I grab the fuel can. Minutes later, we are chugging slowly across the Two Mile, then through the passage where the Bombah Point ferry crosses, and out into the Broadwater. It's a calm afternoon, the water like an immense sheet of glass extending a couple of miles to the shore in the distance.

The lake brings back so many memories. Uncle Alan, dad and I in the boat, setting the net, the calming rhythm of the boat chugging along, the net running out over the transom. Sometimes, Uncle Alan would say, 'Here he comes,' pointing. A little dot is in the distance, growing slowly larger, and then you could make out the jet coming straight at us, the huge bang as it goes overhead, pulling up and barrel rolling, Uncle Alan laughing.

'He's been trying to scare the pants off me for years, but I see him coming every time.' There are no Mirage fly-pasts today, which is a shame, it would just cap things off nicely. I feel sure these memories are a large part of why I have joined up, and why I feel so determined to work on these beautiful French fighters.

We set the net between Mungo and Tamboy and then he goes back to where he dropped the first piece, pulling it up and extracting two Niggers, before heading for White Tree Bay. The boat settles on the sand about fifty yards off the beach.

'You clean those two and I'll start the fire.' He heads ashore with gear. When I get there, it's going pretty well and he clamps the two fish in the wire grill. He disappears for five minutes and comes back with four lemons.

'There's a tree about fifty yards in there.' He points, 'Secret!'

Fifteen minutes later, we are drizzling the fish in lemon juice, eating with our fingers off the tin plates.

I don't know if there is a heaven, but if there is, it must be eating blackfish beside the Myall Lakes.

Around four in the morning, we head back to Mungo and pick up the net. The catch is deposited at the co-op in Tea Gardens by seven and we are back at grandma's having a cuppa by eight.

Uncle Alan drops me off at the pub in Stroud a little late, he shakes my hand, and tells me stay in touch, disappearing back down the road. I get a middie and sit on the veranda waiting for grandad, thinking about the calm waters of the Myall Lakes, Uncle Alan, and Mirage Fighters.

Thursday afternoon, I'm sitting in the shed contemplating changing the plough on the tractor when grandma yells out, 'Tim, phone.'

It's Nev. 'Dougie, I got a new car. You want a ride back to Wagga?'

'What'd you get?'

'HQ Premier, mate, 253, 4 on the floor, beautiful.'

'Cool. Why don't you come down Saturday and stay the night?' I give him some directions and go back to changing the plough.

Saturday afternoon we are milking when a HQ Holden pulls up at the house. I can see the short, skinny blackfella get out, sunglasses on. I walk down from the dairy and shake his hand.

'It's good to see you, mate.' I introduce Nev to grandad and Uncle Bert. They all shake hands.

'Come on you two, get to work,' says grandad.

I instruct Nev on the art of controlling the girls and pushing one into the bails, cleaning the teats, applying the cups, and checking there is some feed available. He picks it up quickly. The dairy is quite small and having the extra set of hands means grandad can take it a little easy. He sets about checking the girls' health in more detail than he normally would. Healthy cows mean high volume yields.

Uncle Bert is not as welcoming, standing off. It's not the same attitude as when people make remarks about him behind his back, I just get bad vibes from Bert. Maybe it's just in my mind.

When we go down to the house, grandma gives him a big hug and his face goes red. Not sure whether it's the lack of oxygen, or embarrassment. We have a cup of tea and get changed, into the Valiant and off to the RSL. Mr and Mrs Bennett and Lou are there. Lou and Nev hit it off straight away. They both share a love of silly jokes and they give me the full catalogue. They seem to instinctively know all of the worst jokes known to mankind, and me rolling my eyes doesn't slow them for a second.

Next morning, we join the others for a pre-dawn cuppa before milking. At the dairy, Dorrie Evans comes in and gives Nev the once over. She seems to offer some sort of approval, I can't be completely sure. Uncle Bert calls Nev over to offer some deep and meaningful advice. As Nev stoops to look, he is hit with a squirt of milk straight from the teat. We all fracture laughing. While he's more than a little embarrassed by the practical joke, I sense him relaxing a little, feeling some level of acceptance, something he doesn't get everywhere he goes.

We leave straight after milking taking the road to Gresford, then on to Singleton. It's a nice car, straight, dash and upholstery in good shape, the V8 has a healthy note to it.

'Where'd you pick this up?'

'The father of a friend of mum is going blind, can't drive anymore. He let me have it for two grand.'

'Nice.' There is a short silence.

'You didn't break it off with her, did you?'

'No.' More silence. 'We slept together.'

'Shit, Dougie. Why'd you go and do a stupid thing like that for?'

I shrug. 'Seemed like a good idea at the time, and she was pretty happy with the outcome.'

He's right, it's not the smartest thing I have ever done.

The ride back to Wagga is a laugh, playing music, telling yarns, and sightseeing, down the Putty Road, Bells Line of Road, and then through Bathurst, Cowra, and Young, stopping at Merv's place for a cuppa.

There is a large crowd on hand when we arrive late in the afternoon. The Apprentice Car Park is overflowing with newly acquired vehicles, proud owners, and a critical acquisition review committee.

What year? How big's the donk? How much did you pay for it? You were ripped off. It's a tough crowd. Gilley's HG van is there with some new mags.

Nev ignores the interrogation and we grab our bags from the boot and head to the room. We have not long walked in when Gilley kicks our door open.

'So, which one of you pricks dobbed me in?'

I wonder if the explanation is going to calm him and put my hand up anyway. He glares at me as I run through the measles story, the questions from Sergeant Davies, and them checking with Medical.

'They wised up pretty quickly,' I tell him. A smile starts to come to his face.

'I was under the van patching up the exhaust with a Coke can when the white Valiant station wagon pulled up outside Thommo's place. Two sets of black shoes and drab socks walk up the driveway, one kicks my ankles. I tell him to fuck off and slide out from under the car. Sorry Corporal, I say.' Gilley is giggling, enjoying himself.

'One of them says, 'Are you Apprentice Thompson?' I say 'No.' He says, 'Are you Apprentice Gilmore?' 'Yes,' I tell him.

'He says, You know why we are here? And I say, I don't suppose I won Hurry Scurry.' He laughs loudly. As he walks out the door, he stops and looks back at me. 'Measles, contagious, not bad on short notice, Dougie.'

Over the next few days, Gilley regales us with various stories of his Christmas crime spree.

Over lunch, 'We were about twenty miles out of Coonabarabran doing about a hundred and fifty Ks, when the front tyre blows. By the way, they don't call it Coonabarabran for nothing,' accentuating the 'coon'. He looks sideways at Nev, has a little shake of the head, and keeps going.

'We are off the road heading into the bush towards a fucking big tree before I manage to drag the car back on the road and stop. There's a spare, but no fucking jack. I get on the CB radio to find a truckie, one stops and gives us a hand to lift the car onto a log. We change the tyre, drive off the log and keep going.'

Over dinner, 'They took us to Amberley and gave us a room at the transit accommodation. There's fuck-all to do, so we head for the boozer and get hammered. The WOD, Adams, shows up the next morning and a RAAF car drives us to Brisbane Airport. While we are waiting for the flight, he buys us two beers. Great guy WOD Adams. They flew us back on a Fokker F27.'

Over a snooker game, 'Anyway, we get back here, the CO hears the charge and gives us ten days CB. We spend the whole time working in the Mess. Those guys are great. They fill us full of Bundy and Coke every night and we have to bluff our way through the last call. I was half pissed most of the time.'

Over breakfast, 'On the way back, I was about fifteen miles out Narrabri and I run out of fuel. This cop turns up, gives me a lift into town to get some fuel, and drops me back to the car, then tells me to have a safe trip back to Base. Stupid bastard didn't even check my licence … or my rego …' We all laugh, everyone knows Gilley has no licence or rego.

Saturday, we are playing a forty-over game at The Rock. Nige and I bum a ride from one of the Thicks, Ken James. He has a burnt orange coloured Datsun 1600 done up to rally, thinks he's Alan Moffat. He gets it sideways going over the railway bridge at Kapooka and scares the shit out of us. Luckily, the road out through Uranquinty is almost dead straight. He definitely has overestimated his ambition to skill ratio.

Our match is an absolute disaster, all out for sixty-eight and they chase it down in eighteen overs, eight wickets in hand. We are definitely rusty. Nige and I grab a six pack from The Kings Own to drown our sorrows and calm our nerves for the trip back to Base.

Arriving in one piece, we're in time to watch the last hour of the A-Grade game, finishing the beer in the process. When I go to the sheds for more, Nancy and Allison are there.

'Hello, Tim, how was your Christmas?' Nancy asks me.

Normally, I would keep the chat to a minimum, but I am already lubricated. I give them a few stories about Christmas with my grandparents, the farm, and seeing the girls.

'What do your parents do?' she asks innocently.

'Residents of the Dungog cemetery,' I tell her without much emotion. 'Car accident,' I add.

'I am sorry' she says, obviously shaken. Allison has a stunned look on her face and there is an uneasy pause in conversation. I realise that I have been a little too flippant, came out all wrong, the beer is talking. It's been six years now and I have come to terms with it, but I forgot it can be quite confronting for some people.

'Can I get three beers, please?' I break the silence. Nancy can't serve me quick enough and I make a hasty exit to save further embarrassment.

Later at the barbecue, Allison fusses over me, getting me a steak sandwich, hanging close, holding hands.

Is it some maternal instinct kicking in?

Later, we are sitting side-by-side on a bench seat engrossed in a conversation on the merits of women in the Armed Forces.

'Girls can't go into combat roles,' I tell her. They'd never carry all the equipment, packs, rifle. They simply don't have the physical strength.'

'That's bull, Tim. It's only because women have been kept in the house barefoot and pregnant for so long. If we get the training right, there would be no physical barrier.' The arguments bounce back and forth, I am trying hard to have an open mind here, but it's not proving to be easy.

'You keep your hands where I can see them, Dougie!' interrupts Bob in his best military voice and everyone has a laugh.

Friday before Australia Day, Warrant Officer Foley and Flight Sergeant Bourke walk into the room, Sergeant Davies yells, 'Sit Fast.'

'Well, gentlemen, it seems you all have almost mastered the theory and practical elements of becoming an Armament Fitter. There is not long to go and I do not want any of you to become complacent. There are rules to be obeyed and I don't want any of you getting into trouble before you depart.' He gives Gilley and me a quick glance.

'Your postings have just come in from DPA. I will read them out, and I will provide a copy to Sergeant Davies so you can quote the authority for your removal.'

'Arnott, 482 Squadron.'

'Sir,' replies Biscuits.

'Beach, 492 Squadron.'

'Sir,' from Sandy, and so on.

Brownie and Terry O'Reilly get ICAMD, glum looks there. Stan gets Maintenance Squadron East Sale. Gus 38 and Gilley get 77 Squadron. Fraz, Johnno, Nev and Merv get 481 Squadron, Jerry and Watto get Number 2 OCU, Nicko gets 492 Squadron, Smithy 482 Squadron, Rosco 9 Squadron, and Sharpie 3AD. I am awaiting my fate.

'Walsh,' he looks up.

'Sir.'

'77 Squadron.' He looks a bit puzzled. 'I might give Mac a ring,' he says to Flight Sergeant Bourke. 'Edwards, Gilmore and Walsh in one Squadron might be too much of a handful.' There are sniggers from around the room.

Once Warrant Officer Foley leaves the room, there is an outburst of chatter, some elated, some dejected, but overall some relief we at least know. We all get a texta and put our new Squadron onto our name tag. It's an overt sign commonly used to signify that one has done their time. As promised, I ring home and Louise to give them the news.

We finish cricket at five-thirty Saturday. I manage to get to the Mess before it closes. There's plenty of time for a shower and change, before heading to the married patch. Another babysitting extravaganza in the offing.

It's a repeat performance. A kissing session, before her top comes off and my hand is inside her shorts. The only difference is that, this time she has my jeans undone and hands on me.

It's funny how it's never the same when a girl does it. They haven't quite got the right technique.

I wonder if she is thinking the same about my technique. Maybe not, she goes off intensely again and I am left all dressed up with nowhere to go.

Sunday, I get to the pool at 1500 sharp. She's already there with her two sisters, Kerry and Janice.

The two girls say 'Hello' politely before running to the pool's edge.

'Chaperones?' I ask. Allison just smiles back at me. She peels off her sun dress to reveal a modest, green bikini.

'Last one in is a rotten egg,' she says, quickly getting into a run and then diving into the pool. She has a good turn of speed, along with a decent head start on me and I dive in behind her. The months of summer heat has the pool pretty warm, but it's still refreshing in the thirty-six-degree heat.

Being the Sunday of the long weekend, there are not many people around, except for the poor unfortunate Thick who has pool duty. He's asleep in a chair, already a pretty bright shade of pink. I try a few summersaults and bombs off the low diving board and the girls give it a try too, they are pretty fearless. Young Janice has taken a shine to me and I introduce her to the art of back throws. We are in the shallow end and she has her hands around my neck, foot in my interlinked hands, knees bent. My knees are also bent.

'One, two, threeeee,' we say in unison, as we extend our legs and I lift my hands. She goes flying through the air backwards and enters the water, head first, some way away. She doesn't tire easily and the process is repeated for some time. I ask her how old she is.

'Ten in March,' she says.

A bit younger than Susan.

There is a tinge of guilt I am not in Newcastle doing the same thing with my sisters, I make a promise to myself to take some time and do it.

Around five, Allison herds us out of the pool and says it's time to get home for dinner. There is a goodbye peck on the cheek and she asks if I want to go to the pictures tomorrow night.

Monday night, Allison lets me in the front door again, a hello kiss on the cheek. She has a skirt and blouse on today, same perfume. It's hard to figure out exactly what it smells like. It reminds me of grandma's roses, it's subtle, not overdone.

'How'd you guys go Saturday, Dougie?' Bob asks.

'We made a hundred and sixty, Ken got fifty and we knocked them off for eighty-nine. Nige got four for,' I recount.

'Good. Better results than the Test team. West Indies belted them around the Adelaide Oval all weekend.' He takes a swig from his beer. 'Did you see the Australia Day honours list?' he asks picking up the newspaper.

I don't usually look at that stuff. Grandad always did and says it's generally some dickhead getting a gong for someone else's work. I realise Bob is actually waiting for some sort of response from me.

'Grandad used to go on about it every year. He reckoned the honours didn't usually end up going to the people who do all the work.'

'He's spot-on, Dougie, bloody Dave Edgeworth,' Bob says. 'He was our CO when I was in Phan Rang on my last tour. Even his troops wanted to shoot him.' He shakes his head putting the paper back on the coffee table. 'Remember, Tim, no one ever got a gong for just doing your job well. You have to be seen as well, but it's a fine line.'

'Must be a bit like Apprentice promotions,' I surmise.

'Exactly,' he says, looking up at me for the first time in the discussion. 'Don't go around arse kissing, but you still need to be doing the right things and getting noticed for the right reasons,' he says.

'Robert,' comes Nancy's chastising voice from the kitchen, Allison is rolling her eyes.

It's becoming an interest of mine to observe various standards of behaviour in different households. In some households, it is absolutely verboten to mention anything bordering on crass, 'damn' or 'arse' would not be tolerated. In the Gardner house, it appears that arsekissing is over the line.

'Let's go, Tim, we'll be late.'

Gus, Pete Johnson, Merv, Nev and Heather are waiting outside the pictures.

'How was the weekend, boys?'

A couple of mumbled responses, they all look tired.

'I picked up that *Cold Chisel* album and one by *Blondie*,' Gus says.

'Blondie, how hot is Debbie Harry?' I ask.

'Tim, she's old enough to be your mum,' Allison says, and I can see she regrets it straight away. 'She's thirty-five years old and trying to recover.

'No, get out. Well, I don't care if she is old, she's still hot.' I reply acting like it didn't happen.

The movie is a bit of a drag, the *Village People*. For a bunch of poofs, they sing alright, but the story is lame.

Allison and I chat incessantly on the walk home holding hands. Most of the talk is about life after Wagga Wagga. The goodnight kiss is long, soft, and her smell has me in a blissful delirium.

The following weekend, it's Merv's eighteenth. We have all been invited up to the farm for the party. Most of the boys head up Saturday morning. Heather is allowed to go after her mum rings Merv's mum to make sure there is somewhere safe for Heather to sleep. If only she knew.

I am playing cricket at Lake Albert and catch a ride up with Rob Beckett. He's a trainee Clerk Financial Accounting who played rugby with us, he's now our opening bowler. He drives and I have a few cans on the way.

Allison wasn't allowed to come, despite reassurances from me she would be sleeping in the house and we are all in the shed. Merv even offered to get his mum to call.

She's got her starting date at Sydney Uni, over the moon that she got accepted into law there. It also means we only have two weeks left together. Every night I am away from her, is a moment lost.

It's a great party. The shed is decked out with streamers, everyone from the surrounding farms has arrived with arms full of food, there is a pig on a spit, and there are a couple of kegs set up in a trailer. Merv's sister Narelle has control of the turntable and a record collection which would rival a radio station.

Merv introduces us to his girlfriend, Karen, a tall girl with a wide mouth, and an infectious smile. They went to school together and have been going out for four months now. She finished school in October and is working as a secretary at the truck business in town.

Merv's mum is a laugh. We have let her in on the story about Merv, Heather, and Nev. She kills herself laughing.

'I'd love to be a fly on the wall when they find out,' she giggles. 'Guess who's coming to dinner?' she laughs again. We word Karen up she might have to be Nev's date for the Graduation Ball, because Heather is going with Merv. More laughs, you couldn't make this shit up.

The beer is cold, food amazing, and the music excellent. Narelle has Bob Seger on.

'What's next?' I ask her.

'A bit of *Steely Dan,* then *Linda Ronstadt, The Doobies,* and *Midnight Oil,*' she says.

I thought I had a reasonable musical vocabulary, but not after spending time with her. She is like an encyclopaedia, this blues band, that rhythm and blues band, rock bands, pop bands.

Who knew there was so many different types of music?

'This is *Midnight Oil,* a track called 'Wedding Cake Island'. It's an instrumental. I have caught them a few times in Sydney. They are going to be big.' I block out all other noise and focus on the music.

How cool is this?

I can tell Gilley and the boys are up to something. They are sitting with Merv's Uncle Pete and Auntie Doreen and there are Air Force warries being told. Nicko turns up with a Vodka bottle and asks Gilley if he wants a drink.

'Give it here,' Gilley grabs the bottle. He pauses, looking around what is now a crowd. 'Can I have a moment's silence please?' It goes quiet, and he makes a drama of breaking the seal and tearing off the lid. He tips the bottle to his lips and starts swallowing, swallowing, swallowing. The whole bottle disappears, Gilley places it on his leg, and burps louder than a foghorn. He starts to rock back and forth from the hips.

'Holy shit,' says Uncle Pete. 'I've never seen anyone do that in all my forty years.' Auntie Doreen looks worried. Gilley is now starting to close his eyes, swaying more.

'Is he okay?' she asks.

'It's his party trick,' Nicko says. 'He'll be asleep soon enough.'

'You can't let him go to sleep, he'll drown in his own vomit,' she continues, worried. Uncle Pete gets up, goes to Merv's dad and says they need to call an ambulance. He rushes over to give Gilley the once over.

'Shit, he's about to collapse.' He supports Gilley in his arms.

'Merv,' he yells. Merv, comes over.

'What's up, Dad?'

'Get an ambulance, your mate here has skulled a bottle of vodka, he's about to become unconscious.'

'Don't fall for that one, Dad, he's bullshitting you. It's water.' Gilley bursts out laughing and sits up grinning.

'Fucking smart-arse RAAFies,' says Uncle Pete.

I spend most of the night with Narelle, playing records, and discussing various tracks, bands, musical styles. My eyes are certainly opened to a wider selection and she is a good instructor, happily sharing without bias or agenda, it's kind of refreshing.

'You said you were living in Sydney?'

'Yep, working at NIDA.'

'NIDA?'

'The National Institute of Dramatic Art, NIDA, they train actors. I am training to be a sound technician.'

'Wow, never knew there was such a thing.'

'Oh, yeah, and we get some interesting, famous, infamous, outrageous characters through there, I can tell you. Anyone who lives to be an actor or an entertainer is a bit of a self-obsessed narcissistic freakshow, probably sexually confused, and that's just the cleaners!'

We get lost in conversation, she lives in a whole other world, almost like a parallel universe, so different to our relatively humdrum existence.

Before long, people are saying goodnight and the crowd is thinning out. Merv is three parts pissed and got a hold of one of the shed posts to stand up, although according to him, he's holding the post up. Mrs Humphries does the right thing and makes sure Heather goes to bed in the house, Merv gets put out on the hay in the shed with a pillow and a blanket and lapses into unconsciousness.

Narelle packs up the music about 0200 and disappears to bed, I have enjoyed her company, but suddenly realise there is something different about her. The rest of us sit around sipping on beers.

'Mate, you really didn't think you'd be throwing your leg over with that one, did you?' asks Johnno. The boys are having a bit of a laugh.

'What?' I wasn't thinking about screwing her, we just got along well, that's all.

'You know, she probably bats for the other team?'

'What?'

'Likes girls, Dougie,' he persists. It finally dawns on me.

'A lezzo?' They all start laughing.

Sometime after, we all find a blankets and a soft place to lie down.

A lezzo, hey? I've never met a lezzo before. There's none in Dungog. And she seemed really normal.

Sunday morning, Mr Humphries is up early. The barbie is going, enough bacon, sausages and eggs to feed an army, and hot coffee. Mrs H comes out with a basket full of rolls and we fill up, it eases the pain, along with the plenty of Bex.

Just before lunch time, I jump into the passenger seat of Gilley's van and we head into town to buy a couple for the trip. Well, not so much a trip, more like a low level, high speed run over the target. We cover the one hundred kilometres back to Forrest Hill in a little over forty minutes. The beers disappear quickly to keep me calm.

When did he learn to drive like a fucking lunatic?

We go past Allison's house on our way back into Base.

Only a week till she goes to Uni.

Time is a funny thing. When you aren't having a good time, it drags on, and when things are going well, it flies by. Our last weeks in Wagga are just so. For the past two years, time has dragged. But now, I have a relationship with the most beautiful girl in the world, I have confidence in my skills and abilities of my new trade, and I have a group of mates who I trust, and they trust me. Time is flying.

I am invited to Allison's for dinner on Saturday night. Nancy is driving her to Sydney tomorrow. The dinner isn't formal, but I put on a good pair of trousers, best shoes, and a button-up shirt. It's pasta and salad, Nancy picked the recipes from the *Woman's Weekly* and Bob has even got a bottle of wine for the occasion. After sweets, Bob makes a little speech about Allison going off to find her place in the world, and how proud he is of her achievements. He does it well.

I hope one day I can be half as good.

Later, we take a long walk around the golf course, laughing, holding hands. The February heat and a buzz from the wine making it all a little dizzying. She tells me she'll write to me and I should come and visit her when I get settled in Williamtown. The goodbye kiss at the front gate is short but intense.

When we first started at Wagga Wagga, the idea of graduation seemed like a dream, miles off in our future. Now it looms big in our lives, front and centre every day. There have been months of planning, and with only two weeks to go, the final touches are being put in place.

With Allison and Louise both at Uni, I have no date and, to be frank, I don't want one. Grandad, grandma, and Mrs Bennett are going to make the trip down from Dungog and it's probably better I have my whole focus on them. I have considered whether I would introduce Mrs Bennett to Bob and Nancy and, come to the conclusion, I will if the opportunity arises.

Most of the other guys have dates. A few have girls from their hometown coming with their mums and dads. Johnno is bringing Michelle, Merv is standing in for Nev with Heather, and Nev is escorting Merv's girlfriend, Karen. Karen thinks it's cool we would go to such lengths to support our mate.

'I always wanted to know whether it's true what they say about black guys.'

'Oh, it's true, baby, and once you go black, you can't go back,' Nev, smooth as ever, and always the modest one.

Even Jerry Holmes has a date, Jenny Adams. Jerry and Jenny, it has a ring to it. They started going out together two weeks ago. If you believe what he says, she has been screwing him senseless. I guess she has sorted out the whole contraception thing. Each Monday morning, he turns up with love bites all over his neck.

'Are you dating a vampire, Holmes?' asks Warrant Officer Foley.

Practice for the Graduation Parade has started. It's a pretty large contingent graduating, about a hundred of us, grouped into three Flights. There is a Colour Party, and the escorting Squadrons from 34 and 35 Intake. In the last week, there are two practices each day, dispersed with cleaning shoes, belts, gators, trips to the pool, and evening drinks at the Airman's Club.

On the day before graduation, grandad arrives at 1700 and I take him to the RSL for dinner.

'A bit grander than the Dungog RSL,' he observes.

They drop me back to Base at eight and I join the boys for a beer.

The Graduation Parade goes off relatively well. There is a whole bunch of pomp and ceremony, Air Commodore this, Group Captain that. Lots of gold braid in attendance. Hell, the Reviewing Officer is the Governor General. He turns up in a Rolls. Four Iroquois Helicopters fly overhead as we do the *Advance in Review Order* and *Royal Salute*, complete with *God Save the Queen* and the band plays *Auld Lang Syne* as we march off.

We spend the afternoon showing our guests around the Base. Grandma and Mrs Bennett are impressed with the order of everything and comment that it appears like everyone knows exactly what is happening, and when it is meant to happen. I'd never really gave it much thought, but it is interesting to get the outsiders view of things.

Grandad seems impressed with my knowledge of all things, guns, bombs and ejection seats. Flight Lieutenant Jennings presents each of us with our certificates, with Smithy the dux of the course and Nev getting an honourable mention.

The Graduation Ball is to be held in the hangar where Engine Fitter training is conducted. It has a highly polished parquet floor, a great dancefloor. The place is decked out with tables, decorations, bar, and some mood lighting in the two helicopters either side of the band. Grandma and Mrs Bennett look gobsmacked, it's not something you see every day.

With the boring speeches and better-than-average dinner out of the way, the music kicks in and the dancefloor fills quickly with old and young. I duck off and say hello to Bob and Nancy, leaving grandad in a deep discussion with Merv's dad about fertiliser. Gran, Mrs Bennett, and Nev's mum are all talking CWA business with Merv's mum. Everybody seems to get along just fine. Around ten, grandad tells us its way past his bedtime. Grandma and Mrs Bennett give me a kiss on their way out.

'See you Friday afternoon,' I tell them. Somehow the statement seems different this time around.

I take a look around to see who I am going to annoy now that the family have all scarpered, spotting Gilley sitting on his own.

'Where are your parents, Gilley?'

'Had something else on. Maybe they had to update their mirror collection, comb their bloody hair, who gives a fuck.' He looks around, 'it's a dry old argument.' He wanders off, coming back minutes later with two bottles of wine in hand.

'You driving to Williamtown tomorrow?'

'No, I had to get rid of the HG. The diff shit itself and I sold it to a wrecker. I am going with Fraz on Saturday.' Jenny appears over his left shoulder and sits down.

'Are you going to share that?' picking up a wine glass and waving it in my face. I shrug and pour her some and the three of us chink glasses.

'Where's Jerry?'

'In the toilet throwing his guts up,' she says. 'He started shovelling it in as soon as the bar opened and now is somewhere the other side of plastered.'

I was just about a say to myself, 'Well, you won't be getting laid tonight,' when I spot her looking me up and down like a side of beef hanging at the butcher.

'How's Allison,' she asks, taking a large swig.

'Settling in. She is staying at the Women's College, says there are a lot of other girls like her there.'

'I bet there are.' She pauses. 'She just couldn't be happy to have you, could she? She had to go and have a career, make a name for herself. She'll end up regretting letting you go and not getting married. I don't know what you see in her.'

'She and I have a lot in common, similar sense of humour. We hit it off straight away. And, we're in love.'

'I thought you and I hit it off straight away. Or, was that, got it off?'

'How's things going with Jerry?' I ask, trying to change the subject.

'Oh, it's okay. He's funny, if not a little immature and he's got a big dick. Could do with some lessons on how to use it properly, maybe you could help him out?'

What sort of girls talk like this?

Gilley finds the whole discussion more than a little amusing and starts giggling, she giggles with him.

'Well, I'm not going to give him any tips. I'm a virgin,' announces Gilley proudly.

'No,' she says with shock.

'Yes,' he says, sitting more upright getting a little serious. She takes another long deliberate swig from the glass.

'Well, we better fix that,' she says getting up and grabbing him by the hand, a bottle of wine in the other. They disappear out through a door on the side of the hangar, she's almost dragging him.

'You have to admire a girl who knows what she wants, and gets on with it,' I say to no one in particular.

The party starts to get a little rougher and louder. The lads have joined a few tables together, end-to-end, and poured on a good cover of beer. Run in, dive, belly first, arms out imitating wings, slipping across the top, and often off the side onto the floor, it's called Carrier Landings.

There are a small group of enthusiastic participants and just as enthusiastic crowd along each side of the tables cheering them on. Naturally, it's not long before someone gets hurt. Stan is escorted from the hangar, looks like a broken collar bone to me, but he's feeling no pain. It doesn't subdue the players for a second.

I grab another glass of wine and sit down next to Nev, Heather, Merv, Karen, and Gus.

'Remember the first day?' asks Merv.

Nev laughs, 'Yep, hot, noisy, ADGies running around screaming at everyone, I learnt five new swear words in the first five minutes.'

'I heard one guy just got off the Herc and just kept walking out the front gate and got a cab to the train station.'

The noise level has gone up a couple of notches as more landing aircraft exit the far end of the carrier deck.

Those boys are gonna be sore tomorrow.

Gus is sitting back, feet on the table, glass of champagne in one hand and a cigar in the other. The white shirt and bow tie make him look like something out of *Casablanca*.

'Take a good look around boys, you won't be an Apprentice tomorrow.' Always the realist our Gus, he offers me a cigar.

I am about to take the piss out of him, when I realise he is right, he's philosophical again, on a roll.

'It's easy being an Apprentice in the RAAF,' he announces. 'We are mollycoddled to a fair degree, hell, we are treated with kid gloves. The Instructors look after us like their own kids, we get our own line at the Mess, they coach our footy teams, and we get cut more slack than anyone else on the Base, because we are apparently growing boys.'

He's right, and have the advantage of being the longest serving students on the base. We know our way around the place better than anyone. We know how to stay out of the way of nasty NCOs, and we know which fences to jump after midnight without being caught, well almost.

'Boys, tomorrow, we'll be just another Aircraftsman in the RAAF and by next week, just another face in the crowd at RAAF Base Williamtown. From kings of our little domain, to the bottom of the pecking order.'

I light the cigar and chug on it, the smoke makes me cough a little. Looking around the room, I am feeling a little thoughtful. We are not the only ones having a reflective moment, little groups here and there. The place is starting to empty out, drunks being carried off. A few more wines, then back to the block and into the sack.

I so wish Alison could've been here tonight.

In my sleep, I can hear someone yelling at me, calling my name. As my consciousness grows, and the dream fades I realise I am being shaken as well.

'Dougie, Dougie, wake the fuck up.'

It's Gilley.

'What time is it, Gilley?' He doesn't answer the question, why would I even expect an answer from the look of him.

'Dougie, you gotta come drinking with us, time's a fuckin' wastin'.'

I try and focus my eyes on the clock, fuck it's one-thirty in the morning. I look back toward him and realise there is someone with him.

Fuck, it's Jenny.

She is standing there with a shit-eating grin on her face, swaying like she is being blown around in the wind. There's no wind in my room, well not the weather kind. Both of them have a bottle of wine in hand, it's a great look.

'Gilley, do you know what's going to happen when Warrant

Officer Adams works out his daughter hasn't come home from the Graduation Ball?' Gilley blinks and shakes his head, but there is little in the way of comprehension, the lights are on but no one's home. As I get out from under the sheet, she looks me up and down with a leer, still swaying.

'Don't get up, I'll get in,' she slurs, trying to move towards the bed, thankfully without much luck. I might need a hand here, so I wake Gus.

'Hey, mate, these two clowns are completely hammered. You get him to bed, I'll get her home.' Thumbs up, we have a plan, but then so did Custer.

I manage to coax her out the door, past the Apprentice Club, and across to ASCO. As we get to the married patch, she turns and puts her arms around me, collapsing in a boneless heap. I throw her over my shoulder and carry on to her house. On the front verandah, I prop her up against the wall and arrange her with her legs crossed to protect her modesty I catch my breath for a little while, then hit the door bell and run like shit. I am two houses away and at full sprint before the front light comes on.

The HQ purrs up the Hume Highway, Nev at the wheel, sunglasses on, *East* is in the cassette player, Jimmy screaming through the speakers, Nev singing along.

'Cheap wine and a three-legged goat, cheap wine and a ...'

The small towns along the way intrigue me, Yass, Jugiong, Bookham, Gunning, and Breadalbane. I weigh up each one as we pass. There will be a grocer, butcher, a bakery, a dirty-finger nails mechanic who can fix anything, and a hairdresser who knows everyone's business, and takes great pride in sharing it with anyone who will listen. Somehow, there is often a Chinese restaurant in there as well. It never looks busy, but they survive and seem completely happy with their lot. It's clear to me these country towns, and the locals, are the at the core of the Australian way of life and our sense of humour.

The land looks dirt dry and I am thinking they are probably hand- feeding. I find myself wondering if the feed affects the wool quality or quantity, and the cash flow.

Where did that come from?

I have worked on the land most of my life but it's different out here I am trying to imagine what life is like. The cycles of flood and drought are more pronounced than near the coast. Shit, the seasonal changes are bad enough in Dungog. I reckon these blokes have their bank manager looking over their shoulder all the time.

The semi-trailers are never ending, roaring past at speed, the wash swaying the Holden each time. Every now and again there is a DMR truck filling potholes, and a guy on the paddle-pop stick, usually with a durry hanging out the corner of his mouth.

I am not sure I could handle that job.

I turn and find Nev looking at me with his lips moving but I am miles away.

'Need a piss,' he says matter-of-factly. 'We'll stop at Goulburn, fill the tank, grab a Coke or something, okay?' I give him the thumbs-up and go back to my daydreaming.

Coming into town, there is an oval with a little wooden grandstand on the right, probably supporting a footy club in winter and a cricket club in summer. Both clubs would have a guy named Chook, Blu, or Tubbie, or all three.

It's just like home, only different. Then again, where's home?

After filling up, he eases the car into the main street, and we get a park not far from the Astor Hotel. Hamburgers and coke from the Paragon Café, then a smoke before continuing. Between Marulan and Berrima, the land changes. It's still dry, but they obviously get a bit more rain here and I sense it's closer to the coast. The buildings in Berrima are striking and have the old-stone look, I am guessing local sandstone. Craftsmen who came out as settlers built these towns with their bare hands, no power tools, and they still stand proudly all these years later. They might not be the pyramids of Egypt, but I can't help but be impressed.

The route through Sydney is an absolute contrast. Too many people going nowhere fast. They drive like maniacs, constantly changing lanes, and the horn is the weapon of choice.

Why is it they don't know how to use indicators here, or are they that lazy?

Nev swears more in the one-hour transit across Sydney than I have heard him swear in the past three months. I am happy to see the back of the joint as we head out through the Berowra Toll Gates.

When we get to Doyalson, I recall the way Sergeant Falconer took us and ask Nev to chuck a left, heading up north through Wyee, Morisset, and Cooranbong to Kurri Kurri. I know enough of the local area to avoid Swansea and Charlestown. From Kurri Kurri, its Maitland, Paterson, and into Dungog.

Every time I come home the mixed emotions hit me like a hard slap. You would have thought after being away for a couple of years, the effect would diminish, but it's as strong as ever. Nev gives me a slightly worried look as if he can sense my torment. Sometimes, I think he has some extra sense we white people miss.

I know I shouldn't be dwelling on this. Everyone will be happy to see me and we'll have a great weekend. The lifestyle is like an old boot, well worn, and all too easy to slip back on almost without noticing. And, of course, grandma will be asking a million questions, particularly if I have written to Lou. If she had her way, we would be booking the wedding date and buying the pram.

But, there's the rub. I know I don't belong here anymore, and I am about to start my Air Force career proper. Two-and-a-bit years of training and I am ready to join Australia's top fighter squadron — 77 Squadron. It's exciting.

The milking is finished by the time we pull up. Grandad and grandma come out the back to greet us. She gives Nev a big hug and his face goes red again. Uncle Bert is standoffish yet again.

It's disappointing to me, but Nev doesn't seem to notice, I guess he's used to it. We eat and turn in early, tired from the long drive.

We're enjoying a few drinks at the RSL on Saturday night when I notice that not everyone is as pleased with Nev's presence as we are — a few sideways glances and comments behind the back of the hand. It's not everyone, of course, just a few, and a few that are big wigs in the town.

When Nev goes to the bar, I give grandad a signal. 'This shit ain't right.' He looks around, shrugging his shoulders.

'It's the same wherever you go, Tim,' he theorises. 'Country towns, in the big cities, they all think they own the place. They'd think differently if they'd ever taken the time to talk with some of the old black fellas. They can teach us something about living with countryside and not trying to turn it into something it's not.' Nev comes back with the drinks and he changes the subject.

'Dougie, the portrait next to the Queen is Doug Walters? What happened to Phil the Greek?'

'This is Dungog, Nev. Doug is the biggest thing to happen to this place since sliced toast,' grandad chips in.

'Neville, we all need our heroes. It gives the community a rallying point and Doug is the NSW hero; the boy from the bush who beat the world. Doug is the only guy in the world who could get a duck at the SCG and still get a standing ovation on his way off. Even Bradman wouldn't get that.'

'Yep, if they drop him for the Ashes this year, there will be riots in the streets. Well in Dowling Street, Dungog, anyway.' Nev ponders the information.

'I guess that's a bit like Artie Beetson and Larry Corowa for the black fellas?'

'Exactly,' replies grandad, 'and that, Neville, is the little paradox that is modern Australia. You're a star if you play first grade in Sydney, but if you are just an ordinary black man, then people look down their nose at you.' There isn't any malice in grandad's words and Nev understands, again pondering the advice.

'You'll need a car,' grandad announces, changing the subject.

It takes me a few ticks to catch up. He's right, I will need a car to get home on weekends. I can't bludge rides from the boys for the rest of my life.

'I'll get Max to have a look at what he's got in the yard. What sort of car are you thinking about?'

'I kind of like Nev's HQ, or maybe something a little older, a HR? The Holden's are easy to work on and sound good enough on the road.'

'I'll call him in the morning.'

At lunch on Sunday, he tells me Max has a green Corolla that would suit.

'He'll let you have it for three-and-a-half grand. It's a Hiroshima Screamer, but it'll be economical and reliable. If you come up with half, I will pay the other half from your trust account.' Sounds okay to me. While I need a car, I don't want to spend a *motza*. I will probably go to Malaysia in the next two years, so a relatively cheap option seems sensible.

Washing up after lunch, the interrogation starts, 'Have you called Louise yet?'

'Yes, grandma, I called her before we left Wagga Wagga and told her all about the graduation. She said to say hello.' Grandma looks down her nose at me, obviously not convinced.

'When are you going up to see her?'

'As soon as I get a car, and some leave. I haven't started yet and I don't know when they will let me take leave.'

'Well, don't leave it too long.' It's not advice.

We finish the milking before four and head off to Williamtown, stopping at Max's yard to look at the Corolla.

'It's in good shape, Dougie,' Nev tells me.

'A Corolla. Young Normie didn't pick up chicks cruising Hunter Street, Newcastle. Not in a cow-shit green Corolla.' I'm not convinced.

From Dungog, we turn left at Clarence Town, over the bridge toward Limeburners Creek, with ABBA on the radio. We start singing along.

'Ring, ring, why don't you give me a call?' pausing, 'Hey you, our best Norman Gunston impersonation.'

At Twelve Mile Creek its right onto the Highway and then Medowie Road to Williamtown. Being a Sunday, the Base is pretty quiet. As we get out of the car at the Screw's office, I take a look around. The green sporting fields contrast with the brown grass around the airfield, and beyond the Base, Nelson Bay Road with a steady stream of traffic heading back to Newcastle, and then the sand dunes of Stockton Beach.

I can sense the ocean being close. It's a different feeling than being in the country around Dungog or Wagga Wagga. It's like there is a large beast slumbering just beyond those dunes.

The beach, Williamtown, and I have a strong connection. I remember going fishing with dad and Pop Walsh on the beach at Yagon. We'd dig pipis from the sand to use them as bait and spend hours pulling in snapper. You'd have to keep your eyes peeled though, as Mirages from Williamtown would fly down the beach at zero feet scaring the bejesus out of unsuspecting fishermen. You wouldn't hear them coming, just a colossal boom as they went past. I swear you could see the pilots looking over their shoulder with a grin from ear to ear. I reckon they took great delight at seeing fishermen face down in the sand.

Maybe they painted them on the side of their jets as kills.

The corporal at the Screw's office hands us some keys to the transit accommodation — the bedding is in the room. We throw our bags in, dismiss any thought of making the bed, and head for the boozer. The rest of the boys are there and we sit around drinking and talking, comparing notes on the drive up. Apparently, Gus came past a Leyland P76 Club coming out of Newcastle in convoy.

'Didn't know they'd even sold that many!'

'So, Gerry, how'd you finish up on grad night?' Gus asks.

'Don't remember much after about nine. Woke up in my bed at eight-thirty the next morning, covered in spew, and old man Adams poking his pace stick at me demanding to know what I did to his daughter the previous night. Fuck, I don't even remember taking her home.'

'Maybe she took herself home?'

'Na, he reckons I took her home pissed, left her unconscious on the patio, hit the doorbell and ran. I spent half of Thursday in his office, him screaming at me, telling me he would charge me with indecent assault.'

'Shit, mate,' Gus grins, 'How'd you get out of it?'

'He let me go for lunch, so I packed the car and fucked off

as fast as I could.' We all laugh. The story has most of the guys rivetted, particularly Gilley. He leans over to me.

'Hey, Dougie,' he whispers, 'she was with me till about one in the morning. We got up to some horizontal gymnastics in the OIC's office. She screamed so loud I thought people would hear her over the band. The girl can suck a grapefruit through a garden hose.'

'Maybe you took her home, Gilley?'

'Yer, maybe? Don't tell Gerry, will ya? If old man Adams comes looking for him, he'll point the finger straight at me.'

'Your secret is safe with me, mate,' I tell him, laughing like shit on the inside.

Monday morning, we are eager. Up early, dressed in blues, and get breakfast at the Mess. After brushing our teeth, we part ways. Nev is off to 481 Squadron along with Merv, Johnno, and Tex. Holmes and Watson to 2 OCU. Gus, Gilley and I head for 77 Squadron.

When we arrive at the Orderly Room, there are a couple of 33 Intake guys already there, O'Hare and Rixon, the framies, and Johnson, the Sumpie. We take our turn handing over envelopes full of documents and are issued with a clearance form. Several of the lines are signed off by the corporal behind the desk and he allocates us a room in the accommodation block.

Out of the Orderly Room, we head for Gunnies Section. Inside the hangar, one of the LACs directs us to the Flight Sergeant's office. We approach and see a dark-haired, middle-aged guy behind the desk busy writing something or other. He has a pair of eyebrows that are twitching as if they have a mind of their own. We knock nervously.

Without looking up, he tells us to wait and he will be with us shortly. Or at least, that's what I think he said. The Scottish accent is thick, I think one of the eyebrows is scowling at me.

'Alright,' he says, looking up, and quickly assessing the three young aircraftmen before him.

'What's your name, lad,' he asks, looking at Gilley.

'Gilmore, Flight.'

'Well, A C Gilmore, I suggest you find some polish for those shoes before I see you again.'

'Yes, Flight.'

'And you two?'

'Walsh and Edwards,' Gus says promptly, with associated gesturing as to who is who.

'Right, well welcome to 77 Squadron, lads. I am Flight Sergeant McIntosh. Can I have those please?' he says, pointing at the envelopes in our hands. He unpacks various bits of paper and enters information in the Roll Book and other ledgers.

'Happy to be free at Wagga Wagga?' he asks.

'Very much so, Flight,' I answer. 'Looking forward to doing some real work.'

'You'll get plenty of that, lad. Who did you have instructing you?'

'Corporals O'Brien, Pike, and Sanders, and Sergeants Tait, Gould, McGleash, Sergeant Davies and Flight Sergeant Bourke.'

'Ah, Dynamite Davies. Did he tell you about the time he had a box of hand grenades to blow up and decided throwing them would be more fun?'

'No,' we all say in unison.

'Aye, next time you see him, ask. And, ask how they fixed the holes in the section truck,' he grins. 'Let's go meet the boss.'

After the meeting, the Armament Officer, Flight Lieutenant Martin, and Flight Sergeant McIntosh sends us to Equipment Section to get issued with ear muffs and a tarmac jacket. One of our highest priorities is to get ourselves a Squadron cap. While we are in blues at the moment and thus have our dress cap on, when we pull on our overalls, it will be giggle hats if don't get a Squadron cap. We'll stick out like dog's balls making you a target for any ridicule, or a lurking WOD.

One of the guys in Equipment Section directs us to Safety Equipment Section where the sergeant relieves us of five dollars each in exchange for a green 77 Squadron cap. The cap bears the symbol from the Squadron crest known as the 'Grumpy Monkey'.

With the clearances finished, we pack our gear away in our new room, change into overalls, and head back to the section with bright Squadron caps firmly on our heads.

'You'll be starting your Mirage course on Tuesday next week,' Flight Sergeant McIntosh tells us. 'Till then, you can work in Carrier Bay with Corporal Mills.' He walks out and we follow through the hangar to a bay in the annexe along the eastern side. We are introduced to the corporal and Flight Sergeant McIntosh disappears. Corporal Mills is a weedy looking guy, probably late twenties, dressed in safety boots, brown RAAF drab socks, and a pair of blue stubbies, pocket on the front right leg with a flap, another pocket right rear, and elastic only at the back.

I don't recall being issued with these.

He instructs us on cleaning barrels and rams from the SUU-20 Practice Bomb Dispenser. He turns a barrel on the wire brush explaining that we should get all the 'black shit' off the outside, but there is no need for it to be shiny and pristine.

'Yes, Corporal,' I respond.

He frowns at me. 'You don't want to be carrying on with that corporal crap around here, mate. Everyone will just think you are an arse kisser.' He looks at me sternly, 'Are you an arse kisser?' He turns and offers me the bared left cheek of his arse. I politely decline and he continues with the instruction without missing a beat.

Wow, that's different.

The rest of the week is spent cleaning black shit from SUU-20s and testing them. It's pretty routine work and doesn't exactly stretch the mind. At each break, the members of the section gather in the Smoko Room for card games. In the first instance, we sit and watch a rowdy exchange of cards which concludes with the loser buying the other players a can of Coke. The Coke comes from the fridge in the Smoko Room which is the sort of fridge you would have in a shop. I have no idea where they got it from. The air is blue with cigarette smoke, ash trays and coffee mugs everywhere, and the odd pie being eaten.

There are various card games played in the Smoko Room. I recognise Euchre and Five Hundred, but there is one game where I have no idea what is going on. It appears you have to follow suit, and there is some sort of points system running, but I cannot quite get it. Eventually, one of the guys calls us over and starts to explain.

'The idea here is not to get points. The one with the most points gets to buy the Cokes,' he says. 'Hearts are all worth points,' he continues. 'Each one is worth one point except the two of hearts which is worth twenty, and the ten of hearts which is worth ten points. The only other card worth anything is the queen of spades, which is worth thirty points. It's known as the "pisser",' he tells us. The dealer takes up the instruction.

'The person on the left of the dealer leads,' he says, nodding to the guy on his left. 'He can lead anything you like except hearts. You can only lead hearts if it's all you have left; same with the queen of spades. Passing to the left,' he says to the participants. Each person picks three cards from their hands and passes them to the player on their left, they then pick up three from the person on their right and add them to their hand. There is some mild cursing from some participants.

At the next hand, the cards are passed right, and the following hand, there is no passing. This is repeated throughout the game. Points are tallied after each hand. At one point, a guy with Reynolds on his name tag leads, a heart early in the hand.

'Burt, you got other suits?'

'Oh, yer.'

'Dickhead,' one of the guys leans over and gives him a smack over the back of the head.

Somewhere in a gentler, more sophisticated world the game is called Rickety Kate or Chase the Lady; here, it's Hunt the Cunt.

The Smoko Room is an interesting place. It's a World War II Nissen Hut, a change room with lockers at one end and Smoko Room at the other. There is a bar, fridge, pie oven, hot water urn, and a table. The walls are festooned with an impressive selection of centrefolds; plenty of boobs on display. A stack of magazines sits atop the bar. Everything from *Australasian Post*, to *Penthouse* and some more intense stuff. There is one magazine with people using whips, ominously titled *Swish*, another featuring anal sex.

Where the hell do they get this stuff?

Intermingled with the centrefolds is a selection of signs apparently 'borrowed' from various locations where the boys have been on exercise. There is a 35 Squadron Orderly Room sign, a Base Squadron Darwin sign, something in Maori I can't pronounce, signs from several different hotels, a COBS sign with a finger pointing, and several WOD Office signs.

The characters in the Smoko Room are likewise diverse. Our first mentor, Corporal Wally Mills, is a man of few words, like grandad, but, when he speaks, you should be listening and he is particularly adept at the one liner. He doesn't take part in the card games and takes his breaks sitting on a bench outside in the sun, dragging on rollies, Tally Ho papers and a tin of Drum tobacco on the seat beside him.

LAC Dan Stewart is usually not too far away. They are good mates and from what I can gather from overhearing the occasional story, they were in Malaysia together not too long ago, and would both prefer to be back there.

Inside the Smoko Room, LAC Joe Byrne holds court. It's like he commands which game gets played, who gets excluded, and has a small and seemingly loyal group of conspirators. Through eye contact and gestures, they connive to land some unsuspecting, wet behind the ears, airman with the Coke bill. There is Misty Reyn, Hipshot, and Hollywood, amongst others, with Terry Evans providing running commentary. Some names bear resemblance to the nametag on their shorts or overalls, some don't.

There must be a story behind them?

The events inside the Smoko Room bear little resemblance to the way guys approach their work tasks. When they walk into the hangar, or onto the flight line, it's all professional. Everyone knows what is going on, helping each other, anticipating the next steps. If you fall behind, there is a helping hand, but only if you have a go. There is a high level of professional pride and attention to detail. No fuck-ups. Do it once, do it right, and no room for any bludgers.

While Mac runs the section, the actual work is controlled by the sergeants; three of them, Lefty Wright, Bob Horn and Toad Williams. They sit in a separate room to everyone else and don't partake in the Smoko Room games. It seems like there is a large social separation between the junior NCOs and those who go to the Sergeants' Mess.

Thursday is pay day and a unique series of events unfold. Pay parade is in the bottom hangar with the entire squadron lining up over a two-hour period, and between aircraft sorties. We shuffle along, hand our pay book over, get the money counted out, step back, salute, 'Pay correct, sir,' left turn, march off only to be intercepted by a corporal selling Hurry Scurry tickets.

Back at the section, there are several women hovering at the Smoko Room door with their hands out — the wives. Respective husbands are approached, the money changes hands, a small amount is returned, and they are off with some haste. Inside the Smoko Room, Squizzy Taylor is sitting in the corner with a cash tin and ledger. He looks at me.

'Walsh, that will be six dollars-twenty.' I am a little taken back.

'I only had a couple of Cokes,' I state, sheepishly.

'Yep, three dollars for the Section Social Club, a dollar for the Squadron Social Club, a dollar for tea, coffee and milk, and three Cokes. Six-twenty.' He puts his hand out. I am still on Apprentice wages and only get one hundred and thirty-four dollars, I am going to have to watch my pennies till full Airmen wages come through.

'Going to the Knuck tonight?' he asks.

'The Knuck?'

'Yer, the Knuck and Fuck.' I must still look perplexed. 'There is a dance on at the Airmen's Club every pay night. They put on a band, or a disco, and a free keg. You can generally expect to get into a fight, or get a fuck, and if you are really lucky, you might get both, Knuck and Fuck,' he laughs.

'Oh, yer, sure.'

I am not sure I need both.

The Knuck turns out to be rowdy affair. A large portion of the Base's enlisted ranks are there; well, a large portion of the single ones, at least. It's easy to tell the Base Squadron guys from the Flying Squadron people. They are the well dressed and courteous ones. The dirty, loud-mouth, guys are from 2 OCU, 77 Squadron which is considered the 'pointy end', or 481 Squadron, and generally clustered by trade, Electricians, RADTECHs, Clock Winders, Truckies, Framies, Sumpies and Gunnies, our mob being particularly rowdy.

Being the new boys, we sit back and watch the exchanges between the groups. Every female who works at the Base seems to be here along with a few from off the Base, but they are still outnumbered by at least three to one. There's too much competition here to get any small talk even started.

Friday morning, and the mail comes in around ten, a letter from Allison included. I quickly devour the words, picking up the scent of the paper. It's small sized paper with flowers along the bottom, only something a girl would do. My letters are usually penned on a bit of foolscap paper, or a sheet from an old exercise book. Lines are essential or I tend to run the words down the page.

Back into it, Gilley is tasked with going to 481 Squadron to pick up some SUU-20 spares. He hops onto the Clarktor and starts the engine. There is the familiar sound of the Holden 186 engine coming to life and Gilley revs it for all it worth.

'You sure you should be driving that?' I ask him. 'We haven't been signed off to operate it yet.'

'Signed off, Dougie? When did you become Mr RAAF Dick? I'm only going to 481. No one will know,' he replies, slipping it into gear and pushing the pedal to the floor. The front end nearly lifts off the ground and he disappears out of the hangar at high speed. Half an hour later, Flight Sergeant McIntosh comes out of his office.

'Which one of you guys took the Clarktor out a half hour ago?' Blank looks all around.

'You boys daren't fuck me around. Two can play that game, and I have a lot more options up my sleeve than you do,' he warns, almost menacingly. Gilley immediately puts his hand up.

'It was me, Flight.'

Mac is shaking his head. It's as if he already knew who the likely culprit was.

'The fucking SENGO just called me and said you were doing about sixty down the tarmac. He wants your arse. And to top it off, you don't even have a fucking licence to drive it, lad.'

'It was never sixty, Flight. The bloody thing wouldn't go that fast. Oh, well, hang on, unless you took the governor off.'

Fuck, Gilley, you are playing with fire here. How the fuck did you manage to say that with a straight face?

Flight Sergeant McIntosh explodes into a series of swear words and Scottishisms, most of which cannot be understood, spit flying and eyebrows twitching. I don't know what he just said, but it sounds really terrible. He might just blow a gasket.

'Into my office, NOW.' Gilley comes back with a glum look.

'He gave me Guard Duty for the weekend.'

'Does Mr RAAF Dick get to say I told you so?'

Thursday, the elation of our first week at the sharp-end is broken with the announcement of the Ashes side to tour England. They have dropped one K D Walters. I listen to news on the radio dumbfounded. My mind goes back to the Perth Test, 1974, a century in a session hooking Bob Willis over the fence on the last ball of the day. I remember grandad telling me about his debut against England in Brisbane, 1965. He came in at 4 for 125 and got 155.

'He just saved our arses against India and New Zealand,' I plead back at the radio. My words at the RSL last weekend come back to me ominously.

Friday afternoon, Nev, Gus and I head into Newcastle in Nev's HQ. My recollection of Newcastle is pretty vague, but I manage to get us over Kooragang Island, along the Industrial Highway past the steel works, down past the wool sheds, and onto Wharf Road. We go past the RAAF crash boat on Wharf Road, the ice works, and we find somewhere to park down near the train station. We walk up Watt Street to Hunter Street.

We peruse a few clothes shops and get a couple of pairs of stubbies that are close to the colour of our overalls. They look pretty much the same as the ones CPL Mills has. We then purchase a couple of records at Palings and wander back down Watt Street stopping at The George for a quick sherbet. While I am still six months off my eighteenth birthday, I have mastered the art of acting like I am an old hand, and if I ever get challenged about my age, flashing the RAAF ID Card is usually enough to bluff my way out of any possible trouble.

'What'd you get, Dougie?' Nev enquires, looking at the Palings bag.

I pull a 45 vinyl out of the bag. 'It's a Pommie band, *The Bureau.* The song's called 'Only for Sheep'.'

'Sounds like something Merv would get off on, or is this one for EWE?' Nev asks. He has to spell it out for us; the joke is a little too agricultural for some. Gus gets on board, albeit a little slow on the uptake,

'Don't be thinking you can pull the wool over my eyes there, Dougie.'

'Yeah, thanks, boys, I think I'll head back to the baaaaaar, it must be my shout."

The quick sherbet turns into three and we have a little glow by the time we get back into the HQ. The ride back to Base is a little quicker, singing along to Creedence on the radio.

'There's a bathroom on the right.'

Back at Base, Gilley is checking credentials at the front gate. We just cruise through getting the finger in return. The evening meal is waived in favour of more beer at the boozer.

Saturday is a quick trip to Dungog. We pick up the Corolla from Max, have lunch at home, and then help with the afternoon milking, driving the Corolla back to Base afterwards.

Sunday after breakfast, I find a sunny spot and start scribbling an account of my first week at RAAF Base, Williamtown, to Allison. It's kind of fun describing the Base and the characters that are now part of my life. I never imagined I would be working with such a crazy mob. If you believe the TV commercials, they are our country's finest.

Sunday afternoon we take the Corolla out to Shoal Bay for a swim and a few beers at the country club. Gilley gives us the finger again as we come back though the main gate. He's not a happy camper.

Tuesday morning rolls around and we report for the Mirage course at 481 Squadron, Field Training Flight. It's the usual suspects, Nev, Merv, Fraz, Jerry, Watto, Johnno, Gus, Gilley and me, all newly arrived ACs. There are two other guys on the course, a corporal from Edinburgh who is posted to 75 Squadron and an LAC from Amberley posted to 3 Squadron. Both need a Mirage course before going to Malaysia.

Our instructor is Sergeant Anderson. He's been around Mirages for years and there isn't much he doesn't know about this jet; a walking encyclopaedia. The first few days are spent on the general aircraft safety and familiarisation including engine performance, the various fuel loads, oxy system, etcetera. By weeks end, we have passed the first progress test and moved onto the egress system.

It's Saturday and Nev has fucked off to Wagga Wagga to visit Heather. Merv is at his sister's place in Sydney.

What the fuck am I going to do today?

I am reluctant to go home to Dungog. Grandma will only

pester me about Louise again and I don't have the strength to think about it.

I start writing another letter to Allison; more stories of my first two weeks. I would have gone to Sydney to see her, but in her last letter, she said she had tutorials on most weekends. She reckons Easter is the best time to come.

Letter done. What now? Town perhaps?

Some of the guys are going to The Terrace for a session at the JI, I could always go in there. I am contemplating my movements when Gilley throws my door open.

'What's happening, Dougie?' he asks, taking a seat and picking up the *Australasian Post*, thumbing through the pages.

'I'm thinking of buying another car,' he goes on without waiting for my response. 'Can you give me a lift to town to check out some?'

'Sure. I'll just have a quick tub.' By the time I am back, Gus has joined us and wants to come along. On the way into town, we try and tease out what sort of car he is after.

'Dunno.' He contemplates the question. 'Wanted another V8, but not sure I can afford the fuel. A four cylinder would be most economical, but it's for bloody poofters.

'You could always walk,' I respond, giving the dash of the Corolla a stroke.

'Maybe a Commodore,' he goes on. Gus gives me a cheeky smile, the one that says that one has gone through to the keeper without so much as a swish of the bat.

We spend the next few hours walking around yards on Tudor Street, looking at every second-hand car in town. Most are either way outside Gilley's budget, and far too *poncie* for him to be seen in. I tell him I get 35 miles to the gallon out of the Corolla, but he is not impressed.

'How about we head to the Terrace,' Gus suggests. 'There's a couple of yards there and we could drop into the JI for a couple. This is bloody thirsty work.'

I take the car up over the railway line and onto Maitland Road into Islington.

Gilley suddenly gets all excited, 'Stop the car, Dougie. That's it there,' he says, pointing. I pull the Corolla up out the front of a used car yard. It looks pretty sleazy to me. Gilley almost runs to the gate, walking around a bronze Falcon. A salesman saunters out of the office.

'Might be a bit tough for you to handle, young fella. It's got a 351 Cleveland under the bonnet with extractors, a high-rise manifold and a four-barrel Holley, not to mention ported and polished heads, oversized valves, lumpy cam and a few other bits and pieces. Guy had the engine built for his racing boat and decided it was a waste in the water.'

I take a look at the sales slip in the window. It's a 74 XB GT and they want four grand for it — only got two months rego.

'You might need to tow a fuel tanker,' I suggest, giving the engine bay a look. Gus is in the passenger seat opening the glove box and pushing buttons, checking to see if the cassette player works. Gilley is in the driver's seat, running his hands over the Aunga steering wheel. He won't take much encouragement; he's foaming at the mouth and the salesman can smell the kill.

'You can get twenty-five to the gallon if you drive it right.'

'What? Downhill with the engine off and a tailwind?' I ask. The salesman gives me a dirty look.

I definitely wouldn't buy a used car off this guy. Shit, I wouldn't buy a can of Coke from this guy!

'How much?' Gilley is cutting to the chase.

'I'll just duck into the office and see what I can do for you,' the salesman calls over his shoulder.

'You sure about this one?' I try to get Gilley to reconsider. 'It's got a bit of rust here and there.'

'It's only surface stuff, Dougie. We can cut that out.'

'Who's we, white man?' The salesman comes back.

'I can do it for three-seven, less for cash, the bloody donk is worth more than that,' he says.

'I'll have to go and see the bank for a loan,' he's thinking out loud. Bad move, the salesman is moving in for the final kill.

'I can do finance for you if you like and you can have the car today,' salesman smiles.

Gilley's eyes light up. The salesman has the keys in his hand and gets in and turns it over. The noise that follows is a strange mix of violence and sex, mixed in with how a 3000-pound kitten might purr. Gilley is sold.

Gus and I wait until most of the paperwork is done. I am not sure exactly how much this will cost him, but my simple arithmetic has worked out somewhere around five-and-a-half thousand dollars. Expensive car.

'Hey, Gilley, we are heading to the JI. See you there,' I tell him. He gives us the thumbs up.

Gus and I are just going over Ironbark Creek bridge when I see the bronze Falcon approaching in the mirror.

'Take a look at this, Gus,' I say, gesturing to the mirror. It's not in my mirror for long, going past us at speed. 'I'm doing ninety,' I tell Gus.

'Fuck,' is all Gus can muster.

On arrival at the JI, Gilley is in the front bar, half a schooner gone, telling a sceptical audience what a great deal he got, the bronze Falcon on display out the window. From a distance it doesn't look bad, but I know it doesn't stand up well to close scrutiny.

Over the coming weeks, Gilley offers to chauffeur us on most outings, movies, shopping, drinking trips. We attend the end-of-course piss-up at the Spinning Wheel Hotel, Sergeant Anderson holding court, regaling us with stories of pilots stuffing up bombing runs, nearly hitting the troops doing the scoring, and missiles almost shooting down the aircraft they were fired from. Gilley drives us back to Base. I've noticed he actually drives better with four of five schooners in him, or maybe I'm less frightened after a few beers, who can tell.

One thing's for sure, the car is fast, very fast, and Gilley's driving seems to be finding the limits of what it will do, while we hang on for dear life. The car has been dubbed 'The Interceptor' after Mad Max's XB Falcon.

Perhaps I need a nickname for the Corolla? Dougie's Green Sewing Machine? The DGSM?

First Monday in April and I'm in early, excited to get out and work at the real pointy end on the flight line. I'm on my second coffee and don't want to be late, I'm getting antsy. My assigned trainer for the next week, Billy Gibson, turns up with about thirty seconds to spare. Billy is one of the senior troops in the section.

He gives me a 'what's your problem' look as he changes into overalls and pulls on his boots, slowly and deliberately makes himself a brew and inhales a cigarette in about five long drags.

We amble towards the flight line. I can feel my eagerness is acting like a handbrake on Billy. We enter the line hut and run straight into Flight Sergeant McIntosh who stops us in our tracks and makes a point of taking a long look at his watch. He's not happy — those eyebrows are doing their thing — Billy is completely unfazed. Mac heads out the door and we head into a second room where what looks like a row of logbooks are laid out.

The place is buzzing with people, NCOs giving instructions, a sergeant listing aircraft tail numbers on a blackboard; it's all pretty hectic. Billy is not a big talker. All I can do at this point is become his shadow and ask questions. He has scribbled a few numbers on his palm, turns and heads out to the line of jets.

I get shoulder to shoulder with him as we head out to a jet.

'What are we doing?'

'BFs,' he says. BF is short for Before Flight Servicing, making sure the aircraft is fit to fly. For us today that's pretty easy, there is no armament on these jets so our only area of responsibility is the ejection seat. It's kind of important if everything goes to shit and the pilot has to get out in a hurry.

Billy climbs up the ladder, does a quick check of the safety pins for the ejection seat, and then steps in to stand on the seat cushion. He looks down and motions for me to climb the ladder. He points out various components around the seat. We are looking to make sure connections are correct, that lock-wiring is secure, and the parachute and harness neatly arranged just so. Billy is done here and motions me to climb down.

We wander over to the next jet and he nudges me up the ladder first. Okay, brain in gear, safety pins in place, step into the seat, start working my way clockwise around the seat. Billy is leaning against one of the supersonic tanks, watching the tarmac traffic. When I am done, he escorts me to the next jet. Once I have finished the task, I have no idea whether I did it right or not.

What is it with this guy?

Four more jets and we head back into the line hut. Billy signs for all the BFs, then tells me he is going for a brew. He disappears and I settle into a seat; *Romper Room* on the TV.

Ten minutes later, the Desk Sergeant calls for Crew 3 to launch a jet. I realise that Billy's name is up against Crew 3; him and Andy Stephens. I look around and see a tall guy with yellow earmuffs gathering his tools. I approach him sheepishly.

'You working with Billy?' he asks.

'Yeah, mate.'

'Our jet is going a little earlier than planned. Test flight. Where is he?' I tell him Billy went for a brew. He's not perturbed.

'Come on, I'll walk you through this till he gets here, it's all pretty simple.'

As we wander out to the line of jets, Andy explains the tasks sequentially, the basic signals, what not to do, where not to go, and how to operate the blower.

We start the power cart next to the jet and plug it in, Andy climbs the ladder, removing the cockpit safety harness, checking the ejection seat safety pins are in, and making sure the power cart is actually providing power.

'Take the covers off, Dougie,' he yells above the noise.

Shortly after, a guy in a green flying overalls and G suit strides purposefully in our direction. I stand back and Andy greets him.

'Morning, Sir.'

'Morning, Andy.' He's a young Flying Officer, only looks a

couple of years older than me. He hangs his helmet on the ladder and starts looking around the jet, tapping on this, shoving that, leaning on something else, giving the tyres a kick, it all looks part of a well thought out procedure. I take a look around to see if Billy is on his way, still nowhere to be seen.

Why am I not surprised?

Our pilot is up the ladder and into the cockpit. Andy follows and he's helping him to strap in. Within a couple of minutes, the helmet is passed up and connected. He calls for the third undercarriage handle to be reset. The ejection seat safety pins are then pulled out and stashed. Andy climbs down and pulls the ladder, motioning to me to get the blower started and into position.

The pilot gives the start engine signal twirling a finger to Andy who passes it along to me. I rev the blower up and hold it, the tube inside the intake, pushing air to the front of the engine. I can hear the engine starter turning and a few seconds later there is a roar as the engine winds up.

The combination of air sucking down the intake, and the intense noise is incredible. While that is happening, the undercarriage doors come up as the hydraulic pressure builds. The jet settles to idle.

I crouch down and run back under the jet, squatting next to the power plugs. Andy is already giving me the signal to pull them out and I give them a sharp tug, carefully closing the panel. Andy now gives the signal to pull out the wheel chocks and I have to kick the back one out before dragging them out of the way.

I position myself under the tail pipe where I can see both wings. I can feel the heat from the exhaust just above my head.

He gives a thumbs-up to the pilot and seconds later our jet is revving up, moving forward, the noise increasing, me following in a low crouch. The aircraft suddenly stops, nose bouncing up and down. I look to check both pitch dampers are working as they should, opposite to the movement of the aircraft's nose. Two thumbs-up from me, and Andy gives two thumbs to the pilot. I make my way to the power cart as the pilot quickly reapplies the throttle and taxies away, waving goodbye as he goes. Andy wanders my way and pats me on the shoulder.

'Perfect, Dougie, absolutely perfect.'

What a relief that is.

A Mirage flight line operation is an interesting thing to watch. At times there are multiple jets coming and going simultaneously, the Line Corporal coordinating the various teams of two who launch and recover the jets. Inside, the Desk Sergeant controls which aircraft gets allocated to which pilot to meet the flying program.

While this is happening, there are various other people literally crawling all over the jets. The Brake Chute guy is pulling out the spent brake chute container from above the engine exhaust and replacing it, the Engine Oils guy topping things up, the Oxygen guy is with his Mini Moke and oxy cart, and Queer-Traders are reading the fatigue meter. It seems frenetic, but everyone seems to know exactly what they are doing and what each other are doing.

There are no airs and graces at 77 Squadron. Everyone is called by their nickname, the sergeants, corporals, everyone. It's a completely different experience to Wagga Wagga where everyone was addressed by their rank. Even the Warrant Officer

Engineering, the WOE, is called by his nickname, Bones. That is until something goes wrong, then he is most definitely Sir.

Mid-afternoon, there is a ruckus. Something has gone wrong in the hangar during an undercarriage retraction test and everyone has gathered to watch the inquisition. I don't know what it was, but there is a sergeant saying, 'Sorry, Sir. Yes, Sir. We will check that, sir,' to Bones. He doesn't look happy.

Mental note. Don't fuck with Bones.

After the jets are covered for the night, I return to the section and find Billy in the Smoko Room sucking on a fag.

'Are we done for the day?'

'Yer, everything is locked, blocked and chocked,' I say, proudly.

'Good, I'm bushed.' He gets up, stubs out his smoke, and heads for the change room.

Bushed. He hasn't lifted a screwdriver in anger all day!

My blood is started to bubble.

I am about to head to the piss shack for a beer and see the bronze Falcon in the hangar with Gilley under the bonnet.

'What's going on, Gilley?'

'Fitting a tacho, Dougie. This thing has a lot of torque and I want to make sure I don't tear the arse out of it or over rev it.'

'Need a hand?'

'No, mate, this is easy. I'll see you at the shack shortly.'

On Tuesday and Wednesday, work isn't too dissimilar from Monday's training, Andy guiding me through the various tasks that I have to master, and Billy making cameo appearances, mostly at times when his absence would attract attention. He is the master of doing nothing.

Thursday is night flying, so we get a sleep-in, have lunch, and rock into work around 1600. We are assigned a launch at 1900, the tasks are becoming routine for me and I am confident. After going through the pre-flight checks and strap-in, the pilot hits the 'start' button. It's turning but the customary roar doesn't eventuate. He tries a second time, to no avail.

Andy runs over to the Line Corporal and they exchange signals. He comes back to the jet, and a couple of minutes later I see two guys on a Clarktor with a metal rubbish bin sitting on the front. They pull up near our jet, grab the bin, which looks heavy, and then manoeuvre it up to the jet exhaust and empty it — it's full of water.

The bin is out of the way and Andy is signalling the pilot to try again. I crank the blower up again and the engine is starting to wind up. There is a little smoke and then the more familiar sound of a proper start. As the air starts sucking into the intake, I withdraw the blower and look back. A fireball starts flicking from the exhaust, it's getting bigger, and bigger. A huge flame and flaming liquid running out of the jet exhaust onto the ground.

Fuck, a fire.

I quickly throw the blower aside and feel myself run around in a circle, twice.

Where is the fire extinguisher? Fuck, what do I do?

The Line Corporal appears at my side, putting a calming hand on my shoulder. He signals that I should remove the power cables and the chocks.

That's okay for you to say. There's a fucking fire under there!

He pushes me forward and I hurriedly remove the power and the chocks. Andy, cool as a cucumber, just signals the pilot to taxi the aircraft forward, the jet blast extinguishing the flame on the tarmac. There is no panic. Everything is under control. It looks like something that happens every day.

I think I have shat myself.

Back inside, Bones is waiting for me.

'You didn't know what to do when the fire started,' he challenges. Andy has a concerned look and jumps to my defence.

'Fair go, Sir. He's OJT this week.'

'OJT?' There is surprise in Bone's voice. 'Who is rostered on with him?' I realise this is serious and think quickly.

'Billy. He's got a dose of the shits, sir. Ran off to the dunny right before engine start,' I lie.

'You better get him in here.' Bones is standing, waiting, there is no room for negotiation. I run off and find Billy watching Sale of the Century in the Smoko Room. When we get back, there is an interrogation.

'Walsh is under training, where were you?'

'I went to get dinner and told them to come and get me if our pilot walked.' Billy's response is convincing and my gut tightens.

Bones is considering the response. He has just had two conflicting versions of events and I can tell he is not in the mood. He looks us both in the eye.

'You fucking Gunnies had better get your shit together. That incident out there nearly got someone hurt, and I am not about to let that happen. Now, the two of you fuck off and come back tomorrow. And, you had better have your shit in a nice, neat, organised pile when you do.'

I look at Andy and he shrugs in resignation. Bones is glaring at us. I follow Billy out the door.

'You never said to come and get you. You never said anything like it. You have been sitting on your arse all week letting me do all the work.' He turns, glaring back at me.

'You bloody people and your "jump when I say jump" horseshit can go get fucked. I am sick of you people. Nothing ever runs on time here, but they always want us there ahead of time so we can stand around scratching our balls looking at each other.'

He gathers himself a little and starts again.

'I arrive on time and get shit for it. I get the fucking job done. Why does everything have to be a race? They don't hand out medals for being first around here. So, in future, you let me worry about where I am and when I'm there. It's none of your fucking business, fucking pimply-faced little RAAF dick.' He storms off.

Friday morning, and I am greeted by Mac as I walk into work. He pulls me into his office and closes the door behind me.

'Problem, Flight?' I ask.

'There was a problem last night.' The eyebrows are twitching. He's obviously not happy. 'I was told you saw out an aircraft without Billy and there was a fire. Where the bloody hell was he?'

I explain that Billy had gone off for dinner and our pilot walked early, and I didn't get a chance to go after him. He's looking at me, summing up what I have said. His look changes slightly.

'Okay, it's your last day of training. Make sure you have covered off on everything with Billy today, including the wet start procedure. You will be on your own next week. Off you go.'

Billy and I get into the flight line right on 0730. Bones is there and eyeballs us straight away. Over the course of the morning, I sense Bones' oversight, and Billy hasn't left my side.

Friday afternoon, and we are finished by 1300 and I head

back to the section. I am only a few weeks into my new posting and still finding it intriguing. The Squadron Warrant Officer is happy to be called Bones, depending on the circumstances, but our Gunnies' Flight Sergeant still requires us to call him 'Flight'.

Upon arrival, I find Gilley has the bonnet of the bronze Falcon up again, Dan Stewart and Wally Mills providing oversight.

'What are you fitting now, Gilley?'

'He's still trying to get the tacho working,' replies Dan.

'Like everything he does, it's at a million miles an hour, with no attention to detail.'

'Hey, Tacho, I've got five bucks you will be here again Monday afternoon,' Dan says.

'No one is going to take you on with odds like this,' Wally replies, 'though I could sell tickets just for the comic relief.'

The boys are not disappointed. When I knock off flight line on Monday afternoon, Gilley has the Falcon in the hangar again trying to fault-find the tacho.

'Bloody Hell, I can't stand this any fucking more,' Wally motions Gilley out of the way. Within ten minutes, the engine is revving, tacho functioning perfectly, and Wal is explaining to Gilley the problem and some basic fault-finding techniques.

'You didn't ground the gauge properly, Tacho,' almost spitting out the word 'tacho'.

'When we get to do this on aircraft, I need you to use your brain. You got it, Tacho?'

'Thanks, Wal, I will remember it.'

Over the ensuing weeks, the Falcon gets a hiding, and Tacho has been firmly embraced by everyone as Gilley's new nickname. His favourite party trick is to see what speed he can get the

Falcon up to on the short straight between Nelson Bay Road and the main gate to the Base, usually with detailed commentary.

'When you get to here, you point the nose of the car a little short of the apex allowing for a bit of understeer to drop back into second. We are doing forty here.' I can hear the tyres fighting for something like traction and feel the front end pushing, not wanting to go where it's being pointed. As the car starts to change direction, he applies a less than subtle amount of throttle.

'You have to dial in some opposite lock here. It goes from understeer to oversteer. Feel that? Second, third, 70mph and 6500rpm, third to fourth at 115mph and 7000rpm.' The front gate is looming fast. Suddenly, both feet go on the brake pedal trying to push it through the floor panel.

'Back into second gear, the brakes have done all they can.' Both back wheels are locked by the gearbox and the car starts to drift sideways. As he lines up with the main drag, he hits the pedal again. ID is flashed at the guard, and down the main drag at a speed considerably faster than the 30k limit. He looks over at me with the widest grin. It's great for a laugh, even better half pissed.

'Mach 1.2 have to work out how to carry more speed through that corner.' For some reason he has started to use 100mph as Mach 1. I guess this working on fighter jets is wearing off on him.

Easter has snuck up, and it's going to be pretty quiet around Williamtown. Merv's off to Cootamundra, Gus is going camping at Seal Rocks with some of the guys from the section, and Tacho and Nev are off to Wagga Wagga. It's quite funny how we all complained about being at Wagga Wagga while we were posted there, and now half the boys are spending their weekends down there.

Fascinating what the prospect of sex will do to a bloke.

Tacho has been calling Jenny Adams and he seems to think she is up for a bit more horizontal gymnastics. He is going to ride shotgun with Nev. They'll stay in the Apprentice Block with the remaining guys from our Intake. Heather's old man still doesn't know anything about Nev. She is eighteen now and doesn't have to justify her presence as much. They spend a lot of time in town, at the pictures, or shagging in the back seat of his car.

I don't think it's going to last, though. Heather's old man is posted to Adelaide and there's no real doubt she will be going with her parents. Nev asked her if she wanted to move in with him in Newcastle, but she is pretty close to her mum and it's a bit too much for her. We are all a bit young to be getting that serious anyway.

Speaking of getting serious, my own love life is in need of some serious consideration. I was supposed to be heading to Sydney to see Allison this weekend, but she is heading back to Wagga Wagga to see Bob and Nancy. I would have taken her down there, but the letter said 'see you in a couple of weeks'. Clearly not an invitation to Wagga.

Maybe I have been given the arse?

I haven't had any contact from Louise either. I really should go up and see her, but that's a bit rich, deciding to see one girl because the other one won't see me. Although I am feeling a little lonely, it's not the right thing to do. I think a trip to the farm is in order.

The road will be full of lunatics going north for the weekend on Thursday afternoon so I decide to shift my stuff into Andy's room. The guy he was sharing with went to Butterworth and he offered the room to me rather than have some cock he doesn't know moving in. Besides, he's got a stereo set-up, a good collection of records, a lounge chair, fridge, and a bean bag; very comfortable.

Friday morning, we sleep in and grab some breakfast at the Mess. Andy is going up to the Bay for the day and I take a leisurely drive up to the farm. Grandad is finishing morning tea when I arrive.

'Couldn't be here for the milking? They are making you soft. You can start with spreading some super down on the river paddock.' He walks off towards the hay shed. Gran's welcome is a little more pleasant. There's a cup of tea, iced VoVos, the standard enquiry about contact with Louise, before telling me to get on with my jobs too.

Last year, I started to think I didn't fit in here anymore. I might have been a little hasty. I can hide out here for a few days, think about things, then get back into the rat race.

ANZAC Day rolls around. I'd really like to go to Dungog and march with grandad and Uncle Bert, but Mac tells me we are marching in Newcastle and attendance is not optional. A RAAF bus leaves the Airmen's Club at eight. We line up and march down Hunter street and then to the service in Civic Park.

Afterwards, Gus, Andy and I have a few drinks at the RSL, then the Air Force Association on Scott Street. The old guys in the Air Force Association are a hoot. They love telling a story. I muse over the various historical items, flags, and honour boards around the room; loads of items, some dating back to World War I. It strikes me that some squadrons are actually older than the Air Force, and the RAAF wasn't officially created until 1921.

Then I start wondering why they didn't teach us any of this stuff during basic training. These old guys have been shot at, starved, and now they are commemorating their losses, remembering their mates who didn't come home. Seems to me that my generation should be a whole lot more involved with them, and that the RAAF really doesn't encourage that connection.

I wonder if the other services do any better.

The ladies are badgering us now to eat. There is a table full of sandwiches, little boys, sausage rolls, lamingtons, cakes, and there is no more beer until we have. One lady takes a particular shine to Gus.

'You look so handsome in that uniform. Just like my Dicky when he was young.'

'Might be time for us to push on, Dougie. I don't want to be impolite, but she has a gleam in her eye that is a little scary.'

'Okay, Nev and the boys are over at Stockton. You want to catch the ferry over and join them?'

As we cross the railway overpass to Wharf Road, there are three girls going the other way, probably about our age.

I give them a 'Hi' and put on my most charming smile. They just giggle a little and laugh loudly once we are past them, obviously not looking for a boy in uniform. As we wait for the ferry, I am contemplating my love life, or lack of it.

Allison in Sydney, Lou is in Armidale, and neither are showing signs of interest in me. And right now, I can't even strike up a conversation with a couple of Newcastle scrubbers.

'You are a million miles away, Dougie. What's going on in that head of yours?'

'Not much, Gus, just thinking about girls.' I survey the harbour for a while. He waits. 'It's not that I am looking for marriage or anything weird like that, but I would like to have a decent run at a relationship that lasts more than a few weeks. It would be nice to go out dancing with someone and go to the pictures.'

'Early days yet, Dougie. Cool it and try the field a bit,' he suggests.

'Yep, maybe you're right, but first I want to find out if there is any chance that Allison and I are going to be in a relationship.'

Off the ferry, we stop at The Washtub for one drink, but they are three-deep at the bar, so we continue on to the RSL.

The boys are engrossed in a Two-Up game. Nev is half tanked and taking fifty-dollar bets, Merv acting as his bagman. Every time Nev has more than two hundred in his hands, Merv relieves him of it. He has the Midas touch today; everything he touches is turning to gold. As we watch, he takes a grunt for fifty on four consecutive throws. The grunt is getting pissed off and decides to drop out. Nev then fleeces a RADTECH from 2OCU for a hundred. It's amazing to watch.

I had seen Two-Up rings at the Dungog RSL, but nothing as intense as this. They are four-deep around a large piece of carpet on the dance floor. The noise is incredible and could be compared to a Mirage running with a full after-burner. Various denominations are changing hands from one- and two-dollar notes, right up to fifties. The predominant bet is five dollars.

A half hour later, the grunt is back looking to exact revenge. After Nev takes him for another two fifties in succession, it's on. The grunt throws a hay maker at Nev's head which he ducks with some ease, landing one on the grunt's chin in return. Merv takes the money from Nev's other hand and backs off, these boys might need some room to sort this out.

It's a real David and Goliath match with weedy little Nev taking on a six-foot Artillery private, built like the proverbial brick shithouse. The Two Up is suspended whist Nev toys with him around the ring, some bets are exchanged on the outcome of the fight. The grunt has enough sense to know that if he stands back, Nev is going to dodge him, so he comes in close grabbing Nev around the shoulders and head. He's a tough little bugger and give his larger opponent sound resistance. Then there is a blood curdling scream. The grunt releases Nev grabbing his arm.

'The little black cunt bit me,' he screams. The room goes quiet. There is an obvious set of teeth marks on his forearm.

'You shouldn't stick your arm in my mouth you dickhead.' Nev laughs.

Two big guys appear out of nowhere and separate the two, one grabbing Nev in an arm lock. He is frogmarched from the room and to the front door, Merv, Gus and I in pursuit. He throws Nev down the front steps.

'Fuck off you little black prick, and don't come back.'

I take a step forward thinking I am going to knock this dickhead's block off. Gus grabs me and pulls me away.

'Not the time for it, Dougie,' Merv nodding agreement.

'And you other RAAF cocks had better fuck off too if you know what's good for you.' The big guy disappears back inside, Gus and Merv have probably just saved the situation getting out of control. Realising my stupidity, I turn to Nev.

'You right, mate?'

'Yer, I am okay.' He takes his time straightening his uniform and taking his hat from Merv.

'I have seen this all before. Black fella having a good time, some guy takes a dislike and a swing, black fella defends himself, and it's the black fella that gets thrown out. I should know by now.'

'Bullshit, Nev, fact is that idiot grunt was just a sore loser.' I tell him. But none of us really have any answers and we all look a little dumbfounded. It's hard for Nev, harder than any of us could possibly imagine.

'Well, what are we going to do now trendsetters, stand around like stale bottles of piss or what?' asks Merv.

As if on cue, the bronze Falcon roars into view, a four-wheel slide, turning one hundred and eighty degrees, blue smoke coming off the wheels, sliding almost gracefully into the parking space opposite the RSL. The window is down and Tacho leans out grinning from ear to ear, sunglasses on.

'You ladies need a lift somewhere?' We all look at each other and piss ourselves laughing, piling into the car giving Tacho the story on the end of the Two Up game.

'What about pizza boys?' he asks.

'Pizzas gotta taste better than that fuckin' grunt's hairy arm, I'm in,' responds Nev, with a grin.

Soon after, we are sitting by the harbour watching the big ships come and go, eating, and drinking cans. 'One Hundred, two, three' Merv is counting intently. 'Nev, you are thirteen hundred and forty dollars richer, congratulations, I think it might be your shout.' We all piss ourselves laughing again.

'That grunt can shout us a few more beers I reckon,' Nev

holding up fifty bucks. Supplies are refilled before Tacho runs us back to Base at speed, 'The Boys Light Up' is on the tape player, and everyone's singing.

'Beautiful people, got a rubber politician in their travel bag.'

What a great day, Lest We Forget.

The following week, we are getting ready for Air to Air Gunnery. I get dispatched with Corporal Henry Lawson and Stan Lee, alias 'the knife', to undertake ammunition preparation. We grab the section Clarktor, hook up a couple of F-Type trolleys, and off we go down the taxiway toward the engine run up area. When we pull up at J Group, there is an LAC sitting in the little office at the entrance, feet on the desk, reading porn.

We jump off the Clarktor and approach the office, Henry leading. He walks in, greets the LAC like they have known each other for years, and picks three red disks from the off the hooks, hand one each to Stan and I.

'How's things, Matt?'

'Not too bad, Henry. You here for the ammo?'

'Nah, mate, thought maybe you could help me out with my haemorrhoids.' The LAC gets up, walking out the door, mumbling.

'You want Vaseline this time?' Hopping onto the forklift and roaring off down the road into J Group, we get onto the Clarktor and take off in hot pursuit. A half hour later, we head off to Ammo Prep to start the work. I am looking at the size of the task.

This isn't going to be a fun day.

With three trailers, each holding four pallets, and each pallet holding sixty-four galleys, we have our work cut out for us. A galley is a round steel container with a steel lid holding thirty rounds of linked 30mm DEFA ammunition, in this case is practice ammunition. The rounds are belted with steel links and come out of the galley rolled in a coil. All up, each galley full of ammunition weighs about 20kg.

Throughout the day, we proceed to unload the galleys from the pallets, take the lid off, remove the 30 round belts and put them nose down on the floor, apply an 'Empty Label' to the galley, and repack the empty galleys onto the pallet. A single evolution of this process is not back breaking, but the repetitive nature of the work gets my blood pumping. My two team mates have obviously done this before and work like machines.

I have had hard days working on the farm, particularly if you are doing something like digging post holes by hand, or loading hay bales, but this is some bloody tough stuff. By lunch time, I am well and truly ready for food.

After lunch, eight different colours of paint are poured into small trays to a prescribed depth. Then we insert the nose of the bullets into the paint leaving a heavy cover on the projectiles, then leave each belt to dry on brown paper.

The different colours of paint are important. When the guns are fired at the air to air target, each aircraft has ammo with different coloured paint. When the projectile hits the target, which is a mesh banner, its leaves a trace of paint on the target. After the target is recovered, we can count how many hits each pilot has made on the target ... or not!

This dipping process is even more back breaking than the unpacking. But Henry and Stan just keep going and going, long after I have reached what I thought was my physical limit. Those beers will go down well tonight!

Monday morning, it's an early start. I am still rostered onto a crew with Henry and Stan and they give me instructions on how to arm the Gun Pack.

'The idea here, Dougie, is to get a round under the firing pin of each gun. How many times will we need to turn the gun over to get a round up the spout?' I think back to my Wagga Wagga training. There are five chambers in the cylinder, that means it would take four evolutions to arm the gun.

'Four.'

'Good, Dougie. Okay, it's a two-person job. Stan is going to operate the speed brace. Your job is to make sure rounds are coming down into the gun properly and to rack the gun over. I'll show you.'

While Henry is putting a strap up through the feed unit and pulling the ammo down into the gun, Stan is inserting the worm drive and gear box. A speed brace goes onto the gear box and he starts winding.

'See how the rounds have started to come down into the gun.' He's gesturing with is head. 'That means the slides are coming toward the back. See the sprockets turning in the feed unit?' I look over his shoulder into the unit.

'Yep.' Stan stops winding.

'Okay, the slides are all the way back. I am going to rack the gun over and Stan is going to let the slides go forward.' I am listening intently. 'Now, you need to remember this tip as long as you live.' He looks me square in the eye. 'Never, never, stand behind the gun when it's being armed. You know why?' Again, I stretch my mind back to my training, sifting through information, searching for the answer.

'No,' I say, hesitantly.

Henry racks the gun and an instant later Stan lets the slides go forward. There is the sound of metal objects operating at high speed, the return springs doing their job. Then a metal object comes hurtling out the back of the gun. Henry stands and walks over to pick it up.

'Because, there is always some cunt who forgot to take the test round out of the gun when they serviced it,' he says, holding up a dummy 30mm bullet.

'Or some cunt didn't disarm it properly last time,' chips in Stan.

'It's right at balls height too. You wouldn't want to cop one in the gonads. Might damage your plans to have children. Now, your turn on the strap.'

We finish arming the gun pack and then I have the privilege of getting on the speed brace when we arm the second one. By the third pack, I am feeling semi comfortable with what I'm doing.

Next step is arming the jet. Stan's on the Jammer. A Jammer is a little, low, bomb lift truck with rear wheel steering, hydraulic lift arms and an adjustable tray. I have no idea why it's called a 'Jammer'. It just is. Stan picks up the first gun pack and drives toward the aircraft while Henry shows me how to put the barrels into the aircraft. Stan drives forward then operates the hydraulics lifting the pack under the Aircraft's gun bay.

'The good Jammer drivers can get the gun pack into position without any adjustment from the tray,' Henry tells me. 'Now we clip the three cables into place. You get that one there,' pointing.

In the time it takes for me to get one cable hooked in, he's done the other two. He checks my cable then thumbs up to Stan, the tray drops and he reverses away quickly.

'Get the winch, Dougie.' When I get back, he continues the instruction.

'Speed brace goes in here and you wind until the pack is all the way up. I'll check to see that it's going in straight. Once it's up, tighten the four bolts here, here, here and here,' he says, pointing. 'Stan will lock the barrels in and do the Type 15 test on both guns. Then we do the SEAM test. Got it?' I nod.

By the time we have armed three jets, I am semi-confident. Henry and Stan make it easy, it's like they both know when I am about to fuck something up, let me make the mistake if it's not dangerous, then explain what I did wrong. There isn't any finger pointing.

Soon after arming, there is a loud hissing noise and I look up the tarmac toward a Canberra Bomber. There's black smoke blowing from ports on an engine.

'What the fuck is that?'

'Engine starter cartridge going off, Dougie.' Henry tells me like it happens every day. It hasn't happened every day for me. Scared the fuck out of me.

Our pilots arrive and sign for the first four jets. The walk around is completed with no issues, engines running, pitch dampers checked, taxiing. Stan pulls up in the section truck.

'Get in, Dougie, we are on unplug.' He navigates his way down the taxi way toward the engine run up area, then left toward the tower, passing Ammo Prep, SAR Choppers and the revetments to the north-west end of the runway where he parks. There is a Canberra on the runway with some dude marshalling it forward.

'That's the tug,' says Stan. 'Bryan Phillips from 481 is marshalling. He's positioning the Canberra so they can hook up the banner.' He points across the runway. 'See the guys over there?'

'Yep.'

'Once the cable is connected to the Canberra, Bryan will marshal it forward and take the slack out of the cable. Then it will take off.' We sit and watch. After getting everything connected and the cable straightened, they clear the runway. Soon after, the Canberra's engines come to life and it speeds down the runway. It seems to take a long time to rotate, but when it does, it goes almost vertical. The thick wing span impressive in the vertical climb, banner trailing behind. I look up the taxiway and our jets are approaching.

'They will park over there facing south,' he points. 'I will go out and stand in front of them. Once I see all the pilot's hands are out of the cockpit, I will put my hands on my head. That's so that we don't have some knucklehead playing with the flight controls or switches while you are running around under the jet. As soon as you see my hands on my head, you can run along and remove the butterfly safety pins from the gun packs, understand?'

'I got it.'

Stan gets out of the truck and waits till they line up, then runs into position, they aren't fucking around. I can see all hands clear of the cockpit and Stan quickly gets his hands on his head. I sprint from jet to jet, removing the safety pins. At the other end, I stop and give Stan the 'thumbs up' which he relays to the waiting knuckleheads.

Canopies are quickly locked down and engines revved as they taxi into take-off position, two forward, two aft.

I can see each pilot finishing final checks then looking at the leader, engine revs now getting to a high pitch. The pilot in the lead jet looks up, then dips his head forward. As he does, the front two jets start rolling, the engines moving to afterburner. There is a glow from the tail pipes as they move down the runway, the entire world vibrating. The second two jets start running up their engines.

I watch the first two rotate as the second two release brakes and go to afterburner, our vehicle shaking as they increase speed.

'Keep hold of those safety pins,' Stan tells me. 'We have four more to launch, and then make all eight safe again when they get back.' It's 0900 and we have only launched four jets. Today's flying program is for six waves of four jets, twenty-four sorties in all.

I am going to be knackered by the end of this.

Twenty minutes later, the next four jets taxi toward us. It's the same routine and all four are airborne quickly. It's fascinating watching the Mirages come to life as they jump into the sky.

How good is this?

Stan and I return to the squadron lines quickly to grab a Coke each before heading to the south-east end of the runway. We are standing beside the truck watching a couple of Macchi jets take off above us when he spies them.

'There, Dougie,' he says, pointing. 'Get those safety pins ready. They will be here before you know it.'

He isn't wrong. The first four jets enter the circuit in echelon, pitching into the pattern in a clinical way. As they head down wind, the gear comes down and the aircraft nose appears to get higher, engine noise increasing. The first one hits the deck quickly, brake chute deployed, slowing and releasing the chute.

It pulls up on the Aircraft Safety Point next to us with the other three close behind. Once we have safetied the guns, they taxi back toward the squadron lines, Stan and I following in the truck.

It's great fun belonging to a well-oiled machine like 77 Squadron. Orders are given, and things just happen automatically. Everybody has their role, all cogs in a complex machine. There is little guidance from the officers, and the only time we see the Squadron Warrant Officer Engineering, or the Flight Sergeants, is when something goes wrong, or there is a disciplinary issue.

The squadron motto is 'Swift to Destroy' and it seems appropriate for a fighter squadron, but the guys at the piss-shack have a different version. It's also affectionately known as 'Malfunction Junction' and there is great joy to be had in telling 77 Squadron fuck-up stories. From what I had seen, it appeared to be unfair, well, until the second week of gunnery.

Thursday morning, we are rearming after the first wave and its quite obvious one of the teams is lagging in the turnaround. As I wander past to our second jet, I take a peek at what is going on. Wally has a screwdriver up the back of the gun pack trying to dislodge something. Dan Stewart handing him tools, Billy is the other team member looking on from the Jammer seat, of course.

'What's happening?' I ask the Sergeant Wright.

'Some dick forgot to lock the return springs on the right-hand gun properly. They are jammed against the back wall of the gun bay and the gun jammed with the slides at the rear, so there is live ammo jammed up and probably chewed up in the gun.'

This is not good. The springs would be exerting a lot of pressure against the back wall and there will be pretty much no chance of winching the pack down. If anyone can sort it out, it's Wally. After ten minutes of dropping the pack slightly and working a big screwdriver as a lever to move the springs down with the weight of the pack, they manage to drop the pack for re-arming. Not a catastrophe, but it really shouldn't have happened. We later find out it was Billy who put the springs back in the gun, but didn't rotate them to where they lock in.

He really needs to be more careful.

Each day, I go back to the section after the mail has arrived in the hope I will hear from Allison, and each day I am disappointed. It would seem I am just not that important to her these days. Maybe I should be calling time on this and moving on.

Mid-May, pay day, at breakfast, I am contemplating whether I should go into town for Thursday night shopping.

'Going to the Knuck and Fuck tonight?' Nev asks between mouthfuls of toast.

I'd forgotten about that.

'Yer, probably. Nothing much else to do.'

'You still hanging out for a letter?' I nod without enthusiasm.

'A few beers at the Knuck won't hurt you Dougie. See ya this arvo.'

Instead of simply heading to the boozer after work as usual, we hit the Mess for a quick meal and then do our best to make ourselves look and smell presentable to whoever might by chance show an interest in us. Tacho sweeps into the room as Gus and I are about ready to leave and has obviously decided we need to know his strategy for the evening.

He has 'knocked the top off it' in the shower, so if by chance a member of the opposite sex might take an interest in him, his 'interest' might last longer than four seconds.

There are times when I wish he was less communicative.

We wander over to the boozer and get a round in, the DJ is already setting his gear up on the small stage down the other end. Occasionally, they have a local band, but most of the time it's a guy with a couple of turntables, big speakers, a few flashing lights and a strobe.

Looking at the DJ in his slick, shiny shirt, boots with heels and a moustache that seems to go on forever, I wonder if we are a bit underdressed for the evening. None of us is particularly fashion conscious, although Tacho seems to have found a shirt loud enough to be seen from space.

'Does that thing have batteries?'

'Jealousy is a curse, Nev. Chicks dig it,' he winks.

The boys are getting warmed up early, another couple of rounds of drinks, and the boozer is starting to get busy. Most of the female population of the Base are in attendance and a smattering of local girls. We grab a table near the dance floor to check out the action.

Tacho wanders down to have a chat with shiny shirt, perhaps he's looking for fashion tips. He comes back and tells us this guy takes requests, we should jot down a list and give it to him. I'm about to sarcastically ask where one might find a notepad and a pen when he produces one from his pocket while muttering something about using it to take down phone numbers, he's certainly been planning for this evening.

We make our list, some Aussie Crawl, Cold Chisel, AC/DC, Nev comes up with a couple neither Tacho nor I have ever heard of. 'Great to dance to,' he assures us. When does Nev dance? The list is entrusted to shiny shirt and, after another round of drinks, he's on the microphone welcoming us and the other one hundred or so others who are now starting to fill the place.

There are a few WRAAFs we know here and a few local girls who look about our age, each with an army of admirers trying out their latest pick up line. First impression on the music is not inspiring, KC and the Sunshine Band? I check with Nev.

'Was this one of your requests?' The response is fairly clear and concise.

'No fucking way!'

Some guy approaches shiny shirt, he looks familiar, but in the dim light I don't recognise him, then it hits me, fucking Faulkner. He is giving shiny shirt a few tips. From the finger pointing and facial expression, I am guessing it's not a cordial conversation, certainly not fashion advice. As he leaves, Shiny shirt pokes his tongue out at him.

Dickheads never change their spots.

I come back from the bar to find Nev leaning over one of the local girls. She seems unhappy about being first on the dance floor, but I can tell Nev is working his magic and she succumbs quickly. She's a big, robust, girl.

He does like the larger girls, our Nev.

He looks tiny out there with her. But he's got some moves. 'Rasputin' is powering through the speakers, Nev doing his Russian Cossack thing, arms folded, alternate legs extending and she's smiling from ear to ear watching his every wiggle and thrust.

I scan the room for Faulkner. He's sitting with a group against the far wall. Looks like they are off to a fast start, tables full of empties, loud and obnoxious already. Merv follows my gaze.

'Queer Traders, Dougie.' They've had their two middies. Give them another one and they will pass out.'

'Nothing would make me happier, mate.'

Ten minutes later, Faulkner is up and wandering across the dance floor, more like staggering across the dance floor, which now has about ten couples on it. Nev sees him coming and is trying to get out of his way, but his trajectory isn't predictable and seems to home in on Nev, almost knocking him over.

There is an exchange of words, but Nev's not taking the bait, the big girl is looking a little worried. Nev grabs her hand and they move to another part of the dance floor. Faulkner is continuing with the verbal to Nev over his shoulder and then directs his attention back to the DJ.

A few minutes later a couple of Corporal Screws turn up and make their way over to Faulkner's table. Somebody obviously gave them a call, and of course, they are all sweetness and light now, butter wouldn't melt in their mouths. Words exchanges and the Screws head back out the door, elephants to track somewhere in their trusty Valiant station wagon.

The music slows down a little and I see Nev moving in, his head is now literally lodged between this girl's breasts, and they both look pretty happy about it.

Can he breathe in there?

The music stops and they uncouple, moving towards the door hand in hand. As they head out the door, I notice Faulkner getting up to head out as well, not sure whether he is heading after Nev or not.

'Hold the fort, Tacho. I'm going for a slash.'

Out the door I turn and head for the Men's. Nev's girl is sitting in a chair in the beer garden. She gives me a smile and a wave. I smile and wave back. Seems Nev had to go as well?

As I get closer, I can hear raised voices and break into a jog. The first thing I see is Faulkner leaning all over Nev who has his face planted in the tiles above the trough, obviously off balance, and probably caught mid piss.

'Gotcha, ya little fuckin' coon.'

I've heard enough. I grab Faulkner by the collar of his shirt and his right arm pulling him off and shoving him towards the toilet doors on the other side of the room. He's obviously hammered and pretty much falls through the door and ends up with his face against a toilet bowl. I follow him in pinning him down with my foot. I'm aware of Nev behind me trying to pull me away.

Faulkner is trying to get up but struggling he turns to face me and he's obviously hit his head somewhere, there's blood pouring down the side of his face.

'Fuck off, Nev, you don't need to be here. Go and check how your girl is, mate.' Nev is looking at me obviously concerned at what I might do. 'Don't worry, this guy's had enough. We should probably get him to Medical. He's bleeding like a stuck pig.' He nods in agreement and washes his hands.

'You alright, Dougie?' that same worried but inquiring look on his face.

'All good, mate.'

Faulkner is obviously not in a good way. I grab a handful of paper towel and instruct him to hold it against the side of his head. He looks up at me and there is murder in those eyes. I manage to get him up and prop him against the wall as Tacho sprints in.

Where would we be without mates.

'Go grab one of his mates and tell 'em he slipped and fell over in here and needs someone to walk him over to Medical.

'No worries, Dougie, I'm on it,' is the reply.

Faulkner is not in a good way, but at least he's quiet and doesn't make a scene when a couple of his mates come in. I must look like I'm trying to help out because they thank me and carefully navigate their way out with him supported between them. I've managed to get some blood on me. I head to the basin and wash it off, checking myself over in the mirror and combing my hair.

It's probably only been three minutes since I walked in, but it seems like a bloody long time, and I can still feel my heart thumping away in my chest. I notice Tacho quietly standing there staring at me inquiringly.

'What?'

'Your shout, Dougie.'

We head back inside, there are a few murmurs around the place, a few guys watching me as I head to the bar.

'Alright, Dougie? asks Tina, the barmaid.

'All good, Tina, thanks.'

'These are on the house, luv,' as she pushes the beers across the bar.

News travel fast around here.

Tacho is in my ear immediately, 'Well, say "thank you Tacho",' he says. I have no idea what he's talking about, which is obvious from the bewildered look I give him. 'I told Tina what happened. She doesn't like that dirtbag either. She's the one who called the Screws earlier, hence the free beer.' I can feel my heart starting to slow. The beer is gone in a couple of swallows, I push the empty across to Tacho.

'Your shout.' He gives me a knowing grin, finishes his and heads back to the bar for another.

The rest of the evening goes by without much drama, the action in the Men's room seems to have made me thirsty, I have a couple more than I should and I definitely have the wobbly boots on heading back to the block. Tacho has convinced a couple of girls to dance with him towards the end, he has a phone number jotted down in his notebook. Back at the block Nev is nowhere to be seen, I reckon between the three of us we have a full Knuck and Fuck set.

As I grab a coffee in the Smoko Room in the morning a couple of the guys are humming the Rocky theme tune — news travel fast around here. Mac interrupts them and requests my presence in his office. He doesn't seem to be in a foul mood, at least not yet. He closes the door behind me and asks me to sit down, there's a first. He tells me he's heard a story and would like some details from my perspective. I retell the events of the evening. He takes a couple of notes, the eyebrows twitching.

He is quietly staring at me, his eyes literally boring into me, not with any malice, searching it seems for something.

'Do you have some history with this guy Faulkner?' he asks.

Oh, shit! I was told this guy had a sixth and a seventh sense.

I confess that we had an altercation of sorts back in Wagga.

'An altercation?' he asks.

'Well, Flight, he was messing with a mate, took a swing at me and missed' I took a swing, or maybe two, and didn't miss. Nothing more to it, but somehow I ended up getting charged for it.'

A bemused look momentarily crosses his face. I wouldn't have believed it if I hadn't seen it. It's quickly back to business.

'There is a reasonable possibility the Screws will press charges here, Dougie. He needed twelve stitches in the side of his head and your previous history is not going to stand you in good stead, no matter who might be at fault.' This is not good. I can feel my face going red and my blood starting to boil.

'That's bullshit, Flight, in both cases it was basically self-defence. They called the Screws on this guy before we crossed paths last night. He was hammered and being a dickhead, one of the barmaids thanked me, not to mention the racist comments he was making to Nev!'

'Dougie, first, careful with your tone in this office. I am here to help you where I can and where I believe it is the right thing to do for someone who is my responsibility, and while I want to believe your story, the fact that there's prior history here gives me cause for doubt.'

There is a long uncomfortable silence. His look reminds me of grandad after he has given me advice; fatherly, trying to educate, to guide. I relax a little. I really need this guy on my side. Pissing him off or carrying on like a sulking teenager is not going to help.

'Sorry, Flight, lost the plot there for a bit,' I mumble. His look is less stern, warmer, more supportive. My respect for him has grown tenfold in the last few minutes.

'Get back to work. Keep your head down. Don't react to the crap the boys will undoubtedly give you over this. I'll do what I can to keep this from going any further, no promises. And if you think of anything else that might be important for me to know, find me.'

'Will do, thanks, Flight,' and with that I head back to the Smoko Room for another brew ... and another *Rocky* serenade.

Late in the afternoon Mac finds me and invites me back for another chat in his office. He closes the door behind me.

'The Screws are going to charge you for assaulting Faulkner. Nothing I could do about it. The CO really has a thing about fighting, no matter the circumstances, and your previous run-in with this guy certainly didn't help your cause.' I nod, resigned to the fact, trying to keep calm when inside I'm about ready to explode, but this is not the time or the place ... is that maturity?

Mac was right, the CO didn't take too kindly to fighting. Nev comes in to give his account. Even the Screws come in and tell him they had been called earlier in the night. At least he's good enough to take all the evidence into consideration.

'Gentlemen, last year in East Sale, there was a fight in the Airmen's Club resulting in one airman receiving a bad cut. The investigating officer reported that no one saw anything and that most people were in the toilet at the time, all one hundred and fifteen of them. This time, no one is in the toilet, except for the three Airmen involved. I find it hard to believe.' He pauses. 'Flight Sergeant McIntosh and Warrant Officer Bailey?'

The two Senior Non-Commissioned Officers stand. 'Yes, sir.'

'I have had enough of this fighting in the ranks. We have a belief here where people seem to think it's okay to sort out issues with fisticuffs. Please ensure you convey my complete opposition to any violence to every enlisted man in this squadron. If anyone turns up here again for fighting, they can bring their toothbrush with them.'

'Yes, sir, they say collectively, looking like they have just been to the principal's office. First time I have seen Mac lost for words and now I am shitting myself.

He's going to send me to Ingleburn, the Military Correction Centre.

'AC Walsh.'

'Sir.'

'I understand you were breaking up an altercation, but your enthusiasm needs to be tempered. I also note this is not the first time you have been in trouble for fighting, but given the circumstances, I doubt you were acting with malice. I award you four days *Confined to Barracks*.'

'Thank you, sir.'

'LAC Faulkner.'

'Sir.' Faulkner stands up.

'I am instructing the Adjutant to review the evidence presented here to see if you have a case to answer.'

I nearly piss myself laughing. The CO has summed everything up pretty well. I can't argue with four days CB and on top of it, Faulkner is going to get what's coming to him.

Who says crime doesn't pay?

The following Friday afternoon I am sitting around the Gunnery tent. There are showers rolling through from the south and we are on a weather hold, waiting to see if they will suspend flying for the day. The pilots aren't allowed to bomb the range unless they can see the target, seems almost sensible given that we have personnel out there to keep track of where their bombs are landing.

The crap weather adds to my lonely feeling. It's been a while since I have been intimate with a woman, and it's not that I want, or need sex. Without doubt, it would be fun. I just need the emotional companionship. Having mates is one thing, but intimacy with a woman is a whole other thing. It's been a while.

My thoughts are with Allison and what she might be doing in Sydney. I am going to find out once and for all whether she still has any feelings for me. I have a letter from back in February where she said she was living in the Women's College. I decide I am going to ring the Uni and see if they will put the call through to the College.

As soon as we have packed up for the day, I am back to my room, changed, and down the Post Office. I try the number five times, its rings out each time. Without success, I join the others at the boozer. It's a long session and not exactly joyous.

Saturday morning, I wake up late. Head's a bit sore, I get dressed and head for the Post Office again. It rings for a long time before a woman picks it up. 'Allison Gardner? Hang on, I will see if she's in her room.' I wait for several minutes.

'Not in, I am afraid. Bye.'

'Shit.' I try three more times before lunch, nothing. It's an STD call to Sydney and I am burning all my twenty-cent pieces.

After lunch, we are sitting around Gus' room playing records. 'She's been out all morning,' I tell him, my mind clearly somewhere else.

'Who?'

'Oh! Sorry, Allison. I've been calling her all morning.'

'Mate, you really are in a state, aren't you? If it's that bad, why don't you just drive down there and talk to her.'

'I think I will do just that, but I am going to call her one more time.' I take my last few twenty-cent coins to the Post Office. This time the voice on the other end of the phone is familiar.

'Tim, hi. There were notes on my door. I was hoping this was you.' That is reassuring, at least she is happy to hear from me. I press my case to come down for a visit.

'Next weekend, sure. I have exams through the week and have been studying every spare moment, but I'll be free by then.' I think Gus can sense the relief when I get back to his room.

'I am going to Sydney and will see her.'

'Good plan, mate.'

'You coming?'

'Why not. I haven't been to Sydney for a while.' Tacho walks in on the back end of the conversation.

'Are we going to Sydney?'

The following week, we finish the last of the Air to Ground sorties. By Wednesday, we have repacked all the leftover ammunition and bombs. The gun packs, bomb beams, and SUU-20s are back in the hangar where we will spend the next two months returning everything to pristine condition for the next time we need it.

Tacho and I are assigned to Gun Bay and Gus is cleaning SUU-20s. In Gun Bay, we separate the two 30mm DEFA Cannons from each gun pack and clean them. There is an expectation that each tradesman can service a single gun in a day. It's simple. All you gotta do is disassemble the gun, clean each of the components, which is no mean feat in itself, then inspect everything before you reassemble, lube, and test it.

The section routine drops back to a less hectic level. There is the early morning brew and cigarette where the news of the previous day, or the latest TV offering, are discussed. The mid-morning and afternoon smoko breaks are again centred on a card game and Joe Byrne recovers his control.

Patience has never been one of my strong points, and I think Tacho has an even deeper weakness when it comes to that virtue. He has been busting to get a seat at Joe Byrne's game since we arrived, and Joe has been giving him the 'junior woodchuck' treatment.

Thursday morning, I notice Tacho slipping away from us a few minutes before smoko time. When we get there, he's holding the deck of cards hostage standing up on the bench, surrounded by the usual players, tempers are getting frayed. Realising some level of violence is imminent, Tacho announces a new game, 52 pickup, throwing the cards across the Smoko Room and trying to make a run for the door. He doesn't get far, and within minutes he has been strapped to the card table with a couple of cargo straps. Then with another, they carry him into the hangar and with the aid of a forklift he is suspended from a steel beam in the hangar ceiling. With hardly a break in proceedings, and perhaps only missing two hands of the game, the boys are back in the Smoko Room with a makeshift table and the game in full flow, while a stream of expletives flow from a suspended Tacho. Flight Sergeant McIntosh wanders into the hangar a few minutes later obviously amused at what he finds, and suggests someone might want to get him down, and then have him report to his office. Tacho has managed to endear himself to Flight Sergeant McIntosh again. It's becoming repetitive.

I don't know what it is, but there are those among us who seem at times to be unbelievably courageous, reacting to potentially dangerous situations in altogether unexpected ways as things are not always as they appear. Tacho is becoming one of those guys who is seemingly bulletproof, putting himself in situations that are often life-threatening, but not based on anything remotely resembling courage. Here is a guy with a complete lack of any sense of self, someone who hasn't worked out where he fits in the world, and this has led to a dangerous self-destructive streak that neither he, nor those of us around him, have been fully conscious of. Until now …

Saturday morning, I am up early and keen to get going. I walk down to Tacho's room and go in without knocking. He's busy under the sheets and I do an abrupt about-turn. Gus is up and I sit in his chair, thumbing through a *Penthouse*. It's not a good option, maybe the *Post*.

'What about some food?' he says. We grab some toast and coffee at the Mess and head back to the block. Tacho arrives about eight-thirty.

'Let's hit the road, boys.'

The Interceptor departs the front gate at speed. We head down through Jesmond, Toronto, and Morrisset, taking the back road at Wyee to Wyong, then onto Peats Ridge. As we approach the toll gates at Berowra, Tacho calmly tells us that a RADTECH at the squadron told him that if you go through the gates at over seventy miles an hour without paying, its fast enough to avoid being captured in the photo, thus escaping the fine. He executes the manoeuvre through the narrow opening with some skill, while Gus and I try to make ourselves skinnier somehow, closing our eyes tight.

There is no fear in Tacho's driving. Whether it's a two-lane freeway, suburban road, or narrow country road, everything is at high speed. Nothing under eighty kilometres an hour into the city. We fumble around in our pockets to gather enough coins for the bridge toll, then over the bridge at ninety kilometres and into the city.

Does he know the road well enough to be doing this speed? No fucking way.

'She said the Uni is up Parramatta Road, just follow George Street and it eventually changes to Parramatta Road.' We nearly miss it because Tacho is going so fast. When we get off the road and find a park, I give her a call.

She looks amazing when she turns up. Light blue blouse, jeans, sandshoes, hair pulled back in a ponytail and a touch of makeup. She greets me with a big smile and a kiss on the lips. Gus and Tacho get one on the cheek. After pleasantries are exchanged, she asks us what we want to do. We all look at each other a little dumbfounded.

'Well, how about we start with the zoo. You lot look like you can assimilate there.' She hasn't lost any of that sense of humour.

After the trip to Taronga, we drop Allison back at the Uni and find a room at Commercial Hotel, then a shower, and change. A few beers downstairs before heading back to the Uni.

She said to meet her at the Sports Bar. It's in the grandstand at the footy oval.

It's fairly packed when we walk in. Lots of burly rugby forwards and clean-cut pretty boy backs. She's in conversation with a couple of other girls.

'Jane, Cheryl, and Narelle,' pointing to each one, 'this is Tim, Gus, and Gilley.'

The boys lose no time in engaging the other girls, allowing Allison and me to talk. She's having a great time, the study is hard, but the other girls are great and really help when she struggles.

Apparently, they're all very intelligent and are becoming a tight-knit group.

'There are a lot of lecturers who still think a woman's place is in the kitchen chained to the sink. They are pretty tough on us, tougher than on the guys.'

Oh, there's Tony. You really should meet him, Tim. He's a good rugby player, has a law degree, and is about to finish an economics degree.' She waves her hand excitedly and he comes over, giving her a peck on the lips.

'Tony Barrett, this is Tim Walsh.' We shake hands and I start some small talk about rugby. He's a fairly serious sort of bloke, not the type I would take for a rugby forward. He's into politics and has strong opinions on various topics from deregulation of the banks, to the Queen.

He also has a funny way about him. The speech is slow and deliberate, laughs are almost forced, and although he is interesting to talk with, I get a feeling that he is humouring me, maybe even patronising me. His smile is a little too contrived.

'You said your grandad was a member of the Country Party, Tim. Whereabouts?'

'Little place called Dungog, north west of Newcastle.'

'Oh, yes, lovely, lovely,' he chortles. I doubt he knows where Dungog is.

'You?'

'North Shore, Chatswood. Went to school at Riverview, St Ignatius.'

Is that supposed to mean something?

Not only do I feel he is humouring me, but he's got his eyes on Allison most of the time.

'So, Ali, what's on the agenda for tonight?' he asks.

'Well, Tim is down from Williamtown for the weekend. We are old friends from Wagga Wagga and I thought I would hang around with him.'

'Oh,' he says, as if he is a little put out. 'I guess I will see you later then. Nice to meet you, Tim,' he says, shaking my hand, and wanders off, stopping to chat with various people as he goes. She watches him go.

'Well, la de fuckin' da, he's a posh bastard.'

'He can come across a little like that, but he is really a nice guy when you get to know him.'

We down a few more drinks and cut out early, disappearing back to her room. I am not supposed to be there, but apparently everyone turns a blind eye to guys in the building on Saturday nights. We aren't in the room long before the clothes are off. She pushes me back onto the bed, kissing me, working her way to my neck and chest, a hand around me. Soon after she is on top, riding me. She knows exactly what she wants.

She's developed some skills since we last kissed in February. No prizes for guessing who helped her practise.

An image of the pretentious prat, Barrett, comes into my head and the red mist is descending. It's a weird circumstance being full of rage at the same time as making love to the girl I adore. I manage to keep my anger under wraps until she's finished, throwing herself onto my chest.

I'll show her who is best.

I turn her onto her back and keep the momentum going. Thrusting hard, then applying pressure to her pelvis with mine. She comes again and I keep going till she sighs a third time.

The following weekend, I decide to take the Corolla to Sydney alone. Allison and I get ourselves a room in a cheap joint in the Cross. We spend the weekend making love, dispersed with meals and a few beers at a pub. I am still filled with jealousy and each session is a little marathon. I am determined to show that I'm the superior lover. As I leave, I ask about the following weekend.

'I'm busy,' she says. 'There is a party on at Bondi Junction, it's invitation only and I only have one ticket.'

'Oh, okay, the weekend after?'

'Not sure, Tim, I have a feeling there is something on that weekend too.'

'I suppose you are going with that Tony guy?' There's accusation in my voice. She pauses and looks at me.

'So, that's what this is all about? Tony?

'You've been sleeping with him, haven't you?' She looks at me a little bewildered.

'Look, Tim, who I sleep with is my business. I am not your personal property.' I can't believe what she is saying.

'I thought you loved me?' Another pause.

'I do, Tim. But now is not the time for me to be faithfully yours. I am going to finish my degree, have a career, and while I do, I'm going to sample the things life has to offer. Besides, you keep telling me you are going to Malaysia. I'm not going to sit here waiting for you while you are humping some Asian floosy.'

I still can't believe what she is telling me. She's happy to sleep with that tosser, Barrett, complete flog.

'Fine, I guess we have a rather different concept of love then.' I say, getting into the car with regret already flooding my brain.

'Fine, I guess we do,' she folds her arms and watches me drive off.

Well, that went well.

The drive back to Williamtown is not pleasant, seems I have monumentally screwed that up.

You're a fucking dickhead, Tim.

The following week, I am on afternoon shift. We start at midday and usually knock off around nine. It's not tough work, but we are kept busy with safety equipment changes and removing ejection seats. By Wednesday, I am well and truly regretting my exchange with Allison and I try calling her several times, leaving messages. There aren't any return calls. We knock off around five on Friday.

'You coming for a beer, Dougie?'

I don't have the heart for this.

'Na, thought I might head home to the farm for the weekend. I'll see you Monday.'

I manage to get to the farm by 1900. Grandma and grandad haven't gone to bed yet, I get a warm welcome and a cup of tea.

Saturday, up early, milking complete and breakfast over, grandma's relentless project to get Lou and me together is ready for the next round.

'Louise is home from Uni. It's the semester break,' I am told. 'I'll arrange us to all get together at the RSL this evening.' I give her a grin and a nod.

'Sounds good, Gran.'

When we walk in, I can see Louise sitting with Mr and Mrs Bennett over by the kitchen. Grandad offers to get drinks and I wander over, shaking hands with Mr Bennett and kissing Mrs

Bennett on the cheek. Lou stands and we come together, me expecting lips on lips, she tilts her head and I kiss her on the cheek.

She has a lot to say about Uni, the lecturers, the other students, orientation week, the social life. It reminds me of my first time home from Wagga Wagga. There is lots to tell and she is obviously in awe of her new surroundings. A bit like me two-and-a-half years ago.

We get up to go to the bar. I am comparing her Armidale stories to my Wagga Wagga stories. It's uncanny how we have both found some comfort in rural towns the other side of the Great Dividing Range.

She stops and turns to me, 'Tim, I have something to tell you.' She looks anxious and I wait, not wanting to make her any more nervous. 'I have met someone.' I force a smile.

'Good for you.' Our drinks turn up and we silently and awkwardly head back to the table. She is trying to stifle a grin. Grandma's antennae are already picking something up.

We sit a long way apart, the reality now starting to hit me, but I am happy for Lou, she deserves to be happy.

You're well and truly single now, Tim.

July, Mac calls a section meeting and says there is a short trip to Townsville coming up.

'The CO wants to sharpen up the heavy bombing skills before the fire power demonstration in August, so I will need two bombing crews, flight line, and a rectifications shift. Get your names to me by lunch time tomorrow.'

According to Dan, Mac will give all the Baggers an opportunity to go home and negotiate with the missus.

'Some of them will just put their name down and tell the missus that it's mandatory attendance, others have to ask permission,' he laughs. Gus, Tacho and I go straight in and put our names in the book. A week later, we are boarding a C-130 for Townsville.

It's just after lunch on Sunday when we throw our bags into the room at Transit Accommodation. Gus, Tacho, and I are have just pulled on shorts, T-shirt and thongs when Stan comes up the hall in uniform.

'No time for that shit, boys. We have work to do. Get changed.'

While the rest of the squadron departs for town, we jump in the back of a Landcruiser, Henry driving and Stan riding shotgun. He takes us around the airfield, past 35 Squadron, and toward the control tower, turning left toward the swamp. He pulls up on an old, overgrown, World War II runaway. Toad and Wally are waiting for us, Wal seated on a large Tow Truck with several F-Type bomb trolleys and a tool trolley behind.

'We'll set up the prep here,' says Toad. 'Stan, take Gus and Dougie and get the jammers. Wal, H, and Tacho, you guys get the bombs.'

Preparing bombs isn't tough work, like dipping ammunition, but it's constant physical work and even in the North Queensland winter, we raise a good sweat. All the heavy lifting is done with the jammer; all we have to do is unpack all the components and assemble them. First, the fuses and boosters are set and delay elements fitted. Then, they are screwed into the nose and tail-fusing wells, the bomb tail, anemometer, lugs, and arming wires fitted.

By 1600, we have four trolleys of fully fused Mk82 low drag bombs ready to go, and another lot unpacked ready to be fused. Toad arrives with a cold carton of XXXX, handing them out.

Gus looks around, 'Where's the bottle opener?'

'See here,' Henry points at a metal assembly screwed to the side of the tool trolley. 'A Mirage undercarriage door stop.' He puts his stubby lid inside the bracket and pulls outward, the lid flying off. 'The best bottle opener in the country.' The rest of us follow suit except Stan; he just rests the lid of his on the mudguard of a trolley and hits it downward, the top flies off.

There are no chairs and so we sit amongst the bombs in the late afternoon glow drinking cold beer. Gus leans over to me.

'This is a little surreal, Dougie.'

I nod like I know what he is talking about. I don't.

'Six months ago, who would have thought we'd be sitting on a Mk82 bomb, in tropical North Queensland, drinking piss on a Sunday afternoon?'

He's right, it's a little weird.

The lull gives me time to check the place out. It isn't the tropical wonderland I had envisaged. We have set up ammo prep next to a mangrove swamp. I won't be venturing far in there I can tell you, crocodiles and I don't get along.

The hills around the town have a smattering of scraggy-looking trees and it's rocky, dusty, and dry. The only palm trees I can see are the ones planted around the Base and suburbs.

It's a pretty hilly place. There are large mountains to the south and a couple of larger hills around the town. At the north end of the runway, I can make out large hills in the distance. Henry follows my gaze.

'The ocean is off the end of the runway. That's Magnetic Island you can see, and over there is Castle Hill. The town centre is the other side of that hill.' The word 'town' shakes Tacho into life.

'Hey, Toad, can you give us lift to town?'

'Not much use, Tacho, this is Queensland. The land of slow talk, scantily-dressed *sheilas*, and pubs that close at six o'clock on a Sunday.'

'You know why they call it Fourex, Dougie?' asks Stan.

'No.'

'Because they can't spell beer,' Toad goes on as if Stan hadn't spoken.

'Your best bet is to get a carton and some ice and settle into the beer garden at the boozer,' which is exactly what we do.

The next morning, it's a leisurely start with a cooked breakfast at the Mess, then setting up our tent on the airfield, camp table and chairs, and cold-water urn. Toad has borrowed a barbecue from someone along with firewood. It's a standard

RAAF apparatus manufactured from a forty-four-gallon drum cut lengthways, three-eight plate on top, angle iron for legs, and gal water pipe for a chimney.

The rest of the squadron guys are setting up power carts, ladders, and chocks. The first of the jets are overhead by 1100 hours and all on the deck by midday, all ten.

To load big bombs, the jets are parked on the cross runway and there is a long safety distance separating them. They are configured with large centreline tanks, and RPK10 fuel tanks on the wings. The RPK10s each have four-bomb racks, so each jet could conceivably carry eight bombs. We are only going to use the outboard stations, four bombs per jet, there's not enough runway on the planet to get a Mirage off the ground with eight 500lb bombs onboard.

The first four bombing sorties launch by 1400, and we have another four ready to go a short time after. The bombing-up process doesn't take long. The trolley stops at the front of the jet and the jammer picks up one at a time. Once the hooks on the rack are closed, the jammer tray is dropped and we have to screw the rack back into the tank using handles until the bomb is rigid against the sway braces. The arming wires are then connected and finally the cartridges are fitted to the rack and connected.

After the second four jets launch, we take the trolleys back to Ammo Prep where we get another load of bombs ready. We only have enough trolleys to fully prepare thirty-six bombs and so it's a constant challenge to keep enough bombs ready to support the rate at which they are being dropped.

Each day is a scramble to bomb-up, prepare more bombs, then bomb- up again. We grab lunch off the barbecue on the run;

usually a steak sandwich or sausage, a smattering of sauce and onions, and some salad if you get in early enough.

By Thursday afternoon, the CO is satisfied that we, ground and aircrew, have reached a level of competence to make the Fire Power Demonstration successful. There are drinks in the hangar Thursday afternoon and the jets launch back to Williamtown on Friday morning. After packing our gear away, Toad drops us at the ferry terminal. He is dressed in his best shirt, shorts, and thongs.

'Not coming, Toad?'

'No, Wal, I've got a date with a WRAAF I know from Kingswood.' Wal looks slightly bemused.

I shudder to think about what this WRAAF might look like. Maybe she'll have to chew her own arm off in the morning?

Henry and Wal are leading the push and as soon as the ferry pulls into Picnic Bay, we are led directly to the pub. Wal orders ten XXXX stubbies explaining that stubbies are better, drinking pots will get us hammered, and they tend to get warm up here. I do the maths; ten ounces per serve versus fifteen. It's not making sense.

The afternoon commences relatively sedately, but declines sharply after about six shouts. Wal and Henry are in deep discussion about who are dickheads around the armament trade, and who might be the biggest dickhead. Stan is amusing the rest of us with war stories from previous bombing camps, especially the ones in Malaysia.

Returning from the toilet, Billy catches me alone and proceeds to bitch that he was stuck on flight line duties all week, complaining that Gus, Tacho and me were the 'Junior Woodchucks' and we should have been on flight line.

Maybe they couldn't risk you loading real bombs, Bill?

'Mac said we needed the training.'

He rolls his eyes, 'You lot are the golden-haired children.'

'I doubt that, Billy, Tacho and I seem to spend a lot of time in his office, and it's not for morning tea, I can tell you. Tacho actually has the entire fly shit pattern on his ceiling memorised.'

'Last ferry is at half four,' announces Wal, looking at his watch. 'Who hasn't shouted yet?' Billy and I raise our hands.

'Better get both shouts in now. We can drink one on the way to the ferry.' It's not a command, but no room for argument either.

There's a fair amount of laughing and pushing as we stumble to the ferry. The whistle blows and we have to run the last hundred metres giggling like kids.

The ride home is highlighted with songs, rugby songs, pop songs, stupid little ditties, all much to the amusement of the locals.

'I stuck my finger in the woodpecker's hole and the woodpecker said, "god bless my soul".' Wal, H and Stan know them all. At some point, Stan stands and gives us a rousing version of 'New York, New York', followed by the 'Banana Boat Song', with singing the reply, 'Daylight come and me wanna go home.' The boy can really sing, eat your heart out, Harry Belafonte.

His final number before the ferry berths is 'Piano Man', the full version.

> 'Now Paul is a real estate novelist
> Who never had time for a wife,
> And he's talking with Tacho
> Who's still in the Air Force
> And probably will be for life.'

Billy leans over to me with a sneer, Yer, you and Tacho are

lifers, Dougie,' like it's some sort of death sentence. 'I'll be out of this joint before you can say boo.'

If it's so bad, Billy, why doesn't he just fuck off now?

Saturday morning, we are all lying around with sore heads when Wal comes in in overalls.

'If you boys want a feed before the flight, you'd better get to the Mess now or you'll miss out.' Gus and I just moan and pull the covers over our heads.

Later, I am walking out onto the tarmac to get onto the C-130 when I look north, with Magnetic Island sitting in the background. All I remember of Magnetic Island is the inside of the Picnic Bay Hotel, the ferry, and the singalong. Not exactly Terry Tourist.

'Maybe next time.'

The following week is the Fire Power Demonstration at Puckapunyal. The jets are armed with Mk82 high explosive bombs and HE Ammunition. Compared to last week, this couple of missions are a walk in the park.

The pilots manage to drop each 500-pounder near enough to the target, and apparently the HE 30mm ammo really lit the place up. After disarming the gun packs and storing everything away, most of the guys head for the boozer, even Mac.

Mac says that the CO is happy with how everything has gone over the past two weeks. Wal reckons that if the CO is happy, then Mac is happy. Apparently, Mac has been overlooked for promotion recently and he's not going to fuck it up this time.

Having brought a few rounds, Mac heads off and the rest of the Baggers gradually slink away now that they have to pay for their own drinks. The live-in guys from the other squadrons have joined us and there is a healthy glow from both the beer and the achievements, then the Screws walk in.

There are two of them, a corporal and a female sergeant. I recognise the sergeant from Wagga Wagga. The boys start a few elephant and pig noises as they wander over to our table.

'Talent night, boys?' she enquires. There is no response. She walks around and stands behind me. The corporal moves opposite to her.

'IDs please, gentlemen.' She puts her hand out to Lash sitting beside me. He hands over his ID and she peruses both sides.

One of the corporals from 481 makes a respectful plea that we are not doing anything except enjoying a quiet beer. She dismisses the claim and puts her hand out in front of me. It's a small hand, neat nails and a light pink polish. Nail polish is a no-no and I suspect that she is playing the game. I hand over my ID.

After a short review, she asks me over to the side of the rooms pulling out her note book. As I walk over, I reaffirm my previous assessment. It's the sergeant from Wagga.

'AC Walsh.'

Yes, Sergeant.'

'You are the Apprentice from Dungog, aren't you?'

'Yes, Sergeant.

'At the sharp end now,' she continues, pausing. 'Bit young to be hanging out with this mob, aren't you?' She is looking at the date of birth on my ID.

'Yes, Sergeant,' I agree.

'You could also be a bit more judicious about the company you keep,' she raises an eyebrow.

Her eyes are shifting between me and the ID, I dare not break the silence. I sense there is some connection and I don't want to be up on a charge, again.

'Maybe there is something we can do to make sure a young man like you is not corrupted by this drunken rabble.'

I am instructed to be at the ASCO service station near the back gate when she knocks off. At this at time of night, it's all closed up and there is little chance of either of us being seen. So many questions are running through my head. Am I doing the right thing? What in the hell is going to happen? Why the hell am I analysing the shit out of this?

As the time approaches, I am hurrying through the married quarters. For some reason, I want to be there a few minutes early. My stomach is filled with so many butterflies I think I might start coughing up brightly coloured wings. What the hell am I doing?

She arrives promptly, driving a shiny little Celica, gesturing me to get in. She smiles, a genuine happy to see you smile. This is good. She smells great. Momentarily, I think about giving her a peck on the cheek or something more, but the butterflies take over.

I put my seatbelt on and have a look about. I'm not sure if I have ever been in a cleaner car. Everything is neat, cassette player and large speakers on the parcel shelf. I look back at her and the smile has turned into something else completely.

Have I done something wrong, or maybe I didn't do something?

Her hand appears from the pocket in her door with something shiny. Before I realise what's happening, both my hands are cuffed. Fuck, I barely had time to blink. She has definitely done that before, and not necessarily as part of her day job. So, what do I say now? Do I ask what the fuck the handcuffs are for? Do I smile and go with the flow?

She quickly pushes the stick into gear, lets the clutch out smoothly and proceeds through the married patch toward the main gate. Her driving is just like her; neat, ordered, with the minimum of fuss. I briefly think about raising my hands to show off the cuffs to the guards as we go through the gate, but what would that achieve? I have signed up for this, or something like this. Hell, I don't have a clue what I have signed up for.

Out of the gate, she turns left and accelerates quickly along Medowie Road, not shy to use the car's power. I finally have a clear thought.

'Where are we going,' simple question, that can't be confidential. I'm only handcuffed, not blindfolded.

'Raymond Terrace,' she responds, curtly. 'I have a flat there. My flatmate is away on exercise so we won't be interrupted.'

Okay, we're speaking now at least. That has cut the tension down a couple of notches. Some of the butterflies are finally taking a rest. Then it strikes me that no one knows where I have gone.

Maybe she's a mass murderer from South Australia?

After turning left onto Richardson Road, I gather enough courage to ask another question.

'So, what's with the handcuffs?'

'Just setting the tone,' she responds matter-of-factly. 'If you don't think it's for you, we can just turn around and drop your missionary-style arse off at the gate.'

Now we were really cutting through the bullshit!

'I'm good,' I reply, hiding my agitation. When she suggested it, it was all exciting, but now I am frightened, excited, anxious, almost aroused. Did I say frightened?

We arrive at her flat; nice quiet street down near the river, nobody around at this time of the evening, nobody sees us heading inside. Nobody knows where I am, or who I'm with. The flat is clean and nicely decorated; not too feminine, classy. She points to the lounge and asks if I want something to drink.

'Whatever you're having,' I reply, as I try to make myself comfortable in my handcuffs. She brings me a short glass with a thick base. It's half full of a brown liquid and ice. I take a sip and almost cough. It's straight Scotch.

She heads to the bedroom and closes the door behind her. I take a large swig from the glass to calm the nerves, the heat from the liquor invoking another little cough.

Well, this is a first, drinking in handcuffs.

I can hear the shower running for a couple of minutes and I rack my brain.

Did I put clean underwear on? Of course, I did, my favourites, in fact.

It's just nerves and the rapidly building anticipation, and I already need another drink.

The bedroom door opens and, as I search my glass for the last drops of Scotch with my tongue, I feel sure my eyes are as large as saucers. What a sight before me!

There are women who look good with their clothes on, but sometimes when everything comes off it doesn't quite live up to expectations, and then there is what stands before me. Curvy, very curvy — full without being fat — and obviously fit. Easily the most mature woman I have seen semi-dressed.

There is some lace and some leather, even a few metal studs, but there isn't a lot of it. It's just enough to make me want to see more, leaving a lot to the imagination. Then again, I get a feeling she is also making a statement. She's in control, absolute control.

The handcuffs had made me think I was in for the full bondage experience, but this is altogether much sexier. She moves smoothly across the room. It's as if she doesn't even disturb the air. She reaches down and takes the glass from my hands, turns and heads to the kitchen. I don't know where to look, her whole body is toned in parts, soft where it should be, and moving rhythmically together.

She returns with another glass of Scotch and ice, and with the other hand, firmly grips the chain of the handcuffs, dragging me to my feet, heading to the bedroom. There is already a party going on in my underwear, she gives me a look that tells me she is aware of it, almost a smirk, confident but sexy.

I look around the bedroom, all pretty standard, except for the bed, there are loops and chains on the posts and bedhead, one of which she has smoothly attached me to without me even realising it.

How do I drink my drink with my hands chained to the bedhead?

She tips the glass to my lips for a sip of Scotch, and then attaches her lips to mine, her tongue exploring, begging my tongue to play.

The handcuffs and chain are making me crazy, to have all of this in front of me and I can't get my hands on any of it. I have never experienced anything like it. She unbuttons my shirt, pinching my nipples, then moves to my jeans, pulling them down; no secrets now, I am happy to be there. I am repositioned on the bed and she straddles me, leaning over to the bedside table.

She has what appears to be a vibrator, the first one I've seen in the flesh. She adjusts something and it comes alive, buzzing quietly. She touches it to her nipples through the lace, and then makes tracks south until it is firmly between those strong thighs. I can see that she is getting lost in the moment.

If only I could get my hands free.

Now the vibrator is on me. Fuck, that feels good. That's when I realise that, other than the long, wet kiss, there has been no physical contact between our two highly aroused bodies. Almost violently, my underwear is pulled down and away actually tearing the fabric. I spring out and she gives me that sly smile again, almost deliriously.

Then in one movement, with no hands or guidance, she is on me, sliding all the way down until our bodies touch, and then up until I am almost out and back down. As she rides up, I can feel her muscles gripping me, it feels like she might just lift me off the bed, it's almost painful.

How does she do that?

Her hands are gripping the bedhead and she is riding up and down on me. I suddenly have the sensation that I am about to lose control and she senses it and stops right at the top of the cycle, with just the tip of me inside her, she seems to hover there without any effort at all while studying me closely. After what seems an eternity, the feeling subsides and somehow sensing it, I am again fully engulfed in her, being held, being controlled.

With one hand she scoops up the vibrator and is rubbing it against herself as she rides up and down on me, the motion all so smooth, I can feel the vibrations through her, I am definitely going to lose it any second.

Just at the point she lets out a low, growling sound, shudders, almost misses a stroke and looks down at me like a predator might look at their prey, her muscles pulsing around me. I try to return the look as my own orgasm rips through me, and keeps coming, like no orgasm I have ever had before. She finally comes to rest on top of me, the look is softening, heading in the direction of a smile. Seems like everybody is happy.

She reaches over for the Scotch, takes a long sip and then presses the glass to my lips. I finish it with one swallow. There is that sly smile again, and a glint in her eye. It seems I have managed to perform somewhere close to expectations. Knowing she has been satiated enhances my own glow.

Within minutes, round two is initiated, then round three, and I think round four. The theme is the same. She has complete control and somehow seems to have something beyond a sixth sense with where my body is the whole time, and how to exploit and extract the maximum possible pleasure from the situation. At some point I fall asleep, utterly exhausted, spent.

I am abruptly awoken at 5am and instructed to shower. I have no idea how long I have slept. Did I sleep? Did I pass out from exhaustion and alcohol? The shower is good and bad, as parts of me are stinging. I am aware of pain across my upper back with no concept of how it happened.

I dress quickly and she is waiting for me with a cup of tea. She looks completely rested and ready for a normal day's work. I feel like I got hit by a bus, and then it reversed back over me.

The ride back to Base is mostly quiet. She seems to be deep in thought, I am only barely conscious. We approach the gate and get our IDs out to show the guard.

'Are you okay to do the same tonight?'

For a couple of seconds, I am lost for words. I think I get away with it as the gate guard gives our IDs a cursory look. What can I say? This was without doubt the most unique night of my life. Why wouldn't I sign up for more? I agree. Pick up will be same place, same time, and I'm asked to wear something nice, as we might go out for a drink.

She drops me off and I amble to my room to find Andy sitting on the edge of his bed scratching his balls. Women rub their eyes in the morning, men scratch their balls. This brings me crashing back to reality.

'You look like shit.' But then, he tells me that pretty much every morning. Perhaps I do look like shit every morning. I haven't thought about it. I strip off my shirt and jeans and he lets out a low whistle.

'What the fuck happened to you,' he asks, looking at my back.

I angle myself to have a look in the mirror. Wow, what a mess. I look like I've seen a few good lashes from a cat-o-nine tails, and I don't actually recall when it happened. Did I even feel it at the time … and I've signed up for another night?

Did you date a cat?

I have no reply and quickly pull on a T-shirt, overalls and lace up my boots before scampering over to the Mess for some food.

There is an old military adage that cooks are 'Fitters and Turners' based on their ability to fit food into pots and turn it into shit. However, on this morning, I have a different view.

The eggs that swim in oil, the bacon slowly congealing in fat, the beans burnt to the bottom of the tub, and the milky coffee concoction, tastes like the most scrumptious delights I have ever eaten. I go back for seconds, which draws several comments regarding my sanity from both sides of the serving counter.

With my stomach full, I make the short walk up to the squadron and into the section Smoko Room, making sure enough people of prominence note my presence. I am not too sure how long I can maintain this charade and I need them to know I was at work on time.

Into the flight line, Stan and I knock over the BFs and head back to the section for a caffeine top-up before the first wave. On the way back, Mac looks me up and down.

'Are you okay, Dougie? You're looking a little pale, lad.'

'Yes, Flight, I'm fine.' Still, he looks sceptical.

I manage to stay coherent until after we launch the first wave and things start to go downhill from there. By the time the jets return, my eyes are burning and my stomach turning. I am fighting to stay alert during the turnaround checks.

The refuelling truck arrives and I start with the big jug on the port wing, fully opening the fuel nozzle. These large tanks always take a while to fill. Maybe I can just close my eyes for a few seconds. They are burning like they have sand in them.

I have a Ted Mulry song playing in my head and I am swaying to music; happy days. Then I hear someone yelling, and then I feel someone shaking me, screaming at me. I get my eyes open and wonder at what the commotion is.

It's a known fact of military life that when someone screws something up badly, somehow everyone within ten miles turns up quicker than what would seems possible. A crowd has gathered.

I release the handle on the fuel nozzle and look down. There is a steady stream from the fuel dump and a couple of hundred gallons of AVTUR running down the tarmac.

Fuck, I have forgotten to reset the fuel dump valve.

Before I can get down to it, Mac is standing there glaring at me and yelling. My lip-reading is not great, but I can gather he is not a happy camper. He's ready to burst a blood vessel, and he would like me to accompany him immediately. I manage to hand the nozzle to my offsider and follow at a discreet distance, stepping over the river of fuel that has made its way almost to the hangar.

This is really not good.

Inside the line hut, earmuffs come off and I really get an earful. Why am I asleep while refuelling an aircraft? Where can he send the bill for several hundred gallons of fuel I have just wasted? Why is it that my actions are known to his doctor who's treating his ulcer? Where would I suggest he gets me posted to so I am as far away from him as possible? Did my mother drop me on my head at some point?

I am escorted back to his office, the Armament Officer standing outside his office as we approach. I note that he quickly disappears inside and closes his door.

I am not the only one scared of Mac.

Mac closes the door behind me and continues to question my intellect, breeding, and reason for being alive, among other things. His tone finally softens and he inquires how in the hell I could fall asleep refuelling a jet, standing up.

'I'm having some troubles with my girlfriend, Flight, and haven't slept well.'

'Foocking girlfriend,' he explodes again. 'We are running a foocking fighter squadron here, lad, not a foocking dating service.' He ponders for a while and seems to settle again.

'Alright, I suggest you go and get some sleep. I need you here tomorrow, rested. And, you can volunteer to be Duty Armourer for the next two weeks. Think yourself lucky, Bones wanted to throw the foocking book at you.'

Back in my room, I collapse on the bed and realise that my back is starting to sting and there is a dull ache between my legs. I set an alarm on the clock radio for the evening meal and the next thing I know, it is shrieking at me. I look around. I am still in my overalls and boots. It takes me a while to drag myself upright and to the shower. The application of soap is handled gingerly.

Gus, Andy, and Nev are in the Mess when I walk in. I grab some brown curried stuff, some beans and some mash and take a seat at the table. I figure it's easier to take my medicine from these guys now. Let them have their fun and hopefully move on.

They greet me as Sleeping Beauty, Rip Van Winkle and a couple of other new and amusing names. The official tally of fuel dumped on the tarmac is apparently 140 gallons. This may be a new record for the squadron, other than the guy who actually jettisoned the wing tanks onto the tarmac and split them. That was over 700 gallons!

'So, what's the story, Dougie,' enquires Andy. 'Are you rooting some nympho?'

I just shake my head and let them speculate. I have other things to think about. How the fuck am I going to get through another night like that and turn up as fresh as a daisy?

Later, I find something I deem suitable to wear, and wander over to the pick-up point at the ASCO service station. I'm early, but Helen's already there waiting. There are no handcuffs this time, which is a slight relief. Out of the main gate, we turn right towards Newcastle. I am told my attire is acceptable, and there is actually some small talk on the drive.

'My Flight Sergeant wants me in bright and early, and switched on,' I tell her. She just smiles back and nods.

We pull up out the back of the Criterion Hotel in Islington. I've heard of this pub, but never been here before. Somebody told me it was either a gay hangout or a bit on the rough side. As we walk in through the back door and head for the bar, it seems the assessment was pretty accurate. On a small stage in the front corner, an unattractive female is lip-syncing to a disco track, while a pretty and effeminate guy is being pummelled by possibly the largest and least feminine female I have ever seen. It's not a pretty sight.

Somebody pinches my arse. Holy shit, it's a guy. I nudge closer to Helen in the hope she might shield me a little, but she gives me a look lacking any sympathy at all.

She orders a drink before I realise it. She obviously knows the girl behind the bar. No money changes hands and drinks arrive. I put my back to the bar, trying to protect my arse, and realise that the ugly woman on the stage in the corner is, in fact, a guy in drag, and he could stand a little closer to the razor next time.

Helen chats with the girl behind the bar. Another drink comes. My back is still firmly pressed against the bar. A random guy looks me up and down and then looks across at Helen, and back at me questioningly. He smiles and gives me a big thumbs-up. I smile back stupidly, not sure what that was about, but it seems pretty good.

Helen nudges me to drink up, which, of course, I do obediently. I turn to put my glass back on the bar as she is giving the girl behind the bar a long, deep pash.

What the fuck?

We head back to the car. With a couple of drinks under my belt, I am feeling pretty good. Helen asks if I'm okay to drive. I nod and she passes me the keys. As soon as we get into the car, the handcuffs appear as if from nowhere and my right wrist is attached to the steering wheel. I give her a look as if to inquire how the hell I'm supposed to drive like this. She points for me to get on with it.

I guess we are going to her place.

With some initial difficulty, I negotiate our way out of the car park and onto the main drag. Once on the road, it's actually not a problem and I take it easy as we head out of Newcastle.

As we get into the eighty kilometres zone at Sandgate, she leans over and starts playing with my ear, finger running up and down my neck. I glance across at her and there is that almost evil leer.

Her other hand joins the party, undoing my top button and slipping her hand inside my shirt, a little squeeze of the nipple, then rubbing it, and a harder squeeze. As we pass the Big Mozzie at the Hexham Bowling Club, the hand has roamed to my jeans, gently rubbing. I become aware that my right foot is pushing down in sync with the rubbing, the car is wandering across lanes. She has my full attention.

As we approach the lights at the Hexham Bridge, I have to force myself to concentrate and maintain some control of the car. Her efforts don't diminish and as I glance over again, she now has a smug look that I have gained some amount of control. The rest of the trip to her flat is a test of my concentration.

When we arrive, she reaches over and unlocks the handcuffs, and we head inside. She grabs a couple of short, fat glasses and fills them with ice and Scotch before handing me one. She takes a large swig from her glass.

What now?

I figure that I have reached a level of trust where I can now be more forward. I put my glass down and move towards her, hands moving to her bottom. Out of nowhere, she turns quickly, slaps my face, then drops a shoulder, skilfully pushing me to the ground. She is now standing over me, screaming.

'I decide the how, the where, and the when. You got that?' I try to get up and she puts a stiletto heel on my chest, pinning me there.

What the hell? That'll leave a mark!

She pushes harder — now this is really hurting — then lifts her foot, turning for the bedroom.

'Don't move.' She reappears a few seconds later with what looks like some sort of mask. With one quick movement, she is astride me, knees pinning my arms. The mask goes over my face and everything goes dark. She deftly releases the pressure on my arms and quickly cuffs me again.

I am helped to my feet and led to the bedroom where she removes my jeans and undies. My shirt is unbuttoned, and the handcuffs secured to something.

Maybe it's the bedpost?

I hear her moving around the room. Music comes on. The Kinks! That's ominous. Some more movement and something comes to my lips.

'Drink,' she commands. The liquid hits my mouth with a rush. It's whisky, straight. She tips a fair bit in and I struggle to swallow, coughing, but keep it all in.

'I heard you were a naughty boy at work today.' She tips more whisky into my mouth. It goes down easier this time.

'And you have been disrespectful to me tonight, haven't you, Tim?' My mind is racing.

What is her game?

'Haven't you, Tim,' she insists. I nod.

More whisky is tipped in and my stomach is starting to churn. I hear the glass being placed down and refilled. She steps back near me, close to my ear. I can feel her breath.

'Do you know what we do with naughty boys, Tim?' she whispers. I shake my head.

'They are punished.'

I hear her step back, then a swishing sound, then it strikes me. The pain is intense and I try to move my hands to cover my unprotected backside. The cuffs are secure and I can sense her bracing for another go. I am trying to move my torso to escape the next hit.

Is she fucking crazy?

A half hour later, she allows me to wash. It's a delicate process, every movement inducing sharp pain from my bruised bum. It's a really weird sensation. A strange mix of pain and afterglow from the sex.

She really got off on the dominance thing.

When I go back to bedroom, the riding crop is on the floor, and the bedside lamp is on. Helen is in the bed, sheets covering her ample breasts, glasses on, reading. She looks so demure. Butter wouldn't melt in her mouth. The contrast is striking. She looks up and smiles at me.

What is going on in that twisted mind of hers?

She puts the book down. 'Do you like this situation?' she asks.

This is crazy. Fucking riding crop on my arse and wild sex.

'Yes,' is all I can blurt out.

'We can do this regularly, if you like.' She is looking at me over the top of her glasses now, watching me. 'But you need to do something for me.'

My experiences with Helen thus far have been fairly outrageous. This could be anything. Despite the prospect, I find myself reluctantly nodding.

'I need someone I can trust to pass on some information on some activities on the Base.' She pauses. 'Some illegal activities.' She pauses again, letting the information sink in. I start thinking it over. 'It will be worth your while.' There is the evil smile. It could have been a whole bunch more extreme and it only takes me a few seconds to respond.

'Okay, I think I can do that.'

I hope I don't regret this.

She smiles a smile that says '*he was never going to say no*', and puts her finger up motioning me toward her.

It turns out someone is pinching petrol, and lots of it. She tells me the Accounting Officers do a gross check every month of mileage/running hours for each vehicle on the Base, and the fuel consumed.

'It's not an exact science, but the figures have been stable for three years. After the fuel strike back in March, the fuel consumption went up, a lot, with no increase in total miles or hours. We reckon there is about two hundred gallons going missing every month.'

'How can I help?'

'We have no idea how it's happening, but it's going missing from the vehicles in the flying squadrons, Clarktors, cars, crew vans, bomb lift trucks, those sorts of things. Nothing is disappearing from the fuel farm or from Base squadron. Just keep your eyes open, okay?'

'Yer, sure.' I am not actually convinced I can help.

'Just our squadron, or OCU as well?'

'Both,' she says.

Back at work, we have slipped into an Air-to-Air combat phase, training versions of Sidewinder and Matra R530 missiles on the jets. We spend most of our days fault-finding any problems and playing musical missiles when a jet has to go into the hangar; missiles off this jet and onto that jet. That and playing cards, of course.

I haven't noticed anything abnormal. All the vehicles look to be operated routinely, the GSE tanker comes around every morning topping up fuel levels on power carts, Clarktors, and jammers. Cars are topped up at the bowser at the transport section. It's difficult to tell how anyone would be knocking fuel off.

The first week of August, I get afternoon shift for two weeks. We start at 1400 each day with a break for the evening meal and knock off when the work is finished. Generally, there isn't much on after about seven each night and it should have been a good chance to watch a bit of Ashes cricket, but it's not going well. The boys capitulated on day four at Edgbaston. We are now two-one down for the series and need to win the last two Tests.

The third test at Headingly was a real embarrassment, making the Poms follow on, then letting Botham score a hundred and fifty, before surrendering for a hundred and eleven, just eighteen short.

It wouldn't have happened if Dougie was playing.

The afternoon shift allows me time to reflect on my relationship with Helen. She has been on day shift for the period and our romantic interludes are most convenient on Friday nights. Romantic interlude is probably not the right term; more like violent, lust-filled collisions.

Maybe I should have a girlfriend that likes to go to the pictures, or out for dinner, rather than sessions with handcuffs, vibrator and riding crop?

Two weeks flight line follow. It's now become a low-thinking activity, much of the work done instinctively. Before, flight servicing's in the morning, launch aircraft, recover aircraft, refuel aircraft, then do it again. The time on the black hose is actually therapeutic. But the less taxing periods allow the mind to wander and I often think of Allison and what she might be doing. Then, I get a picture in my head of that wanker, Barrett, and dismiss thoughts of her.

Shit, I don't really want to think about Helen either. What fucking mess have I gotten myself into?

Between the operations of Mirages of No. 2 OCU and 77 Squadron, the SAR chopper, and the Macchi trainers from OCU, it's a busy airfield. Then there are visiting aircraft like Caribous and Hercules. Standing on the wing of a jet refuelling is a good way to watch what is going on around the Base. The crash alarm has been getting a workout over recent weeks and its comical to watch the fire trucks chase a jet down the runway, only for the pilot to report a loss of radio.

Sometimes, it is very serious. Mirages are known for their undercarriage problems and the application of the Emergency Undercarriage Handle is not that rare.

The other thing that becomes noticeable is the amount of traffic around the tarmac. It seems every man and his dog have some sort of vehicle to move around on or in. Everything from crew vans, to Moke with the oxy trolley, Kombis, Clarktors, tankers, Jammers, and air traffic station wagon. You name it, there is one here.

That's when I spot a Clarktor from OCU coming toward us towing a trailer loaded with forty-four-gallon drums. It's a guy from the OCU GSE section and it pulls up outside the 77 Squadron GSE section. Kingy, the Corporal MT Fitter, walks out and they push the trolley inside the workshop.

That's a little odd.

September kicks off with another two weeks on afternoon shift. With the Ashes lost, all talk turns to the football finals. Eastern Suburbs are the minor premiers and they will have a week off awaiting the winner of the Parramatta versus Newtown match on Saturday. Manly and Cronulla will fight out the other semi on Sunday.

I have been making an appearance in Dungog every second weekend to help with the milking and get some home cooking. While everyone complains about Mess food, there is nothing actually wrong with it — it's the same week in and week out — I just need something different. The state election is coming up and grandad is busy attending meetings and getting the Country Party messages out in newspapers, so the extra hands are useful.

Alternate weekends I hang around Newcastle with the boys. Merv and Nev are playing league for the RAAF team and Gus the RAAF Aussie Rules team and we generally try to get to both games. Gerry, Doc, and I make up the cheer squad.

Friday nights I am in some form of activity with Helen. It seems to range from a couple of hours of various erotic activities to a little rougher exploit with leather and cuffs, depending on her mood. At the end of one interlude, I happen to mention the strange behaviour of the GSE guys.

'Corporal King, you said?'

Yep, there was another guy from 2 OCU, but I don't know him.'

Saturday night is often the dance at Stewarts and Lloyds Recreation Club in Mayfield. They have a good band, ironically called JAB, Just Another Band, and there are always a few girls around. I never seem to be able to get any of them interested in me.

It would be nice to get into a real relationship.

The final Friday of the shift is a no-flying day to catch up on maintenance, and there is a squadron piss-up. Well, almost no flying, we have one test flight launching at 1130 and Andy and I are the crew for that sortie. As we go through the start-up routine, I can smell cooking onions.

'It looks like the party has started,' says Dave Heffernan, the test pilot, looking over his shoulder.

'You'll have to hurry if you want a feed,' I tell him.

'We might have our own little barbecue at the end of this,' he winks.

As soon as the jet taxies, there is a mass exodus toward the middle hangar. Within minutes, there are guys standing around in various forms of uniform, and other apparel, drinking beers and eating steak sandwiches, the crowd spilling out of the northern side of the hangar. Andy and I stay out on the line, watching, waiting. Something is going to happen.

Fifteen minutes after take-off, Andy spots him, pointing, 'there'.

I follow his finger and catch the Delta wings descending south over Grahamstown Dam, turning toward us and disappearing behind the Macchi hangar. We run up the tarmac to get a better view and just catch a glimpse as the aircraft dips below the tree line. We wait and watch.

Within seconds, it reappears just above the treetops at high speed, descending again once clear of the trees above J Group. As it gets to the taxiway, it descends further, maybe twenty feet above the ground, maybe lower, maximum speed, coming almost straight at us, between the OCU Mirage and Macchi hangars.

The jet goes past us and banks slightly to the right, over the top of the crowd outside the hangar. There is a loud bang that follows the jet, people running and diving for cover, falling over, beers in the air. The jet banks slightly between the water tower and the parachute training tower, a climb, barrel roll, and into the circuit. I reckon I have seen that barrel roll before.

In the quiet, following the mayhem, people are picking themselves off the ground and dusting themselves off. The mob within the hangar have now come out to watch. As the jet taxies onto the tarmac, the entire squadron lines up and applauds. The CO looks a little annoyed.

After refuelling and putting the jet to bed, Andy and I head to the hangar for a beer. All the boys are standing around two garbage bins full of ice and beer.

I find a Tooheys New and seek out Dave Heffernan. He's surrounded by a group of younger pilots, Bog Rats, hanging off his every word. He sees me coming and finishes his story.

'Well, we lit this little party up,' he says, laughing.

'That's for sure. You should have seen everyone hitting the deck as you went past. Sensational! I reckon there were at least forty beers thrown into the air.'

'All in a day's work, as long as they didn't go down the intake,' he says. 'I had to volunteer for Orderly Officer for the next two weeks though. The CO wasn't impressed.'

'That's a shame. All the boys loved it.' I am thinking whether I should ask, *Why the fuck not?* 'I reckon I've seen that barrel roll somewhere before,' I suggest.

'And where would that be?' he hesitates and looks at my name tag.

'Dougie. My real name is Tim Walsh, but everyone calls me Dougie.'

'I don't do barrel rolls over the Base every day, Dougie.'

'My uncle goes fishing on the Myall Lakes. I've been on the boat with him when a Mirage has gone over the top just like today.'

'There's loads of Mirage flights out of here every day, Dougie. We all fly over the Myall Lakes. It could be anyone.' Then he winks again and shakes my hand. I leave him to it. There is a fan club waiting for a chat.

I find Gus and Tacho with the rest of the boys from the Gunnies section. Beer flows, stories are told, things get messy and we end up in the boozer still in our overalls until they tell us to go home.

Saturday morning, I am on my way to Dungog for the weekend. It's my eighteenth birthday on Monday and I have the day off; a long weekend. I hop in the Corolla and head toward the front gate. As I go down the main drag, I spot a white Valiant station wagon coming the other way. It stops and she gets out, walking toward me. I pull the Corolla over and wind the window down. She has sunglasses on her head to hold her hair back.

'On your way to my place by chance?'

'Um, no, Helen. I was just heading off to Dungog for the weekend to see grandma and grandad.' There is a slight look of annoyance which quickly turns back to a smile.

'It's your birthday on Monday, isn't it? How about you drop in on your way home, and I'll have something for you,' she says, leaning in and dropping her hand onto my shoulder.

'Oh, okay. It won't be till after milking is finished. After six, okay?'

'That will be lovely, Tim,' she smiles. It's not a nice smile, one of those that says she means business. She backs away from the car.

'I've been missing you.'

It's not the typical Dungog weekend. While Saturday night we still manage to get to the RSL, Sunday is a picnic by the river beneath Chichester Dam. Grandma has packed cold meat and pickle sandwiches, Sao biscuits with cheese and tomato, and a Thermos for the tea. It's even warm enough to ditch my shirt, catch a few rays, and dip my feet in the river.

The Sunday roast has been delayed till Monday. Grandma and grandad have got me a new watch inscribed on the back, 'Happy 18th, Love, Gran and Pa'.

After lunch, grandma organises a chat with Louise on the phone. She is really enjoying life at Uni, but the cold got to her over winter, Armidale is a shit load colder than Dungog.

'How's what's-his-name?'

'Tim, it's Darren.'

Shit, that didn't go well.

I pull up at Helen's around ten-past-six. Her car is in the carport and there is a lamp on in the front window. Not too many other signs of life. I knock lightly on the door. A few seconds later, it opens and she ushers me in. She is dressed in a silk robe, hair up, makeup on, cherry-red lipstick. Strangely, she puts her finger to her lips, indicating I should remain quiet, and then motions me to sit on the lounge.

She goes to the kitchen, returning with my standard drink, Scotch and ice. She signals that I should drain the glass. It's quickly refilled and she indicates that I should wait. She disappears into the bedroom.

About ten minutes later, she reappears looking a little flustered. She refills my glass, then takes my hand and guides me to the door.

Inside, the bedroom is dimly lit with soft music playing, everything is in its usual place, with one minor exception. She has a woman in lace underwear standing with her back against the far wall. I look a little harder and can that she is blindfolded with hands behind her back. From experience, I would say she is cuffed. There is also a chair placed several feet in front of her. Helen motions me to sit in the chair.

'Have you missed me?' There is a nodding response and the woman turns her head toward Helen's voice. Looking harder now, I can see that the woman is highly strung, probably aroused. 'Did you think about the proposal?' She nods again. 'Well, what is it to be?'

'Yes, ma'am,' the woman says, in a low husky voice.

'Yes, you want what?'

'Yes, I want to fuck you, ma'am.'

'Just me?'

'No, ma'am, you and a man.' I can see her chest heaving, breathing heavily.

'That's right. I will let you do anything you like to me, but first you have to fuck a man.'

'Yes, ma'am.'

Helen moves toward her, the back of her hand running down her red cheeks.

'That's my girl.'

8 — Kangaroos and Tail Gunners

An alarm erupts somewhere waking me, thankfully it's not squawking long.

Where the fuck am I? Dungog? Helen's? Where?

I open my eyes, focusing, and realise I am in my bed on Base. A short time later, Andy gets out of bed, farts, and heads off to the ablutions.

Fuck, it's Tuesday morning. How the fuck did I get home?

My mind goes back to last night. There's a flash of holding the backside of a young, slim woman. She is on her knees yelling as I am pushing into her. She is pushing back, and I can make out Helen under her. For some reason, I am focused on the birthmark behind the young woman's right ear. It's roughly shaped like a love heart. Focusing on something keeps me from losing it. I have to save myself. Helen isn't satisfied yet.

The whole night was odd. Helen and I didn't actually have intercourse. She seemed to be getting off watching me screw the woman with the blindfold. After, she'd top our drinks and use her rare skills to get us ready for the next event.

Fucking crazy.

After a shower and some water, I go straight to work. Mac has me rostered to Gun Bay this week and maybe I can convince Wal I should be allowed some time to sleep off my eighteenth birthday.

No fucking chance. Every jet in the squadron has dirty blast panels and Mac is on the warpath.

'Those fooking blast panels should have been cleaned a week ago,' he yells at Toad. 'Get the fooking things cleaned this week.' Toad looks over at me. Message received and understood. Looks like I'm cleaning blast panels.

Removing blast panels from the jets is a major pain-in-the-arse. Being the place where bullets exit the gun barrels, there is a large build-up of carbon deposits which makes it really hard to undo the screws, all sixty of them. The best technique is to take a large hammer with me to bash the screwdriver into the screw heads, then turn them. It dislodges some of the carbon build-up.

Once removed, cleaning them is another thing. The crap that has accumulated is glued on. A good soak in the kero bath, and attack them with Deoxidine. It's a phosphoric acid and solvent-type metal cleaner which leaves your hands numb; nasty stuff. The steel baffles can be cleaned with a sonic blaster, a needle gun powered by compressed air that sounds like a machine gun.

By Thursday afternoon, we have most of the jets clean and panels refitted, and getting a little flippant about the task. I am getting that adept at using a Dassault screwdriver that I can now bounce one out of my hand, land it on its handle end, and catch it back in the hand while walking. Tacho does his party trick of ambushing people with the sonic blaster and strafing the hangar.

As with most things, he takes it that one step too far. Bones and Mac are not impressed at a surprise attack as they walk into our hangar. He jumps back behind the door, but the damage is done.

Joe Byrne wanders out fifteen minutes later and tells him to report to Mac's office immediately. He takes off his earmuffs and gloves and hands them to me.

'Off to see if there's any new fly shit on Mac's ceiling.'

Always in the shit, it's only the depth that varies.

The following Wednesday, Mac announces that Exercise Kangaroo 81 is coming up in October. The squadron will be deploying to Rockhampton and he wants volunteers. Again, Tacho, Gus and I put our hands up, and, as usual, the Baggers have to go home to ask permission.

Early October, the Herc lands on the Rockhampton Airport strip just after 1300 and the heat and humidity hit us as soon as the ramp comes down. I have a quick flashback of arriving in Wagga Wagga, only this time, there isn't the yelling. We head into a tent on the side of the tarmac and drop our gear. As quickly as the forklifts deposit the pallets, we swarm over them, removing tie-down straps and unpacking equipment. We don't have too long before the jets start landing.

The Flight Line Operations Hut is set up in two adjoined tents and Sergeant Clark is giving orders getting everything set for the arrival of the jets. They are overhead by 1500 and we set about refuelling and covering them up for the night. We are then directed to a city of tents and allocated a stretcher. Misty and I are in the same tent. Joe Byrne and Tacho are next door, and Gus and Billy two down. Misty instructs me to change, and a short time later a heavy truck pulls up, driven by one of our Equipment Section guys.

'Get in, boys.'

The truck stops at various locations around the camp and by the time we leave the camp, people are spilling onto the tail gate.

It's not a long ride into town and shortly after, the truck pulls up outside the Criterion Hotel.

I hope the crowd here is different to the Criterion in Newcastle.

I follow the boys out and survey the scene. It's a busy street with a wide, brown river opposite. The building itself has a lot of arches across the front and what looks like a bell tower. I follow the boys into the public bar and Joe gestures to follow him further to the lounge.

Apparently, Joe knows the manager, a chubby guy called Fitzy, and we get our drinks at a special rate. After introductions, Joe gets the first round. I don't see money changing hands.

The boys set a cracking pace and we are not politely urged to keep up with the shout. Joe is holding court in his usual style, telling warries about previous Kangaroo exercises and associated drinking escapades.

It's funny how the stories are never about the war games, just the drinking that goes with it.

During the chat, there is a surprise for me. I overhear Joe telling two Baggers how their 'special fuel supply' had dried up.

'What happened?'

'Screws searched Kingy's place and found ten full five-gallon drums. Him and Bugsy are being done for theft.'

Bill leans over towards Jo, speaking softly. 'Fuck, I hope they don't come looking for more at my place. I'll be fucked for sure.'

'Na, mate, we'll be right. Kingy told them it was only for himself. He won't dob.'

Around 2100, the pub is closing and the truck miraculously appears again. Back to the airport and into the stretcher falling unconscious, until the effects of the booze wear off and I can feel the mosquitoes biting.

Around six, I have had enough of the scratching and Misty's snoring and get out of bed, going in search of a shower. There's a tin shed with a row of cubicles, a boiler on the side providing the hot water, and although the early morning air is quite warm, I use it to soothe the mozzie bites.

Dressed, I find a field Mess set up in a large tent. It's an Army operation. There are no encouraging words from the staff and service is delivered begrudgingly. Apparently, they don't like us Fighter Squadron guys. We come in last, after they have set everything up, then bugger off and leave them to pack it all up.

I ask for two grilled eggs and the cook slaps them onto my plate, a dirty look on his face. I am starving and shovel down the eggs, baked beans and toast quickly, now remembering we didn't eat last night.

The first few days' work isn't hard, mostly familiarisation flights. There is one jet set up with the camera pack to do recon flights and another with chaff dispensers and an ECM pod. My job is to assist Misty with replenishing the chaff; that and to sunbake.

The ample time between sorties allows my mind to wander. Just thinking about all manner of shit, what Amy and Susan might be doing, what's happening on the farm, what's Allison up to?

I really fucked that one up.

My mind shifts to Helen and I have a moment of both excitement and anxiety. I can't deny that the sex we have is pretty outrageous. I haven't shared any of the detail with the boys, not even admitted who it is I am seeing. I reckon they wouldn't believe me anyway. The trouble is, I don't love her, I'm not even sure I like her much. I can never see us getting married.

Could you imagine the look on grandma's face when I walk in the door with Helen.

It's not a thought that brings a smile to my face and that's the moment when I know it's not going to last much longer. It's time to declare that innings.

The after-work routine is a quick couple at the makeshift club within Tent City, shower and change, evening meal, followed by a trip into the Criterion in the back of the truck. Back in the stretcher before eleven with enough liquid sleeping pills on board to knock out half of Dungog.

Towards the end of the week, we start Combat Air Patrol, or CAP for short. That usually involves two jets stooging around off the coast over the top of some navy ships and two jets on two-minute alerts, pilots strapped in and ready to go.

It can't be comfortable for them in there. Seat straps done up tight, dressed in flying suit, G suit, gloves and helmet. There are umbrellas to keep the direct sun off them, but the Queensland heat is cruel. Every now and again, the boys start the blower and shove the nozzle into the cockpit just to move the air around.

If you are not out on the tarmac working, the options to keep busy and cool are limited. The favoured pastime is reading. Sleeping is an option if you can find something soft the put your head on. Most guys opt for rolling their T-shirt into a ball. The smart guys have stashed a piece of foam into the Fly Away Kit — foam is becoming a saleable commodity.

Sunday is a no-flying day. Apparently, there is a big briefing on at Exercise HQ and everyone is getting ready for the big push to start. We have all the jets ready to go and so we are at Fitzy's door when he opens at midday on Sunday.

'Hey, Gus, shouldn't we at least try some sightseeing?'

'I've done the research, Dougie.' Of course, he has; that's just who Gus is.

'Unless you have the money to get to Yeppoon and then out onto the reef, there's fuck-all to see around here. You may as well settle in and watch the end of Bathurst.' Disappointingly, the race ends early as there is a huge pile-up that blocks the track. Dick Johnson is declared the winner, making the Queenslanders happy at least.

At the start of week two, the squadron has been split into two shifts. Day shift starting before dawn and the flying starting around 0700, continuing throughout the day. Afternoon shift comes in around 1400 and there is a half hour handover. They continue flying till around 2200, then fix any jets that are broken. I reckon we'd be flying twenty-four hours a day if the CO had his way, but I guess the Rockhampton residents might have something to say about the racket. War is noisy, even when we are just practising.

Most people are pushing Mac to roster them onto day shift. Aside from the fact that it doesn't mess with your body clock, there is the added bonus of getting to sleep through the night.

Many of the afternoon shift boys never get to bed till three or four in the morning and the sound of Mirage afterburners, and the Rockhampton heat, makes sleeping during the day almost impossible. A lot of guys have taken up walking to the Rockhampton swimming pool for a few hours before work, cooling off in the pool, and then sleeping under the trees.

Most of week two, it's the CAP and two-minute alert routine, with a few Recon sorties thrown in. A typical Mirage sortie lasts around an hour and so there is a constant push to get the next two jets airborne before the two airborne run out of fuel. As that happens, another two jets go onto two-minute alert. My critical role in the whole event is lying under the two-minute alert jets for a shift, launching one every hour and then strapping a pilot to the next jet going onto alert. It's more fun than reading a book.

Week three and we have shifted to a different phase of the exercise. Day shift is starting earlier and the first wave of jets launches in darkness — it's a dawn strike. Through the day there are various Close Air Support and Recon missions.

There are even a few General Flying sorties, passengers joyriding in the back seat of our two-seat fighter, everyone from the general in charge of the exercise, to the cooks in our Mess. The relationship with the army cooks, along with the standard of the meals, has steadily improved over the course of the exercise and a ride in a supersonic jet cements that improved rapport.

The flying tempo goes up a notch and it seems that as soon as we finish refuelling there is a pilot there to sign for the jet and get going again.

Mid-afternoon Wednesday, Slug and I are told to launch A3-29. Our pilot walks out as we are plugging in the power cart. He's a baby-faced Bog Rat who I haven't seen before. He must be new. I follow him on his walkaround. On closer inspection, I reckon he's just out of school, definitely wet behind the ears.

We go through the usual strap-in, engine start, and after-start routine before he pushes the throttle forward and taxies. Our steely-eyed killer is about to take on the yellow hordes, well, at least Flying Officer Wet- Behind-the-Ears is.

Forty minutes later, our jet pitches into the circuit and Waz and I wander out to our assigned slot. As the jet approaches, something looks amiss, but I can't tell what it is from this distance. As it gets closer, we can see what looks like a tree branch hanging from the port supersonic wing tank. I marshal him into position, chocks in, he shuts the engine down and I put the ladder on and climb up.

Flying Officer Wet-Behind-The-Ears looks like a ghost. He is drenched in sweat, is trying to smile as I make the ejection seat safe, but looks as stressed as any human I have ever seen in my life.

He climbs out, inspecting the branch as he walks past the wing. No major damage done. He seems relieved and some colour returns to his face.

'Bird strike,' he says, hesitantly. Waz and I look at each other slightly bewildered.

'Was it in a nest, Sir?'

Over the weekend and into week four, the flying is hectic. Pilots will fly anything remotely serviceable and, in some cases, the next pilot is doing his walk around while we finish refuelling from the previous sortie. The Desk Sergeant has the aircraft EE500 on the wing so we can sign up the fuel. He releases the jet, and the pilot straps in. Luckily, the Line Corporal is ferrying cold water out to us.

On Wednesday afternoon it goes quiet, nothing. Pilots are lying around, sunning themselves. There isn't an unserviceable jet in the place, but we have no tasking orders.

Joe has acquired a large piece of canvas from somewhere — no sense in asking where — and he's busy arranging empty forty-four-gallon drums in a circle.

'What the fook is this?' asks Mac.

'A swimming pool, Flight.'

A look of astonishment comes across Mac's face, then a shake of the head, walking off. It doesn't look much like a pool to me and I sit and watch progress for a while. The canvas is laid across the top of the drums and the centre is pushed down to ground level and held using shoring that we usually use underneath aircraft pallets.

That's a fucking big pool. He's never going to find enough water to fill it.

The next morning, we are still lying around awaiting task orders. A game of cricket is underway on the tarmac, the bat, fashioned from a piece of scrap timber, and the ball — a tennis ball wrapped tightly in cloth, instant airframe, tape.

Don't get wrapped on the pads. It hurts like hell.

It's a high stakes game and even the CO turns his hand to bowling, a crafty bit of leg spin, catching out a few young wannabes. Around nine- thirty, the cooks turn up with morning tea and play is suspended. We're all sitting around eating lamingtons and scones, mug of tea in hand, when the truck arrives; the green Army water truck, with Joe in the passenger seat. He and the driver get out, a boom is extended over the pool and the pump comes on. Three minutes later, we have one fully functional swimming pool.

It's never a good idea for military personnel to have too much time on their hands. Within the hour, the pool is overflowing with bodies, some with floaties and an inflatable swan. Where did they come from? Yellow beach umbrellas have appeared embellished with Queensland favourite liquid and deck chairs have been manufactured from pallets, blokes sunning their already tanned bodies. There are even a couple of the female Air Traffic Controllers in bikini tops and shorts joining the fun.

Gus and I are admiring the spectacle when Mac walks over. There is a flurry of words in Scottish, most of which I don't understand, except for 'fooking Joe Byrne.' Gus and I look at each other and grin, just as Tacho wanders over. Mac looks him up and down.

'What, no inflatable pink flamingo in ye bag,' enquires Mac, with a heavy hit of sarcasm. 'I would have thought you'd be in the middle of that lot.'

'No, Flight.' The look of astonishment on Mac's face is remarkable.

'What, are ya ill, lad?'

'No, Flight, not at all. I was, um, hoping to ask you for the afternoon off.' Mac hasn't lost the astonished look.

'I can na go giving you the day off, lad, not without giving everyone a day off. What makes you so special?'

'Um, it's my eighteenth birthday.' The look of astonishment still on Mac's face, the cogs turning internally. Gus and I exchange glances and an unsaid, *Did you know? No. Did you? No.*

'Fookin' hell, lad, why didn't ye say.'

'Okay, you boys have been working morning and night for a couple of weeks, and you're mostly good lads. Seems only fair that you should celebrate together. I'll get the other lads to cover for yer.'

Shortly after, Gus, Tacho and I are deposited at the Criterion Hotel, Fitzy is counting money at the bar. He looks us up and down.

'Aren't you boys Joe's mates?'

'Yep.'

'You get a leave pass? I notice it's been quiet this morning.'

'Yer, not much flying happening, and it's Tacho's eighteenth,' I say gesturing toward him. 'The boss gave us the afternoon off.'

His face cycles through several looks, some of them more than a little scary, but in the end there is a shrug. I doubt that he really cares someone under eighteen has been getting hammered in his pub off and on, for the past two weeks. A Bundy and Coke and two XXXX pots appear on the bar with his compliments.

'So, what's the plan, boys' Tacho enquires. Gus and I sip our beers, deliberating.

'Is there a brothel in town?' I enquire. 'We could buy you one for your birthday?' Tacho doesn't look convinced. Heads go back down, thinking.

'There's a florist around the corner. We could get you a bunch of roses and a nice card?'

'Fuck off, Gus, I am expecting that from my mother.' More heads down, thinking.

'I've never been on a pub crawl, I mean a proper pub crawl,' he says, eagerly.

'Well, fuck, neither have we.' Three empty glasses are placed back on the bar, and Tacho buys a round. We discuss the plan for the day, how many pubs do we think we can get around?

'One of the boys said that there are forty-six pubs in Rockhampton. I reckon we should aim for at least half.' Tacho tells us, 'One in each.'

By 1400, we are on pub number five. We meet a couple of older guys who are veterans of WWII. I explain to them that we are in Rocky on exercise. The blokes closest to me pipes in.

'Air Force, you say? Isn't the exercise a little further north?'

'We have supersonic aircraft that require a long runway and Rockhampton Airport is the closest one to the action.'

'That's a civilised way to go to war. I was in the Army during the war. No bloody pubs in New Guinea, I can tell you,' he says, chuckling.

'And what do you young fellas do in the Air Force?' asks another.

'We are tail-gunners on F-111s,' Gus calmly tells them. There is a pregnant pause while this information is digested. His mate leans back over with a serious look on his face.

'Doesn't it get hot back there?'

'There is air conditioning, and even a little window we can open if we are travelling at subsonic speeds,' I explain. The old boy looks satisfied, a nod, and an 'Oh, really'. As we leave, we wish them well thinking we are the smartest three blokes to ever drink in a Rockhampton pub.

We take a turn off the main street and look around. There's a pub on the opposite side of the road, halfway down. We cross and walk in with purpose. It's quite noisy inside and just as we approach the bar, it goes quiet. I look around, and there are black faces everywhere.

Where's Nev when you need him?

'You fallas get lost,' an old guy by the window asks, the others laugh. He looks straight at me.

'You, boy,' now pointing. 'You can stay. You other white fallas can fuck off,' now pointing at the door. Gus ducks an empty beer bottle and it smashes on the tiles behind him.

We all back out like it's a standoff inside a western saloon, hands ready to grab imaginary six guns, a couple more stubbies flying through the air. Outside, we run like shit. Through the thumping of my heart, I can make out laughter coming from inside.

The late afternoon light is fading and the last rays hit the east side of the street as we enter the Commercial Hotel. This is pub number twelve. There's a pay night crowd in and we have to lurk over a number of tables before one is vacated. No sense in sitting at the bar, Gus keeps falling off the stools.

I am feeling pretty good and go to the bar for the shout. Gus and Tacho are in some ridiculous conversation about the merits of rock music versus blues. I get the order and when I turn away from the bar, there's a girl waiting behind me.

'Hi,' I say. She smiles, not too dissimilar a smile from Louise's.

'Hi.' I am stopped in my tracks, looking at her. She smiles again.

'Do you mind,' and she gestures to get past me.

'Oh, yer, sorry, sorry.' I keep my eyes on hers as I weave past. Back at the table the boys are still talking music; country rock classics.

Is Mexican Girl really country rock? More like soft porn.

I look back at the bar and I can't see her. That's disappointing. Maybe it's the booze, maybe not, but I am feeling lonely. I need some love and I reiterate my pledge to cut the relationship with Helen.

Fuck, that's not a relationship; it's bordering on an obsession, and not mine.

'Do you live locally?' I snap out of my daydream and look up. It's her.

'Sorry.'

'Do you live locally,' she repeats. My mind coming back to the present.

'No, no, we are here on exercise with the Air Force,' pointing at Gus and Tacho.

'You?'

'No, well, sort of. I am at tech college and live in town, but I am from Roma. That's kind of local.' I used to room with Jim Wenke in Wagga. He was from Roma. While it is in the same state, I know it's not exactly local.

There is movement at my side and now I realise the conversation has got Tacho's attention. He stands awkwardly from his chair, extending his hand.

'Beautiful lady, my name is Michael. It's my birthday and you may offer your congratulations by kissing my hand,' he sways slightly.

'Hello Michael, happy birthday,' followed by a sweet smile, ignoring the offer. She looks back at me. 'Would you guys like to come and sit at our table?' She points to the far corner where two girls, who look about our age, wave at us. Tacho almost trips getting up to move. Gus requires assistance out of his chair.

Concealed in the corner, the boys start regaling the girls with various war stories, mostly bullshit. The other two girls are sisters, probably eighteen or nineteen, and seemingly captivated by the stories. I get back to the original conversation.

'Roma local to Rockhampton, that's like saying Adelaide and

Melbourne are local.' I smile so she doesn't think I am taking the piss.

'When you live in Roma, anywhere within two hundred miles is local,' she pauses. 'What's your name?'

'Tim. Yours?'

'Dee.'

'Short for?

'Darlene'

'What are you doing in Rockhampton?'

She sighs, 'Long story. Mum and dad have fifty thousand acres west of Roma, beef country. Dad sent me here to learn office administration at tech college, and accounting. I'm currently working at a local accountant's office, an old mate of dad's, and heading home at the end of November.'

I think of my own circumstance and the family farm, 'They have a plan for you.' A statement, not a question. She seems surprised.

'My brother got to go to the agriculture college in Longreach, but he fell for one of the girls and now he's chasing her around Brisbane. I get to go home and learn how to run the farm.' She says it all without emotion; it's like she is resigned to her future, almost relishing it.

'It's a big challenge for a girl.' As I say it, I know it's come out all wrong. Her face has gone red with anger. It matches her hair. I change the subject quickly.

'How do you know those two,' I ask, nodding sideways, and her complexion returns quickly.

'Oh, I played netball with Jane and Kym this year. They are locals, real locals.'

'You want a drink?'

'Sure, Bundy and Coke please.' I look over to see if the boys need one. They haven't touched theirs; too busy talking.

When I get back with the drinks, she starts asking questions.

'Where are you from, Tim?'

'A town by the name of Dungog, north-west of Newcastle.'

'What do your parents do?'

'I live, lived, with my grandparents before I joined up. They have a dairy farm ten miles out of town.'

A smile comes to her face, I can tell she clearly understands the jumbled bits of information I have just conveyed. Firstly, for some reason or other, I don't live with my parents and life has not been kind to me. That story would be familiar to her. Secondly, she's acknowledging I am from a farm and I am familiar with hard work and life on the land. Finally, there would be some pressure on me to go home and work the farm.

'You're not going back full time then?'

'Not right now. Maybe in a few years, who knows?' She nods.

'Dad always wanted my brother to take on the farm and with him spellbound by some chick, I feel the obligation to take it on. I haven't ruled out a different career after I get it running right, but not till then,' she says with a determination.

It is a bit of a shock to see such tenacity in someone my age, let alone a girl. She doesn't talk about having a family and I get the impression she isn't out tonight to find a boyfriend; it's a social drink.

The talk turns to farms and cattle. We compare notes about herds and daily routines — they couldn't be more different. It makes me wonder how anyone ever makes any money from beef cattle, but then again, I have never taken too much notice of how grandad makes a living.

Tacho stands, 'Dougie, isn't it time we moved along? One drink per pub is the rule.'

I look across at Dee and gesture enquiringly.

She starts to gather her handbag, 'Come on girls, looks like we are going on a pub crawl.'

The new mob makes its way around several more pubs, Tacho dribbling endlessly to Jane, Kym walking arm-in-arm with Gus. I think she is holding him up. Around 2200, we find a pub that has a band doing some classics, Creedence, Daddy Cool, and T Rex. Dee and I manage to dance a bit before they take a break. Tacho has shouted the drinks and somehow is now chatting with the drummer from the band.

The band comes back on, a heavy bass line playing. It's an Angels' song. She grabs my hand and we dance again. The load of grog has dropped my inhibitions and I reckon I am moving like John Travolta. The lead singer is doing a credible Doc Neeson impersonation. They must like the Angels, because they do two more songs. He has the crowd going. 'No way, get fucked, fuck off.'

Taking a breather, she looks at her watch. 'Hey, it's late and I have to work tomorrow. Are you around tomorrow night?'

'Yer, we don't fly out till Saturday. Do you want to catch a movie or a dance?'

'Sure.'

'I'll meet you at the Criterion at six?' She screws up her nose.

'How about here. It's nicer than the Criterion.'

It takes me another hour to coax Tacho out of the place. He

wants to be friends with everyone. In the end, they shove him out and close the doors behind him. I manage to find us a cab.

Back at tent city, he is in full voice, singing something that only remotely resembles 'Bohemian Rhapsody'. I am too busy holding Gus up to shut him down and thankfully Joe appears grabbing him by the collar, pulling him towards their tent. He's now doing his best Jack Thompson impersonation from *The Man from Snowy River*.

The sound of Mirage engines wakes me. I can still taste Fourex, and I have a slight headache.

Hey, I don't feel too bad.

I look over and Misty's stretcher is empty, then I look at my watch. It's five o'clock. Fuck, it must be another dawn strike. I hope the boys are covering for us. Surely Mac would have got word to us if we were expected to work early?

Within what seems like two shakes of a lamb's tail of my eyes closing again, I am awoken by the physical presence and the airhorns of a Clarktor that is parked halfway into our tent. It's Joe.

'Mac says you, Tacho and Gus should get some breakfast and be there by 0800. You right to wake them up?'

'Yer, sure.' Now I have a headache and a mouth that feels like the bottom of a bird cage. Mac is waiting when we arrive. He has that look on his face like he knows how much we are hurting and he is enjoying it.

'Are you gentlemen sober enough to work on aircraft yet,' he asks, looking at Gus.

'I think so, Flight.'

He looks at me and I nod.

Tacho is grinning, I think he's still pissed.

'Right, all the jets are back on the deck now. We are refuelling and they will launch back to Williamtown at 1100; all of them. After that, all this shite has to be packed up ready for the Hercules tomorrow. You two,' pointing at Gus and me, 'go and relieve Billy and Joe. They'll be having the day off. Tacho, you come with me.' He walks off with Tacho in tow.

The rest of Friday is packing shit up, lots of it. There are three full C-130 loads of crap and every bit of gear has to go onto an aircraft pallet. After the jets leave, we get all the ladders, blowers, and power carts on pallets. Tents are taken down and packed quickly. In the heat, I look around for the swimming pool. It has been flattened long ago. By 1600 hours, there are a bunch of pallets ready to go. Except for the marks on the ground where our tents once stood, you would barely know we had been here.

We hitch a ride into town just before 1800 and head to The Brunswick. The girls are in the front bar and give us a wave. I get a kiss on the cheek from Dee and the other girls greet Tacho and Gus with more intimate moves. Tacho goes to the bar.

'What's on this weekend?'

'Weekends in Rockhampton are fairly standard. Friday night, everyone goes out and gets plastered. Saturday morning, you sleep off the hangover, and then play sport Saturday afternoon. Saturday night is the after-sport bragging session followed by mad dancing and then the midnight sack race.'

'Sack race?'

'Everyone runs around the pub at midnight looking for someone to get into the sack with.' She smiles, but it's a forced smile.

The boys are in deep conversation with the other girls. Apparently, they are twins. How did we not notice that? How pissed were we last night? There's a quick discussion about what we are going to do. Dee and I decide to see a movie and we all part ways.

There is a limited choice in movies at the cinema. She wants to see the *Cannonball Run*, looks like a sort of *Smokey and the Bandit* thing. Halfway through, she grabs my hand and escorts me outside. Apparently, it wasn't what she was expecting.

We walk for about fifteen minutes, talking about nothing of any importance, sharing a laugh.

'Where are we heading?' She looks back with mischief in her eyes.

'My place. Well, not quite, it's a boarding house, and there are strict rules about having boys in the room, so keep your voice down.'

It's a two-storey building, not that different from my accommodation block in Wagga, only older. It might have been a nurse's home in its day. She finds a side gate and we go round the back, through a back door and down a corridor. She fumbles with the keys before opening the door and switching on the light.

It's a small room, a bit smaller than my room at Williamtown, but manages to squeeze in a single bed, record player and a bunch of records standing on their edge. There's also a hand basin, desk and a cupboard. Showers must be down the hall.

'You want a beer?'

There is a small fridge inside her cupboard, extension cord running out to a power point. She opens it and there are a couple of Fourex stubbies inside. Two come out and she grapples for a string hanging from the wardrobe door. There is a bottle opener on the end of the string.

I have to hand it to these Queensland girls; they are down-to-earth.

She takes a big swig and goes to the record player, picking out an album and putting it on the turntable. The speakers coming to life as the needle hits vinyl, a little static before the first track.

Bloody Johnny Horton, Way Up North.

We both sing along with me doing the low down 'way up north' lines. This was one of dad's favourites and I know it by heart. The next track is unfamiliar. It starts with a banjo picking. I can't place it, and look at her questioning.

'The Battle of New Orleans.'

'Never heard of it.'

She sings each line with gusto and I slowly pick up on the chorus. My hands imitating the snare drums as it closes.

'I can't believe you've never heard of that?'

'Nope, I know 'North to Alaska', but not any others.' She decides to change the record to *Silk Degrees*. We have a dance around to 'Lido' before an embrace. I am looking into her eyes. A soft kiss and then it gets a little more intense.

I manage to get her shirt unbuttoned and off, the shoulder strap of her bra down her arm, a pert little breast free in my hand. I touch the nipple and it's hard. The brakes are starting to come off. My hands are on her bum and undoing her jeans. It seems there is nothing impeding us. My hand slides down into her panties and there is a sudden reaction. She pushes me away, panting.

'No,' she tells me, her eyes wild. Something tells me that it's not me she can't handle, it is something else. I hold her close.

The music is still going and so I start to rock to the beat, holding her head in my hands and her body close, not intimate. She is sobbing. Eventually, we manage to lie down and I hold her close. The sobbing has stopped and we just lie there.

Two hours later, I get up and put my shirt back on, gathering myself. She comes to me, wrapping her arms around me.

'If we ever meet again, it won't be the same, I promise.'

The next morning, having showered and changed, I am eating breakfast when the boys come into the Mess. They fill their plates and take a seat next to me. By the look of them, it's been another night on it.

'Big night, Dougie,' says Gus. 'Big night,' emphasis on the big. I am looking on, waiting for the details.

'Those girls do everything together,' Tacho tells me, buttering toast.

'Everything,' Gus confirms, staring at his baked beans and letting rip with a fart that brings tears to our eyes. 'That's better,' he says, digging into his beans.

'The four of us were out the back of the pub at eleven last night. They had their tongues and hands everywhere.'

'Yer, I reckon they have done that before. It was like they were egging each other on.'

'Before we knew it, they undid our jeans and dropped to their knees; synchronised head jobs. You should have seen him, he rested his Bundy and Coke on the top of her head,' pointing at Tacho.

'Then they stood up and bent over up against the pub wall. I didn't need an invitation. Not quite as synchronised as the head job, but it was close.'

'When it was all done, we went back inside and I shouted the drinks. The girls hung around for another hour, Tacho got their phone number and then they just fucked off into the night, just disappeared,' Gus is shaking his head, eyes somewhere else.

A bit like Billy when his shout comes around.

I ponder.

We land in Williamtown around 1400 Saturday afternoon, trudge back to our room, drop our bags and change. The washing can wait. Tacho is going to check on the Interceptor, maybe go for a drive, and Gus just throws himself onto his bed, fucked. Andy and I decide to go and find out what Nev is up to, wandering over to his block. He and Merv are sitting out the front in the sun on bean bags drinking cans from an esky.

'You've picked up a tan,' Nev says. 'Any darker and we'll admit you to the brotherhood.'

'Grandad always reckons I was a throwback. I've got the same complexion as Grandma Walsh. I only have to stand in front of a window to get a tan.' Merv puts his hand into the esky and throws us a can each.

'What's on the program for today, boys?'

'Well, after we hear your war stories from Rockie, we thought we'd head into town and see whether there's any good bands playing,' says Merv.

'Or, we could always drop by the Workers Club and grab a grannie,' adds Nev.

The thought of grabbing a grannie isn't that enticing. Apparently, it involves going to Workers Club and picking up a twenty-five-year-old, single mum from Mayfield. The experience in Rockhampton has reminded me that it's probably best to hang around girls my own age; it just seems more normal. As I am thinking about it some more, a picture of Dee drops into my head, then Helen.

I really have to put an end to that innings.

'Where's Tacho?' asks Nev.

'Gone to see if the Interceptor will start.'

'He'll probably be there most of the afternoon,' Andy speculates.

'Well, grab a seat and tell us all your war stories. We'll see if he'll take us into town later.'

The boys share a couple of cans as I regale them of the story of Tacho's eighteenth, the subsequent double-header, and trying to stay out of Mac's way.

'Did you guys do any work, or just drink piss and chase chicks for three weeks?' Merv asks, incredulously.

'Oh, plenty of work. We flew every day and had aircraft on standby all day, so we had plenty of time on the line, hence the suntan.'

'Sounds like 77 Fucking Squadron Whitsunday tours if you ask me,' says Nev. I think about that a little and don't respond.

Probably true. So much for Australia's premier fighter Squadron.

Tacho appears around five, greasy hands and arms, grabbing a beer without invitation.

'What's on the program for tonight, boys?'

'Well, it depends on whether the Interceptor is serviceable,' Nev tells him.

'It's serviceable, just needed a little fine-tuning and some fuel. How about we head off about six-thirty?'

On the way into town, we drop into the servo on Maitland

Road and throw five bucks each at Tacho for fuel. Then, on through Islington and onto Hunter Street. He adopts the typical slow pace, scanning ahead and behind for potential competitors.

We pull up at the lights at Hannell Street. There is a small crowd inside the Bellevue and I am confirming my assumption that only sailors and misfits drink in there, when an HQ Monaro rolls through the lights. Our light goes green and Tacho is beside the HQ within seconds, rolling slowly side by side toward the next traffic light. I can actually hear the Monaro's engine over the Interceptor; it's making a racket. The driver is a few years older than us, long hair well down over the collar, a few tattoos up his arm. As we stop at the light, he leans over.

'You wanna fucking race RAAF cock?' Tacho has been here before.

'Why don't you race home to your fucking mum.'

The light changes to green catching everyone by surprise and nobody makes a particularly good getaway. I can hear the noise of both cars reverberating between the buildings and I look over at the speedo. First to second at about 85 kilometres, we are side by side, second to third at about 130 kilometres, still locked side by side. We crack 160 kilometres and the Monaro finally backs off, and we are running out of street quickly. Tacho keeps the pedal down for another couple of seconds to prove his point and then backs off, giving the brake pedal a stab.

Merv, Nev and I all look at each other. I think we've all been holding our breath for the past fifteen seconds. There is a collective sigh of relief. We might live through yet another one of these.

The Monaro turns off, doesn't want to play anymore, it seems. At the end of Scott Street, we turn left toward Nobbys, past Fort

Scratchley, then right, around the Esplanade past the rock pools and Ocean Baths, then Newcastle Beach. The pace is modest and we check out the groups of wax heads drying themselves off. Then, he crests the rise at Newcastle Hospital, and the pedal is mashed to the floor as we go past South Newcastle Beach and head for the Boogie Hole. At the end of the straight, it kicks left, then right. As he gets to the turn, he has both feet on the brake pedal, back two gears, right turn up the hill, into King Edward Park, the gardens appearing on our right. He careens through the narrow gap, up the hill and left turn, back west, climbing through the park.

The road makes another U-turn and we are now heading directly east at high speed. Here, there is nothing between us and a two hundred feet fall into the Pacific. We follow the curve around to the right at high speed. The moon has risen and I can clearly see the ocean below, and say a little prayer. As we approach the hairpin bend, he has both feet on the brake again. The car drifts sideways around the turn, and then he kicks the pedal again, fishtailing up the hill. Another left-hand curve at high speed and the tyres screaming, the car straightens and I look at the speedo. We are doing one hundred and thirty and the T-intersection at the top of the hill is looming. Tacho backs off and we turn right to head back towards town at what now seems like a snail's pace.

I wake Sunday feeling better than I have any morning for what seems like forever. A lazy day is in order; definitely need to get some washing done. I ponder my love life. Helen, she always wanting to be in control of every situation. All interactions always on her terms, and demanding on every level.

There has to be something more normal.

We have a date. Well, as much of a date as you get with Helen. As I leave the Base, some part of me is chastising myself for allowing myself to get sucked back into her web.

I should have broken it off when I came back from K81.

When I arrive, there aren't too many lights on, though her car is in the carport. I get out of the Corolla, walk up the driveway and knock on the door. It's all quiet but after several moments, the lock turns and the door opens. She unlocks the screen door, lets me in, firmly closing it and the wooden door behind me. She walks to her room, standing inside, awaiting my entry. As I walk in, I note enough light to make out she is covered with a bathrobe.

She methodically removes my shirt, shoes, socks and jeans, her hand brushing across the front of my underwear, then walks to the dressing table and picks up the leather belt, returning, holding it out for me to take. It's like it's a test every time.

Does the boy have the balls to take it from her and punish her? Or is he going to be the goody-two-shoes and back away, saying it's just not right.

At least, that is what is going on in my mind and I think she knows it. She cocks her head to the side slightly, raising her eyebrows, as if to push me to a decision, and smiles as I take it from her hand. The robe comes off and I feel a surge of adrenalin coursing through my body, among other things.

As she walks to the bed, I can make out a lace bra and panties, but there is something else. She kneels on the bed, pushing the panties down over her backside, exposing both cheeks, then pushes her two hands forward, making her backside thrust out more prominently. Her head bows in some sort of show of submission.

I know it's now my time to join the fray and walk forward. As always, she is orchestrating every move to meet her own specific needs. I put my hand on one of her arse cheeks and rub it slowly, kneading it, then the other, slowly, then withdraw. I have just noticed there are cuffs on her wrists. She turns to me with a mock look of being frightened.

'I've been a bad girl. I need to be punished!' I give that arse cheek a slap. She obviously likes it. 'I've been very, very bad.' Another couple of harder slaps that actually sting my hand and I enter her roughly from behind. This one is not for her. This time it's all about me. I am pumping her hard. I reach under and roughly tweak her nipples and she lets out a little squeal. I feel good to have the upper hand with her just for once. I thrust harder and harder and add a few more slaps, until I lose it and we fall together on our sides. She seems very happy.

That was fucking amazing.

As I am dressing, she tells me she is posted.

'Posted? Where to?'

'I am going to Canberra at the end of the year to a position in the Special Investigative Unit. Not too many people get selected for this, Tim. I am excited. It's probably my best shot at moving further up the chain; put some of these boys in their place once and for all.' A variety of thoughts go through my head.

Thank God. I might be free of her for a while.

The second thought is about her. I am wondering if all of her career aspirations will be satisfied with this move?

Friday, 04 Dec 1981, St Barbara's Day. It starts with a bus trip to Morna Point and a ritual walk through the old Air Weapons Range looking for Unexploded Ordnance, UXO. As the sand shifts over time, an old UXO comes to the surface and has to be destroyed by detonation. The job is finished quickly, but it's already hot.

Back to the hangar, Joe has a keg set up in the Smoko Room. The barbecue has been lit and Misty is turning meat. The onions get a douse of beer. He sees me watching.

'Enhances the flavour, Dougie.'

A few bullshit stories are told and within an hour, there are several pairs of wobbly boots being worn. Toad throws his empty Coke can into the bin from a good five feet.

'I'm off, boys. Got a hot date this arvo.'

There are some sceptical looks and Stan can't help himself.

'Who's the hot date, Toad? Mother Theresa?' Laughter all round.

'For your information, I am having dinner with Veronica Jacobs from the Orderly Room.' He has a smart grin on his face.

I have met her. She is a bottle-blonde Corporal with a big hooter. She keeps her hair down around the side of her face to hide the nose, seems nice enough.

'You've got a stunner there, Toad.'

He smiles and puts on his best posh English accent.

'One doesn't look at the mantelpiece while one is stoking the fire.'

Tacho is beside me, murmuring, 'What? You or her?'

He's right, Toad's not exactly an oil painting, hence the nickname.

'How does he do it? He's got a face like a busted arse,' Gus wonders.

'I hear he's hung like a horse,' murmurs Tacho again.

'Apparently, that information gets around the WRAAFery pretty quickly.'

Some of the Baggers head home early, which signals a turn in the tone of proceedings. The drinking becomes more aggressive. Things are getting out of control pretty quickly.

Joe Byrne is smashed. He's standing outside the Smoko Room with a beer and smoke in one hand, a burger in the other. He announces that he really needs to take a piss.

'I'm not holding it for you,' announces Hollywood.

Joe's face contorts and, shortly afterwards, a stain appears down the front of his overalls. He is relieving himself there and then. A grin starts to spread across his face.

The depravity starts to ramp up as if there is some sort of competition underway. Someone has thrown up into a jug, drinking from it. Ashtrays are being emptied into beer glasses and drunk, even a cockroach going into one glass. There is little adult supervision. The boys are going rogue.

'I'm getting the fuck out of here,' I announce, and make for a quiet exit out the back door. I can't afford to get entangled in something like this. I have enough marks on my service record. Just for once, Tacho sees the sense and joins me.

Fuck, St Barbara's Day in Wagga last year was a different kettle of fish. While it involved drinking, it was respectful, almost ceremonial. I would have been happy to take my gran. What I have just witnessed was nothing like that. It's just plain stupid.

'What about a swim,' suggests Tacho. A few nods, we grab a couple of cans and head to town in the Interceptor at speed. He takes wharf road down past the railway station and to Nobbies. The Esplanade is littered with crappy panel vans, surfboards on the roof racks or hanging over the tailgate, Waxheads leaning against the mudguard smoking, long hair blowing across their faces.

'You know that most of these guys don't know how to surf,' announces Gus. 'They just stand around and look cool. The boards are actually bolted to the roof racks,' he laughs.

With the north-easter blowing, the surf at Newcastle Beach is the pick and I get beyond the breakers, just floating around on my back pondering my situation.

Thankfully, Helen has gone to Canberra. That was starting to get out of hand. She had taken up getting the riding crop out and asking me to hit her. It was strangely exciting to watch her after each smack, savouring the pain, then tensing her backside for the next hit. She practically rode me senseless afterward.

But the whole thing was only ever about the sex. We only ever went out once, and that was weird. No, I need a normal date.

Fuck, I would be happy to just go Saturday morning shopping with someone.

We get back in the car with wet board shorts, a towel wrapped around the waste and a T-Shirt on. In the early evening traffic, Tacho carefully weaves his way out of town, sucking on a can. Once we get over Stockton Bridge, the traffic thins and normal service is returned, and we don't drop under one hundred and fifty kilometres heading through Fern Bay.

As we pass the caravan park, there is a quick flash of a cop car half hidden behind the bus shelter. I yell a warning, but Tacho has already seen it. It's one of those moments where Tacho's instincts and reflexes amaze me. Within what seems like a millisecond he has turned off the lights, changed down a gear and flattened it. I can see he has one eye on the road ahead and one on the mirror. I look back to see if the cop is giving chase, the headlights and flashing lights have come on.

Tacho keeps his foot down, and I realise I am now most certainly going faster on land than I have ever been. I look back again, no lights this time.

'He's not following,' I yell over the noise of engine and wind, getting more than a little nervous.

'If he's got a mate up this way, he will have let him know. I want to get through the front gate as soon as we can.'

We arrive back at Base without incident, Tacho diverting to the car park behind the boozer. Getting out, Gus and I look at each other in shock. Gus is pale.

'How fast were we going back there,' he asks.

Tacho looks a little pensive. 'I wasn't looking at the speedo. But, based on the revs and the gearing, I reckon we would've been doing about two- thirty to two-forty klicks, nearly four klicks a minute.' He walks around the front of the car, looking. 'I definitely need a spoiler on the front, though. We nearly lifted off at one point. Steering was vague.' He is laughing about it.

I'm glad he didn't mention that at the time.

Gus and I shovel in a couple more drinks and the nerves stop jingling quite so bad. Ten minutes later, a couple of the squadron guys comes in.

'Who owns the brown XB out the back?' Tacho puts his hand up, mid- drink.

'You went past us at the Fullerton Cove turn. Nearly blew us off the road. What's the fucking rush, Fangio?'

'Cops were chasing us,' I tell him.

'Well, they probably should have had their afterburner going.' He doesn't seem impressed. I am about to brag that we covered the last twelve klicks in three minutes. But he doesn't seem in the mood.

Saturday is pretty cruisy. Andy and I play a few records, have lunch, and take a dip at the Base pool. There's a game of cricket on the oval and it strikes me that I haven't even looked at a Test match, not to mention having a game myself. With Helen now gone, I promise myself that I will play after Christmas.

Early evening, we hit the Workers Club. After grabbing a beer, we find a table where we can observe the dance floor. It's mostly chicks dancing with each other, and the blokes holding up the bar. I scan for a little while to see if there is anyone around our age. Not too many candidates.

Tacho grabs my arm, points to two girls close to the stage, and stands. We are becoming quite a team, Tacho and I. They accept our request to dance. Between songs, I manage to find out her name is Karen.

She has a bit of a freckly face that goes well with her brown hair. The neat skirt and blouse frame her well. If you walked past her in the street, you'd definitely take a second look. When the band takes a break, we go back and sit with the boys and suss out whether they are with anyone. They aren't. Tacho and I grab our drinks and head over.

The night seems to go pretty well and we even drop the girls at home before going back for Andy, Nev and Merv.

The following week, word gets around about the ride back to Base. Tacho is getting plenty of attention from the boys and I get an invite to Mac's office.

'What happened on St Barbara's Day?'

'Sorry, Flight?' He has caught me by surprise. I thought this would be about Tacho's drive the previous Friday.

'What happened here on St Barbara's Day.'

'We had a barbecue and a few beers and went home,' I stammer. His eyebrows are twitching, so I know he's on edge.

'Someone has painted a moustache on the Grumpy Monkey on every jet and the fooking Smoko Room looks like a bomb hit it. Bones wants blood and I am going to hang the people who did it.' He is eyeing me, his face red with anger.

'Sorry, Flight, I can't help you. Gus, Tacho and I left at the same time as Toad.' I have stretched the truth. 'We didn't go anywhere near the flight line.' His eyes burn into me, trying to discern any flaw.

'Okay,' he agrees. His face lightens slightly. 'If you hear anything, you come and tell me. I might be able to pacify Bones if I know what happened. They might get away with a few weeks' extra duties.' I am slipping out the door with some relief when he interrupts.

'Oh, and one more thing, Dougie. I am sure that your grandparents wouldn't be pleased if they knew you were getting around in a V8 at high speed. You might want to think about who ye get in a car with.'

'Yes, Flight,' I say, glumly.

Fuck, where does he get his information?

One by one, the boys are called to Mac's office to give an account of last Friday's celebrations. Despite his best interrogation efforts, the boys hold their tongues. Mac isn't happy. He knows some serious crap went on, but he can't disclose enough to lay charges; not yet.

On the last Friday before Christmas, there is a golf game at

Muree followed by beers and a barbecue. Mac is firmly in control, overseeing all activities. Nothing outrageous is going to happen today. Everyone wishes each other a merry Christmas and it's over by 1300. Gus, Pete, Tacho and I pile into Gus' Valiant.

'So, what now, boys? There's going to be nothing happening on the Base. Do you want to go up to the Bay?'

'I've got a date with Karen late this arvo. Can you drop me back to Base?'

I have been looking forward to this all week; some opportunity for some normal interaction with the fairer sex. I arrive about ten minutes early at the Cambridge and belly up to the bar with a beer. There's a good crowd in, anticipating the band setting up in the corner.

A girl about my age bumps into me trying to get to the bar. We both apologise and look each other up and down.

If I wasn't here to meet another girl, I'd see what you were doing for the rest of the night.

She departs with two drinks and sits with a friend by the window. I sit and wait.

I am aware of the time. Karen is now fifteen minutes late. I order another beer. The band are warming up as I work through my beer checking my watch every two minutes. I order another and she's now half an hour late.

Have I been stood up?

I grab another beer. My confidence is leaking away quicker than the beer. She's forty-five minutes late. I have to assume I've been stood up. I look back over to where the other girl was and she's not there anymore.

Fuck this, what is it about me and girls?

I don't have a lot of leave, so there isn't too much time spent on the farm over Christmas. There are the standard Christmas Eve and Christmas Day events, but it's low key. Grandma even kept her tongue with respect to Louise. I don't suppose it matters now anyway, but the 'I told you so' stuff was getting monotonous.

Louise and I had a chat at the RSL on New Year's Eve, but it was brief, the conversation forced. She really has moved along and it's apparent that we no longer have a lot in common. I need to move on as well.

I do the ritual trip to Bulahdelah to see Grandma Walsh, and have a night on the lake with Uncle Alan. It's as relaxing as ever. I tell him about the breakup with Allison, how Louise went to Uni and got a boyfriend, and Karen standing me up.

'It seems like every girl I ever get sweet on finds another guy or just dumps me. Is there something wrong with me?'

'Plenty of time yet for the serious stuff, Tim. Just keep your head down at work and the relationship stuff will sort itself out in good time.' Wise words. Somehow, he has this way of making things less of a drama when my own brain does the complete opposite every time without fail.

I get myself back onto Base the second week in January. Work is pretty casual. there is a lot of time spent checking supplies, sweeping floors, watching cricket and playing hangar badminton.

After hours, I am at a bit of loss as to what to do with myself. I spent so much time with Helen last year that I kind of lost the connection with Nev, Gus, and Andy; my best mates. I have vowed to get that back and we have thrown ourselves into a routine of work, beach, and booze. That, and sleep, plenty of it.

A week later, the rest of the section start arriving back at work. There are debriefs on various adventures from around the country, followed by a lengthy game of cards before the boys settle into some work. It's uncanny how, collectively, they need the game of cards to re-establish the pecking order, but then this invisible switch goes on and they all knuckle down to their jobs. There aren't too many slouches here — they get exposed pretty quick — Billy and Chubby Checker being the notable ones.

I have been assigned to Carrier Bay with Joe Byrne and Corporal Squizzy Taylor is in charge. I am a little apprehensive because I have never worked with Squizzy before. They are both prominent in the unofficial pecking order of the section and the combination of the two could be interesting.

'What's first, Squizz?'

'Just start on the SUU-20s, Dougie. I know you've done this before, but here are the work sheets anyway,' he says, handing over a clipboard with check sheets attached. 'It's all pretty simple, just follow the sheet and not even you can fuck it up.' He looks over at Joe. 'Joe and I have to go to K Group and pick up some Range fuel. We'll see you in an hour.'

I am not thirty seconds into the job when the phone rings, 'Squizzy?'

'It's AC Walsh. Squizzy isn't in at the moment, can I take a message?'

'No, I will ring back.'

It goes off four more times in thirty minutes. I have just got back to removing the ejector units when they walk back in. Squizz looks down at the job.

'You been playing with your cock, Dougie?' That's a bit frustrating.

'The phone has been going off its nut, Squizz. I would have had this half done if I wasn't your fucking secretary.'

He just shakes his head from side to side while rolling his eyes, 'Well, la de da, smart-arse.' The phone rings again.

'Squizzy. Yep. Nope. Usual place? Tomorrow at ten. Yep, see ya.' He writes something in his notebook. 'Joe, can you start on the PM3s. I have to go and see Mac.' He disappears.

Joe asks me to help him get one of the dirty PM3 bomb beams off the trailer and then starts removing the release units. He doesn't fuck around either, disassembling the release units quickly and putting them into the kero bath to soak. That's when I notice that Squizz and Joe didn't bring anything back with them.

Maybe K Group was out of Range fuel?

As the week progresses, it turns out that Squizz and Joe are really interesting people to work with. Joe goes like a maniac for half the day and then spends the other half a day on errands. 'Just popping off to see Clem. I'll pick up those pies. Off to ASCO, boys. Just gotta go home for a tick first.'

Who am I to complain? He's done twice the work I have in half the time. I do wonder if he sneaks back in at night to keep up.

Squizzy is the master of organisation. He knows exactly where every task is up to, and where we are with respect to the overall workload. He lets me know when I am falling behind and he tells me to take a break when he thinks we're getting too far ahead.

'Steady, Dougie, we don't have to use this shit in anger for another six weeks yet. If you get too enthusiastic, I can organise an aircraft wash for you?'

No one likes an aircraft wash.

He is forever on the phone ordering spares, or organising this or that. As the President of the section social club, he is also forever picking up cans of cordial, chips, sausage rolls, pies, you name it. I reckon if you wanted a new TV, or some obscure bottle of Scotch, Squizz could organise it, cheap.

Mac announces a trip to New Zealand and puts a nomination list of the noticeboard. Tacho, Gus and I put our names down quickly.

'Don't even bother, Dougie, you're not senior enough,' Joe tells me. 'There are only six spots for the Troops and Junior Woodchucks like you have to wait their turn.'

It's not like the Townsville and Rockhampton trips; everyone has their name down within minutes. Even the guys who would normally ask permission from their wives have jumped in. I get a sense that Joe might be right.

Tuesday morning after the Australia Day long weekend, the squadron is buzzing with people walking in with duffel bags and some of the ugliest pieces of luggage ever exposed to the light of day.

We've configured the jets for long distance flights, large 374 gallon drop tanks on the wings, big jugs. The squadron deployment to New Zealand is about to get underway.

We drop Gus and the rest of the boys down to Air Movements

Section to catch the Herc; it's scheduled to launch at 1000, and in a surprising twist of military precision, it actually does.

The afternoon is spent watching cricket in the Smoko Room. We are leading by a hundred and fifty with six wickets in hand. There's a chance if Hughes, Marsh and Chappell can get some runs.

Wednesday morning, everything is ready for the jets to push across the Tasman. A P3 takes off at 0800. It will hold station over the Tasman Sea as the SAR aircraft in case one of the boys has to ditch, or as they like to say, 'jettison the jet'. We launch the first wave at 0900, and the second at 1000. They are flying to Ohakea where the RNZAF have their A4 Skyhawks based. They are more commonly known as 'Shithawks', although they are tough little aeroplanes. They can carry almost their own weight in ordnance.

Life, or at least work, gets pretty cruisy from then on. There's a leisurely start time because there's no flying, a good hour for lunch, then an early knock-off, every second day to a pub somewhere. I am getting the last of the SUU-20s and PM3 Beams ready for the impending Air to Ground program, and Tacho, as usual, is preparing the gun packs.

'Fuck me, Gun Bay again, just for something different,' he moans. Most of us know it's so that Mac can keep a closer eye on him. It's not that his technical skills or quality of work are in question — certainly not — but Tacho has a unique ability to get into the shit, or piss someone off, or both. Mac's taking no chances, and still I see Tacho coming out of his office cursing under his breath almost every day.

Wednesday arvo, the Aussies finally succumb in Adelaide. We were half a chance when Thommo got Des Haynes early, but it was one-way traffic after that, Larry Gomes quietly amassing runs without raising a sweat, and looking hardly interested in even being there. The Windies make it look so easy.

Not sure why they dropped Terry Alderman? Thommo isn't exactly a spring chicken anymore.

With Joe away, Squizz pulls me in under his wing and starts to task me with a few less conventional Jobs.

'Dougie, can you run into Woolies and pick up a couple of cartons of Coke and some lemonade?' handing me twenty bucks. He hesitates and gives me another forty. 'Get a carton of Wini Reds, a carton of Wini Blues, and a carton of B&H Special Filter while you are there.'

Friday rolls around and Tacho and I are sitting in Gun Bay smoking fags. 'What's on for the weekend, Dougie?'

'I might drop around to see the girls after work, then hit a pub. You?'

'Dunno. Roger Wills asked me to go around and see if his missus is okay while he is in New Zealand. Apparently, she gets spooked and just wants some reassurance that everything is okay. I might do that late this afternoon and join you in town after that. Where should I meet you?'

'What about the Family?'

Nev and I bum a ride into town with one of Nev's corporals after work, Gus is going to meet us there later. We pile out at Aunty Elsie's and hang around with Susan and Amy for a while. They are doing homework and so there are strict orders to complete the homework before any other discussions or distractions are allowed. They are growing up fast. Some part of me feels guilty that I can't take a larger role in their life, but I can't even begin to imagine how that might work right now.

Around six, we excuse ourselves and manage to grab a bus into town, commandeering a table in the front bar of the Family Hotel. There's a band setting up.

Tacho arrives at seven with a girl in tow. Both Nev and I do a double take. She's a slight girl — you could call her petite — about five-six, nice dress, shortish permed hair, and big tits, very big tits. They are not only big, but they're on full display. It's a low-cut dress that doesn't hide much. If she falls over face first, her teeth will be just fine.

'Hi, guys, this is Kirsten. Kirsten, this is Dougie and Nev.'

'Hi,' we both say, trying desperately to look at her eyes.

It's a male thing. I am sure we are all hardwired to look, and when they are this big, it's almost irresistible. She smiles, she knows, and she's obviously proud.

'Drink, Kirsten?' Tacho enquires.

'Tequila Sunrise please, Michael.' He smiles, but it's more of a grimace than a smile.

Michael? I had forgotten he had a proper name.

I am just musing how old Kirsten is, maybe twenty-five, and then notice that she is married, gold wedding ring clearly on display. Then the penny drops.

Holy fuck, its Roger's missus.

'So, what do you do for a crust, Kirsten?' Nev asks, always the gentleman.

'I am a secretary at a solicitor's office in Lambton.'

Nev goes on with the small talk while Michael gets the drinks. For a black guy in a white man's world, Nev doesn't have any inhibitions about chatting up the white girls. I remember asking him about it once.

'No use waiting around for an invite, Dougie. There's a lot of black fellas out there with a chip on their shoulders, blaming the white fellas for all their problems. I don't have time for that shit, I am going to live it up while I can.'

He can definitely hold his own with the ladies; has a bit of a gift there it seems, though not always so good on the piss. I cast my eyes around the room. Small crowd so far. It will get busy later when the band comes on. There are lots of blokes having a beer after work. The band is putting a banner up behind the drum kit. Noxious Weed is the name, it has a drawing of a joint and a marijuana leaf, and a phone number.

Fucking dope-smoking hippies, I hope their music is better than their banner.

The side door opens and two *sheilas* step in, both in that mid-twenties age group. The shorter one is in boots, skirt, blouse, and a wide belt with a big buckle, the taller in jeans and a sleeveless top. Kirsten sees them, stands, and waves, motioning them in our direction. They come over and hover awaiting an introduction.

'Michael, Dougie, Neville, this is Angela and Vicki.'

'Hi, Ang, Hi, Vicki.' It's a chorus.

Tacho asks Ang where her 'buckin' ears' are. It goes through to the keeper without so much as a swing and a miss.

After rearranging the seating, there's the usual chat, where they work, the weather, apparently the band here is good, have you heard the new Cold Chisel album, did you know Split Enz are playing at the Palais next weekend. Vicki tells me she is a Nursing Sister and works at the Royal in the Intensive Care ward.

'I've got a couple of RDOs and for once it's on a weekend. I am not going back onto afternoon shift until Monday.'

'Intensive Care? I bet you get some really badly hurt people in there.'

You dumb shit, Dougie, that was clever.

'Oh, yer, mostly car accidents, but you also get a lot of industrial accidents. Guys are always dropping heavy shit on themselves or running over each other with forklifts. Farmers are the worst. Those guys are either rolling a tractor on themselves or getting their shirt sleeve caught in the PTO. It gets pretty ugly.'

I have a flash of a memory. Uncle Bert is scolding me for going near the PTO on the tractor back at the farm. Since working in the RAAF, we have had safety bashed into us, and I now have more respect for the dangers of farming, and Uncle Bert.

Vicki is a real nice girl to talk to. She's down to earth, no airs and graces, knows her music, it's great to just sit and talk with someone who's not in the bloody Air Force. A bit later, the band starts up and girls were right, they're not too bad, covers of Canned Heat, Creedence, and Eric Clapton. We dance a bit and share a few jokes.

'There's a good band on at the Workers Club. Do you want to go up there?'

'Sure, why not.'

'We'll see you up there in a bit,' says Ang, sitting snugly with Nev.

Outside, she tucks her arm through mine, walking closely, chatting about stupid shit we did at school. We cross at the traffic lights on King Street, and she stops.

'Do you really want to go to the Workers Club?' It's an offer.

'Na.'

Monday morning, I get into work exhausted. Vicki and I

spent most of yesterday in bed. We didn't sleep much. I reckon I can get a little respite on the foam bed we have installed under the bench in Carrier Bay. It's hidden by a canvas flap.

'You'd better get that SUU finished, Dougie, I have a special job for you this afternoon,' Squizzy tells me.

Fuck, that's all I need, another errand. I need sleep!

After lunch, Squizz tells me to go back to my room and change into civvies. I am to meet him at the Base car park. Just before 1300, he pulls up in a ute with a cool room fit-out on the back. It's a plain white ute, no signs on the side.

'Do you know the OAK milk bar at Peats Ridge?'

'Yer,' I am feeling nervous about this.

'Just pull into the car park and there will be a bloke with another ute, just like this one. You drive his ute back here, and he will take this one.'

I must have a sceptical look on my face.

'Don't worry, Dougie, it's all above board. The guy's name is Debbie Reynolds.' Now I am almost certain this is not above board.

'Does Mac know we are doing this?'

'Of course, Dougie.' He's waving his hands, dismissing me to the driver's seat.

Sure enough, I get down to Peats Ridge and pull into the car park at the OAK, there is an identical white ute there. I pull in next to it and get out. The other driver gets out and we exchange looks.

'Gunnie?' he asks, quizzically.

'Yep, you?'

'Yep, they told me your name is Dougie. That right?'

'Yep, are you Debbie Reynolds?'

'Yep.' We are both looking at each other with some uncertainty.

'Which course are you off?' I ask, just to be certain.

'31 Apprentices. You?'

'33 Apprentices. I think you guys had graduated before we got to Wagga.'

'Yer, we left in December '78.'

'Oh, yer, we got there in January '79.'

There is an awkward silence before I ask the obvious.

'Do you know what's in the back?' There's an immediate look of relief on his face.

'Sure,' he walks to the back of my ute and pulls out some keys. I follow him. He takes the lock off and opens the door. I peer in. The air inside is cold and the box is full of fish boxes. Fish boxes full of prawns.

'I have to make two drops on my way back to Kingswood, one to the Sergeants' Mess at Richmond and the other to the Officers' Mess at Glenbrook. The rest we'll fill with orders from the guys at Kingswood.'

'What's in the other ute?'

'Empty boxes, mate,' he laughs, as if it's a dumb question. He walks back to my ute, holding up his keys. We exchange.

'I'll see you next Monday,' getting in and driving off.

Since seeing the load of prawns, I'm now certain that Squizzy is running a business far beyond anything that could be interpreted as social club activity. When I get the next job, I stop and look at him with scepticism.

'I don't know, Squizz, you sure this is legit?'

'Dougie, if Gus asked you to drop his car to a mechanic, you wouldn't think twice, would you?'

'Probably not.'

'It's the same thing, Dougie. You drop the ute off and drive my car back. Here's the keys, go on, get moving.' He pushes me out the door.

Thursday, 'Dougie, can you take the ute down to Peats Ridge this arvo?' I must have that look on my face again.

'Take it easy, Dougie, this is social club business. All proceeds go into the account. I am not benefiting from any of this.'

'Alright,' but I am not convinced, not even slightly.

Sunday, I wake late with a pounding head, my face is aching and I am not sure I will be able to hold down water. The drinks in town last night went a bit longer than I thought they would, and I really should stay away from the Bundy. Shit, I can't actually remember how we got home.

I find a mirror and check the damage, swollen cheek and black eye. The fuckwit caught me with a backhander by surprise.

I would have taught him a lesson if Gus hadn't intervened. Oh, well, it's only a bit of swelling. What time is it? Ten-thirty, I'm actually not too bad for ten-thirty.

I get to the Mess before midday and check the menu. There's roast chicken, lamb, and baked vegies, nice. Then it hits me. I do a double take.

Sunday lunch? That is a worry. We went to town on Friday night and I don't have much of a recollection of anything since.

Picking up a plate, I opt for the lamb, vegies, and spinach. The cook on the servery looks vaguely familiar and when she turns to get some gravy, I can see the birthmark below her ear, heart shaped.

'Thank you, Corporal Shoobridge,' I say, smiling.

Maybe she recognises me?

No sign of it. She's ignoring me. She is there to serve food.

I wonder whether Helen and her were as much an item as Helen and I were?

Over lunch, I push the birthmark out of my mind and try to contemplate the previous forty-eight hours. There is a vague memory of a trip to Vicki's late on Friday night coming back, then going to the pub for lunch before she started work yesterday. Shit, I am not sure what happened after that. Tacho appears at my door a little before two, looking visibly worse for wear, again.

'Don't tell me. You picked up last night and she almost clawed you to death, again.'

'Close, Dougie, and there's a chance you might just be a fucking psychic. You know how I said Roger Wills asked me to duck around and check on his missus?'

'Yerrrr,' he has my attention.

'You met her at the pub in town the other night. Kirsten, the one with the rather large ...' his hands gesturing like he's fondling both breasts.

'Oh, yer, Kirsten. How could I forget. Mate, those were big enough to have their own postcode.' An image of a twenty-five-year-old woman with big tits appears in my head. It's a nice image, but now I am getting concerned.

'Well, I turned up yesterday and she was getting ready to go out. Just out of the shower. Answered the door wrapped up in a towel, and well, one thing led to another, as they say. She has definitely been looked after, if you know what I'm saying.' He is polishing his fingernails on his shirt.

The mist starts to rise and my thinking goes cloudy. I feel like smacking him in the mouth.

'Mate, how fucking stupid are you. You're not going to die in that bloody death trap of a car of yours, some fucking Bagger is going to cut your cock off and choke you to death with it for diddling with his missus. What were you thinking? No, don't answer. I know there's no thinking going on. Two heads and only enough blood to power one at a time.' I am feeling really angry and my mother's face briefly flicks into my mind.

Who the fuck does he think he is? Shagging a married woman?

Tacho looks hurt by my outburst, but I don't give a fuck. Maybe, just maybe, he'll engage brain the next time something like this crosses his path … but probably not. He's shaking his head at me; he's not happy.

'You've got a hide going off at me for screwing someone's missus, Dougie.' He's obviously not impressed with me. I have no idea where this is going. 'Did it ever occur to you to ask Vicki who her boyfriend is?'

It stops me in my tracks, I hadn't figured or even given a thought to the possibility that Vicki might have a boyfriend. I look at him with my mouth open.

'She's Dale Wilson's chick, Dougie.'

I feel sick. The only possible point of justification I have is that, at least she isn't married, but it's thin. I don't know Dale well, but it doesn't matter. I have really fucked this up.

'Fuck it,' I storm out of the room and leave him standing there. I need some air. The memory of my parents arguing the night before they were killed is on repeat in my head, again and again.

What the fuck is wrong with me?

Monday morning, I get to the Mess early, eat and get out before Tacho might arrive. He's a late starter. I get to work and Squizz is there.

'Any deliveries today, Squizz?' He turns with a smart-arse look.

'Change your mind, Dougie?' I think about my response for an instant.

'I just thought I would help out the social club, Squizz.' He obliges with a trip to Nelsons Bay to get the ute, then onto Peats Ridge for the drop off. During the drive, I have time to think about what I have done. Knocking off another guy's girlfriend isn't something I am proud of. And, what the fuck was he thinking rooting Roger Will's missus?

Fucking idiot.

My mind wanders a bit on the drive, thoughts of Louise and Allison.

Allison, I really fucked that one up.

I remember the night with Michelle in Wagga, and the following night with Jenny Adams. Then, the penny drops.

You're not bloody Snow White yourself, Tim Walsh.

It doesn't sit well with me.

I manage to avoid Tacho through the rest of the week. He's in Gun Bay and when I'm not on one of Squizzy's errands, I keep a low profile in Carrier Bay. After hours, I make sure I am not in the Mess at the same time as him and avoid the boozer like the plague. It gives me plenty more time to contemplate my, our, actions.

I think I know he doesn't feel the same as I do. This is all fair game to him.

He'd root a rattlesnake if it was the only thing around.

Thursday, I take the weekend delivery to Peats Ridge and get back in the early afternoon, I am in the Smoko Room having a durry, flicking through the latest *Post* magazine, when he walks in. There's a bit of an awkward silence. He breaks first.

'You going to the Knuck tonight?' I think it over for a few seconds.

'Probably. Have you seen Nev? Is he going?'

'Yer, Nev, Watto and Johnno are going. There's a bit of a celebration, Jerry got posted to Butterworth this morning.'

That's news, the first guy from our course to go overseas. I guess this will be the first of a few farewell drinks.

'Sounds good.' I get up and walk out. The Knuck ends up being a subdued affair. With our squadron away and half of OCU in Amberley for something or other, the place is almost morgue-like. I have a few with Nev and go home early.

Friday morning, we sit around the Smoko Room talking shit, drinking coffee, and having a fag. Mac walks in just after eight.

'The first jets are coming in from New Zealand about ten, second wave an hour later. Dougie, Burt, and Terry, can you guys go over to the flight line and check in with Bones. The rest of you guys can sweep the hangar, mop the floors in the offices, and clean this fooking Mess up. As soon as the jets are fuelled and covered, and this place looks respectable, you can all knock off.'

Saturday, the Herc from Ohakea comes in about eleven and I go down to greet Gus. During the walk back to the block, he is bursting with stories from his time overseas.

'Dougie, the place is amazing. It's like being in Australia ten years ago, beautiful, everyone is polite, even the Maoris. They are all happy to show you around, and the Kiwi *sheilas*, they are just so, so ...' His hands are active and from the look on his face, I can tell that he got lucky.

'Dougie, I reckon we should go on a holiday over there.'

'Sounds great, mate. Did you meet someone in particular?'

'Yer, there was this chick named Mary. Dougie, I gotta tell you, she is the prettiest chick I have ever met.'

He did get lucky.

Afterwards, we are all at the boozer getting the umpteenth story from Gus.

'I reckon there wasn't a guy on the trip that didn't get some.'

'What? Even the Baggers?' asks Tacho, with one eye on me.

'Mate, the fucking Baggers are the worst. They were getting laid while we were still unpacking our bags.' Tacho gives me a 'I told you so' look.

Life returns to something like normal after that.

I am assigned to aircraft rectifications. It's mostly seat work, changing the safety equipment, or cartridges, removing ejection seats when needed. There is a lot of it, ejection seats out, ejection seats in, seat out, seat in. Some pilot has dropped his pen in the cockpit and I spend an hour upside down, my head under the seat, hands behind the rudder pedals, looking for it. The only option after looking, is to remove the ejection seat.

Mid-March, Mac writes up the new postings out and in. Lefty is going to 3 Squadron, and Dan to 75 Squadron. There are two new guys coming in from Wagga Wagga, Jones and Marella.

By the end of March, I am well and truly over seat work. I reckon I could do this in my sleep. My mind briefly goes back to my refuelling incident last year when I actually went to sleep standing up, but this is different. My hands move almost without prompting, undoing lock wire, removing cartridges, undoing trip rods and leg restraint lines, guiding the seat up the rails; it's a piece of piss.

Saturday, Nev and I do a bit of shopping in Newcastle and get a counter lunch at the Crown and Anchor before heading back to Base to veg out for the arvo, sharing a few beers and a laugh.

Around five, I take a run through the dip and put on my best. There's a farewell function for Lefty and Dan tonight at Muree Golf Club, both being off to Butterworth. Someone says that it's Lefty's third posting to Butterworth.

For some dumb reason, this is the first mixed function the section has had since we arrived. All of the other functions have been just blokes sitting around a pub, or the Smoko Room, drinking piss.

Tacho has pressured Pete into driving us there. Gus and I are in the back, Tacho in the front telling him how to drive, urging him to 'get into it'. I take a couple with me; it keeps me calm.

The function is in the auditorium and when we walk in most of the boys and their respective other halves are there. They are all clustered into groups which pretty well reflect the section command structure and the carpooling arrangements most of the Baggers have for their daily commute.

Mac is seated at a table with the ARMO, Flight Lieutenant Martin and Bob Horn. Bob is usually about five steps behind Mac and a lot of the boys have nicknamed him Boots. Apparently, he's so far up Mac's arse all you can see are his boots. The lady beside Mac is obviously Mrs Mac, a stately looking lady with a short haircut and an upright pose. There is a younger girl, about my age, sitting beside Mrs Mac.

I didn't know Mac had a daughter?

Squizzy, Hollywood, Joe, and Roger Wills are at one table, and Coxy, Billy, Stan, and Misty are at the another, along with their wives or girlfriends. A bunch of Singlies are at a table further down the room.

'Hey, Gus, do you want a drink?'

'Sure, Dougie,' he contemplates the answer. 'How about Rum and Coke?'

I get three, and hand them out, sitting down with Lefty, Wal and Dan. They introduce their wives, Julie, Carol, and Jane, and we chinwag before dinner. Entrée is prawn cocktail or a pastry filled with spinach, then onto the main: chicken or beef, with mash potato, pumpkin and beans.

The CWA ladies would be proud of this lot.

After dinner, Mac makes a speech, thanking everyone for coming and saying some nice words about Dan and Lefty, presenting each with pewter tankard full of beer, which they obediently scull. Dessert is set out on a table and we all line up to fill our bowls. I am talking with Carol who goes through the usual questions, how old am I, where am I from.

'I work with a girl from Clarence Town, Marie Donnelly.'

'I know of the Donnellys.' Grandad used to buy cattle from them every now and again. But I don't know Marie.'

'She might be just a little bit older than you,' she speculates. 'Maybe you both should come over for dinner sometime.'

'That would be great.' I don't force the response, but I am apprehensive about being set up with a girl. It makes it look like I am desperate; then again, maybe I am.

On the way back to the table, I look around for Gus. It's his shout. I do a double take noticing him sitting with Mrs Mac and the girl. It's not like Gus to be chatty with the girls this early in the night. He usually needs a few in him.

After dinner, people from the main bar start to wander in and the DJ starts up. A couple of slow numbers to start with, more mood music than anything. I look over to see Tacho in fits of laughter with Roger Wills and Kirsten.

He's playing with fire there.

Squizz announces that the tab will go off at nine and so Lefty and Wal get a couple of bottles of both white and red to tide us over, glasses all round. The music is getting lively — the Eagles — the chat rowdier, and there is a general buzz.

'Dougie, come and dance,' Carol grabs me by the hand. 'Wal doesn't dance,' she tells me. We see out a few tracks before sitting back down, drinking wine to quench the thirst, when Mac comes over.

'Dougie, where is Edwards?' I look around thinking he should be here somewhere. 'He went to the bar with my niece a half hour ago.'

Oh, oh, it's never good to get Mac's blood pressure up.

'I'll go and see if I can find them,' I tell him, throwing back my wine. The main bar is largely empty, a few barflies hanging around and the usual pokie players looking to get rich. They're not here.

Outside, I check the back seat of Pete's car, but nothing. They could be anywhere.

'Gus, Gus,' I yell in hushed tones, but nothing. I walk around the ninth green and look around, but nothing, then around the bottom side of the clubhouse and onto the eighteenth.

'Gus, Gus,' listening, listening.

'What do you want, Dougie?' It's Gus' voice from beyond the green.

'Mac is on the warpath, mate. He wants to know where his niece is.' Silence, there is obviously some sort of deliberation going on.

'Snow him, Dougie, we need a few more minutes.' There is a hint of urgency in his voice.

I can't argue with that. The boy has obviously got a little more talent with the ladies than I gave him credit for. Back inside, I am heading toward Mac and I can see Mrs Mac is irritated. Mac looks up as I approach.

'Gus is throwing his guts up outside, Mac. Er, um, sorry, ma'am. Your niece is helping him clean up.' Mrs Mac looks visibly relieved, but I get that look from Mac that says 'don't try and bullshit me, boy'. I manage to slink away and get another drink. Ten minutes later, the two lovers reappear and I fill Gus in on the cover story before they re-join their table.

'Nut Bush' comes on the speakers and most of the crowd hit the floor, evenly spaced, and moving in almost perfect synchronisation. Military trainers couldn't have organised this. Even Mrs Mac and Mac's niece are there, Mac watching proudly from the table.

It's getting late, and the wine is having an unexpected effect. While I am getting plenty of dances with the Baggers' wives, I have had my fill of white wine and my gyro is starting to topple. Carol has to help me off the dance floor. In my cloudy state, I look over at Tacho. He is in deep conversation with an obviously hammered Roger Wills, his missus leaning on Tacho's shoulder.

Now, that is not going to end well.

Sunday, Tacho kicks our door in at eleven. Andy and I are in recovery listening to some Pink Floyd and reading.

'I guess you got laid last night?'

'Well, I had to help Kirsten get Roger home, didn't I,' a smug look on his face. 'He was plastered.' I give him a look of disgust, but its wasted. I just shake my head.

'Did you hear the Argentinians have invaded the Falkland Islands,' he announces. Andy and I look at each other dumbfounded.

'The Falkland Islands, where the fuck is that?'

'Fucked if I know, somewhere down near Argentina, I think. But the Poms own it. Their Marines gave the Argies a touch-up before they were overrun.'

'I can't see the Pommies taking too kindly to that,' says Andy.

No, that is going to end badly.

We run into Gus on our way to the Mess for lunch.

'Where are you off to, Romeo?' I think he was hoping to get out without any interrogation about last night's exploits.

'I got invited to Mac's place for lunch. Well, not so much invited as told to be there. He reckons I should make a good host for his niece's stay.' We all raise eyebrows and laugh as he runs off toward the car park.

The week before Easter goes quickly. Lefty has upped the ante on getting as much preventative maintenance out of the way as possible before the weapons program starts again. There are few opportunities for a smoke between jobs. I would have thought Lefty would give it a rest as he's leaving for Butterworth in less than two weeks.

Each night, Gus is busy showing Mac's niece around Newcastle; well, that and his room for some tonsil hockey. Good Friday, I suggest he shows her around the valley, the vineyards, and come up to Dungog for a night. Mac approves the itinerary given they are staying at grandad's house.

Grandma has them in separate rooms, but that never stopped a red-blooded Scottish lass. Gus gets up bleary-eyed Saturday morning long after the milking is done. Alisha didn't sleep in though. She is an experienced hand in the dairy and her chat had both grandad and Uncle Bert giggling most of the morning. They're like a pair of schoolboys.

'You can come back any time you like,' grandma tells her, as they walk to the car. No acknowledgment of Gus, he's too exhausted to care.

Tuesday after Easter, we start to work up to air to ground sorties. The flying program has the pilots doing navigation exercises which culminate in four jets being overhead a particular landmark simultaneously. While the flying is happening, we are busy getting everything ready to conduct weapons operations. Tool kits are checked, test equipment readied, and ammunition being unpacked and prepared.

Wednesday night, I am invited to Wal and Carol's for dinner. I mess round with the kids for a bit before Marie Donnelly arrives and Carol consigns them to their rooms. It's a lovely dinner and there's a fair bit of chat over dessert. Marie and I insist on doing the washing up before saying good night.

On the way out, I hover around her car looking for an invite to a next meeting, maybe a date, but it's not offered. She drives away before I can ask for her phone number.

Friday morning, the boys are launching the last wave for the week. A four ship NAVEX with a strike at the climax. We have everything ready to go for next week's air to ground program, and I don't have a lot on, so I wander out to watch them taxi. Number three to taxi is Dave Heffernan and I give him a wave as he goes past.

He has the visor down and his mask undone hanging off the right clip. He signals to me he's going to do a fly by, right hand performing the act. I respond by pointing the index and second finger of my right hand to my eyes, then pointing them at the sky, 'I will be watching'. A thumbs-up from him.

After they take off, I have time to wander to the section for a chat, have a durry, and grab another coffee before heading out onto the line. It's ten minutes before they are due back and there are a few other people hanging around expectantly, looking, waiting.

It's a clear morning and the autumn sun hasn't generated any haze. A perfect day for watching aeroplanes fly.

'Over there,' someone says, pointing toward Hexham. I can just make out a black speck coming at us against the backdrop of Mount Sugarloaf. 'Where are the others?' he asks.

I look around and can't see anything, so I watch the black dot. It's getting bigger. As the jet crosses onto the airfield, it drops low, below tree level, banking slightly left toward us. There's a sudden bang from behind, and the air goes out of my lungs. The tail of a jet heading west now visible, it jinks right to miss the oncoming one. The jet coming from Hexham is now overhead, about thirty feet up, then bang, a third jet hits from the north, low and then climbing, flick left, then nose down out over the ocean.

'Fuck,' says no one in particular.

I am looking around. There were four of them. Where is the other one? Others are gathering in groups discussing the strike. I am not convinced it's over, and walk further out onto the tarmac, looking around.

Where is he?

He catches me by surprise coming in from the south over the top of the civil air terminal. I think he just took an antenna off the roof, crossing the runway, getting lower, jinking right and coming up the taxiway.

Fuck, the starboard wing wasn't far off the deck.

I am looking at the side of the jet as he goes past, waving. There is no climb this time, just a loud bang as he just keeps going between the OCU Headquarters building and the tank hangar, disappearing.

Fuck, he hasn't crashed it, has he?

In the aftermath, there are people lying on the ground, bits of paper floating in the air and people running out of buildings to see what just happened.

Ten minutes later, all four jets enter the circuit in formation, land and taxi back onto the line. They shut down, pilots unstrapping. I manage to walk past Dave as he heads in to sign the paperwork.

'No barrel roll today?'

'Not when you're that fucking low, Dougie,' he says, smiling like a Cheshire cat.

Before we knock off, Mac puts up a list of the postings out and in. Terry Evans is going to 3 Squadron and Gus to 75 Squadron. There are two new guys coming in from Wagga Wagga, Chamberlain and Holt.

'Fucking Azaria Chamberlain and Harold Holt,' announces Joe. 'Next thing they'll post Johnnie O'Keefe into this place.' He pauses, 'No, wait, he's dead.' He pauses again, 'No, this place is a fucking circus, maybe they'll post Bozo the Clown in?'

The whole nickname thing is not an exact science, but it seems once you have been christened, it sticks, whether you like it or not. Azaria Chamberlain and Harold Holt are going to be hard names to shake.

Friday night, there is a celebration for Gus, lots of back-slapping and advice on what he might, or might not, get up to while overseas. He is all smiles, but I get a sense that he is nervous. The reality of going overseas for a couple of years is starting to sink in.

Monday morning, we are arming gun packs and bombing up with 25lb poofter bombs again. It's good, honest Gunnie work that raises a sweat, much better than running or doing weights, and it's certainly better than running Squizz's errands. I am on a crew with Chubby Checker and Wal.

Chubby isn't the fittest specimen on the planet and I quickly find out why. He is driving the jammer and positions the gun pack under the jet. I clip the cables into place, signalling him to drop the tray. I winch the pack up, tighten the securing bolts, and fix the barrels in place, looking around to see where Chubby is. He's managed to park the jammer, shift his arse from the seat, and is now wandering over with the Type 15 test set for the guns. He hands it to me and walks back to the jammer.

I test the guns and turnaround again. He hands me the SEAM test tester this time and climbs up the ladder into the cockpit.

What are you, the fucking supervisor?

I hook up the test set and pull the ladder off. It's verboten to do the SEAM test with the ladder on. Apparently, some guy in Malaysia plugged the left-hand gun in after they tested the left-hand circuit, when they tested the right-hand side, and the guy pulling the trigger shot himself off the ladder. I look at Chubby sitting in the cockpit and conclude I might need to stay alert here.

'Where the fuck's Wal?' I sit and wait. He turns up five minutes later.

'Sorry, lads, I was just getting a brief from Hornie. He's given us two more jets to arm. We'll have to get a move on.'

He could have done that earlier. We'd be half done by now.

Wal and I run the SEAM test while Chubby pulls the trigger. The SUU-20 and PM3 are next. Wal and I get everything attached to the jets and tighten the sway braces. I set the intervalometer and pull the ice tongs, looking around for Chubby. I look at Wal, and he gives me a similar bewildered look. We both get out from under the jet and look at the cockpit. He looks back at us.

'I thought you'd need me here to test the SUU,' he explains. We both shake our heads.

'Okay, pickle,' Wal tells him, signalling with his finger to keep pickling. I can hear the intervalometer clicking over. 'Set it to ripple, Dougie.' I click it forward to the ARM position.

'Pickle and hold it.' The intervalometer clicks quickly through the stations. 'Okay, shut it down. Let's get the bombs on.'

By the time Col extracts himself from the cockpit and joins us, Wal and I have loaded all but one practice bomb. I make sure he knows that one is for him and start pushing cartridges into the barrels, screwing them in, and applying the tension wrench. Chubby is still struggling with his solitary bomb.

The rest of the week plays out mostly the same way, Wal and I doing most of the work while Chubby drives the jammer, and operates switches in the cockpit, not much otherwise. It bothers me less and less that Chubby's a lazy tractor arse. It's probably safer to keep him out of the way.

For this program, there are four teams operating, each with a corporal in charge and two troops. There's Tacho and Pete working with Dan, Stu Hunter and Gus are with Don Robertson, Stan and Billy are with Coxy, and Chubby and I are with Wal. Sergeant Bob Horn is in charge.

Arming aircraft is competitive stuff. Each morning, we go through the arming-up routine, bullets into packs, then packs into the jets, then SUU and beam on, and bombs on. Two, sometimes three, jets per team, depending on how many jets the maintenance guys can generate. We race each other to see who is quickest.

Stu and Gus are not in the contest, they are too busy talking to get anything done quickly. Stan and Coxy are weighed down by Billy, like Wal and I with Chubby. The standouts are Tacho, Pete, and Dan. They are all pretty fit, quick thinkers, and don't fuck about. When we get our turnarounds done, they are usually finished and sucking on a can of Coke, watching.

Wal and I are out to break their dominance, working on ways to optimise Chubby's contribution, so we can go faster while not allowing him to get in the way.

Working at this intense pace makes the time fly. Before I know it, it's Thursday and pay day. After lunch, Gus and I are hatching a plan to knock off, eat, shower and change, and get to the Knuck, all before 1900 hours.

'Listen up, boys,' it's Bob. 'I want the barrels and rams on those SUUs changed, half today and half tomorrow. Tomorrow's flying program is short; last wave at eleven. All the barrels and rams have to be cleaned before you go home tomorrow.'

Friday, we have all jets recovered and downloaded by midday. Some of the boys drop the gun packs back to Ammo Prep and reload them while Chubby and I get stuck into cleaning barrels and rams. Wal is wiping down the SUUs with Range fuel. Bob walks in dressed in blues and his bag in hand, inspecting progress.

'Where are you off to?' enquires Chubby.

'There's a function on at the Sergeants' Mess,' he tells us. 'Wal, don't forget run the lights box over those when you're done.' The look on Wal's face is not complimentary.

'You could always help,' I suggest.

'RHIP, young Dougie, RHIP.' He turns and walks out.

'What's this RHIP crap?'

'Rank Has Its Privileges,' Chubby tells me.

'Cock,' even Toad wouldn't pull crap like this, and he'd be making sure there was cold beer in the fridge for when we're finished.

Saturday, we have somehow avoided the mandatory attendance at the ANZAC Day march in Newcastle. I get my dress uniform out and drive to the farm, arriving after lunch to avoid being chipped for being late for the morning session.

Sunday morning, grandad and Uncle Bert are up at four and in their suits, the collection of medals on their chest impressive. It's probably the first time they have both attended the Dawn Service; usually Uncle Bert stays home to milk. I will be doing that today. Grandma also takes the opportunity to get out for the morning.

After milking, I grab a cuppa and some toast, have a quick wash and get my uniform on, jacket, tie, cap, everything in place. In town, I go to the RSL and grandad is in deep conversation with Mr Williams over some element of the main service. With that complete, I walk with him to the main street where we all form up. Uncle Bert comes over and has a chat; obviously had a few this morning already, the Australian Vietnam Medal and the green-and-white Republic of Vietnam Medal proudly on display.

The march is not a long event; a section of veterans with grandad marching at the front, and Uncle Bert is the flag bearer. I get to march in the rear rank, the pipe band immediately behind, and the school kids behind them.

After the service, I get three beers in before heading home to milk. Grandad and Uncle Bert are going to make the most of my presence, they are staying. Grandma will drive them home later.

On my way back to Williamtown that evening, it strikes me just how lucky I am. Few of my workmates can run home for the weekend, see family, march in their hometown on Anzac Day, and get back to Base.

Lest we forget.

Early May, the bright Newcastle autumn has turned towards winter. A low has hung off the coast for a couple of days and the surf has pounded the beaches relentlessly. It's dull, it's dreary, everything is damp and depressing. It's not really raining, but it's not dry either and the moisture- laden wind seems to go through everything. Not as bad as Wagga Wagga in winter, but dreary.

Our latest attempts to bomb the crap out of a minor target on

Salt Ash Range with poofter bombs have been seriously thwarted by the weather. It's hurry up and wait in the extreme and there's nothing any of us can do about it. I have played so many hands of five hundred I can now predict which cards my opponents are going to lead with a high degree of accuracy.

I briefly consider the Argentine Air Force guys attacking the British Task Force. Those boys won't be on any weather hold.

Aren't we supposed to be practising for a war?

I give the cards a miss and walk around thinking, too much time on my hands. My thoughts are wandering somewhere between Louise, Allison, Vicki, Helen, Dee, even Janine. All women I have loved, and cared about, or had a great affection for, none of whom I have any real standing with at present. Shit, I doubt most of them would even talk to me at the moment.

Something is really shitting me. I can't put my finger on it, but I am uneasy, on edge.

Maybe it's my inability to secure a relationship lasting more than a week, or maybe it's inability to find real love in some way. Fuck knows. Maybe I am just a bit lonely and need some companionship? It doesn't even have to be sexual, just sharing a meal would be okay.

Am I doing something wrong that scares them off? Can they sense something in me? It's all a bit of a muddle. Fuck, it's like I am feeling a little crazy. I have to get my head straight.

By mid-May, we have managed to get enough bombing sorties in to meet the pilot's training objectives. All the gear comes off and we start packing away the unused ammo. Now we have to clean everything we have just used, mainly guns, gun packs, Suu-20s, and centreline beams. I am assigned back to Carrier Bay with Squizz.

Following the events in the South Atlantic has become a ritual for us. The Exocet missiles must have a lot of Pommie sailors shitting their pants, the Sheffield and Atlantic Conveyors are at the bottom of the ocean and others have been hit.

The Argentinians have Mirage IIIs of a similar vintage to ours, and they are up against the Royal Navy's harriers. Seems they are getting slaughtered, but according to some of our pilots there's a good reason. The Mirages are having to fly almost to the extent of their range with big jugs on, so their ability to dogfight against the harriers is pretty poor.

They also don't have a lot of time to linger once they are over the islands, or they'll run out of fuel on the way back to their Base. It's interesting how the media have us believing something, but the reality of what's actually going on is different. Tuesday afternoon, the phone in Carrier Bay rings.

'77 Armament, LAC Walsh.'

'Dougie,' it's Nev,' and he's chirpy. 'I just got posted to 75 Squadron.' This is more than a little exciting. We head to the boozer that afternoon for a celebratory drink, or two.

'Did you hear that Doc and Andy have been posted to Butterworth?' says Tacho.

'Andy?'

'Yep, I was talking to a few RADTECHs, they're not all completely queer. They said he'd be going July.'

'I heard Merv got posted too, but he's on leave and no one is saying officially till they can tell him face to face.' Nev adds.

I am wondering when my own posting order might come, I really can't be far behind. I need to ask Mac what he thinks is going on.

'What about you, Tacho? When do you think you'll be posted?'

'Not likely, mate,' he scoffs. 'I took it off my posting preferences. I have enough trouble staying out of gaol around here, let alone a foreign country where gaol is not nearly so pleasant. They've got the fucking death penalty over there.'

'You know it's going to be a tough being away from you bastards, you are more a family to me than anything I ever had,' Nev says. He's right, of course. We have stood by each other, been there for each other, watched each other's backs, kicked each other up the arse.

'But I am glad I don't have to ride in the back seat of that bloody Falcon any more, Tacho. It's a bloody miracle that we haven't been in an accident in that thing!' Even Tacho has to laugh at this.

Saturday night, early June, Nev, Gus and I bum a ride into town with Pete. It's Gus' last weekend in Australia and we are out to make it memorable. There is supposed to be a good band on at the Workers Club so we head there first, settling on a table at the rail above the dance floor.

Just after eight, I need to break the seal and head for the little boys' room. I am standing at the trough when the door opens and two guys walk in. One stands next to me and the other uses a cubicle. I am not paying attention, deep in thought about what Nev said yesterday.

I suddenly realise I need to keep my wits about me, standing there with my prick in my hand, lost in thought, I'm actually pretty vulnerable. I can feel the eyes of the guy next to me sizing me up.

'RAAF cock, hey?' The short hair gives it away, he's no

Einstein. I nod, looking at him. He's probably a few years older than me, hair down over his collar, parted in the middle, your typical Newcastle westy. I give him my meanest stare and zip up.

I try to wave my hands under the water and get out of there as quick as I can, but he gets between me and door, his mate from the cubicle joining him. I weigh it up, they aren't here to give me fashion advice.

Westy throws the first one and I move sideways, it catches me a glancing blow on the cheek. It stings but no real damage done. I manage to use his momentum to push his head into the wall, he slumps to the floor. The other guy is sizing me up, not so cocksure now the odds have changed. I walk slowly past him to the door with my fists raised. He watches me go past.

Newcastle can be a bit wild like that. Someone takes a dislike to the way you looked at them, or they just had a shit day at work, or broke up with the girlfriend and, bang, they hit you. They don't mind a bit of knuckle, the Newcastle boys. You have to have your guard up. Wagga Wagga wasn't this bad and I wonder if other towns are similar?

Monday morning, Tacho and I drop Gus to Air Movements. It's a fairly emotional event. The three of us have barely been apart for the past two- and-a-half years

'See you in a couple of months,' I tell him. We are just walking back into the section when Mac comes past. He does a double take.

'What happened to you?'

'A couple of boys in town took a dislike to me, Flight.' He is shaking his head.

'One thinks he is Fangio, and the other thinks he is Cassius Clay.' Tacho can't leave it alone.

'Nah, he's more like Rocky, Flight.' He gets a glare from Mac for his trouble.

Does he do this just to wind him up?

A few days later, Mike Chamberlain and Dave Holt from number 34 Apprentice Intake arrive. While they are only a year younger than me, they seem so young and innocent. They look a little pale walking out of Mac's office. I remember our first day, Mac telling Tacho to polish his shoes.

In the Smoko Room, they get no let off from the crowd looking for a bit of young blood. Azaria Chamberlain and Harold Holt are introduced to the card school and are soon purchasing Cokes for the pack. Friday morning, Mac comes through Carrier Bay.

'Where is Taylor?'

'Not sure, Flight, he was here a few minutes ago,' I lie.

'When he turns up, tell him to come straight to me.'

A few minutes later Squizzy walks in looking more worried than I have ever seen him and deathly white.

'Mac's looking for you, seemed pissed off.' He's muttering to himself, going through his desk looking for something as Mac walks in. He gives me a look as if to ask if I'd passed on his message.

'I told him, Flight.' I find some reason to exit and wander out into the hangar to get away from the tension, but stay close enough to overhear the conversation.

'I trust you've heard about the Graduation Dinner at the Officers' Mess last night for 2OCU? Your prawns were definitely the star of the show.' Squizzy is still muttering, nothing resembling a word is coming out. 'The CO wants to see you in his office at 1400, he's hoping he can leave his toilet by then, fortunately or maybe not, he wants me there with you.' He goes to leave and turns again.

'If this little side business of yours drags me down, I will personally make sure you never, ever get that third stripe! You will be lucky to keep the two that you have.' Mac storms out, red in the face, the eyebrows independently alive.

I've never seen him so angry, not even with Tacho.

Speak of the devil, Tacho wanders in.

'Did you hear about the Graduation Dinner debacle?'

He goes on to tell me that half the people who went to the dinner have food poisoning, most of the flying on the Base is cancelled for the day. The culprit seems to be Squizzy's prawns.

'Mac was in here going up one side of him and down the other earlier, apparently he has an appointment with the CO at 1400. I would love to be a fly on the wall for that one!' Tacho is shaking his head,

'That might be the end of his little prawn business.'

'At least he won't be getting me to taxi his shit around.'

A week later, the CO hears the charge. The only thing they can get him for is failure to comply with a General Order. Apparently, you are not allowed to have a second job unless the CO approves it, and running a seafood business has been deemed a second job. Squizz gets fined seven days pay, and he loses all his seniority. The seniority hurts, you need at least three years seniority to become a sergeant.

Sunday afternoon, mid-July, we have taken a relatively casual drive to the Bay for a session at the Seabreeze; casual given that Tacho is driving and we didn't exceed the speed limit. Perhaps he's not well. There's a game between St George and Parra on the TV. Saints are not going well and I am not convinced that Roy Masters is the right guy to be coaching them. The way it's going, we won't make the semi-finals.

It's also Nev's last drink with us for a while. He's taking the bus to Sydney tomorrow and onto the Charter to Butterworth on Tuesday. It's called the Charter because a few years ago, the RAAF used to charter a Qantas aircraft to take people back and forth between Australia and Malaysia. These days, it's a RAAF 707, but the label sticks.

He's had a week at his mum's place and is pretty relaxed, taking in the Sunday paper as Tacho and I discuss the merits of Cold Chisel's live double album *Swingshift* which he has been playing to death.

'You'd better take a look at this, Dougie,' Nev says pushing the paper in my direction. 'Here,' he says, pointing to the wedding photos.

Her face catches my attention as soon as I look, resplendent in a white gown with the smug arse-wipe Barrett at her side. The caption reads *'Mr and Mrs Anthony Barrett were married at the Chapel at Riverview, St Ignatius, yesterday followed by a reception at the Australian Golf Club. The groom is the eldest son of Mr and Mrs William Barrett of Chatswood. The bride's parents, Warrant Officer Robert Gardner (RAAF) and his wife, Nancy, of Townsville, Queensland, were in attendance. The couple will honeymoon in Hawaii before establishing a home at Manly.'*

'Fucking bitch.' I feel cheated.

'A bit rich, Dougie. You did tell her you were going to Malaysia. You can't expect her to wait while you're out travelling South-East Asia screwing everything in sight.' Nev takes back the paper.

'She said she wanted a career and marriage could wait. And, he's such a tool. What does she see in him?'

'Fuck knows. Money, hob-knobbing it, big cock, fuck knows,' he says, putting his finger and thumb around his nose and masturbating it. 'When do you reckon you'll get posted?' he asks, changing the subject. I imitate his gesture.

'I would have thought I would get posted by now. I might go and see Mac tomorrow and see whether he knows anything.'

I will remember 10 August 1982 for as long as I live. Around 1030, I am refuelling a jet on the line when Billy wanders past at his usual snail's pace.

'Mac wants to see you straightaway.' I finish the job, sign for the fuel, sign up the aircraft documentation, then head over to the section. Mac is in his office writing, eyebrows twitching. I knock and he looks up from his writing, motioning me to enter and close the door.

'Well, Dougie, you got what you wanted. Here is the posting order for you to join 3 Squadron on 22nd September.' He is watching me closely. I am both excited and nervous. I will get to Butterworth a week after my nineteenth birthday and will be there for at least two years, maybe three. I will be at least twenty-one when I come home to Australia.

'Are you sure that you want to do this?' he asks, looking at me with that Mac '*I am sure you haven't thought this through*' face. 'Your grandparents are not getting any younger. What will happen if one, or both fall ill or die while you are there? Have you thought about that?'

Mac has an uncanny way of zeroing in on the heart of an issue. I often worry about grandma and grandad, and have thought about what might happen while I am overseas. Now, that issue is squarely in front of me.

'You go away and think about that,' he tells me. 'Come back and see me if you have second thoughts or just need a sounding board.'

'Thanks, Flight, I will.'

Word of my posting gets around the section fairly quickly. By afternoon smoko, I am grabbing a Coke when Graeme Billings opens his trap.

'Off to Butterworth, hey, young Dougie? I got ten bucks that says you go up there and fall for one of those slope-head sluts.' I look at him without emotion, tempted to punch his lights out, red mist bubbling softly.

Cocks like Billings aren't worth the effort.

'You know the locals are actually closely related to monkeys? Just out of the trees, they are.' I can feel the red mist rising further now and manage to resist the temptation to put my fist into his nose.

'Just like Geelong then, isn't it, Graeme? Do they drag their knuckles the same way?' I know he is from Geelong and figure it's only fair to throw it back at him, but he only laughs.

'You'll find out, young Dougie. The gooks even walk like monkeys. When you turn up back here with a slope on your arm, I will laugh like shit.' I feel like vomiting.

How does a reasonably well-educated Australian think like that?

'Fucking knob jockey.' I take my Coke and head back to the flight line.

Billings has me thinking. I have never been to Malaysia; I've never even been overseas. How am I to know whether anything

Billings says is even remotely true, no matter how ridiculous it might sound. One of the reasons I wanted to go to Malaysia in the first place was to see a bit of the world. And now, my curiosity has been reinforced. Mac has a point about grandma and grandad, but they are in pretty good shape, and I think I will take my chances. It's not like they'll get any heathier as they get older. It makes sense to go now.

The next few weeks go by quickly and as the date closes in, I am swamped with all manner of advice and stories about Malaysia; what to do, what not to do.

'You should live on the island.'

'Make sure you get an Amah, but don't pay any more than fifty Ringgit a week.'

'You'll have the clap and be in to see Dr Dan within a month, a quick jab and he'll sort you out.'

Everyone is an expert.

I try to spend every spare moment either with the girls, or at the farm in Dungog, soaking up the scenery, the smells, the sounds, my family.

Mac gives me the last Friday off. I've got fifty hours TOIL owing that I will never see again, so it was no great gesture, but everyone is under the pump and letting just one person go puts pressure on the rest of the guys.

I get to the farm around nine, just in time for a cuppa. There are a few questions about time and date of departure, where I will be living.

'Is it hot up there?' grandma enquires.

'Hotter than your English mustard, Gran, and humid, I'm told. Worse than Darwin.'

Later in the morning, she needs some flour and a few other bibs and bobs from Ernie's shop. She gives me a list.

'I'll come with you,' announces Uncle Bert. 'I have to go to the bank.'

The ride into town is pretty quiet. Uncle Bert's never been Mr Chatterbox. It's not like we don't get along, it's just that we don't have much to talk about. He's a farmer and I am a RAAF Armourer.

He was in the Army. Surely we have something in common?

'I got nineteen out of twenty on my range practice the other week.'

'What happened to the twentieth one?'

'Pushed it high right. I didn't have my breathing right.'

'That will do it,' he says, not really paying attention. He's off with the pixies. I back the Corolla into a space just down from the Sunshine café.

'I'll meet you back at the pub,' he instructs.

After the visit to Ernie's, I drop the bags on the back seat of the car and walk down the main street. I haven't been in Dungog on a work day for a long time, but things haven't changed a lot. There's the standard collection of cars and utes, a couple of four-wheel drives amongst them, Dave Turner's red dog pacing up and down the back of his ute inspecting each passer-by.

Inside, it's quiet. Three guys propping up the bar, one in a navy-blue singlet and South Sydney footy shorts, another in long work trousers and matching shirt — both haven't seen a washing machine for a long time — and a fat guy in jeans and a flannie drinking black beer. Uncle Bert is in the corner with a schooner and a copy of *The Land*, his head buried inside. I get a schooner of New, sit next to him and light a smoke.

We don't normally go to the pub. It's a bit odd. Matter of fact, I don't recall being in here more than twice in my whole life, and one of those times was before I joined up. Couldn't have been more than fifteen at the time. I recall Mick, the publican, gave us a beer and when we were nearly finished, he told us the cops were coming. We scampered out a back door pretty quickly. I smile to myself at the memory.

'They're thinking of building another dam out Munni way,' he tells me. I nod and we sit there sipping the beers. The bloke in the flannie orders another black.

'Don't know why they think they need another dam,' he says to no one in particular. 'We've got enough of the fucking things.'

The door opens and a guy in a shirt and tie walks in. He carries himself like he's somebody of importance, puffed up like a peacock. Then, the penny drops.

I know that prick.

I can feel my pulse quicken as I recognise the face, a little older and weather-worn, but it's fucking Neil Jackson. I stand involuntarily, put the smoke out in the ash tray and move toward him, the mist getting heavier, my pulse now pounding. I can hear Uncle Bert say something, but I am not receiving, I am transfixed. He has his back to me ordering a beer. I can see his face in the mirror behind the bar. I tap him on the shoulder and as he turns, I hear Uncle Bert yell.

'No, Tim.'

I get the first one right on his jaw and he spins away, the next one missing. It's not his first fight. He's taken a step away to gather himself, holding his jaw and looking me up and down with a sneer on his face.

I'm gonna wipe that off.

'Now, sonny, you'd better be happy with that one, cause it's the last one you are going to get. I am going to make you cry like a girl.'

I am about to launch back at him, but I get pulled aside, manoeuvred away as Uncle Bert steps in, cleverly holding me back with one hand and pointing with the other.

'I thought I told you to fuck off out of town or I'd cut your balls off?' Jackson's stance changes. He's no longer the aggressor, and is clearly frightened. He gathers himself.

'Who's the kid?'

I lurch forward at him again, Uncle Bert holding me with one hand.

'I'm Tim Walsh, you cock sucker. You'd remember my mum, wouldn't you?'

'Shut up, Tim.' Uncle Bert's grip and strength are surprising. He turns back to Jackson. 'You better get your arse back out of town before I decide to finish the job I started eight years ago.'

I can see Jackson sizing up the situation, regaining a little composure. He's obviously not going to take two of us on, but I can see that he's considering whether to tell Uncle Bert to fuck off.

'A bloke's got to be allowed to say hello to his parents.'

Uncle Bert is considering the request.

'Well, you do just that. If you are still in town at lunch time on Sunday, or I hear of any ladies being harassed, or so much as slightly annoyed by you, I will be visiting with my boning knife. You understand?'

Fuck, who is this guy in my Uncle's skin?

Jackson backs gradually to the door, nodding slowly. He

doesn't take an eye off Uncle Bert. It's only after the door closes that he releases his grip on my arm and walks casually back to the table and finishes his beer, cool as a cucumber.

'We're going,' he announces, picking up the newspaper and walking to the door, me following. The three patrons and barmaid still have their mouths open as we go out the door. It's not till we are out of town on the Fosterton Road that he speaks.

'What the fuck did you think you were doing back there?'

'You know.' I can feel my blood start to boil again.

'Enlighten me, Tim.'

'He's the cunt that caused all the trouble with mum and dad. He killed them, or may as well have.'

'What are you talking about?'

'The affair, I heard them arguing. They were arguing when they had the accident.' He's silent. He knows that I know now.

'Pull over, Tim.' It's not a request.

When the car stops, I can feel him staring at me. 'Who told you that your mum had an affair, Tim?'

'Everyone, there was always people whispering about it when I walked past. The kids at school used to tease me all the time. "Your mum's a slag, your mum's a slag," till I fucking shut their fucking mouths.' I shake my fist at him.

He's looking at me with concern, shaking his head. I don't know whether he has pity for me, or is disgusted. It's confusing, I'm lost.

'Your mum didn't have an affair, Tim.' It's a statement, a solemn one and it takes me aback. I can't believe what I am hearing.

'What about the argument. I was there.'

'Tim, your mum and dad may have had an argument. There were a lot of nasty rumours going around at the time. But, when they drove off for that weekend away, they were happy. I can assure you of that.'

It's not making any sense. What the fuck is Uncle Bert talking about? I am looking at him, shocked, lost for words.

'Have you spent the last eight years believing your mother had an affair with Jackson and that caused the accident?'

I nod, looking down at my shoes. My whole world has been turned upside.

'Fuck, Tim, that explains a few things.'

There is a loud sigh of relief. He looks at me earnestly.

'I'll tell you a few truths, Tim, so you better listen. Your dad was a good bloke. Him and Jackson were playing footy together and they used to hang out together a bit and drink after the game. But Jackson was a bit of a ladies' man, or so he thought, and your dad didn't like the way he treated some of them. So, they weren't mates, but got on okay.'

'Your dad had to go to Sydney for a few weeks on a course with the PMG. While he was away, Jackson started hanging around your house. Calling in during the day when you kids were at school, or later at night, sniffing around your mum.'

'Before you know it, people started to talk. And, talk is cheap around here, Tim. If you paid attention to every rumour in this fucking town, then most of them would be divorced or in bloody gaol.'

'Anyway, we were at home late one Thursday night and your mother turned up in the car with you three kids in the back. She was crying. Apparently, Jackson had turned up at the house half-pissed and pushed himself on her.' He starts to grin, well sort of, more of an evil leer.

'*Fuck, maybe Uncle Bert really has lost it.*'

'Apparently, she kneed him in the balls that hard he was vomiting.' He chuckles again. 'Your mother told him to fuck off or she'd scream the house down. He couldn't get out of there fast enough.' He is still grinning, at least for a bit, and then his face turns serious again.

'Tim, your grandmother is a tough lady. When she saw the state your mother was in, she nodded to me. No words were necessary, and I went into town to have a little chat with Jackson.' He pauses before continuing. 'You know that little boning knife I use to castrate the steers?'

I nod, squirming a little inside. The smile briefly returns to his face.

'He was at his parents' house. It was late and they were in bed. He came to the door, walking like John Wayne, and when he saw me, he told me to fuck off.' Now it's definitely an evil leer.

'That's when I put my fist though the screen door and grabbed him by the throat. I had him face down on the patio before he could blink and put the blade in front of his eyes. He nearly shat himself.'

Now I am smiling.

'Anyway, I told him to get out of town and if I ever saw him again, I would cut his balls off with that knife. He struggled a bit, but when you are face-down on the concrete, with your arm twisted up your back, and a knife in your face, you generally don't argue.'

Now, we are both smiling. It's the best story I have heard in years, no, ever. He turns serious again and looks at me.

'Your dad got home the next night, and there may have been an argument, I don't know, but they turned up on the Saturday morning saying they were going to Seal Rocks for the night and to drop you kids off. It's the last time I saw them and, I can assure you, they were happy. They had the accident on the Lakes Way that morning.' He's still now, just staring ahead. We both go quiet for a while and I let it all sink in.

You fucking idiot, Walsh. For all these years I have believed those kids teasing me, the gossips.

'Why didn't you tell me?'

'We all thought you knew, assumed, I guess.' He's defensive, but compassionate. 'Fuck, Tim, if I'd have realised you didn't know the truth, I would have been the first to tell you.'

I take it in a bit longer. It's like a weight has been lifted and I am free. He looks at his watch.

'Fuck, mum is going to send out a search party if we aren't back for milking. We'd better get going.'

For the rest of Friday, I withdraw, keep to myself and contemplate the events of the day, and my new respect for my Uncle Bert. I am not going to take him on, and I finally feel like I have a clue about who he is. The rest of the weekend is pretty routine, Gran is spoiling me at every opportunity, even a couple of jokes with Uncle Bert.

Before lunch on Sunday, Uncle Bert announces we are going to get a paper. He drives in silence, quietly whistling to himself, the warm spring sun pleasant through my window. He stops at Gilbert's servo. I get out, get the paper, and hop back in. He continues up Hooke Street, then left toward the hospital, pulling up at the lookout. We get out and sit on the bonnet, I light a smoke and contemplate my hometown.

'Dad and I came up here before I left to go to Vietnam,' he tells me. 'We just sat and looked for a while.'

It really is a stunning sight with the bright sun shining on silver tin rooftops, a few chimneys still slowly smoking, spring blossoms amid the trees. The birds are really active, black-and-white magpies on patrol and an eagle circling overhead. There is an odd bit of traffic noise, but for the most part it is birds, cows, and the sound of kids yelling at each other. Ten minutes later, he looks at his watch.

'Fuck, we're late, get in.'

He turns left again back down Mackay Street, slowing the Holden to a crawl and looking intently at the front of a fibro house. A new Commodore is parked out the front. The ute gathers speed again and we turn right up Lord Street, pulling up at Lion's Park. He gets out again and sits on the bonnet, I lean against the fence rail, smoking. Five minutes later, the new Commodore comes slowly past, Jackson driving, looking ahead, no acknowledgment. Uncle Bert's head and eyes track the transit out of town.

I get going before milking, tears from gran, firm handshakes from grandad and Uncle Bert and I am on my way. By the time I get back to Base, I am feeling like a different person. Somehow, I feel clearer and more determined than when I went home. I am confident with my choice to go to Malaysia and I am feeling somewhat released.

On Monday morning, Tacho and Azaria drop me to Air

Movements Section for the bus ride to Sydney, a night in the Cross, then onto the charter to Butterworth on Tuesday morning. A whole new world awaits me.

10 — Char Kway Teow

I become semi-conscious around nine. There is a chopper flying around the airfield somewhere, but it feels like it's inside the room beating my brains into submission. I have visions of the chopper crewie hopping out, opening my front door and running to open the back door so the chopper can fly through.

Fuck, where am I? Oh, yer, Singapore.

The past two weeks have been a drunken blur. It all started with the 707 flight out of Mascot, then Butterworth, Penang, and Thailand.

Shit, those Thai girls know how to put a smile on your face. Noi would give Helen a run for her money, minus the handcuffs.

I look around the room. Tex is snoring in the other bed. I decide I need water and that is when I discover I am still dressed, shoes and all.

'Shit, no wonder my brain hurts.'

I make it to the handbasin and chug down a glass of water, remove my clothes and lie back down. That was a bad idea. The bed feels like it's spinning. The water ends up back in the basin.

'Shit.'

Delicately lying back down, I start ruminating on my South-East Asian tour thus far. Drunken night in Penang drinking Anchor beer, drunken weekend in Hatyai drinking Mekhong, drunken week in Singapore drinking Tiger beer, Fogcutters around the pool at the Hilton.

Fuck, does anyone do anything in this man's Air Force other than drink piss?

An hour goes by and I manage to get some water down.

At least the chopper has fucked off.

'Morning, Sunshine.' I look up and, through the fog, recognise the face.

Fuck, it's Lefty.

'Is this the same fearless Armourer I saw cuddling someone, or something, in the Bugen Strasse last night?'

Fuck, I didn't, did I?

He is standing in the doorway, looking like he'd never touched a drop. Pete is behind him leaning on the veranda rail with a smart-arse grin on his face.

'Come on, get dressed. We are going shopping.'

I have had a crash course in Lefty's version of shopping, and it's got fuck-all to do with shops.

'Fuck off, Lefty,' is the only response I can think of. Not my best snappy comeback.

'Now, now, no need to be like that, young Timothy. Corporal Buchanan and I have your best interests at heart ... Now get up and get dressed.' There is a short pause before he throws back the sheet and starts to drag me from the bed.

'Okay, okay, I give in. But you have to let me have a shower first.' They both have big grins and start on Tex.

Showered and dressed, we follow them downstairs to a waiting crew van, sunglasses firmly entrenched over my eyes so I don't bleed to death. Buck Rogers, one of the Sergeant Framies, is driving.

'Hi, Buck.'

'Morning, Dougie,' he laughs.

What the fuck did I get up to last night?

Buck turns left out the main gate, down Choa Chu Kang Road and left onto Woodlands Road. Despite my sensitive state, the sights and sounds of Asia fascinate me. Here in Singapore, things are pretty civilised. Western-looking houses, lawns manicured. Malaysia and Thailand look almost primitive in comparison.

He drops us at a row of shops on Transit Road. It's mostly electrical goods, juicers, stereos, speakers. Plenty of orders being placed for video recorders. I get myself a Walkman. An amazing thing, this. Not much bigger than a cassette, but can take one, an inbuilt radio, headphones and earplugs.

What will they think of next?

Lefty is true to form, the shopping is over in less than fifteen minutes.

'Methinks it's time for a sharpener. This way,' he points, marching off. Before I know it, we are entrenched in the Paris Bar and three shouts later, leads us to the bus stop. A short ride later, I find myself outside a building proudly labelled as the New Zealand Forces Recreation Club, Fern Leaf.

'So, what do the Kiwis have here?' I enquire. Lefty explains there are a couple of infantry companies and a few choppers stationed at Dieppe Barracks a little way back down the road.

'This is their recreation centre and it has rooms upstairs you can rent if you ever come down here on holidays,' he says, pointing at the building.

'Dieppe, that's in France?' I ask.

'Yep, Poms had some hare-brained idea to cross the channel

before D-Day. Got their arses kicked. They named the barracks after that battle and the name stayed when the Kiwis took over in the early seventies.'

The afternoon goes slowly. Lefty and Pete sharing stories of previous Singapore trips and Malaysia postings. It's Lefty's third posting to Malaysia.

'I reckon I have spent nearly a third of my life here, I just love it.'

Just before seven, Lefty announces it's time to go. We walk out the front and Buck is magically waiting in the crew van. I turn back at Lefty with a 'what the ...?' look and he grins.

'Where to, boys?'

Pete and Lefty look at each other simultaneously saying, 'Za Bugen Strasse', doing their best Adolf impersonation.

No, not again.

Buck drops us at an already buzzing Bugis Street. Pete leads the way and we find a table not too far from the intersection of the two streets. I recognise a number of likely suspects at other tables. Every couple of minutes someone comes up and tries to sell me something, anything. Everything from harmonicas, umbrellas, and cassettes, to vibrators, you name it. I find a stall selling '60s British music and buy a large selection at an outrageous price.

'They're pirate copies,' Pete tells me.

'Pirate?'

'Illegal copies done in someone's back shed,' he tells me. 'They are ay, but you'll find they're fucked after a couple of plays.'

Lefty and Pete keep the beers coming; tall bottles of Tiger. As the night goes on, the crowd grows. A healthy smattering of Australian Navy uniforms amongst it. Before midnight, one of our squadron guys challenges a sailor to the Dance of the Flaming Arseholes. The contestants are hoisted atop the roof of the toilet block where they drop their pants and a roll of newspaper is wedged between the arse cheeks. The two rolls are lit and the two lads dance. The winner is the last to either drop the roll, or extinguish the flame because it's burning their arse. I am told there is a slightly different version where it's a running race.

The sailor wins, but our guy protests that they were late getting their roll ignited. We chant, 'Rematch, rematch, rematch,' but our challenger has some burnt attributes which require soothing. The show goes well into the night. In the drunken haze, I see Tex with a *shim* sitting on his lap and him playing with her tits.

I didn't do that, did I?

Around three in the morning the boys decide we might have had enough and we find a cab. I pour myself into my bed a half hour later.

Sunday, I manage to avoid the boys by going to town before lunch and doing some real shopping. Orchard Road is much different during the day with plenty of Western style shops and cafes. They even have a McDonalds.

Why would anyone want to eat that shit?

Late in the afternoon, I find myself back on Base. A few beers at the ARC Bar and then onto Tengah Village for food. We walk down to the main gate and pass office which, like the rest of the buildings, have a colonial look to them. In the village, Pete suggests a particular venue and we sit down on stools at a round table with a stainless top. The floor is brushed earth and there are chickens clucking around our heels.

Gran would be laughing her head off at this.

The food is exceptional. Satays with spicy peanut sauce and cucumber, fish, pork, prawns, all cooked in some magic sauce. It's hard to describe. Hot, sour, sweet, all at the same time. Everything washed down with loads of Tiger beer.

By the time my head hits the pillow, I am exhausted lying in the heat under the fan. I occurs to me that I have been in three different countries over the past week, four if you count Australia.

You wanted to see some of the world Tim, here you are. Make the most of it.

The next few days go by quickly, the work is routine but the intensity is frantic. We have two waves airborne before 0830. We start Bombing Up on the Turnaround around 1000, then morning tea arrives.

Fucking scones, cream, strawberry jam and mugs of tea. Are you fucking kidding me?

I have grease, oil, and burnt propellant all over me as I shove a scone or two in my mouth, trying not to get any black shit on the scone.

'Back to work, you blokes,' Lefty pushing the pace as usual. We generally get all six waves complete by 1700 each day and wash the day's heat away with more Tiger beer.

Late on Friday we launch half the jets back to Butterworth, and we keep six. There is a hurry to close up; it's going to be a big weekend.

Saturday night, the Mess has been transformed into a function centre with a stage, dance floor, long tables with places set, and decorated in Anchor beer promotional material. There is a band setting up when we get there.

Octoberfest is obviously a big event in the RAAF Support Unit, Tengah, social calendar. The place is bulging with servicemen, partners, locals and invited dignitaries. Half of our squadron personnel are there including the CO, XO, and a few knuckleheads. One of the black handers is already pissed and groping the ladies a little too indiscreetly. He gets unceremoniously ejected.

There is a menu on the table which lists an entrée of Bratwurst with sauerkraut, followed by a main meal of ham hock or schnitzel, potatoes and more sauerkraut, followed by dessert of apple pie or black forest cake. The waiters start to bring out the first course and I am instructed by Pete on which knives and forks to use.

'Start from the outer, and work inward,' he says.

Seems simple enough.

The band cranks up playing German folk music. They are the most German-sounding Chinese men I've ever seen, not having seen too many Chinese men. They are a five-piece ensemble with drummer, accordion player, guy on double bass, flugelhorn player and guitarist. The guitarist and accordion player do the vocals. 'Mein Schatz' is sung with some class over the main meal served with big glasses of Anchor.

After dinner, I notice Pete in the corner talking with two European women. I wander over and he introduces the girls, Sally and Liz. Sally is probably about thirty, a little round, pretty, hair parted down the middle and gathered in a ponytail.

Liz is a tall girl, dark hair over the shoulder. There's a hint of freckles on her cheeks, camouflaged by a minimal amount of makeup, and red lipstick. The most striking feature is her legs;

long legs. Even in relatively flat shoes, those legs are stunning. She is wearing a sleeveless, floral dress that flares from the hips and finishes above the knee, simple white shoes.

Wow.

'What brings you to Singapore?' I ask.

'Oh, we work at the High Commission. I am an Administrative Officer with the Department of Foreign Affairs,' she says.

I'd like to have an affair with you, in a foreign location.

I ask how she came to get a job like this and she tells me her dad was a diplomat. They have lived in various places including London, Taiwan, Saigon, as well as Canberra. She finished sixth form in Canberra, went to ANU to study International Relations.

'Once I finished the degree, I applied to join the department through their graduate program.' It occurs to me she has finished a degree and has had some work experience since. She doesn't look that old, but I am doing the maths and now guessing twenty-four. I ask.

'Twenty-three, twenty-four in April. You?' I concede I am only nineteen. 'Nooooo,' she says. 'You can't have finished school, completed your training, and have enough service up to get overseas?' I explain the whole apprenticeship thing.

'Aaaaaah,' she says.

The band wants everyone to pair up on the dance floor. Liz and I team up. Before the music starts, they take us through the moves. It's basically a fast Pride of Erin to start with, then you turn to face your partner, stomp your feet, clap your hands, slap the hands of your partner, slap your knees and shoes, and then back into the fast waltz.

Having got the instructions, the band cranks up. Holding

her left hand we walk quickly forward, turn and come back. We stop and face each other, feet stomp and hands clap successfully. Then there is a mixture of slapping various parts of the body and each other. She is killing herself laughing. During the third chorus, we get it mostly right. The song concludes and we are left panting and giggling. The tempo changes and I offer both hands. She steps forward and I put my right hand on the small of her back, the other in her left hand.

She moves effortlessly around the dance floor and requires little lead from me. It's almost like she can anticipate my next movement. My mind has shut out most of the room and we become engrossed in each other's presence. We linger on the dance floor hoping for another song, but the band is taking a break. We go back to the seats near Sally and Pete, holding hands.

I ask her about her job and what she does here in Singapore. 'Not a great deal. There are a lot of Australians passing through, or living in, Singapore. Someone is always losing a passport, getting arrested, or something. Or, it's a Singapore national wanting to work in Australia. It's not difficult work, just plenty of it.'

A young Singaporean man gestures to Sally and she announces their ride is here. I think I am broken-hearted at the thought of not spending more time with Liz.

'We have happy hour at the High Commission every Friday night at 6 pm,' Sally says. 'What's your last names so we can put it on the guest list?'

'Buchanan, Peter Buchanan and Walsh, Tim Walsh,' Pete replies. She takes a pen from her handbag and writes the names on a coaster. Liz leans into me, gives me a peck on the cheek, and whispers.

'See you next Friday.' I am jelly.

The party is winding down, so Pete and I grab a couple of half empty bottles of wine and some glasses off the tables before the staff confiscate them. In the corner, I am sitting there contemplating the chance of meeting with the most beautiful girl I have ever met.

'I think I really like Sally,' announces Pete. The statement pulls me from my own reflection and back to reality.

'Aren't you married?'

He looks at me the way Uncle Bert used to look at me when I asked a dumb question. He's taking his time.

'Dougie, sometimes marriage just doesn't work out.' I am looking at him waiting for the rest of the response. I can see there is more, and I can also feel a little anger growing.

What is a married guy doing screwing around?

'You know the whole "to have and to hold, from this day forth, till death do us part" stuff? Well, it happens to probably a quarter of people who get married.'

I know it's not true. Now, I think he is making shit up to justify an affair while his wife is at home in Penang watching TV. I am not too fussed.

'Frogshit, Pete, you are making excuses.'

He tips his head to the side. 'If you say so, Dougie,' taking a swig. He's looking at the band pack up and his eyes change like he isn't really here.

'Deborah and I used to be great dancers. As soon as the band started, we'd be on the floor. Rock, waltz, jive, you name it, we could do it.' He shakes his head. 'Fucked if I know where it all went wrong.' I wait for more, but he's not talking.

'You're just going through a tough patch.'

His eyes come back to life and looks straight at me. 'No, mate, this is terminal.' If I didn't know any better, I would say he about to cry. 'I think we are done.'

My mind is wondering to mum and dad. For a long time, I thought they 'were done' and it caused the car accident. Uncle Bert seemed to think that wasn't the case.

How can I be sure? What's right and what's wrong? Fucked if I know.

My mind comes back to the present. 'Pete, are you sure? This is heavy shit.' He gathers himself and looks at me.

'Dougie, we were going okay when we left Williamtown. We thought we'd start a family here while she wasn't working.' His head drops and I wait, taking a drink and lighting a smoke. I offer him one and he lights up. I have never seen Pete smoke before. He takes a deep draw.

'We'd been screwing each other stupid for months and nothing happened. Then, we went to medical and they did some tests. Seems she has some sort of thing where the fertilised egg doesn't stick and passes when she has a period.'

'Fuck.'

'Yep, that's what she said. That was a year ago and we haven't had sex since.'

'Fuck.'

'It's over, Dougie, at least for her. I am just lonely.'

I sleep in the next morning, only getting out of bed to take a leak. Not even ten o'clock and it feels like ninety-nine per cent humidity. I lie under the fan and try to read a book, but all I can think about is a tall girl, with long legs, and a smile that would melt steel.

The other thing going through my head is the conversation with Pete at stumps.

Why would a woman just stop having sex because she can't have kids?

The week goes fast. Each morning, we launch all six jets to bounce six coming in from Butterworth on a Heavy Bombing and Gunnery mission, four Mk82 GP bombs per jet on the outboard stations of RPK-10s, gun packs with HE ammo, and a centreline tank. They shoot the left-hand gun on the way down. All twelve land at Tengah and we turn them around.

Pete and I are assigned to testing the right-hand gun to make sure it works and lock-wiring the ejector pistons on the RPK-10s to make sure they don't extend and create drag. Pete is a hard worker. I am pretty fit, and giving him at least ten years, but I find it difficult to keep up in the tropical heat. To top it off, the humidity has ratcheted up a level.

Each afternoon, all twelve jets are launched from Tengah, six Shooters and six Bounce, six fighting six. The Shooters do their gunnery mission and return to Butterworth, the Bounce jets recover to Tengah. When they land, Pete and I run around to cover the aircraft while the others are refuelling and fixing minor USs. No one leaves until everyone is finished. The Duty Storm has started arriving at around 1600 each afternoon. It's called the Duty Storm because it is so regular and predictable it may as well have been on duty.

There is plenty of time between sorties to sit and think. I have taken to sitting outside in the heat and letting last night's booze weep from my pores. That and contemplate Liz, and Sally and Pete.

Why can't Pete and his missus just sort stuff out?

Friday, we are both jumpy to get out of work. All six jets come back serviceable. The boys are refuelling, changing brake chutes, filling engine oil, and Pete and I put on the covers. We are out by four, shower, and put on our best. It's pissing down and we have to wait for an opportunity to get out the front gate and to the bus stop. We get out on Bukit Timah Road and get a cab. We only have a vague idea where the High Commission is. It's only a short ride and we arrive at half-past six. The gate guard asks for ID, checks the list, and directs us to the pool.

'Fuck, they have a pool.' I am stunned.

The pool is at the back of the building so it's out of sight of people using the services of the High Commission. There is a wooden shelter at one end with a thatched roof. The crowd is gathered around and as we get closer, I can see a barman in a suit serving drinks under the shelter. Sally steps from the crowd to greet us.

'I thought you guys had stood us up,' she says turning and indicating we should follow. Liz and she are ensconced on the side of the bar farthest from the pool. Sally takes a seat next to Liz and orders us a beer each. I greet Liz with a peck on the cheek and a shy, 'Hello.' Her smile tells me she is happy to see me and I relax a little.

Sally explains the beer and wine prices, and the fact this is one of the few places you can get real Australian beer and wine in Singapore, and it's not Ben Ean Moselle. Pete and Sal start into a discussion on the merits of various wine blends. I have no idea what they are talking about.

'Did you miss me?' she asks.

Fuck, the soap has been getting a workout in the shower all week.
'Yep,' I say.

'Man of few words,' she says, swaying slightly to the music.

We look at each other in silence, looking for something to say. She has her head dipped slightly looking up at me. I am trying hard to be cool, but unsure what that is under this scrutiny. 'Six Months in a Leaky Boat' is coming from the speakers.

'This is cool,' I suggest. 'But I think 'I See Red' is their best.'

'No way, 'I Got You' will be one of the penultimate songs of the eighties.'

I haven't got a clue what the fuck penultimate is, but it sounds important.

'Yer, it's a pretty good song,' I say. 'What's your favourite Beatles song?'

'That's like asking which is the best food you have ever eaten,' she says. 'Maybe 'Hey Jude', 'Strawberry Fields', or 'In My Life',' she offers.

'Good choices, but I can't go past 'A Day in the Life'. It has everything, classic Lennon voice and silly McCartney lyrics.' We both laugh and she sings a few lines of 'Silly Love Songs'. We get engrossed in music. Talking about bands, best front man, best diva, Sinatra, Creedence, Morrison, Cilla, and mum's favourite, Petula Clark. She sings a couple of lines of 'Love, This is my Song' with some skill and I melt.

'Last drinks,' is called, and we look up. It's eight-thirty and we have not taken a breath all night, nor taken our eyes off each other. Unbeknown to us, most of the crowd has dispersed and there are only about ten people left. Sally and Pete get one last round.

'So, kids, what are we going to do?' asks Sal.

'Genevieve's,' says Liz. A statement.

'Great idea,' she says. We down our drinks and move to the exit, Pete and me in tow. We have no idea where we are going or how we are getting there.

The girls lead us to a car park and Liz approaches a sleek-looking, red sports car and unlocks the passenger side door. If Merv was here, he would describe it as a 'dog cock red' car.

'In the back, Sal,' she says, walking to the driver's side and unlocking it. It's a two-door and she rolls the front seat forward. Once Pete and Sal are safe in the back, I find a lever to put the seat back into position and climb in. She starts the car and reverses out, waving to the guard as we go through the gate.

'I have never seen a car like this.'

'It's a 1968 Jensen Interceptor Mk1 with a Chrysler V8. Dad and I took an interest in British cars when we lived in London. When I saw this, I just had to have it.' Tacho would be killing himself with jealousy if he knew I was in a real Interceptor.

She carves her way through narrow streets and traffic, hands gentle on the gear changes, obviously comfortable behind the wheel. Ten minutes later, she pulls up at the front of a hotel. The uniformed concierge opens her door and greets her. 'Good evening, Ms Alexander. Are you staying long?'

'Thank you, Ranjit, only a couple of hours,' she says.

She leads us to the shopping mall next door and into a near deserted ground floor. I can hear music. We enter a bar with a few people on the dance floor, disco lights flashing round and round, and big screen beyond the stage. 'Piano Man' is belting through the speakers and Billy Joel is on the screen. We get a drink and find a booth at the back. Sal and Pete get comfortable.

Liz and I resume our earlier conversation on the Beatles when Blondie comes on. She grabs me and we run to the dance floor. We move easily and in harmony with each other. She is looking over her eyebrows again, finger pointing at me, mouthing the words, 'One way, or another, I'm gonna get ya. I'll get ya, get ya, get ya, get ya.' I am playing hard to get, but it's hardly the case.

The songs are great and we dance away the night, Elton John, Michael Jackson, Queen, Boston, Aerosmith, The Stones. Before midnight, she says it's time to go and we go to the booth to grab her purse. Pete and Sal are in a clinch. I think she has the better of him and I am tempted to start counting to three and hit the table.

'Hey, guys, we are off, catch you tomorrow.' Sally just waves a hand.

Back at the hotel, it's only a short wait before the car reappears. The young Indian guy gets out and closes the door behind her.

'Good evening, Ms Alexander, lovely to see you again.'

''Thank you, Ranjit,' she replies. Another young Indian male opens the passenger side door and I get in. He closes it behind me.

Again, she weaves her way through streets, across a bridge, and into what looks like an older part of Singapore. She finds a space in a dark street and parks.

'Come on,' she says.

She walks down the middle of the street considering the buildings, obviously looking for something. When she spots it, she moves back to the footpath and to a door. She knocks firmly. Seconds later, a slot in the door opens, Chinese eyes assess her, and it closes again. The door opens and we are ushered into a room.

'Ms Alexander, how lovely to see you again.' The Chinese

guy extends his hand, she takes it and they shake briefly. It's a small waiting room with a few seats and a theatre ticket window.

'Mr Leng, this is my colleague, Tim Walsh, from the High Commission in KL.' I try to look earnest and shake his hand.

'Lovely to meet you, Mr Walsh,' he says, sizing me up. 'The show is about to start.' She steps toward the ticket window opening her purse. He waves his hands to remove thoughts of payment and shows us to a curtained doorway. As I go past the ticket window, I note a gorilla-looking Chinese guy behind the counter. I am thinking it would not take much encouragement for him to snap you into small pieces and eat them, perhaps with a little soy sauce.

On the other side of the doorway, the room is dimly lit and clouded with cigarette smoke. It's a small theatre with no more than about sixty seats. Mr Leng shows us to our seats and disappears back to the waiting room. From what I can see, it's about two-thirds full, mostly Chinese couples, but a smattering of Europeans couples and the odd mix of both. I lean over to Liz and whisper.

'This isn't a re-run of the *Sound of Music*, is it?' She smacks my hand lightly with a cheeky smile.

The lights dim and its almost pitch black when the music starts, rhythmic music. Spotlights on the stage start to illuminate two cages with a dancing figure within each one. As the light gets brighter, I can tell its two women dressed in heels, skirts and blouses. One is Chinese, the other a blonde, Caucasian woman. Although the cages are separated by about two yards, they are moving in sync. As the music progresses, the blouses come off in unison followed shortly by the two skirts. Both have tanned and firm bodies. After the obligatory tease period, the brassieres come off, both women with stunning breasts.

'They are silicone,' Liz whispers.

I'll have to ask her later what she means.

As the panties come off, the music reaches a crescendo and stops. The girls take a bow, turn their back to the audience and take another bow.

'Taking our photo,' I remark. The lights go back down.

Over the next half hour, there is a procession of women dancing and stripping, a new gimmick with each. One has a large vibrator as part of the act. Another finds a way to get four ping pong balls inside herself, they get fired, cannon-like, across the stage into a basket. Yet another fires darts at a dart board, the crowd applauding when they stick. The large vibrator girls come back and carefully arrange a stack on coins on a small box, the top coin painted white. She rubs herself up in time to the music and then squats over the coins, they disappear inside her. She stands up and dances around the stage.

'If I pulled her arm, you reckon she'd pay out?' I get another little smack on the arm.

The girl dances back to the box and squats again. When she stands, the coins are deposited back where they started, the white coin now on the bottom. The crowd applauds.

A European-looking couple dance onto the stage. It's the same girl as in the cage. They take off each other's clothes. The strip is obviously not the focus. She starts rubbing him up. He is hung like a horse and it takes a while for it to fully extend. She starts blowing him and, from my limited experience, is no novice. He mounts her and she seems to wince in pain. I grab a quick glance over at Liz and she has a similar expression on her face. Perhaps there is such a thing as too big, not that I would know.

They proceed to do it in pretty well every conceivable position. I am particularly impressed with the one where both of them have their hands and feet on the stage facing up, her feet under his armpits, her above him. She lowers herself onto the monster.

'How did she do that,' I wonder, mouth open.

Several more positions are demonstrated before the pace increases and the grand finale. He pulls it out and unloads over her tits. She rubs it in, then takes him back in her mouth as the lights go down and the curtain closes. The crowd applauds loudly as the main lights come on. I am aware of being aroused and Liz has noticed without being too obvious, giving me a sly grin.

Back outside, Liz opens the driver's side door with a smile. 'Well, you don't get that in Dungog, Tim.'

I get in and look firmly at her. 'I never said I was from Dungog.' There is a long silence.

'No,' she concedes, now with a look of guilt. 'I looked at your file,' she says, in a soft voice.

'My file? What the fuck is my file?'

Who the hell is this woman?

She hesitates. 'Well,' she says slowly. 'Certain departments hold certain files on certain people. You are in the military and so you have a file.' She goes on, 'Tim Walsh, aka Dougie after Doug Walters the cricketer. Born Dungog, NSW, 14 September 1963. Known associates Angus, Gus, Edwards and Nev Walker. Charges include punching people and being drunk. Not much else of note.' She pauses. 'You didn't expect me to go out with someone I'd only met for an hour and not do a character check, much less take you to a Tiger Show?'

I think about it for a bit.

'No,' I concede with a laugh.

'I guess Sally looked at Pete's file too, hey?' She nods. 'She knows he's married?'

'Yep,' she replies. 'Sally prefers the married ones. They don't broadcast it.' There is a pause. She looks over at me. 'What happened to your parents?' she asks, in almost a whisper. I tell her about the car accident and my sisters. A tear runs down her cheek.

The streets are almost empty as she threads her way through the city. The buildings turn from commercial into residential. She slows and turns into a driveway. The house is elevated and she parks underneath. We make our way up the stairs and she unlocks the door. The lounge room is neat, bamboo furniture with a TV and stereo, kitchen and dining area off to the side. The windows are casement and have shutters. It's a real colonial feel.

She pours two Bundy and Cokes, hands me one, and goes to the record player, Australian Crawl starts up, 'Sirocco'. I reflect on the night and wonder whether everything is what it appears. She puts her drink down and comes to me, wrapping her arms around me, and swaying. We kiss, slowly at first, and then more deeply with growing passion. The clothes come off quickly.

With the previous entertainment still on our minds, we are impatient and do it on the lounge floor. By the third track, we are on the kitchen table and I put the B side on as we head to the bedroom, momentarily wondering what language James Reyne is speaking. She dictates the action, rocking her hips back and forth.

What it is about me and dominant women?

We wake around eight, hugging and making love slower this time. I make sure she has plenty to breathe heavy about. We lie under the fan sweating and panting again.

'Well, that wasn't in your file,' she says, with a laugh.

I am hungry and crawl out of bed. I find my undies and pants in the lounge room and put them on. There are several tomatoes on the bench and I hunt for onions. They are in the cupboard under the sink. Sliced onions and a bit of oil into a hot pan, and the house fills with a lovely aroma. The tomatoes go in and start to cook down while I whisk some eggs, adding some fresh milk and letting it sit.

When I walk back into the bedroom, she is sitting up, reading, with glasses on, sheet covering her breasts. Liz looks sexy in glasses. I put a cup of tea on her bedside table and offer the plate of scrambled eggs with grandma's fried tomato and onion. She puts the book down and rubs her hands. She's scoffing it down when I get back with my plate.

'If I ever get a house slave, you are on the top of the list, Mr Walsh.' Breakfast finished, she announces, 'I am going to take you shopping, Dougie boy.'

She used my nickname? That's right, it was on my file.

She grabs me by the pants and drags me to the shower — soap, warm water, her hands on me, my fingers on her. When she orgasms, she closes her eyes, savouring the moment. Out of the shower, I lift her onto the vanity, her long legs wrapped around me, then back into the shower. Around lunch time, we get into the Interceptor.

She threads her way through a couple of suburban streets and then out onto Bukit Timah Road toward the city. It is such a clean place. No rubbish on the side of the road, every bit of grass mown, and the edges trimmed. She turns left on Serangoon Road and finds a park.

'Little India,' she announces. 'You can walk up and down Orchard Road all day looking for a bargain, but you won't get much cheaper than here. But you have to haggle.' She laughs. 'Eleven, this cost me twelve. Are you trying to ruin me,' she says, mimicking Monty Python.

We get out and stroll around the streets. Along the way I pick up some new undies, a shirt, and a toothbrush. We head over to a large building which is obviously some sort of market. Inside is an amazing array of fresh produce, fresh meat of endless varieties, hawker stalls, and retail shop fronts. It's an extremely busy place and the tropical heat seems to add a level of intensity to the experience. The fresh meat and some of the other aromas are overpowering. We stop at a fruit shop.

'What is that?' I ask screwing up my nose.

'Durian,' she says. 'They tell me it's an extremely sweet, yet savoury, taste, if you can get past the smell.'

Liz purchases a couple of steaks, a bit of fruit and veg, and two bottles of Kickapoo Joy juice, handing me one. We meander our way back to the car drinking from the bottles.

Back at the house, I go through her music collection. It's not huge, but definitely well selected. You won't find Air Supply here! I pull out *Silk Degrees* and put it on the record player. She is in the kitchen chopping ingredients.

'It's a pretty impressive selection of music. What's your favourites?' I ask, walking to the kitchen.

'Mad Beatles fan and love the current Aussie music revival,' she says.

'Chisel or Aussie Crawl?' I ask.

She ponders and replies 'Chisel'.

'Best Chisel song?' I ask again.

She ponders, 'Four Walls'.

'I prefer 'Hound Dog'. Best Beatles' song?'

'I told you last night.'

'Oh, yer. Best Stones' song?'

'I do love 'Paint it Black' and 'Brown Sugar'.'

'Robert Redford or Steve McQueen?' I change the subject.

'Steve.'

'Mel Gibson or Mark Lee?'

'Tim Walsh,' she says. 'You are much better looking than those two.'

'Best album of all time?'

She looks at the ceiling in thought. 'Either *Abbey Road*, The *White Album, or Dark Side of the Moon*,' she replies, goes to add something, then decides better of it.

'Country or western?' I ask. She giggles.

'Orange Whip?' she asks, going to the fridge. She gets two cans of Tiger out, cracks both, and hands one to me.

'Not too much, Dougie, you have duties later.' She smirks and takes a swig.

'Who would you have in the best band ever?' I enquire. 'Drummer first.'

'Well,' she says, considering the answer while cutting some cabbage. 'Either Keith Moon or Ringo. Probably Keith Moon; so much energy.'

'Lead guitar?' I push her.

'Clapton, Harrison, Townsend, Richards, or Brian May.

Clapton has a fat head. Townsend, May and Harrison are good, but not as good as Keith Richards.'

'Is that a prerequisite to join the band?' I ask.

'What?' she says.

'First name of Keith.' She laughs. We decide the band should be called the Keiths.

'Front man?' I go on. 'Lennon, Jagger, Barnsey ...' She laughs about Barnsey and then decides Freddie Mercury is our man, or Keith Mercury at least. Keith Janice Joplin and Keith Joe Walsh join the band, Keith John Entwistle gets a start as the bass player. There is some debate about having two members of The Who in the band and no Beatles.

While we are in a questioning mood, I ask what her full name is.

'Elizabeth Mary Alexander,' she replies. 'Born 25 April 1959 in Canberra. Second daughter to Joe and Sara Alexander, two others followed. Educated in various locations around the world. You know the rest.'

'What was Saigon like?' I push. 'It was '65 to '66. I was young. But I do remember playing in the streets with the local kids. I can even speak a Vietnamese dialect fluently. It's what happens when you are young. I don't remember any shooting, but there was a lot of uniformed people around. I do like a man in uniform,' she says, eyeing me up and down.

'Tell me more about my file. How do they get the info?' I ask.

'Not too much more to tell, Tim. It's pretty basic. ASIO has a super computer. It's as big as this house. They pull data from all the computers of the other federal government departments, medical, tax, defence, dole office, feds. They all get mashed together. No one will ever admit it, but the data is there. They are trying to access data from the state governments as well, like your birth certificate and driver licence number. We are not too far off being able to tell what you had for dinner.'

'Fuck, that's impressive.'

This girl is not your average Administrative Clerk.

'What about the Chinese guy last night. Who is he? I ask.

'Oh, Mr Leng,' she replies. 'He's a local gangster. We do him a favour every now and again, and he tips us off on certain shipments to Australia being made by his competitors. If they knew, he'd be very dead, very quickly.' Now I know she is not your average Administrative Officer. 'The European couple on the stage are probably Swedish backpackers. He has a group of them on tap. They will do pretty well anything for some cash and a hit.'

'Hit?'

'Heroin, silly. You're inquisitive,' she says, and asks about my family, changing the subject. I tell her about the farm, grandma and grandad, Uncle Bert, and 'the girls'. She laughs when I tell her about Shit Head and Dorrie Evans.

'What are your sisters' names?' she asks.

'Amy and Susan,' I tell her. 'They are living in Newcastle with Aunty Elsie and Uncle Ron. Grandma and grandad were not able to take all three of us. Too old. Aunty Elsie is one of dad's older sisters. Dad is, was, the youngest of nine children. I think Aunty Elsie is fifteen years older. She and Uncle Ron never had kids themselves. They have money and so the girls are treated like princesses. Having said that, Aunty Elsie is tough when it comes to school. She never went to high school herself and so the girls are expected to be at the top of the class in most subjects.'

She has a tossed salad and coleslaw ready. I get handed a paint scraper and a plate of steaks and sliced onion. 'Medium rare, please, Tim, I'll get the beers.' I go out on the veranda and there is one of those small, round barbecues on three legs. I turn on the gas and put my hand in pocket for a match, realising I have not had a cigarette since lunch time yesterday. It won't hurt me.

'Do you have a match, Liz?' She steps out on the veranda with two beers and a box of matches.

She changes the record while I clean the plate and cook the steak and onions. Its ELO, a new world record. I am no chef, but I sense the steaks have had enough heat. I put them on the plates and she suggests we let them rest. Something else I will have to ask her to explain later. Are they tired?

Soon after, she serves the salad and we tuck in. 'Mr Walsh, are you happy to accept my offer of the house slave position? This is excellent.'

'That would depend on the benefits package,' I say, smiling.

She decides we should talk politics over lunch, late lunch. 'So, your grandad has been a card-carrying member of the Country Party for forty years,' she opens. 'A bit conservative, is he?' I am slightly annoyed she knows so much about my family.

I think she could have asked, even if she already knew. She's direct.

'You are from the city,' I tell her. 'It's hard for people who have never had to struggle through the tough times on the land to understand. Doug Anthony understands and he is our man in Canberra.' I am looking at her and see a change come over her face. She isn't impressed.

'Don't you ever think you have a monopoly on hardship, Timothy Walsh,' she says with scorn, picking up the empty plates and storming off. I sit and contemplate my error. The air is heavy, rain imminent. She comes back with a bottle of Australian wine and two glasses.

'Sorry, my grandfather was a coal miner in the pits around Picton. He got injured in a cave-in and couldn't work. They didn't have two-bob to rub together. If it wasn't for the union, the company would have evicted the whole family.'

'Bastards.'

No one should get kicked out of their house, particularly when they get injured on the job. I guess the union is just a version of the Country Party for men working for big companies.

The Duty Storm rolls in just after four. The intensity of the downpours in the tropics is starting to captivate me and we sit back from the rail, watch the spectacle for a while, and sip the wine, silent. ELO comes to an end and I offer to find some tunes. She gets up and goes to the kitchen. She is over the sink washing up the knives and folks when I walk in.

'If you are going to drown those two pups, I'll have the one with the pink nose?' She looks and smiles.

'You can take the boy out of Dungog ...' leaving the rest unsaid. 'Do you want to go out?' she asks.

'Don't mind. We could sit around here and play records,' I suggest, which is exactly what we do. She finds another bottle of wine and a Chuck Berry track. 'You dance pretty good, let's shake this place up a bit.' She grabs my hands and starts leading; basic rock and roll. Then she shows me how to twirl and spin her several different ways. It's great fun. We go through numerous Chuck Berry numbers getting my technique right.

She slows the tempo. Sinatra songs. She nuzzles into my neck as we sway. I think I am in heaven. Fifteen minutes later, I am, and later she sleeps wrapped in my arms.

I cook again Sunday morning as she sleeps and I have to wake her at nine to eat. She is a bit groggy.

'Morning, house slave. Sleep well?'

'Not as good as you. But, well, yes.'

'I think we should do a little sightseeing,' she says, heading for the shower.

That is the cutest bum I have ever seen!

She declines my offer to wash her back.

'We don't have time for that, Tim.'

The day is a blur. We visit the Changi Memorial Chapel, drive past Raffles Hotel, the Singapore Cricket Club and then out to the Changi Sailing Club for drinks. Back in town, we visit the Teok Ayer Market. 'It's Victorian,' she tells me, in a matter-of-fact way.

It's now mid-afternoon, she makes her way back through town and onto Bukit Timah Road. I think we are heading back to Tengah. She keeps going past Choa Chu Kang Road onto Woodlands Road. She turns off and pulls up in the car park of a cemetery. It no ordinary cemetery; this is Kranji War Cemetery. We walk through the gates onto the manicured lawns.

I am stunned. There are literally thousands of graves in neat rows. The same headstone above each one. At the top of each one is an insignia. The Australian graves typically have Australian Military Forces Rising Sun insignia, but some have the RAAF crest. Some of the graves have names, some just have 'Known Only To God' or 'Unknown Australian Soldier'. Beneath the date of death and age is a cross, and then a short message below.

'Our loving son' or 'Sadly Missed' are the most common. I just stand and look at grave after grave, her following. I just cannot fathom the enormity of the scene and all these young men resting in a cemetery, a long way from home.

'The major service each year is Remembrance Day,' she says.

'It's a little soon.'

'You will have to come down for ANZAC day then, and be my house slave for a few days.' I am extremely interested in both propositions.

We get back in the car and head off down Woodlands Road and then onto Chua Chu Kang Road. It's the moment I am dreading. She pulls up outside the front gate.

'I am out of here on Friday. Can I see you before I go?' almost pleading.

'Of course, you silly bugger. I have a busy week, but will pick you up here about six Thursday night.' I lean over to kiss her and we end up in a serious pash session, with loads of heavy breathing. She breaks it and says 'I have early starts all week, Tim, I can't do this right now.' I get out and just stand looking at her as she drives off. That is a very dedicated Administrative Officer I observe.

I dump my stuff in the room and head to the ARC Bar. The boys are in there playing Killer. I get a beer and join them. 'Big weekend Dougie?' Tex asks me.

'Yep.' I keep the answers brief. They don't need to know too much. It will be all over the Base in Butterworth within hours if I do. Not sure yet how it happens, but it does. And, it's not that I have done anything wrong, but the gossip just shits me.

We break for a feed and go back to play Mickey Mouse. More

questions, few answers. A couple more games and beers, and we retire about nine.

I get up early and head for the shower. Pete is in there cleaning his teeth at a basin. I take a look at his back.

'Shit, mate, you better tell Sally to cut her nails. You be okay when you get home Thursday?'

'Thanks, Dougie, I will be okay. I forget the last time she saw me naked.'

Pete and Sally have been in the back of my mind all weekend.

Is it fair he is messing around on his wife?

A bit over a week ago, I was pretty adamant that it was a no-go thing. But now I think that was a bit naïve.

If I was married to Liz, and it didn't work out for some reason, what would be the point where I say it's off?

Somehow, Pete's crap marriage makes it okay for him to have an affair. But where is the line between right and wrong?

It's worrying me.

Would I ever cheat on Liz? What if we hadn't had sex for a year? Fucked if I know.

I walk into the flight line hut, throw my T-shirt into my bag, and check the aircraft documents.

'You have a date with a vampire, Dougie?' Buck asks from behind the desk, referring to the bites on my neck.

'She might be a vampire, Buck, but she is the sexiest vampire this side of Melbourne.' Buck and a few others raise their eyebrows. I head out onto the line to do my Before Flight Services.

It's not a tough week. Three waves of four aircraft per day of Dissimilar Air Combat Tactics (DACT). Our guys go up against Singaporean A4 Skyhawks. Any flying without bullets, bombs, other stores, or re-configuration is relatively routine. I am on Aircraft Launch and Recover duties.

The first launch of the week, I get the external elements of the jet ready, while my Queer Trade counterpart pulls pins in the cockpit. The pilot appears, completes the walk around, and straps in. I am on the blower.

Twice he hits the tit and it turns over, but fails to start. A Sumpie hops onto the starboard wing and taps the starter box. He hits the tit for the third time and holds it down. The turbine starts to wind up.

'*Fuck, this is going to be something.*'

As the air sucks into the intake and the engine catches, I take the blower out and walk to the wing tip. As the RPM increases, a fireball emerges from the tail pipe, gets longer and longer and longer. A few seconds later, the flames are almost licking the Flight Line Hut.

I have seen a lot of wet starts in the short time I have worked on Mirages, but this is the biggest fireball I have ever seen in my life. At one point, I thought the whole jet was going to catch alight. I am scared shitless.

The fireball subsides, we finish the pre-launch checks and the aircraft taxies shortly after.

Fuck, I might not be too much help to the pilot if the fire did spread, dressed in my safety boots, shorts, earmuffs, and fuck-all else.

Thursday morning, we are launching for the last time. All six jets are heading back to Butterworth. As they taxi, one aircraft stays put. Some sort of problem, and he shuts down and unstraps. By the look on his unmasked face, the Flight Commander is not impressed. Another jet crumps after having some engine problem on take-off. He taxies back, shuts down, and unstraps.

Most of the team have packed everything up into the hangar. They hop into the squadron truck and disappear to get on the Herc back to Butterworth. The remaining guys swarm over the last two unserviceable jets. I help the Sumpies do an engine run on the one that returned from the runway. After some lengthy power runs, they shut it down and I refuel. We get back inside.

'Fucking nothing wrong with it,' announces Phil.

'Not surprised,' says Buck. 'Nothing wrong with the other one either. I reckon those two Bog Rats are on a promise. They are not launching till tomorrow.' I am thinking to myself they could crump again and it would give me a Friday night with Liz.

I am not standing outside the gate long when the red Interceptor comes into view. She isn't at pace and is obviously handling the vehicle with care and finesse. That girl can drive. She pulls up and smiles though the open window.

'What's a nice boy like you doing in a place like this?'

I jump in and we have a short, passionate kiss. 'I am hungry,' she says. 'How was your week?' she asks, entering the traffic on Chua Choo Kang Road.

'Nothing dramatic,' I say, and tell her the story about the two Bog Rats crumping. Liz reckons it might have something to do with the cruise liner in port, with loads of young American girls on board. The Duty Storm is late today but you can feel it building. We go straight to her house and she almost drags me inside. As we hit the lounge, the storm breaks. The rain and the lovemaking are both intense.

'Shit, I really need some food now,' she announces from on

top of my chest. We quickly run through the dip and into the car. Fifteen minutes later, we are amongst a bunch of food stalls at Newton Circus.

'Grab a table, Tim, and I will order.' She vanishes into the crowd.

Five minutes later, she returns with a large bottle of Tiger and two glasses. As we talk about when we might see each other, satays arrive, followed by a shellfish dish, whole fish in sauce, and a prawn dish, rice on the side. One of the staff arrives voluntarily with another beer and she pays, telling him to keep the change.

The trip back to the Base is silent. We both know this is the last time we'll see each other for a while. At the gate, she kisses me passionately but breaks it off, regaining her composure. I get out without talking and watch her drive away.

This is bloody serious.

I get into work at 0800 and do the before flight servicings. The air is heavy and every movement induces sweat. The two Bog Rats turn up about 0830, sign for the jets, and out we go. I am strapping in Flying Officer Walker.

'Have a good night, Nick?' I ask, wanting to know why they were keen to stay the night.

'Yer, Dougie. Stan and I had a date with a couple of Aussie girls on holidays. Cost us a bit for dinner, but it was well worth it,' he says, with a wink. He hands me the seat pan safety pin and I show him the face blind pin before stowing both. As I take the ladder off the side of the aircraft, it starts to rain. Both jets start without a hassle, power cables are removed, chocks out, and pitch dampers checked. I retreat to the crew van. Thumbs up from the passenger seat as they taxi. It is pissing down now.

Buck drives us to the Caribou and we stand under the wing watching the take-off roll. The rain has intensified and the tarmac has two inches of water on it. We can barely see the two jets on the piano keys at the far end of the runway. As the first one rolls and gathers speed, the water plume behind the aircraft builds as the wheels literally plough through. By the time it rotates, the cloud is huge behind the glow of the afterburner. I wonder at how he kept control of it down the runway with all the water on it. The wheels come up, undercarriage doors up, low to the ground, glowing after-burner against the rain; it's a spectacular sight as it disappears into the rain.

The scene is repeated, the second aircraft rotating and then disappearing into the clouds.

Those boys sure know how to fly aeroplanes.

'Okay, let's go,' the Loadie yells and indicates we should jump in through the back ramp. Inside, I pull on my overalls, grab a seat, and strap in. Engines splutter into life and then settle at idle. A short taxi and then the throttles open. The familiar gravely tone is like a lullaby. I close my eyes and all I can see is a smile, the dark hair, green eyes, freckles, and those long legs.

Shit, Elizabeth Mary Alexander, I think I love you.

The following weeks are an education. At work, things are done a little differently in Malaysia — a more hectic schedule. Usually, three waves of eight, or twenty-four sorties, per day and sometimes thirty-two. There always seems to be a jet coming or going. While we are always busy, it's not mentally challenging work and I have plenty time to think about Liz, maybe too much.

After a two-week stint on Flight Line, I am assigned back to

Gun Bay. Hands in a kerosene bath most of the day cleaning, checking and then reassembling and testing DEFA guns.

Every day, I sweat on the mail coming in from the Orderly Room. Grandma wrote last week updating me on life at the farm and the local gossip. Nothing really new, just reassuring to know life back home is going on as normal. There is one from Louise. She is finishing her second year at Uni and heading home for Christmas. She wants to know if I get leave to go home.

Well, I could, but it's awfully expensive and I have something, or rather someone else, on my mind.

On the home front, I move off Base into the house with Gus and Andy. The house is at Bagan Ajam which is a couple of kilometres south of the Base. We pay two hundred Ringgit each into the house kitty each fortnight which pays the rent, the Amah, and groceries, not that we eat at home much. Normally, we'll eat breakfast and lunch at work, and eat at the Boatie, Bat Cave, or local food for dinner. The grocery bill is largely soft drinks and beer.

The local food, or *makan* as it is known, is something else. There are a myriad of little shops, stalls and pushbike-driven carts selling food. One of the favoured foods served from the *makan* carts are noodle dishes, Bee Hoon, Me Goreng, and my favourite, Char Kway Teow. Takeaway dishes are cooked over gas burners and spooned into a plastic bag, tied with a rubber band. We often pick up a feed on the way home, and I can't remember having a bad one, it's all good.

I have inherited Stevo's Malvern Star and so the pushy has become my primary way to get around. Gus has the Morris and some of the other guys in the street own cars. It's a variety of vintages, makes and models, but nothing younger than ten years old. Motor bikes seem to the transport mode of choice, a mixture of small Japanese bikes, and old British bikes, Nortons, BSAs, and Triumphs. The colonial British influence of the '50s and '60s is still evident in the cars, bikes, road signs and architecture.

Every now and again, a road block is set up and identification documents are checked. Gus tells me there are still CTs active in Malaysia.

'CTs?' I ask.

'Communist Terrorists,' he says. 'When the Japs were here, some Chinese were trained by the British to run a guerrilla operation against them. When the war was over, they expected to get a big say in independence, but the British took over again. They wanted influence and started shooting people to get it, which caused the Malayan Emergency. When Malaysia was finally granted independence, the ethnic Malays were handed most of the political power and the Chinese Communists have remained active ever since. Every now and again, you will see the Malaysian F5s bombing up. Apparently, they bomb the shit out of the area around the Thai border.'

'Fuck. How do you know all this stuff?'

'I read books, Dougie, unlike you illiterate heathens.'

Saturday morning, late November, I get up around 0730, pull on some shorts and a T-shirt, go downstairs and grab a 7UP. It's a cool day, with the ground still wet from an early morning deluge.

I take a walk down to the beach enjoying the relative calm of the day. The sea is still, just a slight rolling swell causing a small wave to break on the sand every now and again, the palm trees swaying lightly. A couple of fishing boats putt-putt around. Beyond, the island of Penang sits like a giant, sleeping animal. The island itself is clear, and unusually, I can make out distinct buildings atop its heights. I can tell the giant is about to awaken and there are dark clouds around the island, but it's not yet raining.

I walk along the beach for a while contemplating my life. It's pretty good right now. I have a good job in one of the RAAF's best fighter squadrons, I am living in a foreign country, in a house with my mates, servants to do the house work, and I am in love with the prettiest girl in the world. Even though she is in Singapore, it's not too far away.

I wander back to the house and Gus is making coffee. 'You want one, Dougie?'

'Yer, sure.' He has this knack of making it with condensed milk, so even the shittiest coffee tastes good. We sit at the table and contemplate the world, sipping the brew. I break the silence.

'So, what's the plan for the weekend?

'PSA at the Boatie tomorrow afternoon. Free nibbles, a band, and they are putting a keg on.'

'Shit hot, I guess they have Danny playing?'

'Yep, Lolling, Lolling, Lolling on the Libber,' he sings, doing his best Asian Creedence impersonation. He's funny.

'What about today?' I ask, pushing for ideas. He stops as if deep in thought.

'Not sure, what would you like to do, Dougie?'

'Well, I have only seen Penang at night, and that was through amber glasses. How about we go to Penang and look around?' I see his mind kick into gear and eyes light up.

'Good plan, Dougie. Get your gear on, we'll go and pick up

Nev. I'll get Andy out of bed.' A half hour later, we are at the Tiger's Den cajoling Nev into some clothes, then off for a day of adventure, Nev in the front, Andy and I in the back, Doc Neeson screaming from the ghetto blaster.

Gus eases the Morrie off the ferry and right toward some older-looking buildings, left turn, then left again at the Queen Victoria Clock Tower.

'This is Beach Street, Dougie. The commercial heart of Georgetown. All the banks are here, so if you need to open an account, this is the place to come.'

He turns again, through narrow streets, emerging onto a wider avenue, finding a park of sorts. We get out and we follow. Gus has the commentary going again.

'See that over there?' he points to a building surrounded by a large wall and ornate gates. The walls and the building roof are adorned with human-like figures with multiple arms, the females with multiple breasts, and an assortment of snakes and other animals.

'This is an Indian temple; it dates back to the early nineteenth century.'

It's amazing. Who designs stuff like this?

He scurries off again, crossing the street. This is an effort in itself. All manner of truck, car, plastic, and pushbike to dodge. We approach another temple. This one is covered in dragons and there are burning sticks everywhere.

'What's with the burning sticks,' asks Nev.

'Incense, Neville,' He speaking like he's some sort of authority now. 'Burning the incense is a way of paying homage. In this case, the temple is for the Goddess of Mercy, so they are paying homage to the Goddess. I am not sure what sort of mercy she is known for, but there was obviously a lot of it.'

There is a big steel box to one side, with flowers and more incense inside, the exterior is adorned with a swastika.

'Is that a swastika?'

'Yes, Dougie, well spotted. Different cultures use the swastika as a symbol of different things. Some say it represents the footprints of Buddha, other religions think it represents lightning bolts, or the thunder of God. Just because a couple of loony Nazis highjacked it in the thirties, doesn't make it bad. Don't be mistaken.'

Every day is a school day.

We stand around for a while looking at the crowd coming and going. Finally, Gus turns and gestures us to follow, off up the street at a pace. The sun is hot now and it's easy to sweat just standing still; the walk is actually keeping us cooler. We cross a busy street, successfully dodging all manner of vehicles again.

'This is Chulia Street, Dougie. The ferry is this way,' he says, pointing. 'If you ever get lost, just get directions to Chulia Street, the rest is easy.'

A bit further along, we reach a large building inside a large fenced yard. The building wouldn't look out of place in a Lawrence of Arabia film.

'Boys, this is the Kapitan Keling Mosque, one of Penang's oldest buildings. It dates back to the early nineteenth century.' I note how well the building and grounds are looked after.

'Better outfield than the SCG.'

'Of course, it is, Dougie, staunch Muslims are our Malaysian friends. It means they don't drink and they don't eat pork, no bacon and eggs for breakfast here, mate.'

He turns, walking back toward the car. We dutifully follow as our tour guide continues with his educational dialogue.

'That's not to say everyone is Muslim; a large percentage are, but not all. About a quarter of the population are Chinese, and they run a large portion of business here; there is also a small percentage are Indian. The Indians were brought here by the British as cheap labour and they are still the labourers.'

We cross back over Chulia Street and climb into the Morrie. He guides the car up Chulia Street, still talking.

'That's the Hong Kong Bar there, we had our photo taken in there the night you arrived, Dougie. If you are driving around, don't run into a trishaw, you can get in a lot of shit for hitting a trishaw.'

He turns onto another street. 'This is Penang Road; the shops here sell mostly clothes and souvenirs. You are more likely to see tourists in this part of town.' The Morrie takes the road west and we weave our way through the assorted cars, step-throughs, bicycles and *makan* carts. He pulls up in the foothills and gets out of the car, and we dutifully follow. He's pointing up the hill.

'That is the Kek Lok Si Temple, otherwise known as the Temple of a Thousand Steps, or better known as the Temple of a Thousand Rip-Offs. It's the best place to pick up souvenirs.' He marches off with his students in pursuit.

We go past several shop-fronts, each with differing goods and he turns into some fruit stalls. He turns as he walks in.

'This is the Air Itam Markets, the best place to buy fresh meat, fish, and fruit and veg.' Further along, he pauses at a fruit stall and asks the operator something I don't understand. There is a short exchange with hand gestures. The storekeeper prepares several trays of fruit and Gus parts with five Ringgit.

'Here, try some of this,' he says, offering one of the trays.

Hesitantly, I pick up a piece of something red.

'What's this?'

'Rambutan.'

I nibble at it gingerly with my teeth, not too bad.

'This one?'

'Mangosteen.'

It's not too bad either.

'Here, Nev, try this.' He's offering a yellow-looking thing. The smell hits me quickly and Nev has a look like he has just smelt sewage.

'Fuck, did one of you guys drop your guts?'

'Hold your nose, Nev, it tastes excellent.'

I manage to get it down, and the taste is fine, it's just the smell, something else again.

'What the fuck was that?'

'Durian, the king of fruits,' Gus laughs.

Nev's face is still aghast and he is spitting profusely to rid the taste from his mouth.

'Someone has just shat in my mouth,' he exclaims.

'This way,' Gus turns and walks off. None of us are really sure if we should follow. He stops at a stall with coconuts, and unintelligible words and money are exchanged again.

The guy grabs a machete and quickly opens the top of a coconut, pushing a straw in and handing it over.

'This will take the taste away, Nev,' handing it over. Three more appear and soon we are wandering the market sipping straight from the coconut. It's not my cup of tea, but I reckon its better than the taste of the durian.

'I've had enough of this stuff,' announces Gus. 'You boys need a beer?'

'Is the Pope Polish?' He wanders on looking for something, coming to a stop at an outdoor restaurant.

'Tiger beer?' Nods from the proprietor. 'Four Tiger beers, John,' he commands as we sit.

An hour later, we are back in the Morrie winding its way back into town. We're all singing along to the ghetto blaster, 'It's a long way to the shops if you want a sausage roll.' Gus has to use the bumper bars to shove his way into a park outside the Tiger Bar.

Afternoon drinks turn to evening, the Morrie shuffling us from one bar to the next, Ahchew, Bangkok, TongLok, and NewLumTong. I swear this car has a mind of its own. At the Chung King, Gus decides he's in need of the services of a lady. Mama San gives us a run down on the price list.

'Head job, fifteen dollar, sixteen dollar short time, long time twenty dollar,' she says. 'Special price for you, John.'

Who the fuck is John?

Gus asks if I would like to partake, but I have a sense that I could be at risk of some sort of disease and decline. He jumps up, grabs a lady by the hand and disappears. It's not a brief event.

I hope he didn't pay for long time.

We finish the night with a meal at the Craven A; roti with egg and onion all round, and sweet but tangy curry juice to dip in.

It's now after midnight, and the streets are near deserted. Gus takes a few back streets towards the ferry. Out the window, I can make out people, in large numbers, sleeping on the narrow paths outside the shops, and rats, the size of small cats, scurrying around cleaning up after the night's business. What an amazing place. So vibrant and alive, and yet so poor.

Tuesday morning, the letter arrives. I can tell it's from her without seeing the sender on the back of the envelope. The writing on the front is elegant and it has a Singaporean stamp. In haste, I am tempted to tear it open, but discipline myself to use a knife.

Her parents are coming up for Christmas, but going home before new year. She suggests I go to Singapore for New Year's Eve for a couple of days. I am sitting there contemplating my next move.

'How the fuck do I get to Singapore?' It's a rhetorical question.

'Fly, Dougie,' Tiny answers back, not breaking from his paperwork. 'There's a good travel agent on McAlister Road,' he says, handing me a business card.

St Barbara's Day arrives and we are to have a sports day on the main oval on the Friday. Tiny tells Rob to grab a Clarktor and bring the squadron esky to the Oval.

Why he would need a Clarktor?

Tiny, Doc, and I head for the Boatie to pick up the grog. Tiny is handing cartons of Anchor to me, and I run them outside to Doc, who is stacking them into the section truck. At twenty, I enquire who all the grog is for.

'For us, Dougie. All the guys from 478 and 75 Squadron are coming too,' Tiny explains.

Thirty cartons later, Doc and I are riding shotgun in the back of a nose- high Landcruiser. At the oval, Rob is there with a six-by-four trailer with an aluminium structure on top, the squadron esky. We unload the cartons and start to pack the esky while

Tiny and Rob disappear. A half hour later they reappear with the tray of the Landcruiser full of solid ice blocks. Two Dassault screwdrivers, with the tips ground into a point, are produced and the ice is chipped on top of the beer.

The Landcruiser disappears again and magically reappears with two camp tables, gas barbecues, and trays of steaks, snags, onions, and coleslaw covered in foil. There are twenty loaves of bread.

Fuck, this is a big operation. Even a big party at the RSL in Dungog would only attract a keg, not thirty cartons of beer and all this food.

Tiny senses my bewilderment. 'A guy at catering owes me a couple of favours,' he says. 'Dougie, can you please arc up those barbecues, mate, the hungry hordes will be here soon.'

Around midday, the boys start arriving. 'Don't fuck around, Dougie, throw on as much as you can fit,' directs Tiny, while handing me a beer. Before I know it, there are over a hundred guys drinking, eating, and putting shit on each other. all It's hard to keep up with the names, nicknames, and work out whether the mockery in the exchanges is serious or not.

Tiny has a pork pie hat on and is running around selling raffle tickets. First prize is two nights accommodation at the Rasa Sayang, Batu Feringhi, and dinner for two. The minor prizes include a thirty-dollar voucher at the New Lum Tong and a bottle of Scotch. Apparently, the prizes have all been 'donated'.

That's not worth any detailed thought.

The games begin. There is a three-legged race; beers must be in each participant's hands, and any spills result in disqualification. Trophies are handed to the winners. Tiny has thought of everything.

The practice bomb throw nearly ends in disaster. Most participants use a pendulum technique, but Doc decides on a style like an Olympic hammer throw. It's a high-drag bomb and he has the cup in his hand, rotating on his heels, moving faster with each rotation. He must have got dizzy because he releases and the bomb flies into the crowd. Shouts of warning and laughter all round. The bomb impacts one of the camp tables causing one end to collapse, coleslaw exploding like shrapnel.

The final event is a team event, the Mk82 bomb drag. Each squadron has a team. Rob, Doc, Lew and I represent 3 Squadron. The nose fuse well has a modified bomb lug screwed into it, and there is a rope attached. The idea is the team has to drag it fifty metres and it's timed. We cover the fifty metres in twenty-one seconds. The boys from 75 Squadron run in nineteen seconds and are the winners. Tiny produces a ten-dollar voucher at the Bat Cave for each of them. He stands on a chair to pull tickets from his hat.

'Listen up for the raffle draw. Thirty-dollar voucher at the New Lum Tong. Blue ticket, eighty-seven.'

One of the Baggers from 478SQN puts his hand up and gets a round of booing. He accepts the voucher with a smile. The New Lum Tong is widely known as the 'Head Job Hotel'.

You wouldn't want to be his missus.

Merv wins the Scotch and Blue Sanders the accommodation, to another round of booing and calls for a redraw. Amongst the commotion, blue-and-yellow smoke grenades are set off in the crowd and everyone disperses, dragging the esky with them. No one wants to go thirsty.

To my amazement, the beer runs out before 1600 and everyone

retires to the Boatie to add more fluid to their already lubricated bodies. It's 2200 before I get myself home and into bed.

This overseas posting is turning into a drinking marathon.

December is filled with a seemingly never-ending round of Christmas parties. There is the squadron Christmas function, the Boatie hold a carols-by-candlelight event, and even the volleyball club has a function after the last round of the year.

For our section party, Tiny has booked the poshest restaurant on Penang; the Eden. All the food and drinks are covered. He tells me it's the money from the St Barbara's Day raffle and Coke sales.

We must be shifting a lot of Coke.

I am seated with Lefty Wright and Pete. It's the first time I have met any of the wives. Lefty's wife, Julie, is quietly spoken and shy. I reckon she'd have trouble getting a word in edgeways with Lefty anyway.

Pete's wife, Deborah, is the interesting one; quite pretty and slim without being skinny. She is obviously well educated, speaks with authority on everything from politics to fishing, and they genuinely seem to get along well together. I note a lack of touching or intimacy. She asks what I'm doing for Christmas and the new year.

'I am having new year's in Singapore,' I tell her. 'I met a girl down there who works at the High Commission. I'll stay with her.' I can sense Pete shuffling in his seat and I change the subject.

The period before Christmas is a little slower and gives me a chance to better assess my surroundings and acquaint myself with what life will be like for the next three years. The Butterworth Base has a squadron of RMAF F5 Fighter Aircraft, a RMAF Helicopter Squadron, two RAAF Mirage Fighter Squadrons, a Maintenance Squadron, Base Squadron, an entire Hospital, an Australian Army Rifle Company, and a detachment of RAAF P3 Orion Aircraft from 92 Wing. The Australian Army personnel rotate every three months and the 92 Wing personnel every six weeks.

It's no small community. I reckon there are about a thousand RAAFies between the Base and Penang, plus about a hundred grunts in the Rifle Company, and a whole host of wives and rug-rats. There has to be several thousand Australians in the local area.

It's well organised, and I am not talking about the military operations we undertake. The social aspects are managed to the enth degree. There is a radio station, RAAF Radio Butterworth, known as RRB. Their handle is 'The Voice of the Royal Australian Air Force in Malaysia, where the time is …'

There is a pool, gym, golf course, and an assortment of small clubs, soccer, league and union, scuba, volleyball, softball, cricket, badminton, tennis, photography, and something called Hash House Harriers. From what I can gather, the latter is about running around the jungle following little bits of paper and then getting hammered afterward.

Christmas Eve, all the single guys roam the married patch in groups singing Christmas carols. The Baggers generally have a party on every third or fourth house and the choristers sing until rewarded with a drink. Failure to reward us results in another carol, then another. After singing 'We Wish You a Merry Christmas', the words change.

'We won't go till we get some,

We won't go till we get some,

We won't go till we get some,

So, give us some beer.'

Christmas Day is at Dave Christensen's house. He and his wife, Karen, don't have any kids and so they have invited us Singlies for lunch. Andy and I pick up a carton at the Boatie on the way and are greeted with a tumbler of Stones green ginger wine.

'It helps with digestion,' Dave tells me, the voice of experience speaking.

After a baked lunch, they share presents with us. It's a bit embarrassing because we didn't get anything for them, but Karen dismisses our apologies. Soon everyone is armed with a water pistol and we spend several hours stalking each other through the house and garden. The whole team is drenched by the time drinks is called.

Andy and I have dinner at a seafood place on Dragon Temple Lane before going home. I lie awake wondering what is going on at the farm right now. And, what Liz might be doing.

New Year's Eve can't come quick enough. I get Gus to give me a lift out to the airport at Bayan Lepas. We get out of the car on the ferry and watch the activity on the harbour.

'This is pretty serious then?' he asks.

'Yes, mate. I have been involved with a few girls in the last few years, but this is the first one to match the feelings I had for Allison. I could marry this one.'

'Shit, Dougie, you gotta stop talking like that, mate. There's plenty of fish in the sea; look around you. You should be going to Thailand and enjoying yourself.'

'There is something a bit creepy about that whole thing, Gus, and the possibility of catching something doesn't sit so well. I guess it's just not for me.'

'Dr Dan can sort out anything you bring home. You're not turning gay on me, are you, Dougie?' he says, with a look of grave concern.

When I land at Changi, she is waiting for me at the exit from immigration. God, she is prettier than I remembered. Plain blue blouse, white skirt, flat white shoes, red lipstick, just enough makeup to dull the freckles, and those long legs. She throws her arms around me and hugs me tight to her body.

'I missed you,' she says.

On the way to the car, she fills me in on the plans for the night.

'The party is at the High Commission tonight, beside the pool. 'I don't suppose you've got a Hawaiian Shirt?' she asks.

'No, I am travelling light.'

'No worries, we'll stop at Little India and pick one up.' She is smiling broadly. 'I am off work till Wednesday. It'll give us four whole days together.'

When we get to the High Commission, the large crowd is at all points around the pool. The bar is busy and there is a drink station set up at the opposite end of the pool with a three-piece band nearby playing Jazz. Sally greets me with a kiss on the cheek.

'You didn't bring Peter with you by chance?' she enquires, hopefully.

'I'll tell him you were asking about him.'

'You do that,' she says, with a smile.

Liz and I spend the night either dancing or holding hands, talking with her work colleagues. The High Commissioner is doing the rounds and greets me warmly.

'Tim, yes, I have heard a lot about you. Enjoying Butterworth?' He is obviously well informed.

'Yes, sir, it's an interesting mix of races and cultures. The food is amazing.'

We exchange a few Penang eating experiences before he moves on to the next group.

He is a particularly impressive man with a quick wit and loads of local knowledge. I am even more impressed with Liz. She obviously has shared details about me with her work mates and it means she is fairly committed, or at least it's how I interpret it. Maybe she shares my thoughts about potential marriage?

At midnight, there is the customary countdown before the cheering, whistles, and kisses; intense kisses. On the way home, I pop the question.

'You thought about marriage?' I blurt out.

Boy, Tim Walsh, are you a romantic.

'Is that a proposal, Tim?' she says, looking my way with some shock.

'Well, no, yes, sort of.' I am stuffing this up. 'If I am going to propose, I will do it properly.' I pause, collecting my thoughts. 'I am wondering what your thoughts are at the concept,' I explain.

'Well,' she says, drawing it out to give herself thinking time. 'I definitely want to get married and have children. It's just a question of when.' There isn't much traffic and she does not have to concentrate hard. I can tell she has more to say.

'It's hard for a woman to get ahead in our department, and taking time off to have children could prevent me getting the jobs I want. Does that make sense?' she asks me.

'Perfect sense.' I am silent for a while thinking about what it means. 'So, it's a yes to marriage and children, but not yet.'

'Yes,' she says without conviction, and then after some thought I get a definitive 'Exactly.'

The next afternoon we are lounging around listening to Billy Joel. I still have the marriage thing on my mind.

'How many kids?' I ask her.

'What?' she looks up from her book with a slightly bewildered look.

'How many kids are we going to have?' I persist.

'You are taking this marriage thing way too seriously, Tim,' she frowns, then ponders the question. 'Three or four I reckon. Two is not enough, and I am not going to spend my life bearing children. No more than four. I think three will do.' The answers are thought through and it tells me she is genuine. She is as committed as me and now I am wondering whether I should just pop the question and get it done.

'What are we going to call them.'

'Tim,' she says, putting the book down and standing, a serious expression on her face. 'I won't be ready for children for some time yet,' she says, with intent. 'If you want children soon, you might want to look for someone else.'

'Sorry, I don't want to sound pushy. But I really like you and I am wondering what the potential options are for marriage and children.' She sits next to me with an earnest look.

'Tim, you will be in the Air Force for another five years. In that time, I can expect to go back to Canberra for a while and then get another overseas post. I really want the Director's job in the High Commission in London or a Washington job. I can't see us getting married until after that.' She has actually thought this through.

Five years, I'll only be twenty-five and she will twenty-nine.

'Can I come and visit you in London?'

The four days go by quickly. She is easy company and it's like we have known each other for years, not days. Sex with someone you love is a different experience for me. In the past, it has been about the lust and wicked pleasures. She is relaxed and gentle, which brings out a softer reaction from me. It's much more intense.

She drops me at Changi Airport on Tuesday afternoon. Like the Caribou flight several weeks previous, the flight back to Penang is spent with a picture of her rolling around in my head as I doze.

11 — The Ornithologists Club

January in Butterworth is a quiet period. Most people are on leave, either locally or overseas. A lot of people gravitate to Europe for the White Christmas. Gus has fucked off to Scotland to visit Alisha and Andy is in Phuket. I have the house to myself and it's nice to be alone for a little while, Liz on my mind.

At work, the flying is sporadic and does not generate any real effort. Tiny decides it's a good opportunity to butt test a couple of our 30mm DEFA cannons.

At the northern end of the working area, there is a Deflector Butt. It's called a Deflector Butt because it has a large, thick, metal plate bolted over a pit, which deflects the bullets down into the pit. At the firing point is a heavy steel structure bolted to a concrete slab. We fix the gun to be tested to the steel.

Loading the gun is a little different. Normally when we do it, the guns are on their side on the pack. In this instance, it is upright and higher than normal. We have a little fun getting the ammunition into the gun. Tiny has everything wired up and advises us to put on hearing protection. He yells, fire, and squeezes the button.

I thought I was pretty worldly when it comes to bullets going off, but nothing prepares me for the surprise when the first rounds are fired. The shock wave off the end of the barrel hit me in the chest and I gasp for air. The mixture of shock wave and noise is astonishing. There is a huge amount of smoke generated and we have to wait for it to clear a little between bursts.

'Cease Fire,' he yells. 'Can you blokes break the belt there? I want to show you what it's like for the re-cock cartridge to go off.' He grabs a spare link and a dummy round and puts it into the belt. 'Now, I am going to pull the trigger again. I want you to listen for delay when the dummy round goes under the firing pin. Ready?' We all nod and put our earmuffs on. 'Fire.'

There is a burst of around thirty rounds with a little gap, almost unnoticeable, in the otherwise regular firing sequence.

'*Cease Fire.*' He steps forward and pulls the re-cock cartridge from the front of the gun, picking up the dummy round.

'Did you hear it?' It's a real lesson in how quickly this all happens, and more importantly, when something goes to custard it will happen fast.

We all take turns at the firing point and then try our hand at firing single rounds at a time. The gun usually fires at 1200 rounds per minute, or twenty a second. So, it's quite a challenge to get a single round off.

January is also a slow period on the social front. Most of the sporting competitions are yet to start and so our leisure is generally focused on water skiing and golf. The committee elections are undertaken and, somehow, I manage to become Assistant Bar Member at the Boatie, without opening my mouth or raising an arm. Scarecrow Thomas is the Bar Member.

Being Bar Members require us to monitor stock, place orders, and do a fortnightly stock check. The stock check is officially called a Bar Reconciliation, or Bar Recce. It's a process overseen by the Base Financial Accounting Officer. If work commitments allow, we do it Friday morning, if not, it's Friday after work, but generally before trading starts. Sometimes, it involves sampling the products and when this happens, the Bar Recce can be a dangerous affair.

A letter arrives mid-January. A pale-blue envelope with a Singaporean stamp on it and my name is written in an elegant hand, neat and tidy. I tear it open and devour the words. A little chit chat about work, she found a new night market with excellent Black Pepper Crab, and by the way, I miss you. She doesn't say she loves me, but the 'miss you' is enough to get the butterflies going. I start a response immediately.

At work, the antics in the Smoko Room are not too different to 77 Squadron. It's a different bunch of blokes, and slightly different card games, but the chat and competitiveness are there, the major difference being a much more equal playing field. Around here, they look after their own and you will get your head punched in pretty quick for picking on someone less able to defend themselves.

Another interesting observation is the discussions on personal health. Working in the tropical heat means that most of us have crotch rot and there are intimate comparisons of the severity. At least one of the single guys is generally being treated for venereal disease, typically Gonorrhoea, and there is also a mix of crabs and herpes going around.

When the chat turns to crabs, the Baggers run a mile. If any of them come down with crabs, there is going to be hell to pay at home. Doc informs me he has the best treatment for the crabs.

'Yer, Dougie, if you get them, you just get a can of Mortein and spray on like this,' opening the top of shorts and spraying his crotch liberally. 'Don't light a smoke when you do this and stand back,' his outstretched arm holding me at arm's length. 'The little fuckers can pole vault.' I give him a fair clearance immediately, and for the next few days.

In the last week of January, I have purchased my first motor bike, a 1968 Suzuki 120. Being from the country, we have grown up on bikes, but it's a whole different proposition riding on Malaysian roads. It takes me some time to gain confidence in the manic traffic.

The start of February sees the flying intensify. The pilots are doing some 1 vs. 1, and 2 vs. 2 sorties, and we start to get gun packs and ammunition dipped ready for the upcoming Air to Air Gunnery Programme. We are just putting the last guns onto packs when the mail comes in.

'There's one here for you, Dougie,' Tiny yells.

It's with the same elegant writing, blue envelope, and a Singaporean stamp. She doesn't mess about with pleasantries. She is heading back to Australia and flying out on the tenth. That's tomorrow.

Fuck it, not even a chance to get to Singapore to say goodbye.

At least she has given me an address in Canberra to write to her. It's in a suburb called O'Connor. I think about my only visit to the nation's capital, and that was for a funeral, and it was fucking cold.

Maybe I could get a posting there?

Football training has started. We are getting our line-up ready for the first game against the Saints. Nev has now moved into halfback and I am playing second row. Running around in the heat, on top of the work, has us pretty fit. There isn't an ounce of fat on any of us.

At home, Gus, Andy, and I generally get a takeaway for dinner, then have a beer and a game of cards, Poker or Five-Hundred if we get a fourth player. We sometimes change to Dominos with a wager on points difference. A high scoring tile usually acknowledged with 'Dominoes' and a slow handclap around the table. Gus reckon it's his version of Lawn Bowls.

'What's happening for Chinese New Year, lads,' he asks.

'Fuck knows,' Andy tells him, with the associated fingers around the nose.

'I think I might head for Phuket. You guys want to come?'

Although I have never been there, I'm reliably informed that a trip to Phuket normally involves long days on the beach drinking followed by a pub crawl of various night spots before paying a bar fine for one of the girls and bonking each other half the night.

'I'm pretty sure Liz wouldn't condone a visit to Phuket without her,' Gus frowns at me.

'You don't have to partake in the nocturnal activities, Dougie. There's plenty of sightseeing and fishing to do.'

'True.' I contemplate it for a little, but all I seem to be able to think about is Liz. Her freckly face and those long legs wrapped around me.

The following week, we start Air to Air Gunnery. I am on Ammo Prep with Corporal Dave Kemp. Kempy sustains himself on a diet of Coca-Cola and Benson & Hedges cigarettes; that and Anchor beer of an evening. He is about five-foot-ten, and I reckon nine stone wringing wet. Our task is to pick up pallets of ammunition from the bomb dump and convert them to 120 round belts of 'dipped' ammunition fit for Air to Air Gunnery practice.

The job is more strenuous than doing it at Williamtown; the increase in both temperature and humidity making it good exercise. Our routine revolves around tucking in and getting the physical work done early in the day, then dropping off ammo and picking up expended links during the hotter hours. There is a swim in the firefighting pools at the bomb dump before knock-off.

As Chinese New Year approaches, the crackers and skyrockets start appearing. You have to be ever alert for a large *bunger* being rolled into the Smoko Room, or a string of *jumping jacks* dropped at your feet.

Late afternoons a war has developed between the rival gangs from either side of Jalan Intan. The boys have fortified the front of our house and Gus has acquired a long piece of one-inch water pipe. With Gus aiming, Andy lighting, and me loading, we can lay down a very accurate barrage of *sky rockets*.

It's a wonder someone doesn't lose an eye.

March, we have moved from Air to Air Gunnery, to Air to Ground Missions, guns and 25lb *poofter bombs*. This is a step up in pace and the physical nature of the work is exhausting.

The military has a habit of dropping into a routine and this is no different. It seems like day after day we start early and launch the first two waves of jets. The respite while those first two waves are up is our biggest break of the day. The remainder is a blur of gun packs going up and down, SUU-20 and PM3 coming off and on, guns being armed, and bombs being loaded, over and over again.

The cooks have opened the flight line kitchen next to our hangar and it's a blessing. At least we can take fifteen minutes out to get a decent lunch before going again.

I still haven't heard from Liz. I wander past the mailbox every day and look, the disappointment now starting to tear my stomach.

Maybe she's busy. She did say she wanted the job in Washington or London.

Fortunately, there is no shortage of social activity to keep my mind off it. Footy training is Tuesday and Thursday, and Wednesday night is volleyball. Friday night is darts at the Boatie, Saturday is footy, and Sunday is water skiing, golf, or sleeping off a hangover. It goes on, week in, week out, along with a weekly letter to Liz.

The last week of March, we drop the gunnery and it's just poofter bombing. There's a heap of time between sorties now and some of the guys are rotated back into the workshop to start cleaning the guns. I get off a few more letters to Liz, but there hasn't been anything coming back the other way.

Wednesday afternoon, I am signing up a bomb load when I look around the flight line. People are sleeping on the floors, in chairs, everyone sleeping. I reckon the whole squadron is knackered. We have been going at it for weeks now.

Just as I sign off the load, the last four pilots of the day arrive. They check the documentation, look at the CFUs, sign, and out the door quickly. The Line Sergeant is caught out.

'Crews 2, 3, 4 and 5, your pilots have walked.' The sleeping troops get up quickly running toward aircraft.

It's not cool to let the pilot beat you to the jet.

It's the last sorties for the day and after launch we are all standing around. Almost all of the Flight Line guys, Gunnies, and Rec Crews are on the tarmac having a laugh, poking fun at each other. The odd bucket of water being thrown on unsuspecting Airmen, it's a pretty light-hearted atmosphere. We get interrupted by jets entering the circuit early, way too early. Three jets taxi back in with bombs intact.

'What's the problem, sir?' enquires Lefty.

'The range is closed.'

We pin the bombs and start our after-flight checks. The fourth jets taxies in ten minutes later. I note the SUU-20 is empty. Dave Heffernan unstraps and comes down the ladder.

'Hi, Dougie, how's things?' he asks, removing his helmet.

'Good, sir, um. I thought the range was closed,' I ask looking at the empty SUU.

'It was, Dougie, but I found the work boat.' He winks at me, the same wink I saw nearly two years ago. 'I suspect I am going to volunteer for Orderly Officer again.'

Thursday morning, we arrive to start another day of bombing. Lefty is sitting with the Desk Sergeant and the Line Sergeant drinking coffee and laughing. There is no urgency here.

'What's going on, Lefty?'

'CO has cancelled flying for the day. He reckons we have done enough and, anyway, tomorrow is Good Friday. He reckons we have earned an extra break. I reckon he knows we have all hit the wire.'

'Next week is BFM. You boys can download everything and drop the SUUs. Start cleaning up.' We spend the morning spraying oil into the SUU-20 release units so they don't corrode. We will be pulling them all apart in the next few weeks and oiling will ensure we don't have to chisel the carbon and crap off.

By lunch time, everyone is knocking off, most of the boys

are calling their cabs and heading to Thailand. On my way out, I check the mailbox. Nothing.

Around seven, I get bored and decide to go to the Boat Club. When I arrive, it's quiet; maybe ten people in the whole place. After a drink, I take the bike to the Super Pub. It's a bit livelier; a few Baggers and their wives holding up the bar.

Good Friday isn't too different to any other Friday in Malaysia. Being a Muslim country, they have their usual prayer sessions, but it's the same old. Some of the Chinese businesses are closed, the Catholic ones.

With most of the boys in Thailand, I spend the weekend lounging around the house, or down at the Boatie drinking with Baggers. But mostly, I just sit around wondering whether I will ever hear from her again. The last letter was the farewell over two months ago.

The next few weeks are standard Air to Air Missions, loads are captive and dummy Sidewinder Missiles, and a semi-active R530 Matra Missile on the centreline. I am on aircraft rectifications, seats in and out, safety equipment changes, and the odd missile US. Nothing is stretching the grey matter.

I wander past the mailbox and each day I am disappointed, except for the odd letter from Gran. She is like clockwork. The letter almost always arrives every second Tuesday.

It's frustrating being thousands of miles away. I can't even get in the car and drive to Canberra to ask her what is going on.

Is it something I wrote in a letter? Have I not written enough? Unlikely. I reckon I have been given the arse.

The Friday after ANZAC Day there is no flying. One of the boys said there was a dining-in night at the Officers' Mess last night and they are sleeping off their hangovers. I think they are probably better off to sleep than trying to fly a jet fighter half-pissed. The Bar Recce has to be done today and I check with Tiny before heading to the Boatie.

'Way you go, Dougie, not too much going on here.'

I get down there around 1000 hours and there is some sort of function on. Plenty of Baggers' wives sitting around drinking tea and eating lamingtons. Scarecrow has made a start to the count.

'What's going on here, Crowie?'

'It's a women's support group. They meet once a month and sit around talking about women's stuff. Probably swapping scone recipes,' he offers.

I'm not sure Crowie knows much about women.

The count doesn't take too long and around 1130 I am at the bar finishing next week's order, beer in hand. My mind really isn't on the order. It's been nearly four months since I have been intimate with a woman and I am feeling lonely. Soap in the shower isn't cutting it and Gus has nearly convinced me to take a trip to Thailand for some comfort.

Maybe I could spend a weekend bouncing Noi around a hotel room in Hatyai?

'Hi, Dougie,' it's a soft voice behind me. I turn to come face-to-face with Donna Gibson. Donna is Squadron Leader Gibson's daughter. He is one of our pilots and the Commodore of the Yacht Club. She is often at the Boatie for dinner with her mother and father and, despite being around my age, rarely even acknowledges any of us single guys. I actually considered whether she was a lesbian.

'Do you have a minute?' she says.

'Sure, what's up?'

'I have been invited to a dinner next Friday night at Batu Ferringhi, but I don't have a date. I was wondering whether you might come with me.' After the initial shock at her actually engaging me in conversation, I consider the offer.

Why the hell not. I reckon I have been given the arse by Liz anyway. Might as well see what happens.

'Sure, that would be great. What's the dinner for?'

'It's the Ornithologists Club. I have just joined it; neat casual dress, long pants and collared shirt'.

'Sure, no worries.'

Ornithology, what the fuck is that?

'It's good of you, Dougie, thanks so much. Can I pick you up at the Hostie at 3.00 pm next Friday?'

'Sure, see you there,' I say, although1500 sounds a little early for a function, but maybe she has pre-dinner drinks in mind. I don't really care; a little female company will lift my spirits.

Maybe she's not a lesbian?

'Oh, by the way, my real name is Tim.' She looks a little surprised.

'Oh, okay, it's so much nicer than Doug anyway.'

The following Friday, I throw my gear into a backpack and head for the ferry. I park the bike at the front of the Hostie at about 1445, light a smoke and lean on the seat in wait. A lime-green Cortina rolls in ten minutes later and pulls up next to the bike.

She puts her elbow on the door and drops her chin to look over the top of her sunglasses at me.

'Been waiting long?' she asks.

'Na, just got here.'

'Throw your bag in the back and we'll get going.' The vinyl seats are hot on my legs. She turns right out of the Hostie gate and down the mad mile, competent with the gear changes, but not exactly smooth.

'Don't force the gears,' I tell her. 'Just move the stick to neutral, then add a little pressure toward the next gear. When the car is ready, the stick will move into gear. It's a smoother ride.' On the next gear change, I put my right hand on hers to demonstrate.

'Oh, yer,' she smiles.

'So, what's the Donna Gibson story?' I ask. 'You have obviously finished school?'

'I finished my degree at Newcastle Uni last year and when Dad got posted back here, he asked if I wanted to come. I loved living in Malaysia last time and could not pass it up. Probably stay this year and go home and get a job next year.'

'What sort of work do you think you are going into?'

'I've got a psychology degree so I might look for something with the Health Department. At a pinch, I could always join a private practice.'

It's a pleasant afternoon with the breeze off the ocean taking the sting out of the tropical sun. We have the windows down and her hair is blowing in the wind, not unlike another girl who recently chauffeured me around. She slows the pace coming down the hill into Batu Feringghi and cruises slowly along the tourist strip, easing the car around pedestrians. At the western end, she turns the car into the Bayview Hotel and parks.

I am expecting we would be heading to the bar for a few cleansers before dinner, but she heads to reception. I am hardly a prude, but I am taken back by her brazen approach. Walking to the elevator, she calmly tells me not to get uptight; she will explain.

In the room, I close the door behind me and she is standing there with a smile.

'So, what's the deal? Normally, you don't give any of us single guys the time of day, but here we are in a hotel room, and I am guessing we aren't here for a game of Euchre?'

'Look, Tim, it's not easy being a single girl of our age in this place. Most of the single guys are only interested in the local hookers, and when they do take notice, we are expected to lie back and think of England; not exactly romantic. And to top it off, my father is trying to set me up with every Bog Rat on the Base. Most are arrogant twats. I am just looking for a bit of company, no strings attached, and without it being advertised to every person in Malaysia.' I let it sink in, trying to understand everything she has just told me. It's a little strange. She breaks the silence walking toward me.

'Besides, Tim, there is something smart about you attracting a lot of talk.'

'What do you mean?'

'Every second married woman in Butterworth would happily drop their knickers for you. You are hot gossip, Tim.' I give her a frown.

That's news to me.

'Come on, Tim. You don't knock off the hookers, you don't make smarmy remarks, or pinch girls on the bum. You are polite and you don't hit on the married girls. They just love you. I am just going to see what all the commotion is about.' She now has her hand on my shirt playing with the lapel, reaching up to pull my lips to hers. She pauses.

'Tonight will be different, Tim,' almost a whisper. 'Just keep your cool and enjoy yourself. No strings, no tales.' She breaks off the embrace and goes to the shower, starting the water, and undressing. She is not shy.

I shower after her. When I come back into the bedroom, she has a long red dress on. Splits up either side. She asks me to zip up the back and I can tell it's a dress with a built-in bodice, no bra. I wonder if she has any underwear on at all and feel myself stir at the thought.

'Dinner is at six, sharp,' she says. I get some after-shave and deodorant on and get dressed. We are out the door at five-to.

The function is in a private room. We are greeted at the door by a middle-aged woman who introduces herself as Janet. Bottle blonde, probably about thirty-five, and carrying just enough weight to add to her deep cleavage, without looking fat. Dressed in a frock with stockings and high heels. I have seen her before, but can't quite place where. There is a waiter who offers Donna a glass of champagne and a beer to me.

Inside the room, there are about a dozen couples at a long table sitting opposite each other, girls on the right and boys on the left. As we walk around looking at the name tags, I note Pete's missus is at the table and I don't make eye contact with her. Donna and I are seated at the end farthest from the door. I am introduced to the couples one and two down and we make small talk. I only vaguely recognise most of the people at the table.

Precisely on ten-past, the entrees come out, alternate prawn cocktails and spring rolls, champagne and beer flowing freely. On the stroke of six- thirty, mains are served. Chicken or Beef

Wellington, with vegies, again alternated. After the meal, I am waiting for the official part of the evening to commence.

Janet, rises from her chair and taps her glass with a spoon. The room goes quiet.

'Ladies,' she says. Immediately, the women gather their things and depart the room.

Is this some sort of weird Ornithologist ritual? And, by the way, what the fuck is Ornithology?

All the men are now seated watching her. There is an air about the way Janet walks — it's almost like a march, but with grace. She walks down the back of the men and then around the front looking intently at them. As she approaches the end of the table again, she picks up a tin pail.

She stands again at the head of the table. The first person puts his right hand up and she places a key in it, a room key. He stands and walks from the room. As she progresses, each man puts his right hand up, is handed a key, stands and walks out.

Fuck me, it's a fucking key party.

I am looking around for somewhere to run. She has her eyes intently on me. The guy next to me stands and walks out the door. I look at her for quite some time. There is one key in the pail. No prizes for guessing whose room it is.

'I know what you are thinking,' she says.

'Really? I didn't volunteer for this.'

'Look, Tim, people have different needs and wants, and,' she pauses 'it's hard to get what you need in a country like Malaysia. Donna has needs that are not being met'.

'Well, she didn't have to bring me into it.'

'It's the rules, Tim. Whether people are single or married,

they have to come to the meetings with a partner. It keeps things orderly.' She is sitting opposite me now, leaning forward, cleavage clearly on display. 'Her previous partner was posted home and she spent quite a while deciding on you. She thought you would understand.'

I am sitting watching her, trying to understand what she is telling me.

'So, you have two choices. Well, three, really. You can come upstairs with me, or we can sit here for the next four hours and get hammered. Or ...'

'I can get up and walk out.'

'Yes, you can get up and walk out,' she agrees. 'But, if you leave, you must not say a word about this to anyone. We have enough influence to make your life uncomfortable if you shoot your mouth off,' she tells me, earnestly.

I am sure they have.

If it's one thing I have learned since joining the Air Force, if someone takes a dislike to you, things can get nasty, quickly. I contemplate the options.

'You better get me a drink. Can you make it a Rum and Coke? A double,' I add. She is gone only a short time and sits the drink in front of me. She has a similar tumbler with what looks like the same mixture in it. We sit there contemplating each other for a while. I break the silence.

'So, Janet, how did you get into this?' I ask. She looks a little reflective.

'It was our last posting here. John was always at work, at the pub, or away somewhere. We had an Amah, so there is no housework to do, and she looked after the kids. You can only go to so many morning teas and bingo games. I was bored and lonely,' she pauses.

'A girlfriend suggested I come to a meeting. She explained the rules and I thought, *'What the hell?'* The sex I was getting at home was pretty ordinary and I have been a part of the group ever since. We even had it going to Williamtown for a while, but it's not the same as here and it folded.'

'And, what are the rules?'

'Not too many. For starters, its couples only, and one-on-one. Some of the girls get into group sex on the side, but the official meetings are strictly one-on-one. The couples concept helps us control who comes and goes from the group and makes sure no one misses out. There are usually plenty of girls lonely enough to fill vacancies. The hard part is recruiting the right guys.'

'You'll miss out tonight,' I suggest.

'Yes, but it was a chance we took to get Donna a good partner. We thought you would be the right one,' she says, looking at me intently.

'Partners, and the other members, often have sex outside the official meetings. But the monthly meetings are the glue. The meetings have a twofold effect, keeping the discipline of the rules, and an opportunity to try out people who like what you like. The only other rule is, no sex with people not from the group, except your husband or wife, of course.'

'There are no husband and wife couples?'

'Yes, but only a few. A few of the girls are not lonely, just not getting what they want from their husbands. Jenny and Jason O'Dea are here tonight. He is well endowed but impatient. I usually team him up with the girls who like it hard and fast. She prefers a slow hand. They both get what they want, and now their sex at home is better. It's almost like marriage counselling.' She picks up our empty glasses and leaves the room. I am contemplating her comments.

Lonely women, mismatched sex lives, maybe this Ornithologists Club has genuine value? I just can't get past the adultery.

She comes back with more drinks. 'Well, Tim. Has all that altered your opinions of Donna? She spent a lot of time working out who might be her best partner?'

I am really unsure what to say. I took the date with Donna just hoping for a little female company and I find myself sitting opposite a middle- aged woman who, by the way, is offering to have sex with me, and I am now wondering whether I should start a relationship with Donna, and perhaps even join the club.

How the fuck did I get here?

'I don't know,' I tell her honestly. 'She seems nice, but I hardly know her. And, I don't think I am over my last girlfriend yet.'

'Oh?' she says with a raised eyebrow. 'Do tell.'

I shift in my seat. 'I was involved with an Aussie girl from the High Commission in Singapore. It was pretty serious, and we had even discussed the possibility of marriage. She went back to Canberra in February and I haven't heard from her since. I must have written a letter every week without a reply.' I take a big drink.

'What do you think is going on for her?' she asks.

I am a little taken back by the question. The only thing I have considered is she got cold feet and dumped me.

'What do you mean?'

'Well, girls who have made a serious commitment to a

relationship don't just quit it for no good reason. She probably has some conflict going on. Have you considered what it is?' I take another big drink and think about it.

'Well, she is ambitious. She works for the Department of Foreign Affairs and wants a promotion to get a highflying job in London.'

'That will be it. It's not so much as she has dumped you, she is just focused on that. You might want to back off a little on the whole love and marriage thing for a while. Stay in contact by all means, but back off and let her have time to have her career.' She lets the comment sink in for a bit. 'Need another drink?' she asks.

'Yer,' I tell her from a trance-like state, thinking about what she said. I conclude she might be right and decide I am going to write Liz a letter full of gossip, rather than soppy love letters. If there is a chance we get together in the long run, I want to make sure I am at least in the game. When she comes back, I change the subject.

'And, where is your husband tonight?'

'Oh, he'll be down at the Hostie tonight, playing darts, and drinking. Probably drive home around midnight and fall into bed. Won't even notice I am not there. I told him I was having one of my girls' nights out anyway. He's used to it.' Now it's her taking big drinks.

'The whole drinking thing has been a real eye opener,' I tell her. 'I haven't had a sober day since I got here and have never seen a bunch of blokes drink so much; it's like a sport.' She nods her head in agreement.

'Not so much a sport as an obsession. The women are as bad as the blokes, you know. We have some pretty long lunches.'

'And, I have never seen so many activities based on drinking. There is the Smirnoff Club where they sit around and drink vodka, straight. Another is the Pirate Club. They get shots of rum, throw them back, and one of the others dead-legs the drinker, who makes a sound like a pirate,' I tell her, shaking my head. 'Probably the funniest game is bottles.'

'Bottles?'

'Yer, bottles. It's basically a counting game, best played with five or more people. You start at one, and go around, each person saying the next number. When you get to a number with a seven in it, or a number that is a multiple of seven, you say bottles and the count reverses the other way. Anyone who stuffs up the count, or misses a bottles call, has to drink. You want to try?'

'Sure,' she says, straightening herself in the seat.

'You start,' I tell her. One, two, three, four, five, six, bottles, eight, nine, ten, eleven, twelve, thirteen, bottles, fifteen, sixteen, seventeen, woops. She takes a big drink. We do it again and this time I slip up on twenty-eight. 'I always forget that one,' I say, as she gets up for another round.

When she comes back, I tell her I know one of the other girls.

'Which one?' she asks.

'I can't recall her first name, only met her the once, but her last name is Buchanan. I work with her husband, Pete.'

'Oh, Deborah, she's a funny one. Looks and acts like such a prude, but she's up for anything, and I do mean anything! Likes a bit of group sex, does our Deb, and doesn't mind it both ways either, from what I hear.' I think to myself the drink has loosened her lips a bit. 'I'm not into the group thing myself, but would try it with her, just to see what the fuss is about.'

She then goes on to give me a rundown on the other girls —
who likes group sex, who likes a smack on the bum, who's best
at oral sex, who moans loudest — she doesn't leave much out.

'How do you know all this?'

'Oh, the boys are bigger gossips than the girls. I just ask them.
It also helps me pair people up,' she giggles. 'While I still try to
ensure most of the girls have slept with most of the boys, I still
get a kick out of matchmaking and genuinely try to put together
combinations that will work together.'

She then goes on to describe some of the attributes she uses
to matchmake, size, stamina, rough or gentle, even tall versus
short. It's a fascination view of sexual compatibility I have never
considered before.

She takes another big slug. 'So, what's your thing, Tim?' she
asks. 'I may as well ask as it looks like I am not going to get a
chance to find out.'

'I'm not sure,' I tell her.

I am contemplating the question with another big drink. My
sexual upbringing has been a bit of a roller-coaster ride. My mind
goes to some of the wild things Helen and I got up to that's not
my thing. And sex with Liz was just exhilarating and gentle.

What is my thing?

'I guess I like to have a connection. Sex without affection is
okay, and can be exciting, but I prefer it with care and warmth.'

'A romantic,' she says. 'That figures,' finishing her drink.

'It's what has me uptight about this situation. I can just screw
someone if that's the situation, but I prefer more. And, I don't
have any time for married women. Married people playing
around is just wrong.'

'Don't get on your high horse too quickly, Tim,' she says with some venom, eyes bright glaring at me. 'I am not here for some cheap fling. This,' she waves her hand around, 'is about people getting some basic comfort, whether it is substituting for something they don't get at home, or complementing it. This isn't about power or cheating.'

I feel chastised and don't really have a comeback, and I can see she is feeling a little frustrated. She settles a little.

'Look, Tim. You know, you can have a connection without falling in love. Most of the girls in this group are just after sex with someone who cares, at least for a couple of hours. And, nearly all of us are married. Married to pisspot blokes who only care about their next promotion, their next drink, their mates, and come home once a week sober enough to get their rocks off.'

'If it's that bad, why don't they just leave?'

She throws her head back and laughs loudly. 'If I had a dollar for every time I heard that old chestnut, I would be a rich woman. You don't actually believe that crap, do you, Tim?' I am a little shocked.

What's so crazy about leaving a bad relationship?

I can tell she recognises the misbelief on my face. 'Tim, suppose I decide it's time for me to dump the drunken arse who calls himself my husband, what happens then? Hey?' She is standing now.

'Do I go home to my parents' place in Biloela with three kids. What sort of life will we have? What sort of opportunities will the kids have? With a Leaving Certificate and few other skills, about the best thing I could hope for would be a cleaning job at the local motel. No, Tim, I am staying exactly where I am. If

I need to get a little bit on the side to keep my sanity, then it's what I am going to do.' She sits again, arms folded, lecture over.

But, life's not that simple. You can't just screw around.

I think about Pete a little. I was happy to accept his cheating based on his non-existent relationship with Deb.

Is that okay? What is okay? I don't know.

I am deep in thought having an internal conversation when she interrupts. 'You could get a bit of something out of this yourself, Tim. Think of it as charity, a community service.'

I've never heard of fucking someone as a community service before. But she does have a point. And, it's not like in Australia where you can go out, pick up, and have a one-night stand. Here in Malaysia, there aren't many nineteen-year-old girls looking for some fun. Most of the local girls give us a wide berth. She's still staring at me.

'I'll think about it.'

'What about another game,' she asks.

'Sure, what do you want to do?

'Strip poker,' she says, picking up the empty glasses. 'I'll see if they have a deck of cards at the bar.'

Fucking strip poker, she has to be kidding. There are no prizes for guessing what happens if we get our gear off. I am feeling pretty pissed and wonder what she might look like without the frock. She comes back with more drinks and no cards.

'No luck, hey?'

'No,' she sounds disappointed.

I sit back contemplating what she said and what might happen next. 'We could always do paper, rock, scissors,' I suggest.

'Paper, rock, scissors?' she asks.

'Yer, we use it all the time to decide who buys the Cokes. You shake your fist three times like this, and on the third shake you make a choice, displaying it with your hand.' I demonstrate. 'An open palm like this is paper, a fist is a rock, and two fingers out like this is scissors. Paper wins over rock as you can wrap a rock in paper, scissors wins over paper because you can cut the paper with scissors, and rock wins over scissors because you can crush the scissors with a rock. Get it?'

'Okay, let's try,' she is sitting up, taking another drink.

'Okay, one, two, three,' I say in time with our shaking hands. I have a rock and she had scissors. 'Okay, I win. The rock can crush scissors,' I explain. She starts unzipping her dress. 'Wow, wow, it was just a practice,' I tell her, holding up my hand. 'One more practice. Ready?'

'Yep,' she says, enthusiastically.

'One, two, three.' This time I anticipate her paper, with a scissors. The new ones are always one step behind. 'I win again. Scissors cuts paper.' I can see the recognition in her eyes; no dumb shit, this lady.

'Okay, let's get serious,' she says. 'How many pieces of clothing do you have on?'

'Sorry?' I am a little confused.

'How many pieces of clothing do you have on? Depending on how much clothing we have on, we do this that many times and the loser has to strip for the other one,' she explains.

What the hell. 'Do shoes count as one or two pieces of clothing? I ask.

'Two.'

'Okay, well, I have a shirt, trousers, two shoes, two socks, undies, and belt. Eight pieces of clothing, right?'

'Right, and I have the dress, bra, panties, two shoes, two stockings, and a garter belt on. Oh, and the scarf, nine pieces. You get to nine wins; I strip for you. I get to eight wins; you strip for me.' Its sounds fair and I am too pissed to reason any more.

'One, two, three,' I say, starting the event. I go for the rock again and she outsmarts me with the paper. She claps her hands in celebration and takes a drink. 'It's not a drinking game,' I tell her.

'One, two, three,' I say again, going for the scissors this time. She has the rock. 'Fuck it.'

She giggles this time. 'Why don't we up the stakes?' she says. 'First one to ten wins. Loser not only has to strip, but has to blow the other one.' The booze has me considering whether she is a moaner or not. I am looking at her cleavage when I agree.

The game goes on and the drinks empty. There are no refills. We both know where this is going to end. It's just a matter of time. At seven-to-five in her favour, someone clears his throat and we both look to the door. It's her partner.

'It's after eleven,' he says.

'Is that the time?' she says, grabbing my left arm and looking at my watch. 'Shit,' she is disappointed. 'Time's up, Tim. The rules are you return to your own room at 11.00 pm,' she explains, getting up. 'You owe me one,' she says, departing with the guy. I am left sitting at the table on my own. How the fuck did I get here?

Through the booze haze, I manage to remember which room is ours and knock on the door. She sizes me up and down when she opens the door. 'You're pissed,' she says. 'What did you and Janet get up to?'

'Drinking games,' I tell her, stumbling through the door and onto the bed. She has obviously showered and in a lacey nightie. I lay there contemplating whether I am in a fit state to do my community service when the lights in my head go out.

I wake about seven, head feeling like it has a vice on my temples and smelling like Captain Morgan Rum. I need water. She stirs beside me. Oh yer, I remember now. Donna. Then the previous night comes back to me. The cleavage, drinking games, and paper, rock, scissors. Fuck, did we have sex? Did I have sex with Donna?

Fuck knows.

I come back to the bed with a glass of water. 'You want some?' I ask.

'Sure.' I hand her the glass and she takes a long drink. 'You okay?' she asks.

'Not sure. I have a sore head,' I tell her, taking back the glass. 'Your friend, Janet, can knock them back.' She is looking at me like she is waiting for a verdict.

'So, what do you think?' she asks.

I know what she is asking. 'I am not sure,' I tell her, going back to the bathroom to refill the glass. When I get back, she is up on one elbow, sheets down to her waist, bodice is sight. I can see her nipples are hard.

'I was thinking about you most of the night,' she says, pulling back the sheets and patting the space beside her. Somewhere in the back of my mind, I have someone urging me to do my community service. I take my trousers off and hop into the bed.

Later, in the car, she asks me the direct question. 'Are you going to join the club?'

'I have been thinking about it most of the morning. It seems clinical, just walking into someone's room and having sex with them. Someone you hardly know and a married someone at that. I'm not sure I can do it,' I tell her.

'And sometimes, the sex isn't what you expect,' she adds. 'Last night, everything was over in the first hour. He spent the next three hours talking about himself. I was happy to see him go.'

'You aren't making your case any better,' I tell her, with a smile. She smiles back.

'I'd like you to think seriously, Tim. Most of the girls love having someone who makes them feel special and, judging by this morning's performance, you are good at it.' She smiles at me again.

Driving through Tanjun Bungah she has another go. 'I saw Janet at reception when I checked out. She was particularly impressed with you. What did you two get up to last night?' she asks.

'Just talked a lot and played some drinking games.'

'Well, you have won her over. She reckons she had a great night.'

'That's nice,' In my mind I am working through the implications of becoming a known gentleman in a key club.

'This club is important to her. Her husband is a particular arse. I am not sure why she puts up with his crap. Apparently, he slaps her around a bit.'

'Nooooo?' I look at her.

'Apparently,' she says, glancing back at me, and back to the road, attentive to the driving. 'It's fairly prevalent, you know. The RAAF married patches are not the perfect little houses with the white picket fence people would like you to think.'

I look at her again.

'I've lived in RAAF patches all my life, Tim. It's like any community. There are nice guys, blokes who are drunks, some who slap their wives, some who are perverts, and some who are just arseholes. Three of my dad's so-called mates, have hit on me since I have been here.'

She goes on. 'I know of a bloke who secretly videoed sex with his wife and sold copies to his mates. She only found out when one of the mates asked her to do the same for him.'

'Bastards,' I whisper in disbelief.

'That's why we have the women's groups and so many sporting teams. Many of the girls are depressed and need the draw of social activity, just to survive. Think about it. They are in a foreign country, they can't work, all of the housework is done by a servant, and they are thousands of miles from family. Some girls love the colonial lifestyle, but on the other end of the scale, many are horribly depressed and lonely, especially when the husband spends all day at work, half the night in the pub, and then comes home and expects them to get on their back and be enthusiastic about it.'

'Bastards,' I say again. 'Lucky if I don't fill them in.'

'You'd better warm those knuckles then, Tim,' she says. 'There are a few of them.'

Maybe RAAF recruiting should be doing fuckwit tests rather than IQ tests.

It makes me think about the guys I work with and who might be arseholes.

'Bastards,' I murmur again.

She pulls into the Hostie and parks next to my bike, leaving the car idling, turning to me.

'What about the club?' she asks again.

'Still not sure.'

'What about seeing me every now and again?'

Why not, I think. 'Sure, I'd like that.'

'Okay, I'll call you. Which section do you work at?'

'3 Squadron Armament,' I tell her.

'Okay, see you soon,' she says, as I get out of the Cortina. She backs out and leaves, while I sit on the bike seat, light a smoke, and ponder the last twenty-four hours, wondering whether I was in some sort of dream. I snap out of it, put my helmet on, and start the bike. We are playing footy at three and I need to get home and pick my gear up.

She doesn't take long to call. I am in Gun Bay on Wednesday afternoon when the phone rings. Tiny picks it up.

'Dougie, it's for you, some *sheila*.' I wipe the kerosene off my hands with a rag and pick up the phone.

'Hello.'

'Tim, it's Donna,' she says.

'Hi, how's things?' I ask with interest. I have been thinking about her a fair bit since our trip to Batu Ferringhi, particularly Saturday morning, when the sex was good. She enjoyed herself and was openly affectionate.

'Is there a chance we could catch up during working hours this week?' she asks. I look at Tiny.

He won't have an issue if I fuck off for a while.

'Sure, when are you thinking?'

'How is tomorrow morning? Mum is playing golf and I can get away without too many questions.'

'No worries, where?'

'Your place okay?'

'Sure.' She gets the address off me and tells me she'll be there at ten.

Getting off the phone, I sit for a while and contemplate Donna. She's different to the girls I have previously gone out with before, though this is hardly dating. She's not as wild in the sack, but she does like doing it.

I am starting to build a library of sexual responses and linking them to personality. It's by no means an extensive library. My experience isn't vast, but I think it's a fair sample size for someone my age.

It's a sliding scale. At the extreme right are the crazies, the Helens of the world. These are the ones who have a particular look in their eyes bordering on crazy. They will pretty well do it anywhere, anytime. Some like it hard and fast, some even resort to a little rough play, but they are also the ones who create the most drama, managing to create a scene wherever they go. And it's all about them; they want complete control most of the time.

Then there are those like Janine who are a little less crazy, completely self-centred, but not as unpredictable. They know what they like and demand it. When they orgasm, they make a racket, not really caring if anyone else is satisfied — not as self-centred as the full-on crazies, but still wanting to call the shots most of the time.

In the centre of the scale are the intelligent ones, Allison fits the mould. Demure, smart, always well dressed. Butter wouldn't melt in their mouth, until you get them excited. They like it, are active participants, and are generous lovers, not selfish.

Further left are the subservient and silent ones. They will

pretty well do whatever you want to do, but don't offer any suggestions of their own. If there is to be a change to proceedings, you have to initiate it. If they orgasm, there isn't a lot of noise, you just feel them tense up and release. These ones don't have too many opinions on anything, and are happy to go with the flow. Don't look for stimulating conversation with the silent ones. You get to call the shots.

On the far left of the scale are the damaged ones. Dee comes to mind. There was definitely something about her that was deeply troubled.

Donna is somewhere between intelligent and subservient. She obviously has a high intellect, her review of the social issues within the RAAF community a real eye opener, though as a psychologist, it's not a surprise. I start contemplating my failed relationship with Liz, and where she might be on my scale when Tiny interrupts.

'Earth calling, Dougie, earth calling, Dougie, come in, Dougie.'

'Sorry, Tiny, what did you say?'

'You are a million miles away, Dougie, what's going on?'

Fuck, Tiny actually pays attention to what's going on around him.

'What is it with chicks, Tiny? One minute they love you, the next minute, you are yesterday's news.'

'It's an age-old problem, Dougie, when you get the answer to that one, you will make a lot of money.' He puts his head back down into some sort of ledger — football, social club, who knows.

'I have this theory,' I tell him.

'Oh, yer, on chicks?' He is writing and listening.

'Yer,' I go on and explain the theory, he stops writing halfway through and listens, looking at me. When I finish, he sits back in his chair, looking at the ceiling.

'Not bad, Dougie, not bad at all. I remember these two sisters who used to come into the Apprentice Club when I was at Wagga Wagga. Mad as cut snakes the pair of them, and crazy rooters.' I can see his mind wondering off in reflection. 'The Potaskie twins.' He snaps out of the dream. 'This scale of yours may need some work.'

'Yer?'

'Have you thought about a "y" scale? Some of the ugly ones are the best roots because they never know when they are going to get another one.'

He has a good point. I will have to think this through. More research might be required?

'And one more thing, Dougie, in my experience, you think you know women and then something happens that destroys everything you thought you knew. I reckon they might be at one point on your scale, but then, they can disappear and reappear on any other point. It's random, like golf. Just when you think you've worked the game out, it bites you on the arse and laughs in your face.'

So much for theories.

The next morning, I have a gun stripped and in the kero bath. 'Hey, Tiny, I've got to skip home for an hour or two. A guy is coming to fix our hot water.'

He waves me off. Tiny isn't really paying attention. He is doing some deal with a guy who's printing shirts for our end-of-season footy trip. He's working out the cost, sale price, and profit.

I get home early and tidy things up a little. Right on ten I can hear the wheezy sound of the Cortina coming down the street, stopping out the front. I watch her walk down the drive. She has a light dress on, no sleeves, and ribbons at the top which tie up on the shoulder. She isn't wearing a bra and I am trying not to gawk at her breasts. I greet her at the door with a peck on the cheek and usher her into the lounge.

'Nice,' she says, looking around the house. 'I never get down this way; it's out of bounds. Mum reckons you'll catch something off the furniture in a Singlies house, but this is quite clean. Do you have an Amah?''

'Three days a week. She's off today,' I tell her. 'Want a cuppa?'

I boil the jug and serve up two cups of tea, white, no sugar. She is thumbing her way through the books on the cupboard when I come back.

'You guys read anything other than Wilbur Smith?' she asks. It's a fair point as his novels dominate the collection.

I shrug my shoulders, 'There's a couple of Tom Sharpe's somewhere.'

'Beats Mills and Boon,' I tell her, and she smiles back, sipping the tea.

'Nothing like a bit of soft porn,' she says, walking towards me. 'I prefer the real thing, though,' touching my shoulder.

I am conscious that I am still in my work gear, complete with grease down the front of my T-shirt, shorts, and steel-capped boots.

'I'm hardly dressed for a date,' I tell her. She doesn't seem to mind, kissing me softly on the lips. Her lips feel like warm velvet. It's a touch I have always found hard to resist and the passion escalates. Before long, I have untied the shoulder strings of her dress and let it fall to the floor. Knickers follow. I manage to kick my boots off and she relieves me of my T-shirt and shorts, hands everywhere, mine and hers.

She is wet, and as she approaches orgasm, she asks me to put it in. I take my fingers away and push her towards the table, her arse resting on the edge. She is in a hurry and moves her knees apart, inviting me in.

Afterwards, I show her upstairs, the bedroom, and we do it again. I sense she wants to make the most of the occasion.

We shower and she leaves before 11.30 has come around. On my way back to work, I keep thinking that if I'd known RAAF working dress was so alluring, I'd have been wearing it out to night clubs.

'Get the hot water sorted, Dougie?' Tiny asks.

'What? Oh, yer, it's all working fine.'

The following week, the phone rings again. 'Dougie, it's that *sheila* again.'

It's the same arrangements as last time, she arrives at ten and we are at it like teenagers five minutes later. Afterward, we are lying back in my bed, her head on my chest. She gets onto her elbow.

'I've got a big favour to ask?' I am not sure I am going to like this. The last time she asked me for a favour I ended up at a key party on Penang.

'Shoot,' my voice isn't convincing.

'I have a friend, Maria. She and I go to Penang shopping and have lunch once a week,' she says looking at me, gauging whether I am getting bothered.

'She is a great girl, fun, smart, a pianist no less.'

'Are you going to ask me to do a duet with her?'

'No, silly,' she pauses. 'She is married to a complete tosser who likes blow jobs, hand-on-head style. He's a fucking dickhead, Tim.'

'Do you want me to teach him a lesson?'

'Not exactly,' she smiles a cheeky smile. 'I recommended she try something different, in my professional capacity, of course.'

'You want me to sleep with her?'

'You don't have to be crass, Tim. Think of it as a damsel in distress.'

Boy, every day I am learning something new about the female psyche. In one breath, they want to fall in love and live happily ever after, and in the next, they will advocate casual sex.

Do women actually have any standards?

I am starting to realise just how true Janet's words were. 'Think of it as community service,' she said.

'Can you get away again tomorrow?' she asks, hopefully.

I must have a look of resignation on my face because she squeals and give me a hug. The hug quickly moves to other activities.

Through the afternoon I contemplate what I have signed up for. This goes against the grain. My mind goes back to Williamtown and lecturing Tacho about sleeping with Baggers' wives. Then I think about Janet's view. The world isn't an easy place to work out what is right and what is wrong.

The next morning, I tell Tiny I have a couple of little jobs at the Boatie to finish. I'll stay back late and finish the gun I am working on. No problem with Tiny as long as we don't get behind on the work.

I take the bike to the Boatie and leave it there. I don't want to raise too many eyebrows in the married patch by riding my bike in and leaving it outside someone's house. Whose house, I am not sure, but I expect Donna has this all sorted out.

I take the beach track to Tan Sai Gin and walk down the street. Luckily, I don't have to walk far as number thirty-three is on the beach end of the street, close to the track. I hop over the gate and go to the front door. The curtains are closed and I can't see inside, so I knock gently. Donna pulls the curtains back enough to see me, opens the door and pulls me in. The door and curtains are closed quickly and I follow her in, taking off my boots.

'Fancy a drink Tom, she asks picking up a glass. They are sitting at the kitchen table, each with a short glass of clear liquid. 'Gin and tonic?' she asks, holding the glass up.

'Sorry, Donna, a bit early for me, and I have to work today.' I look around. The house is a typical Tan Sai Gin residence. Semi-detached, with living areas at the front, cane furniture with TV and video recorder. The dining table is between the lounge and the kitchen and curtains with a palm tree print; always the palm trees.

I recognise the other woman. She is not as tall as Donna, with short, mousy-blonde hair, dressed in a white blouse and a pair of blue shorts. Both girls have a slightly glazed look in their eyes; they have had one or two already.

'Tim, this is Maria. Maria, Tim,' she says, introducing us and taking another drink. Maria says 'Hello' and looks me up and down. I feel like this is an audition for something.

'I explained your situation to Tim,' she says, looking at Maria, then getting up and gathering her bag. 'I am going up to the shop for some curry puffs. Does anyone want something?' She doesn't wait for an answer, letting herself out.

Well, this is awkward. I have no idea what I am going to do

next. Maybe it is the booze, but she doesn't share my unease, walking over to the record player and placing the needle onto the vinyl. I recognise the Patsy Cline track, one of mum's favourites. The memory of my mother stings me a bit and I have to shove it aside. She comes over, putting her arms around me and swaying to the music.

She nuzzles her face into my neck. The music, her smell, soft skin, starts to intoxicate me.

Monday morning the Air Defence exercise starts. It's an Integrated Air Defence System exercise with Malaysia, Singapore, New Zealand, United Kingdom and Australian forces involved with a variety of aircraft all attacking or defending key targets, and a host of ground force activities.

We have positioned four jets on both the northern and southern ends of the runway, on two-minute alert. A couple of pilots are strapped in, power connected, ready to launch at a moment's warning. We are lounging around on the concrete, watching the various comings and goings.

New Zealand A4s, RMAF F5s, RAAF F-111s, and some of our Mirages launch early. From such close proximity, both the Mirage and F-111 are spectacular on the take-off roll with after-burners glowing in the pre-dawn light. Not only do the after-burners glow, but the air and ground shake violently.

We have each of the jets loaded with AIM-9 Sidewinder Missiles on the outer wing stations, and a semi-active radar-guided Matra R530 missiles on the centreline. They aren't real missiles, as we don't want to shoot anyone down, but the seekers work and will tell the pilot if he has a target locked up.

It's another one of those hurry-up-and-wait moments the

military is known for. There isn't much to do except sit around. It's entertaining for the first few hours, but as the morning heats up, it becomes increasingly uncomfortable. The knuckleheads swap out of the cockpit every half hour. They are soaked through their flight suits in the heat and humidity. Even having the blower in the cockpit doesn't offer much relief.

Friday morning, the exercise is winding down and I get out early and to the Boatie for the Bar Recce by 11.00. The ladies' function is just concluding; some are staying for lunch, the others walking back to their homes, or hopping into cars. I have to get the count done before the guys start selling drinks at 11.30.

I notice Donna at a table with her mum and several other ladies I don't know well. After lunch, they get up to leave and Donna comes past me at the bar, as I am finishing the paperwork.

'The meeting is next Friday,' she says. 'I'll see you at the Hostie at the usual time.' It's not a question.

That night, we have a section function at a seafood restaurant on Gurney Drive. Tiny has managed to get the section esky in place with about eight cartons, and bit of soft drink and spirits for the ladies. My job is to keep everyone lubricated and so I position myself on a seat next to the esky, handing out drinks as people arrive and making sure I have plenty, it's thirsty work, this.

The food is amazing. I have never seen fish and prawns cooked this way. There is a shell dish which looks like mussels; the boys call them long shells.

'What's this?'

'Satong.'

'Satong?'

'Squid, Dougie, squid.'

I've never had squid before and it's somewhere beyond yummy, especially the accompanying sauce. It's got this sweet, hot, and sour taste, all at once.

'What about this one?' I ask, munching on something looking a bit like chicken.

'Frogs legs, Dougie, paddy chicken,' says Lefty, smiling. I've been eating it for several minutes and so there is no need to feel at all nauseous about it. I form a mental vision of all these frogs getting around in wheelchairs with bandages on their stumps. In the after-dinner racket, I find myself three parts pissed sitting next to Deborah, Pete's wife.

'The meeting's on next week,' she says, flatly and without any emotion, her eyes seemingly boring into mine.

'I heard,' equally flat in response.

'There's a couple of us hanging around on Saturday for some extra group activity,' she says, eyes still firmly looking into mine.

'I'm not sure I can do it, Deb.'

'If you turn up Saturday, you will understand what all the fuss is about,' she says, lifting one eyebrow.

I look her up and down trying to gather a sense of what makes her tick. She's quite attractive and would not be without company in any social setting, particularly if she was single. She is articulate and funny. There is a lot to like about her. But she is married, and to a mate of mine.

As the party breaks up, most agree to go back to the Hostie for a night cap. I bum a ride with Doc. Inside, the place is crowded and everyone loaded. I spy Janet before she spies me. She is seated at a table with a bunch of RAAFies and their wives, all yarning and laughing. She is wearing sandals, a yellow skirt, and a sleeveless, white blouse. The buttons are done up to hide what I know is an ample cleavage.

I am guessing the guy on her left elbow is her husband. I've seen him around, but don't know where he works.

The Hostie is home to the Penang-based guys, mostly Baggers, and they challenge us to a game of Mickey Mouse. My darts skills are limited and the other guys have to carry me for a bit, until I realise, I have an uncanny knack of hitting the bull's eye. I just keep hitting it, and when I miss, it usually ends in knocking off one of the other numbers. The local boys have the shits with me hitting the bull.

'Your shout, Dougie.'

I head to the bar, waiting my turn for the order, and feel something touch my right arm. I turn and Janet is standing there. It wasn't her hand touching my arm.

'Hi.'

'Hello, Tim, it's nice to see you.' I smile and nod.

'I see you have been out with Deborah?'

I nod again. 'Social club function.' She nods. I can see she has something to say, she's shifting on her feet, holding her tongue between her teeth.

'The meeting is next week.' It's an enquiry.

'You are the second person to tell me that tonight.'

'Oh!' She raises an eye and looks Deborah's way. 'She is keen on you.'

I shake my head. 'Look, Janet, I really like Donna. She's nice. So, I will be there next week, but don't team me up with her, okay? It's just way too close to home.' As I say it, I am thinking *'It's just too close to work.'*

'Okay. Are you staying long tonight? We could finish that game of paper, rock, scissors?'

'Sorry, Janet. I am playing footy tomorrow afternoon and we are heading home after this one.'

'Shame. See you next week.'

The week goes slowly, we are doing General Flying sorties and reconfiguring the jets with large external tanks for some navigation exercises.

Friday, I have to ask Dennis for a favour to get out early, get home, change, and manage to get to the Hostie by 1430. It gives me some time to think. I take a walk around the bar, down to the foreshore, and have a cigarette and a Coke.

Do I really want to do this? What the hell. Donna is cute, if not a little fun. We could make a pretty good couple if she would only decide it's okay to go out with me in public.

Back out the front, I adopt the standard pose, leaning up against the bike. She is ten minutes late, apologising, getting out of the car to give me a kiss on the lips. On the way out to Batu Ferringhi, I chat my head off. The guys at work are giving me the shits, lazy bastards some of them, turning up late for work and sleeping off a hangover while the rest of us do the work.

'That says more about your supervisors than your colleagues, Tim.'

I think about it a bit. She's right, I hadn't thought about it from that point of view. Somehow, it's even more disappointing.

'How's Maria?'

'She is well, Tim. In fact, she went home on the charter last week. She told him she needed to go home to see her parents. She's not coming back.'

'If he's as big an arsehole as you say, I am not surprised.'

'She left this for you,' handing me an envelope. It's scented, the same perfume she was wearing when we met. The paper is light blue, with stylish writing, almost graceful.

> *Dear Tim*
>
> *Thank you for a wonderful morning and helping me to understand what love really is. If you are ever in Adelaide, please come and see me.*
>
> *M*

I put the note into my bag and daydream for the rest of the ride. Maybe it turned out for the best, Janet's words about community service in my ear again.

When we get to the room, she throws her bag on the bed, turns, and kisses me strongly. I can tell she is excited and in a rush. It's literally takes ten seconds for her to get her skirt and blouse off and pull me to her.

At the end of dinner, Janet rises from her chair, grabs her glass and raises it. She taps it with a spoon and the room goes quiet. She pauses for a moment before lifting her chin and calling 'Ladies!' Just like last time, all the women gather their things and leave the room.

Janet walks around the room eyeballing all the guys. She's a bit of a queen of the dramatic, our Janet, gown flowing behind her, ample breasts and cleavage out front. She picks up the tin pail, not taking her eyes off the group.

Now I am wondering how she knows which keys gets handed to which bloke. She must have some system. She marches down the line, handing out the keys, the guys dutifully leaving the room. I am third last and I guess the guy at the end is the one for Janet.

I take my key and get up, walking to the elevator, Room 314. Well, I know it's not Donna or Janet. It had better not be Deb.

I put the key in to the door and turn the handle. Inside, she is seated at the table facing the door, upright, with her right knee over her left, a drink in hand. She stands and walks to the door, closing it behind me, and hands me a drink.

I note she is slim, no higher than five foot four, short, dark hair, eyes and cheeks made up. Taking a sip, Canadian Club and Coke, I am trying to remember her name.

She walks back to the chair and looks for something on her bag. She pulls out a blonde wig and gives me a questioning look. I nod. She arranges it on her head, adjusting it, looking in the mirror. Then, she pulls out a lipstick applying it, cherry red. Her dress is strapless, tight across small breasts, a split up the side, stockinged legs with high heels. She is going for the Marilyn Monroe look, minus the big tits and arse, but close.

She comes back to me, eyes on mine, I chug down some more CC and Coke. She unbuttons my shirt slowly, rubbing her hands over my chest. The hot weather and high physical workload have left me pretty fit and she appreciates the muscles on my stomach, undoing my belt.

She starts singing 'Happy birthday' in the girlie Marilyn voice. 'Happy Birthday to you,' the zip comes down and the button is undone.

'Happy Birthday to you.'

'Happy Birthday, Mr President,' her hand groping around.

'Happy birthday to you,' she has her hands on me and I involuntarily thrust. She takes the hand away and waves a finger at me like I have been a naughty boy.

She goes to the bed, lying back, motioning me to join her. The dress has ridden up, I can see the tops of her stockings and the white flesh above. Her arms welcome me and we embrace strongly. She pulls my mouth to her neck and sighs, then suddenly pushing me back down onto the bed.

It takes several minutes for our breathing to return to normal. She lays back, pulls the wig off, then gets to her feet. The wig goes into the bag and she sits in front of the mirror adjusting the makeup.

'What would you like to do next?' she asks. 'We can do the Cat Woman and Batman thing if you like,' she says matter-of-factly, adjusting her makeup some more.

'Or, we can do Samantha from Bewitched, or Mrs Brady. They are dirty girls, particularly Mrs Brady. She likes Greg giving it to her bent over the table. Or, you can come back tomorrow and my friend and I will do a Marcia and Jan Brady act for you.' I am actually intrigued as to what the Cat Woman and Batman thing might entail.

'Okay, can we do the Batman thing?'

She scrummages around in the bag again looking for something else. A dark wig appears this time and she spends some time adjusting it and the makeup. She is intent and it seems the look has to be just right.

She pulls out an outfit and disappears into the bathroom. I grab a beer from the fridge and settle in; this is intriguing. Several minutes pass and the door opens. She is in a black jumpsuit complete with cat's ears and a mask, and zips in unexpected places. She looks more like Cat Woman than Cat Woman. Now, I am also wondering what Mrs Brady might look like.

She goes to the bag again and a Batman mask and cape appear. 'Here, put this on.'

Saturday morning, Donna and I check out early and head back to the Hostie. Her old man is having a party at their house and she has to help her mum with the cooking. We are in a hurry.

'So, who is the chick that dresses up?'

'Mandy? Did Janet set you up with Mandy?'

'Is she the one that does the Cat Woman and Batman thing?'

'That's Mandy. Apparently, she is really talented. Used to be on TV in Perth; *Romper Room*, I think.'

'She certainly gives *Romper Room* and the *Brady Bunch* a whole new feel.'

'You sound like you enjoyed it all.' A pause before she drops the bombshell. 'I have been thinking about going back to Australia, Tim.'

I look at her a little stunned, 'Yer? I thought you liked it here?'

'I do. But, being with you has made me realise I should be at home, get a job, live life normally. Maria had the right idea. Here, it's like some sort of colonial zoo for alcoholics and sex maniacs.'

No, not much normal about it, for sure.

Mid-June, the working routine isn't overly taxing. The Rugby League season has finished and so there's no training through the week, the Rugby Union season won't start for another month or so. I am servicing gun packs, writing the odd letter home, and doing a little work on Scarecrow's boat in the evenings.

Most nights, I leave the Boatie, grab a Char Keow Teow from Dragon Temple Lane and take Gus for a few dollars playing poker. He never learns; each time he has a good hand his hands tremble slightly and I just throw in. I reckon I have taken him for twenty bucks over the last week.

Every now and again Andy joins us. He's taken up drinking Cappoes in a big way — not sure what is going on there, but he has got this great party trick. He can get his jocks off, while still wearing his shorts, and playing cards, and no one is much the wiser. He then pulls his jocks over his head with his ears sticking out of the leg holes. He calls it the 'Russian Cosmonaut' manoeuvre.

The boys are bored.

Friday afternoon, we knock off around 1500 and head for the Boatie. It's a popular choice, half of 75 Squadron and 3 Squadron are there, wall to wall RAAFies, most of the Baggers in drab uniform. Tiny has the boys corralled out the front delivering a briefing on the end-of-season footy trip.

'Listen up, lads, and we will get this over with quickly. The flight to Bangkok is leaving Bayan Lepas at 1330 tomorrow. We will meet at Sumie's on Beach Street at 1000 for pre-departure drinks and then form groups into taxies to the airport. Please make sure you are all checked in by 1230.' There is a fair amount of chatter about these arrangements and Tiny sticks two finger into his mouth and whistles loudly, and they all shut up.

'I will be the sheriff for this trip and Andy is the deputy,' Andy stands and waves like he is the Queen. A piece of fruit passes his head and he ducks. 'I am not sure whether that was a good idea, the sheriff and his trusted deputy can make your life difficult on a footy trip.'

'Okay, okay, here are the starting rules.' He pauses for effect.

'Rule 1   the Sherriff has absolute discretion,

Rule 2   no touching females,

Rule 3   no entering or leaving a premises before the Sheriff

Rule 4 '.   Tiny pauses and looks up.

The whole crowd joins in.

'No poofters!'

'Rule 5   no eating without permission; eatin's cheaten,

Rule 6   if there is any doubt, refer to Rule 1,

Rule 7.'

He stops again and the crowd responds.

'No poofters.

'Okay, Davo has your shirts over there. Remember, you must be in your shirt at all times.'

I am only a spectator and made up some bullshit story about being broke. Truth be known, it's Donna's last weekend and I am going to enjoy some time with her, rather than drink myself into a stupor for three days and bounce a Thai girl around the bed.

Saturday morning, I am up and dressed by nine.

'I'll go and pick Nev up. You guys get ready and I'll get you on the way back.'

Nev is chatty. I reckon he gets excited at the thought of getting laid. Like me, Nev doesn't use the services offered in the Traps on Penang, he prefers the Thai girls, and by all reports, they just love him. It's funny how girls of all nationalities love the cute, little black fella. He does have a certain charm about him, that and a concealed weapon.

'Sure you won't change your mind, Dougie? There's still time to buy a ticket.'

'No, mate, I am working on Crowy's boat; going to get the heads back on the engine today and see if it'll start. All going well, we'll put it into the water tomorrow.'

He shakes his head. 'Are you sane, Dougie? You'd prefer to work on Crowy's boat than play bedroom gymnastics with a pretty little Thai princess?'

I don't know what it is but I feel the need to brag a little. 'I've got a little more on than just the heads on a boat engine,' there is a hint of adventure in my voice.

'No secrets here, Dougie. Are you bumping some Bagger's wife?' I give him a quick look of contempt.

'Fuck off, Nev, you know I'm not like that.' I let him wait a little while. 'You know Squadron Leader Gibson?' The look on his face is gold.

'Donna Gibson? Dougie, you sly dog, you. She's a good sort.' He stops and thinks for a tick. 'She doesn't even acknowledge our existence. How did you land her?'

'It's a long story.'

Around nine-thirty, I drop Gus, Andy and Nev at the ferry and point the Morris towards the Boat Club, parking out the front of the boat shed. Crowy has already unlocked and we get to work. He cooked the engine water skiing up at Muda River a couple of weeks ago. John Bong at Peria machined the heads and he managed to get a mate in Australia to send him the gaskets. It's not easy to get Holden 308 parts around here. Around three, everything is hooked up, a new battery in place, we push the boat out of the shed and connected the hose. We have attracted a crowd.

It's one of those unwritten laws of RAAF life. Whenever someone is working on something mechanical, there are at least three people watching and giving advice. Lefty reckons if you were lost in the middle of the Sahara Desert, all you have to do is put a spanner on the engine and three people will turn up to give advice. I have tested the theory a couple of times and the ratio is fairly constant. They generally arrive with a *stubbie* in hand.

I turn the key and the engine turns over quickly, giving Crowy enough time to turn the distributor cap slightly — nothing. We try a couple more times.

'What firing order did you use?'

'1-2-7-8-5-6-3-4,' replies Crowy, slightly annoyed.

'Holdens are 1-2-7-8-4-5-6-3,' one of our learned supervisors informs us. Crowy swaps the leads around, the arrangement looks more orderly.

'Hit it, Dougie.'

The engine fires almost straightaway and he fiddles with the dizzy cap getting it running smoothly before tightening it down. The timing light comes out and he makes some fine adjustments. After a few minutes, the temperature comes up and it's idling okay.

'What do you have on the Tacho, Dougie?'

'Twelve hundred.' He starts fiddling with the carbie and it almost stalls.

'Eight hundred, nine hundred.'

He sits back admiring his work, the engine ticking along. With the world a safer place, our audience wanders off.

'Time for a beer, Dougie.'

We sit around for a while, check the tides for tomorrow and discuss a plan. If everything goes well, we'll take the boat to the Springtide Hotel for a beer and seafood. Around five, Squadron Leader Gibson's entourage arrives. It's a fair crowd, many of the blokes are pilots and large group of women, Donna being the guest of honour.

I am about to finish my beer and make myself scarce when she comes over. There is even a peck on the check.

A public show of affection. Now, that's a surprise.

I apologise for being so grubby.

'That's okay, what have you been up to?'

'Just helping a mate fix his boat. We will put it in the water tomorrow. Big night?' I look over at the building crowd.

'Mum invited every busybody in the married patch,' she harrumphs. 'I was happy enough to just have dinner with her and dad, but she wanted to be the centre of attention. Are you going to join us?' she asks, with a cheeky smile.

'I'm hardly dressed for the occasion.'

'Can you go home and get changed? I would really like you to have dinner with us.'

It takes me three-quarters of an hour to get home, shower and change, long trousers and a Hawaiian shirt. I decide to take the bike back, it's quicker than driving the old Morrie.

When I get back, she waves from the centre of a long table of people, pointing, a spare chair beside her. I get a beer and sit down. Plenty of eyes on me.

This will be all over the Base by Monday. I'd better prepare for the interrogation at work.

'Tim, this is my mum, Maureen.'

'Nice to meet you, ma'am,' I nod towards her.

She nods back. It's not an inviting face.

'You know dad.'

'Sir.'

'Hello, Dougie,' he has a happy smile on his face. 'I see you and David have Fishtail ready to go back in the water. It must have been a big job?'

'Yes, sir, we got the heads on this morning and the carbie and water pump weren't too much trouble. We had it running really well.' Mrs Gibson doesn't look too impressed at the easy conversation between us.

The young Chinese bloke from the kitchen arrives at Squadron Leader Gibson's shoulder and he stands. He taps the side of his *stubbie* with a spoon and the chatter dies down.

'Ahem, ladies and gentlemen, maybe more of the ladies than the genteel men in the house,' he has a little chuckle to himself and everyone else chortles in response. 'We are here to farewell our daughter, Donna, who is heading back to Australia to further her career as a psychologist.' One of the ladies next to Donna's mum claps and everyone joins. He waits for the clapping to subside.

'I am sure Donna doesn't want too much fuss and so I am going to propose a toast now and draw a close to any formalities. Please raise your glasses. To Donna, may your journey into the medical world be long and fruitful.' We all take a swig from our drinks.

'Now, Johnnie is here to take your orders and there is a tab at the bar. Please enjoy Donna's farewell.'

It's a great night, with many of the older pilots delighting the crowd with flying stories from previous postings to Butterworth, their wives tempering the hilarity with anecdotes of what really happened. Donna has her knee pressed against mine all night and a memory of Louise flashes through my mind.

Around nine, everyone starts to disperse, a long line of women and young fighter pilots wanting to offer a farewell kiss. I wait patiently. After the masses have gone, Donna's mum stands and extends her hand.

'Lovely to meet you, Tim.'

'Mrs Gibson,' I say, shaking her hand. She looks like she is happy to see the back of me. Squadron Leader Gibson gives me a strong handshake murmuring something about seeing me tomorrow if he has his jobs done. Donna goes to her mother and kisses her on the check.

'Good night, mum.' A look of sudden shock comes across Maureen's face.

'You're not coming home?'

'No, mum, Tim and I are going to have a few more drinks.'

If looks could kill.

She goes to her father and there is a warm hold. He kisses her on the forehead. My guess is Donna is Daddy's girl.

Donna and I stay till close, drinking cocktails. Anything Pete can make, we drink, anything. Tequila Slammers, Harvey Wall Bangers, Gin and Tonics, everything. RAAF Radio Butterworth is on the loud speakers. Donna knows the DJ and she calls several times requesting songs, and he obliges: The Angels, Eagles, Michael Jackson, and Aussie Crawl.

After Pete kicks us out, I give her the helmet and fire up the bike. She hitches her dress up and gets on the back. I have to rev it pretty hard to get the little Suzuki to take off under the load. She is still singing, and swaying as she does, making it hard for me to keep control of the bike on the run up to the main road.

The highway is mostly empty at this time of night and we weave from one side of the road to the other as she sings, hands extended, almost flying, 'I am woman, W-O-M-A-N.' When we get to Bagan Ajam, it is upstairs quickly, make love and sleep.

I wake around seven, head throbbing and mouth dry. Looking around I realise there is someone else in my bed and she is sleeping soundly. Then I remember the night and a smile comes to me. It's really nice having been out with someone I like, and then come home to sleep together. I have a warm feeling in my belly.

Wandering downstairs, I try to keep the noise to a minimum, grab two Cokes, pop the tops off, and head back. Sitting back on my side of the bed, I give her a nudge. There is an awakening before consciousness.

'Fuck off and come back in two hours.'

'Here, drink this,' I offer a bottle of Coke.

She grumbles but gathers herself and sits up, hair a mess. I am looking at her uncovered breasts. She grabs the bottle and downs a half, handing it back and collapsing again. I sit the bottle on her bedside table and lie down. She snuggles in.

Two hours later, I show her to the shower and give her a fresh towel, while I go downstairs and get a cup of tea together, leaving hers on the side of the bath, and then sit outside in the last of the morning cool. She joins me a little later, throwing her arms around me from behind.

'Need another cuppa?'

'No, thanks.' I can feel her surveying the scene. Jalan Intan at ten in the morning, not yet hot, and most people either in Bangkok or sleeping. She walks down the short driveway to the street, dressed in one of my drab uniform shirts and nothing else.

You don't see that every day.

'This is such a nice place, Tim. I can see Penang, the palm trees, and it's quiet. You single guys really have this sorted out.' She leans against the gate, and I have an overwhelming feeling of contentment.

'I promised Crowy I would help him put the boat in at midday,' I say, looking at my watch. She doesn't look in a hurry to go anywhere. 'Have you ever been to the Spring Tide Hotel?'

We decide to take the Morris to the Boatie, via her parents' house to pick up some swimmers. Crowy is waiting, itchy-footed to get going. I look at the tide and it's just high enough to get the boat in.

'Get the fuel, Dougie.'

Ten minutes later we are doing a mach run-up along the beach, the V8 doing away with the Sunday slumber. Tacho would be proud. Crowy is checking the engine for anything loose and any fuel leaks and oil pressure. Thumbs up.

By one o'clock, we are ensconced at the Springtide drinking beer and eating prawns with Donna and Crowy's missus, Sharon. The girls are busy discussing some sort of social group they belong to, who the dominant women are, and who are the leaders. Apparently, the two things are not the same.

It's a nice feeling to have female company; it's almost calming.

Could I live with Donna full time? Maybe?

It wouldn't be a good idea to have a female in amongst all the single guys I live with. It would cause all sorts of problems.

Could you imagine what it would be like if we all had live-in girlfriends? Now, that would end in tears. What if we were married? Now you are talking shit, Dougie.

'We'd better get going,' Crowy announces. 'We'll miss the

tide if we don't.'

Donna gets to drive the boat back to the mainland and supervises while we winch the boat back onto the hardstand in front of the shed and then hose it down. We get a couple more drinks in before climbing back into the Morris.

'So, what's your plans for tonight?' she enquires.

'We usually have dinner at Dragon Temple Lane, but nearly everyone is in Bangkok. It would be just the two of us.' She smiles.

'I like the sound of that. Drop me at home, I'll shower and see you there.'

It's a wonderful evening, great food, cold beer, and silly chat. We go back to my place and put some music on, singing into our stubbies. She leaves around midnight.

'See you tomorrow afternoon.'

Monday morning, the questions start five seconds after I walk in the door.

'The missus said you were out with Squadron Leader Gibson's daughter on Saturday night, Dougie?'

'Maybe.'

'She's a tidy little number. Does she go off?'

Some of these pricks have nothing better to do.

Tuesday night, I decide to cook dinner and get a fresh chook from BGS. She is leaving on the charter tomorrow and I think it will be nice for us to spend time together. She doesn't arrive till after seven.

'Mum and dad have been fussing,' she tells me, 'and there was nearly a full-scale war when I said I was going out, sorry,' kissing me full on the mouth.

The dinner is hardly gourmet stuff, but it's edible and I found a bottle of Mateus to go with it. She doesn't seem to mind and in fact gets a bit sentimental.

'You know what, Tim, I have really enjoyed these last couple of days. It's just like having a boyfriend back home, going out together, having dinner. Why didn't we just do this from the start?'

Mid-July, the monsoon has started. There is usually early morning rain and clear, hot, days. There are a couple of new guys coming in on the charter and Nev, Gus and I are at air movements to greet them, a dozen stubbies in the bag on ice. The 707 taxies in and stops, the power cart is attached, engines shut down, and stairs are put in place. A line of blue uniforms, spouses, and kids, start down the stairs and across the tarmac. We are looking out for our new work mates when I see her.

'Fuck,' I say, ducking out of sight. Nev and Gus are looking at me strangely.

'What's up, Dougie?' asks Gus. I am stooped behind him so she can't see me.

'Remember the year before last when I said one of the Screws at Williamtown had taken a liking to me?' I remind them. They nod. 'Well, it's her.'

'Not bad, Dougie,' Gus says, looking her up and down. 'A little old, but bloody hot,' he says, with a grin.,

'She's not hot, mate. She's a fuckin' animal, not quite right in the head. I'll see you guys at the Boatie,' I say, slinking off before I am noticed.

Over the following weeks, I manage to stay clear of her. The odd time she comes into the Boatie, I manage to slip out without being seen. It's not like I don't want to talk to her, but I am wary of falling under her spell again.

My luck runs out Tuesday night in the first week of August. I am on lock-up duties at the Boatie and it's a quiet night. I tell the barman he can go home and serve the last few customers myself. She comes in around nine, standing at the bar in blue uniform and a gorgeous smile.

'Can I get you something, Sarge?' I say, trying to be as unconnected as I can. Her tongue touches her lips before she replies.

'I'll think about that, Tim. In the meantime, can I have a Lemon, Lime, and Bitters, please?' she says, taking a stool. 'How's life treating you, Tim?'

'Very well, thanks, Helen. What brings you to Butterworth?'

'Just a little relief manning for three months. One of the guys here has taken long service leave. I had to beg them to let me come. It's not RAAF policy to post enlisted women overseas, even officers. It's usually only the nursing sisters who are exempt. They made a special dispensation for this one time,' she is smiling at me smugly, 'and I thought there might be some fringe benefits.'

I am remaining silent. Saying anything could be twisted to suit her agenda.

'What time do you close, Tim? I have some new toys I am just busting to try out.'

I stay silent, unpacking the glasses from the dishwasher.

'Oh, playing that game again, are we, Tim?' She still has the evil smile on her face. 'I don't suppose your friends know about the tip-off on the petrol scam?' She pauses. 'Tim the rat. Ratting on his mates.'

'You wouldn't stoop that low, Helen?' I glare at her.

'Tim, I would do anything for a little taste of that hot body of yours,' the smile has not gone.

What the fuck am I going to do here. The boys would not be impressed if they knew I was an informant for the Screws. I would be treated like a leper, may as well apply for a discharge. And, having sex is one thing, even a bit of S and M would be okay, but it's the control she gets over me I am wary of. I'll just end up being her little puppet again.

Three months?

I am silently pondering whether to just go with it for three months, but she breaks first.

'Okay, Tim, I will make a deal with you,' she goes on. 'I won't blab about the petrol tip-off, and you do two things for me.'

'Depends what they are?' I am willing to consider almost anything to stay out of her spell, but keep a straight face.

'First, I need a little information,' she says, lowering her voice. 'We are investigating a drug ring working out of the Base at Edinburgh in South Australia. They are importing the stuff from Asia and we are pretty sure the shipments are coming in on a P3. We've had dogs through the aircraft after they land but can't find anything. I don't need you to rat on anyone, just make some discreet enquiries with your mates at 492 Squadron. How could they get the drugs in?'

I am thinking this is too easy. 'Second thing?' I ask.

'It's been sometime between drinks, Tim, and a girl has needs, as you well know. If you aren't up to it, find me someone who is.' Her smile has gotten bigger. 'And, someone who knows how to keep their mouth shut, unless I tell them otherwise,' she adds.

'Did you look in the Bomb Bay and the Sonobuoy Launch

Tubes?' I ask her, while still thinking about who might be the best candidate to try to satisfy her.

'Sorry?' the smile is gone. She is all business now.

'A P3 has a bomb bay, they usually put a panier in there for the trip back to Edinburgh. There are also forty-eight external tubes for Sonobuoys. Anyone who knows what they are doing could hide stuff in the bomb bay, inside the panier, or in a Sonobuoy Launch Tube.' I tell her. She has her notebook out, busily scribbling.

'What is a panier?' she asks with all attention on me.

'On a motorbike, they are the bags bolted either side of the seat for carrying shit. On a Mirage, we have a fuel tank converted for carrying things. It has access panels on the side. When we need to shift spares to Singapore urgently, we will use the panier and fly a jet down there. On a P3, it's like a big flat basket with bomb lugs they load to the Bomb Bay. The crew pack their luggage in it. If I were trying to smuggle something, it would go somewhere inside the bomb bay, concealed inside the panier, or inside a Sonobuoy Launch Tube.'

She finishes her notes. 'How do you know this stuff?'

'Dave Nixon is off my Gunnies course. He is up here for six weeks and showed me around a P3 the other day. Do you want to meet him?'

'You bet. This is gold, Tim. Are you sure I can't reward you in some way?' She has that little smile again.

'I will be just fine, but thank you, Helen, though you might get some joy with Nicko. He doesn't mind asking Thai girls to dress up in a school uniform. If you are here Thursday night for the chook run, I will introduce you.'

'I'll be here,' she says, getting up and gathering her bag. 'Oh, I got you something.' She says pulling a small, flat, plastic container from her bag handing it over the counter. 'I know how much you like your music. This is a compact disc. It's the newest thing. Soon, vinyl records will be obsolete.'

I look at the cover. *Midnight Oil, 10, 9, 8, 7, 6, 5, 4, 3, 2, 1.* I have heard about this. Apparently, a good album. Fuck knows how I am going to play it.

'Thank you, Helen, that is kind.'

Sometimes she is surprisingly caring and considerate.

'You sure you don't want to see and perhaps partake of my other presents?' She has one last try. I just give her a smile and then she is gone. I have to admit the sex offer was tempting. She certainly knows how to test the boundaries of lust. Though, from where I stand it's a long way from love, and that fact alone makes it something I can resist … most of the time.

Thursday night the Boatie is full. Pay night and plenty of families out for drinks, rug rats running everywhere. I am selling bats when she walks in, hair back in a bun, makeup with purple lipstick, wearing a sun dress. Every male eye in the place follows her across the room. She greets me with a peck on the lips and a hug.

'Hi, Helen, how is your week going?' I ask, casually.

'Making good progress thank you very much, Tim.' I direct her to our table.

'Helen, this is Nev, Gus, Doc, and Dave.' She greets each one and pulls in close to Nicko, engaging him in conversation straightaway. As I go around selling the next round of bats, I get several enquiries.

'Where do you know her from, Dougie?' Benny Martin asks me.

'She was at Williamtown when I was there, an elephant tracker. I think she tried to charge me for speeding once but took pity on me. Up here for three months on relief manning.' I maintain her story. She doesn't waste any time and leaves with Nicko at about eight-thirty. He's at the Boatie the following afternoon looking bleary-eyed.

'How was your day, Nicko?'

'Mate, that friend of yours, Helen, she a nympho, mate. Kept me up all night, literally.' I smile at him.

'Shit, mate, I didn't know. Always struck me as a little frigid,' I tell him, killing myself laughing on the inside.

Wait till she introduces the riding crop and handcuffs.

Two weeks later, they are at the chook run again. He hasn't said anything further to me about Helen and I suspect she's taken him to the next step. He is attentive, getting her drinks, and ordering her food. She has him eating out of her hand, almost literally. I catch her coming back from the ladies' room.

'How's the investigation going?' I ask.

'The people in Adelaide say you are right. The stuff is in Sonobuoy Launch Tubes. They have some guys under surveillance down there, but we don't know who it is on this end. There are only about ten permanent 92 Wing staff here and it has to be one of them. Just not sure who.'

'Oh, well, let me know if you need any more information,' I offer. 'How's Nicko working out?'

'He's coming along well, thanks, Tim, but I am afraid he's going back to Australia on Tuesday. I am going to make sure this weekend is special.' My mind briefly flicks back to my 'birthday present' two years ago. That was something special. 'You sure you don't want to join us?' While there is a brief stirring in my groin, the sexual benefits don't match the consequences.

'Na, you guys enjoy yourselves. Need a drink?' I ask her, heading to the bar.

Thursday, she comes into the Boatie with some of the other live-in sergeants, looking a little forlorn.

'Cheer up, Helen,' Nev encourages her. You'll be back in Australia in a month or two. You can go down to Adelaide to see him.'

It strikes me I have never seen Helen get emotionally attached to anyone before. She is clearly upset Nicko has gone home. There is a first time for everything. Perhaps the ice block that is her heart has started to melt in the Malaysian sun. I wait for a quiet moment alone and ask her about the investigation.

'There are two real possibilities,' she starts. There is a warrant officer, techo and corporal box packer Hill, and Saunders. They are the only ones with enough access to the aircraft to stash the goods. Still not sure how they are getting things past the techoes who rotate up here from Adelaide and do all the aircraft maintenance work; unless some of them are in on it?'

'What about aircrew?'

'Checked them all out. There's no common denominator, unless a whole bunch of them are in on it?'

'I know this Saunders guy,' I tell her. 'He comes in here sometimes with his missus. He's a weaselly-looking bloke who keeps to himself and doesn't have much to say. The missus looks like she could haunt houses. They are a great pair.' Normally this would prompt a comment on the couple's sexual preferences, but she is deep in thought.

'I gotta work out whether it's him or not. Can't just drag him in and interrogate him without some decent evidence, or it'll just tip him off and he'll shut things down until we lose interest.'

'Never stopped you with me.'

'That's a very different interrogation technique, Tim,' she smiles.

Sunday morning, the humidity didn't subside through the night; it's sticky, and I can't sleep in. The boys are snoring their heads off and I decide to get out and take a ride on the bike. The roads are quiet and I make it to Sungie Patani in three-quarters of an hour, find a café, and order a Roti Canai and a hot Milo. It was my twentieth birthday last Wednesday. It seems I am now bordering on becoming an old fart.

I am feeling a little philosophical. Life has been an interesting journey so far, growing up in the country on a dairy farm, joining the RAAF, and now I am sitting in a foreign country drinking ultra-sweet Milo and eating fried bread with curry juice for breakfast.

I haven't heard from Liz since February and a swell of despair washes over me. I really had thought I might have met the right girl. I shake my head in regret. I wish it had worked out differently.

I am having a great time in Malaysia, but it's a bit of a lonely existence. The rest of the boys make regular conjugal visits to Thailand, but there is something not right about it for me. Maybe it's the paying for it. Gran would be distraught if she knew I had paid for a hooker. Even Donna has gone home. Twenty years old, in a foreign country, and unable to truly connect with anyone of the fairer sex.

I'd better shake myself out of this state. I think I'll head home and see whether the boys have woken up. Being lost in my own thoughts is obviously not what I need right now.

Back on the bike, I get it wound up back down the highway through the rice paddies. As I come past Robina Park, a yellow Mazda 616 comes hurtling onto the highway at speed. Its urgency sticks out a little in the sleepy Sunday morning traffic. As I get closer, I can tell it's a RAAFie at the wheel, Saunders.

I drop back a little to try to be less obvious. He turns into the main gate and I follow him, right towards the cinema, then left towards the flight line. I am a fair way behind, hoping to avoid raising his interest. He's gone down towards Fire Section, so I park at 3 Squadron Headquarters and walk onto the tarmac near 75 Squadron Gunnies Section.

Where did he go now?

I poke my head around the corner of the hangar. The Mazda is outside the 92 Wing Maintenance section with the boot lid up, I wait, keeping myself out of view. He appears a few minutes later with two Sonobuoy Launch Tubes, throws them into the boot and closes it. He climbs into the driver's seat and starts the car.

I make sure he is clear of the area before I get on the bike and head after him. As I come up past the Engine Repair section, I look up towards Air Movements and see the car disappear around the corner, heading for South Gate. I catch up to him on the highway before we get to NAAFI.

Has he seen me?

He takes the road down through Butterworth to the ferry

while I follow at a discreet distance. I line up in the bike lane while keeping an eye on his car. They load the ferry and I get onto the cluster of bikes at the back end. I leave my helmet on to disguise my presence a little. He stays in the car. I can see the storm clouds building on Penang.

I am going to get a wet arse.

Off the ferry, he heads left toward the jetties, then right onto Magazine Road, then left again. I am trying to stay back but not too far back, I might lose him, and I can't push the bike too hard as it has just started to rain cats and dogs. He turns right again, and I get caught by oncoming traffic. I can see him turn left again. By the time I get there, there is no sign of the Mazda.

Where did he go?

The Mazda turned in here, but now I can't see it anywhere. The rain does not help my vision. There is a square with shops surrounding a small park. I do a slow lap. Nothing.

Where did he go?

I pull up, step off the bike and get under the veranda of a closed electrical business to get out of the rain for a moment. I light a smoke and consider the situation.

Where did he go?

I can't see anything. Looking about, not even the locals and the Kampong dogs are venturing out. Something is not right.

Fuck, this isn't a good place to be.

I decide my little dabble in the investigation business is up. I'll let Helen sort this out.

I throw the cigarette butt in the monsoon drain, pull my helmet and sunglasses on, and step out into the rain. The bike fires up first kick and I tap it into gear, cautiously accelerating. The traffic is light, but the slick road is challenging.

Turning out the square, I pull the throttle open, looking around at the weather to gauge how wet I am going to get. When I look back to my front, the Mazda is stopped in front of me. I have just enough speed to make this a really shit situation.

It's really funny how, when things go to shit, the world seems to slow down and it all happens in slow motion. You can't stop it, you can't change it, but it's in slow motion.

The Mazda is in front of me, it's pissing down, and I am on a bike that handles like a cake of Palmolive Gold in the shower. I decide to lay it over rather than impacting directly and going over the top. As the bike hits its side, my arse hits the bitumen and I can feel my jeans ripping. There is no pain, just jeans tearing and skin scraping along on the gravel. It's going to leave a mark. The bike starts to slip from my reach.

It hits the side of the car first and stops, my left leg still under it, and then I come to an abrupt stop against the bike, feeling my left leg literally shatter under the forces. All movement stops and there is no pain, but I am stuck with my left leg jammed under the bike, which is wedged under the side of the Mazda. I put my head back and rest a tick trying to gather my senses.

'Fuck,' the pain starts and grows quickly. I take my helmet and sunglasses off and throw them backward, the rain now hitting my face hard.

I hear the driver's door close and footsteps splashing in the water. He comes around the front of the car with something in his hands.

'Who sent you?' he yells at me.

I just look back at him through the rain. I have no answer.

'Who the fuck sent you?' he yells at me harder. 'Was it Cheng?' he yells.

I have no idea what he means and just look back at him bewildered, the pain in my leg is ramping up by the second. It is when he lifts his hands, a softball bat held firm. He swings hard and drives it into my side. The strike sends a sharp pain down my side into my pelvis. I am helpless to evade him or defend myself, and it seems this is not over by half.

'You don't know what you got yourself into, young fella. Tell me who sent you?' and he hits me in the ribs twice more. I am trying to get my arm between my ribs and the bat. I think he might have already broken a rib or two.

'I don't have time to fuck around with idiots here. Tell me now, or we are going to make this ugly.' He taps the bat against the side of my head. 'Last chance, sonny. Tell me who sent you or we introduce you to the world of drooling spastics,' he says, tapping the side of my head with the bat again.

I am shaking my head, trying to speak, but the words won't come. I have no idea what he is talking about. He raises the bat ready to strike.

'Last chance, sonny. Talk now.'

I can see the muscles in his arm flex as he starts to swing. Suddenly, a fist comes from nowhere and hits him in the side of the head. He goes down like a rag doll, out cold. I look sideways and see the bald Chinese guy from Singapore. He picks up Saunders by the collar and hits him again, square in the jaw. He is definitely out for the count. The Chinese guy picks up the bat, looks at it, then at me. He leans over me.

'You are okay now?' he says, in a very British voice. 'The local constabulary will be here in a moment. I'll call the RAAF police and ambulance.' He drops the bat and walks off into the rain.

I just lie there and wait. At some point it all goes dark.

Epilogue

I don't know how long I was out, but when I come to, the Malaysian Police are there and an ambulance turns up not long after. The cops have cuffed Saunders and he has regained consciousness, face down on the road struggling to breathe above the water on the ground. The cops don't seem too worried about his predicament.

The ambulance guys have put a drip in my arm and I am not feeling much pain. They start to unpack me from underneath the bike and car. During the process, the RAAF ambulance and doctor arrive and it's all I remember for a few hours.

I wake about 1600 and Helen is by the bed. She gets up promptly when she realises I am awake.

'You silly bastard, Tim, you nearly got yourself killed.' I look down at my legs under the sheet.

'How bad is it?'

'Multiple fractures, Tim,' she has a grim look on her face. 'They'll have to send you to Singapore for surgery.'

'How's my dancing career looking?'

'You'll be fine, Fred Astaire, but it'll probably be a lengthy recovery.' I laugh and bolt of pain shoots through my chest from the right side.

'Oh, shit, it hurts,' and she is off in search of a doctor.

In the next few hours, they x-ray every bone in my body and plaster the leg. A Chinese doctor comes in and informs me

I have multiple fractures to the left leg, and two broken ribs on my right side.

Around 2000 hours, two Aussie Medical Orderlies appear and pack me up into the back of a RAAF Ambulance. I am tucked up in bed at 4 RAAF Hospital by 2100 hours. I know I am fairly well sedated because I don't feel too much pain, just a little discomfort, and I am feeling pretty happy.

Monday morning, the procession starts. First, it's a doctor to check my condition and give instructions to the nurses, then it's the ARMO and Bomber, followed by Helen. She is extremely apologetic and fussing over me.

Our Commanding Officer, Wing Commander Reynolds, drops by about 1130 and makes a commotion about me being an important cog in a large machine. Over lunch, Nev and Andy come past and tell a few inane jokes to cheer me up.

I am just nodding off for an afternoon nap when a Squadron Leader appears at my door. He's dressed in drabs, carrying a slouch hat, and wears a string of medals. I recognise the Vietnam Medals, but not the others.

'Hi, Tim, I am Squadron Leader Taylor.' He holds out his hand and we shake. 'Had a little accident?' he is looking down at my leg.

'Yes, sir, a motor bike accident.'

'Indeed, can you tell me anything about it?'

I must look pretty reluctant to talk and so he pulls out a RAAF Police badge and shows me.

'It's okay, Tim, I have most of the details from Sergeant Bryant already. I just need you to fill in some of the things we don't know. How did you end up following Saunders?'

'Oh, that was just by chance. I went for a ride yesterday morning and was coming back past Robina Park when I saw his Mazda pull out. I just followed him on a hunch.'

'You followed him all the way to Penang. That's more than a hunch?'

'Eventually, yes. At first it was just to the Base. He went down to the 92 Wing Maintenance Section and threw a couple of Sonobuoy Launch Tubes into his boot. I followed him from there.'

'That was a little silly, Tim.'

'It just seemed the right thing to do. Helen, I mean Sergeant Bryant, told me he was one of the suspects.'

'Yes, she told me about the information you provided already. That was excellent, thanks Tim.' He looks like he is pressing me for something, and I can't work out what it is.

'How did you end up under his car?'

I am thinking back to yesterday, the ferry trip and following him through the back streets. I remember having a smoke. He is watching me process.

'We came off the ferry and I chased; well, followed him through some back streets. He didn't see me, at least I think he didn't, and then I lost him.'

'Go on.'

'It was raining and I stopped for a smoke to get my head clear. That's when I decided it wasn't a smart place to be. I was just leaving when the Mazda appeared out of nowhere and I had to drop the bike to stop from t-boning him.'

The memory starts to come back to me now — the impact, I can hear him walking around the car, and the rain, then the softball bat hitting me. I recount the story.

'When the local police arrived, Saunders was out cold on the ground. Was there anyone else there?'

I look at him again wondering how much I should say. I am working out whether to mention the previous time I have seen the Chinese guy. I opt for leaving it out.

'Some big, Chinese guy, with no hair, just appeared out of nowhere and hit Saunders. He knocked him out cold and then the Chinese guy gave him another to make sure. Then, the Chinese guy told me the cops would be along soon and just walked away. I remember he spoke in a posh English accent.' The Squadron Leader is nodding.

'That will be Zhao,' he tells me. 'He's a Singaporean Intelligence Officer.' I am not surprised. 'You are pretty lucky. Zhao has infiltrated the drug gang we are after. If he wasn't there, you might have ended up face down in Penang Harbour. Not a story I would want to have to tell your grandparents back in Dungog.'

That shocks me a little. I hadn't given it any thought when I started tailing Saunders. It was a bit of a lark, helping out a friend. Now, I am very much aware of how close I came to an unhappy end.

'We are a little worried about that leg of yours, Tim. We think we'll send you home to get treatment in Sydney. There is a C-130 leaving Wednesday morning, and you are booked on it.'

He gathers his belongings before looking at me sternly. 'It was just a bike accident okay, Tim?' looking at me. 'You never saw Saunders, or the Chinese guy, okay?'

'Sure.'

'Not even to your best mate, okay?'

'Yep, okay,' and then he was gone.

Who was that masked man?

Tuesday afternoon, the boys start drifting in after work, beer bags in hand, full of Anchor stubbies and ice. The nursing sister tells them to keep it quiet or she'll have to throw them out. By six, there are about twenty people on the veranda outside my room, all talking and drinking. She gives up in disgust and joins the chat. There is an Anchor stubbie label on the bag of my intravenous feed and I have a stubby discretely hidden in the sheets. It's a regular party. The boys are making jokes about my inability to control a 120-cc motorbike.

'Heaven help him if he ever gets hold of a Kwaka 900.' Gus lets me know they have picked up my bike.

'How is it?' I ask.

'Fuckin' better than you, mate!' is the response. 'We'll have it good as new for you when you get back.' I am reminded again of the value of mates.

'Oh, one more thing,' says Gus, and pulls my sunglasses out of his pocket. 'You can't go anywhere without these to hold your eyeballs in, mate.' Around eight, the Sister has had enough of them and begins dispersing the crowd.

'Aww, come on Marg, just one more?'

'Get out, you drunken idiots,' Marg tries to put on a stern face, but no one is going for it. 'Come on, you guys, this is my job. I don't try and tell you how to do yours.' There are a couple of apologies and they start picking up their stuff.

'See ya when ya get back, Dougie.'

Wednesday morning, the trip home on the C-130 starts. They have a litter set up on the starboard side of the aircraft, toward the rear. I am strapped to the litter with an intravenous feed in the arm and comfortably covered in blankets, top and bottom. There are two seats beside it, the aircraft is otherwise full of cargo pallets.

I have two companions. One is a tall, officious, Flight Lieutenant with short, dark hair, and I'm thinking if she smiled her face might crack. The other is shorter, mousy-blonde Flying Officer with her hair in a plait, and definitely a whole lot friendlier; at least she seems that way. Both are wearing flying suits, which are not exactly flattering for either of them.

After six hours spent mostly snoozing, with the odd wake-up where they seem to want to move me around for the hell of it, we land in Darwin. They offload me over the rear ramp into the ambulance and onto Medical Section. The two Sisters do a handover to one of the local Sisters and bid me good afternoon.

The next day I am woken early, washed again, dressed in fresh pyjamas, fed and wheeled into the ambulance. We meet my two companions at the back of the Herc where there is a handover and they load me onto the litter. They get everything set for take-off.

Another dreamy seven hours to Richmond with a few bumps here and there and we land in darkness. Offload, into the ambulance, and down to Medical Section.

Friday morning, it's back into the ambulance and off to Concorde Repat Hospital in Sydney. About a fifty-minute ride before we pull up and the ambulance backs into a loading bay. A stretcher comes out and two Medical Orderlies push me through the hospital arriving at Ward Seven. The sign above the door reads Orthopaedic Ward. It's all starch and the smell of bleach, people running everywhere all the time, I'm missing my happy drip.

The weekend arrives and so do the first visitors. Grandma, grandad, and Mrs Bennett turn up just before lunch on Saturday and I am feeling a little guilty as grandad has obviously left the milking to Uncle Bert.

It's been nearly a year since I have seen them and the exchange of information is hectic. They all want to know what it was like living overseas, what the food was like, what did we do after work, and did I meet any girls? Grandma makes a particular point of chastising me for riding a motor bike and hurting myself. I try repeatedly to convince her the accident wasn't my fault, but it's pointless.

The opposite passage of information describes all the local events and comings and goings in Dungog, and that the show girl was little Mandy Brighton.

'She can't possibly be old enough, can she?'

How old does it make me?

While grandma heads down to the cafeteria for a bit of lunch, I press Mrs Bennett on how Lou is going.

'She's good. She will finish her degree in May and then get assigned to a school as a student for six months. A bit like you, I suppose. They could send her anywhere. She is with Darren and he is also studying to be a teacher. His family is from Inverell, they farm beef cattle, he's nice.'

There is a part of me feeling a little jealous about it. I'm not jealous of her boyfriend, I have no right to be. I am jealous I don't have anyone special in my life, and my prospects while lying in this hospital bed are surely less than wonderful.

Grandad informs me the Rugby League Grand Final is on tomorrow; it's Manly versus Parramatta. He says Manly are the red-hot favourites as they have won the Minor Premiership, have half the Queensland team in their line-up, and they won the State of Origin series earlier in the year. However, he wouldn't underestimate the Eels — on their day they could beat anyone. Apparently, St George were narrowly beaten by Canterbury in the semis, who were then knocked out by Parramatta. Grandad reckons had they got past Canterbury, they would have beaten Parramatta, though he did have something rather unkind to say about the coach.

I flick the TV on as they leave and catch the second quarter of the VFL Grand Final at the MCG. It's all one-way traffic with Hawthorn winning by nearly a hundred points, and it's actually good to watch, but my memories of playing it briefly in Wagga remind me it's still a bloody stupid game.

Monday morning, there are a string of x-rays with lots of staying still, followed by a visit from the doctor in the afternoon, Doctor Kelly. He looks at my foot and leg from different angles, making comparisons with various x-rays, and scribbling notes. I am already getting antsy to get out of here.

'You're lucky,' announces the doctor.

Strange that I don't feel too lucky right now.

'You have two fractures to both the tibia and fibula and metatarsal fractures of the foot. The foot problem will heal without our intervention, but will need physio. The bigger problem is the leg fractures. The bones are a little displaced, which is quite serious, but the breaks are relatively clean from what we can see. I think we can use external fixation to get everything straight and a clean mend in the bones so you don't end up with a leg too much shorter than the other.' I don't have a clue what most of it means, except the shorter leg bit, and give him my dumbest look. I think he gets the idea, or would this be a good point to make him aware of my lack of medical training? He picks up one of the x-rays and points.

'Here is your foot, there are the breaks here and here, which is here and here,' he says, pointing to my foot. He picks up another x-ray. 'Here is your leg, there are the breaks here and here, which are here and here,' pointing to two points of the plaster.

'We are going to let the foot fractures heal themselves, nature will sort those out, but the leg fractures will take a little more than just a cast. There is a treatment we call external fixation where we use an external frame around the leg and fix each piece of the puzzle to the frame using special pins inserted into the bones. We'll have to operate on the leg to insert the pins.'

I am a little taken aback. I've never heard of inserting pins into bones before. There's the lack of medical training again. I just assumed they would use some sort of clamp set up for the traction.

'Pins?' I ask, getting more worried by the second.

'Yep, the pins are a special type and we can make adjustments over the weeks to make sure the leg alignment is right. We'll probably operate tomorrow, if it's okay with you?'

'Yep, the sooner the better for me. How many weeks till I'm up and around?'

'It depends. You are relatively fit and healthy, and given the clean nature of the breaks, it might be as early as eight weeks, twelve if you are unlucky.'

'Can I do the lying around at home on the lounge, or do I have to be here the whole time?'

'You have to be pretty immobile the whole time. Any bumps, or too much movement, will cause movement at the break points and delay the healing process. I would strongly recommend you stay here, in bed for the entire time.'

'The whole time?'

'You can move around a bit in a wheelchair but getting out of bed is to be strictly supervised, and not too often, maybe every second day. The nurses know how to help you in and out of bed.' I let the information sink in.

Fuck, two months in bed is a long time.

But it has got to be better than three, or worse, a leg which doesn't set right or is the wrong length. I guess I'll just have to get used to it.

'Okay, thanks doctor. I'm in your hands.'

Tuesday morning after a wash, fresh pyjamas and no breakfast, they insert another drip as they prep me for surgery. I am pretty numb to it all both physically and mentally, and the prospect of two months in bed not moving too much is weighing pretty heavy on my mind. Before I know, I am waking up in recovery with a nurse fussing about me. I am feeling no pain, but more than a little disoriented by the anaesthesia. I am becoming aware of my leg and look down to see a frame around the outside with pins which actually go into the leg. Looks like it might hurt later. A couple of hours later my leg is starting to throb and Doctor Kelly is back.

'Everything went to plan, no complications or anything unexpected. How does the leg feel?' I am relieved to hear things went as well as possible.

'It's starting to throb a bit. Is there likely to be much pain?'

'Your anaesthetic is pretty much worn off, so yes, there will be a bit of pain, which should only last a couple of days. Just keep the nurse apprised of how you are feeling and we will keep it in check. Don't be taking painkillers for the hell of it though, and for now no radical movement of the muscles in the leg, as we need to let everything settle down.'

It's the October long weekend. Friday night I am lying back watching *Kingswood Country* when the Head Nurse walks in. She is a pretty good-looking lady, probably around twenty-six or twenty-seven, dark hair, olive skin, and brown eyes; obviously of European decent.

'Your grandfather just called. Said to say 'Hello' and says to tell you he's not coming down this weekend. To quote him "too many idiots on the road".' She laughs and scurries away.

After she leaves, I briefly contemplate whether she would go out with me. I must be getting horribly lonely because my mind is fantasising about taking out every female of the species I come in contact with. And, I am in no fit state to go out with anyone.

The paper arrives on Sunday morning and I check out the Sydney Grade Cricket scores to see which of the potential Test players have got runs or taken wickets.

But it's only a side interest, the big event of the day is the race at Bathurst. It's been a bit of a tradition to watch it from start to finish and I am settling in for a long day. Peter Brock is starting from the front of the grid again. He has won the last four from five and is almost a sure thing to do it again. I am going through the paper checking where the likely challenges will come from when Tacho and Azaria walk in.

'Dougieeeee, how are you maaaattteeee?'

Boy, how good to see some familiar faces.

I look them both up and down. Tacho looks like he's grown out of his boyish body.

'Tacho, you've filled out a bit?'

'Yes, mate, been hitting the gym. I'm bench pressing 200lbs. Race started yet?' he asks, coming around the side of the bed to see the TV. 'Fuck, the first Ford on the grid is Johnson in 10th, fucking Peter Brock.' One of the nurses drops by to clean the pins forcing Tacho to cull his language, well most of it.

'Did you come down in the Interceptor?'

'No, mate, the Interceptor died,' he says, with a look of grief that you'd be forgiven for thinking his grandma died. 'I was on a run to Canberra last year, somewhere around Lake George. As it was just getting dark, I came up behind an ambulance with all his flashing lights on. He was doing 90 … problem was I was doing 120. I decided I couldn't take the chance he could read my number plate and radio the local constabulary, so I turned the lights off, kicked it down a gear and took off.'

'A little way down the road, I forgot about a rise in the road and got airborne at about 120, engine over-revved, and valves and pistons met in a way they are not designed to. I'm driving a rather nasty Bluebird Turbo now, well more like thrashing the living shit out of it. And, Dougie, you'll be happy to know they still haven't fixed the toll gates at Berowra. We went through there at ninety-five this morning, a new record.'

I look over at Azaria who is shaking his head. He gives me the 'no use getting stressed about it if you ride with Tacho' look. I know it all too well. I contemplate telling him about the Singapore Interceptor but decide against it for some reason. The nurse finishes cleaning the pins, packs up and moves on, Tacho's gaze following her and making faces like he's never seen a woman before.

'How's Mac?'

'As grumpy as ever. When we heard you were here, he mumbled something about young blokes riding around pissed and not understanding the principle of gravity. I think he was actually a little disappointed you had hurt yourself; you know what he's like. Bloody Brock's off again.'

I am not surprised. While Mac was the supreme grumpy Flight Sergeant, he looked after his boys like a father. If you made a dumb mistake, he let you know about it and forgave you. He was unforgiving of a second or third same dumb mistake, and sometimes creative with the punishment for such infringements.

'Tell him I said "Hi".'

'I will. They worked out what they are doing with you yet? Are you going back to Butterworth?'

'I haven't heard anything. All my stuff is still there and so I assume I'll get some sick leave after leaving here, then head back after Christmas.'

'Ha, Brock is in the pits with the bonnet up, bloody wanker, I hope it's terminal! The Falcons are way off the pace this year. I think I'd rather see Fury win in his Bluebird, even though it's not as nasty as mine,' he says, giving me a wink. I have no idea what he's blathering on about. I'll blame the pain killers if there are questions later.

We spend the morning exchanging stories of our last year's adventures. Just before lunch, Brock jumps into another car and continues driving.

'He can't do that,' complains Tacho. 'Fuck this, Dougie, I can't watch this anymore. And, we gotta work tomorrow. Catch you later.' The boys depart as lunch arrives.

It'll be another frightening ride up the Pacific Highway for Azaria.

I am developing a daily routine. After breakfast, I get them to help me into a wheelchair so I can bath myself. There is something a little indignant about a bed bath and it gives me the added bonus of sitting on the veranda to get some fresh air afterward.

The newspaper arrives around nine and I spend the time before morning tea checking sports results and the stock market. I've got a bit of money in the bank and I think I might invest.

After smoko, they wheel me off to physio and we go through a set routine before returning for lunch and the *Mike Walsh Show*.

The afternoons are mixed with listening to a cassette and reading, divided by afternoon tea. Dinner is early evening followed by more TV, then a cup of tea and little reading before lights out.

The nurses and sisters here are a great bunch. Most of them are married but every now and again one of the single girls is rostered onto our ward. That can be a lot of fun, talking about different bands, music, dates they have been on, whether their latest boyfriend is worth keeping or not. Sometimes, I reckon they are using me to get inside information on what men are thinking.

'Sweetie, don't get too concerned about what he's thinking. It's probably about his next beer or meal, or who his footy team is playing this weekend?'

It's funny, the single girls don't usually flirt too much. There is the odd comment about seeing what I can do on the dance floor when I am upright, but by and large, it's not them flirting, it's the married ones.

It's not all the married girls, about half of them. I reckon some just want the reassurance they are still attractive and there is nothing in it, just a bit of fun. A small number are compulsive, and I reckon they'd root anyone, if they were cute enough.

And then there are the quiet ones. They are business-like, and not too chatty, unless they know they are alone. Then, there is the odd little exchange, either a comment or a sideways glance, and you know what they are thinking. I doubt they are about to do anything right away, but I reckon if the right opportunity arose, they'd be in it. Weird!

I have been attached to the Base Squadron Richmond until I get better and every fortnight I get a visit from the Orderly Room Sergeant. He drops off any mail, my pay, and the latest RAAF News. Not that there's much news in it; usually a photo of a Police dog or a WRAAF in a bikini.

Do WRAAFs usually take a bikini to work?

Grandad and grandma drop in every fortnight. Gran usually brings a cake for the nurses and some home cooking food for me, a stew or her tomato and onion concoction. Absolutely yummy. It's not that the hospital food is that bad, it's just so repetitive.

I hand over my pay envelopes to grandad, keeping a little for the paper and some Minties. We've got a plan. We are investing in shares, a select few. Grandad reckons Rupert Murdoch owns half the politicians, so we opt for News Corporation, Woolworths for something different, and the new National Australia Bank.

'There's talk that the young bloke, Keating, is going to deregulate the banks. If that happens, the shares will go through the roof.' No fool, my grandad.

Saturday mid-November, I am now counting down the days. On Tuesday, it will officially be seven weeks since the operation, only ten more days to go, if it's healed well. I have everything crossed except for my eyes. I can already feel the difference in my leg's structure. Subconsciously, I feel greater strength in it, but I am going to have to keep my enthusiasm under control for a little longer. I don't want to fuck anything up after all this time and patience. They helped me out of bed early today so I could take advantage of some great weather and I have found a sunny spot on the veranda.

I have the usual plans, check the newspaper headlines, sport, then the stock market. Remembrance Day was yesterday so there are some photos of the service in Martin Place.

The First Test scores from the WACA are there. I watched most of it yesterday and was surprised to see Yallop finally make some runs, 122 not-out at the close. Even Phillips managed one hundred and fifty. I guess they are only playing Pakistan, and without Sarfraz, the attack is a little ordinary. The left arm bowler, Hafeez, and the leggie, Qadir, were the pick.

I am checking the closing prices on the stock market when I hear the sound of heels heading my way. Looking up from the paper, it's hard to see who it is with the sun in my eyes. I can make out the heels, then the legs. I know those legs, those long legs.

'Rumour has it there is an injured house slave in this hospital,' she says. She has her head dipped slightly looking at me over the top of her sunglasses, then the smile appears. The newspaper hits the floor and I open my arms. She rushes in and plants a wet kiss right on my lips, the embrace doesn't give for some time.

'I missed you,' she says.